The Rest
of the
Story

Sarah Dessen is the bestselling author of over a dozen novels for teens, including *Once and for All*, *Saint Anything* and *Along for the Ride*. Her books have been published in over thirty countries and have sold millions of copies worldwide. Sarah's novels *That Summer* and *Someone Like You* were made into the movie *How to Deal*. Sarah currently lives in Chapel Hill with her family.

Visit Sarah at www.sarahdessen.com or follow her on Twitter @sarahdessen

SARAH DESSEN

The Rest of the Story

HarperCollins *Children's Books*

First published in the United States of America by Balzer + Bray in 2019
Balzer + Bray is an imprint of HarperCollins Publishers
Published simultaneously in Great Britain by HarperCollins *Children's Books* in 2019
HarperCollins *Children's Books* is a division of HarperCollins*Publishers* Ltd,
HarperCollins Publishers
1 London Bridge Street
London SE1 9GF

The HarperCollins website address is:
www.harpercollins.co.uk

1

Text copyright © Sarah Dessen 2019
Jacket art © 2019 by Jenny Carrow
Typography by Jenna Stempel-Lobell
All rights reserved.

ISBN 978–0–00–833439–0

Typeset in Janson Text

Printed and bound in Great Britain by CPI Group (UK) Ltd, Croydon CR0 4YY

MIX
Paper from
responsible sources
FSC™ C007454

This book is produced from independently certified FSC™ paper
to ensure responsible forest management.

For more information visit: www.harpercollins.co.uk/green

For Leigh Feldman.
Even when words fail me, you never do.
Thank you.

PROLOGUE

There weren't a lot of memories, especially good ones. But there was this.

"Tell me a story," I'd say when it was bedtime but I wasn't at all sleepy.

"Oh, honey," my mom would reply. "I'm tired."

She was always tired: that I did remember. Especially in the evenings, after that first or second glass of wine, which most often led to a bottle, once I was asleep. Usually my dad cleaned up before he went to bed, but when he wasn't around, the evidence remained there in the light of day when I came down for breakfast.

"Not a fairy tale," I'd say, because she always said no at first. "A lake story."

At this, she'd smile. "A lake story? Well. That's different."

That was when I knew I could lean back into my pillows, grabbing my stuffed giraffe, George, and settle in.

"Once upon a time," she'd begin, locking a leg around mine or draping an arm over my stomach, because snuggling was part of the telling, "there was a little girl who lived by a big lake that seemed like it went on forever. The trees around the edges had moss, and the water was cold and clear."

This was when I would start to picture it. Seeing the details.

"The little girl loved to swim, and she loved her family, and she loved the creaky old house with the uneven floors and the little bedroom at the top of the stairs, which was all hers."

At this point in the story, she'd look at me, as if checking to see if I'd fallen asleep. I never had, though.

"In the winters, the water was cold, and so was the house. It felt like the world had left the lake all alone, and the girl would get sad."

Here I always pictured the little girl in a window, peering out. I had an image for everything, like she was turning pages in a book.

"When the weather got warm again, though, strangers and travelers came to visit from all over. And they brought boats with loud motors, and floats of many colors and shapes, and crowded the docks through the days and nights, their voices filling the air." A pause, now, as she shifted, maybe closing her own eyes. "And on those nights, the summer nights, the little girl would sit in her yellow bedroom and look across the water and the big sky full of stars and know everything was going to be okay."

I could see it all, the picture so vivid in my mind I felt like I could have touched it. And I'd be getting sleepy, but never so much I couldn't say what came next. "How did she know?"

"Because in the summers, the world came back to the lake," she'd reply. "And that was when it felt like home."

ONE

The wedding was over. But the party had just begun.

"It's just so romantic," my best friend Bridget said, picking up the little glass jar of candy from her place setting and staring at it dreamily. "Like a fairy tale."

"You think everything is like a fairy tale," my other best friend Ryan told her, wincing as she reached down yet again to rub her sore feet. None of us were used to dressing up very much, especially in heels. "All those days of playing Princess when we were kids ruined you."

"I seem to remember *someone* who had a Belle fixation," Bridget said, putting the candy down with a clank. She tucked her short, choppy dark bob behind her ears. "Back before you decided that being cynical and depressed was much cooler."

"I was the one who liked Belle," I reminded her. We all had our roles: they were always bickering about our shared history, while I was the one who remembered all the details.

It had been like this since we'd met on the playground in second grade. "Ryan was all about Jasmine."

"She's right," Ryan said. "And I'll remind you again that I'm not cynical or depressed, I'm realistic. We can't all see the world as rainbows and unicorns."

"I don't even like rainbows and unicorns," Bridget muttered. "They're so overdone."

"The truth is," Ryan continued, "even with cute candy favors, the divorce rate in this country is over fifty percent."

"Oh, my God. Ryan!" Bridget looked horrified. Ryan was right about one thing: she was the biggest optimist I knew. "That is a *horrible* thing to say at Emma's dad's wedding."

"Seriously," I added. "Way to jinx my future. Was my past not bleak enough for you?"

Ryan looked at me, worried. "Oh, crap. Sorry."

"I'm kidding," I told her.

"And I *hate* your humor," she replied. "Have I mentioned that lately?"

She had not. But she didn't need to. Everyone seemed to have a problem with what I found funny. "Despite the statistics," I said, "I really do feel Dad and Tracy will make it."

"She'll always be Dr. Feldman to me," she said, glancing over to the cake table, where the couple in question were now posing for the photographer, their hands arranged together over a knife. "I still can't talk to her without feeling like I need to open wide."

"Ha," I said, although as the kid of a dentist, I'd heard

all *those* jokes, multiple times. What's your dad's favorite day of the week? TOOTHDAY! What do you call your dad's advice? His FLOSSOPHY! Add in the fact that my dad's name was Dr. Payne, and hilarity was always ensuing.

"No, I'm serious," Ryan said. "Even just now, when they came by to say hello, I was worried she'd notice I hadn't been flossing."

"I think she's got bigger things on her mind today," I said, watching as my new stepmother laughed, brushing some frosting off my dad's face with one hand. She looked relaxed, which was a relief after over a year of watching her juggle the details of flowers and her dress and the reception along with her own bustling practice. Even at her most stressed, though, she'd maintained the cheerful demeanor that was her signature. If my mom had been dark and tragic, Tracy was sweetness and light. And, yes, maybe flossing. But she made my dad happy, which was all that really counted to me.

"Nana incoming," Ryan said under her breath. Immediately, we all sat up straighter. Such was the power of my grandmother, who carried herself with such grace that you couldn't help but try to do the same. Also, she'd tell you if you were slouching. Nicely, but she would tell you.

"Girls, you all look so beautiful," she said as she came sweeping up in the simple rose-colored chiffon gown that she'd custom-ordered from New York. "I just can't get over it. Like little princesses!"

At this, Bridget beamed. While Ryan and I had moved

on, she'd never really gotten over her own years of wanting to be Cinderella. "Thank you, Mrs. Payne. The wedding is lovely."

"Isn't it?" Nana looked over to the cake table, where my dad was now feeding Tracy a bite from his fork. "It all came together perfectly. I couldn't be more thrilled for them."

"Me too," I said, and at this she smiled, reaching down to touch my shoulder. When I looked up at her and our eyes met, she gave it a squeeze.

"Are you getting excited about your cruise?" Bridget asked Nana now as the waiters began to move through the room with champagne for the toasts. "I heard you're going to see pyramids!"

"That's what I'm told," Nana replied, taking a flute from a passing tray and holding it up to the light. "And while I'm excited, I'd honestly rather be here overseeing the renovations. Travel is always good for the soul, though, isn't it?"

Bridget nodded, even though I knew for a fact she'd only been on one real trip, to Disney World a few years back. "Renovations are boring, though," she said. "We did our family room last summer. It was all sawdust and noise for *months*."

"You underestimate how ready she is to turn my room into something fabulous, like a Zen garden or formal sitting room," I said. "She's been counting the days."

"Not true," Nana said, looking at me. "You have no idea how much I will miss you."

Just like that, I felt a lump in my throat. I made a point of smiling at her, though, as a man in a suit passing by greeted her and she turned away to talk to him.

There were good changes and bad ones, and I knew that the ones ahead were firmly in the former category for both Nana and myself. After the wedding, my dad, Tracy, and I would live together in a new house they'd purchased in a neighborhood walking distance to my high school. Nana would finally get her apartment back, something she said she didn't care about one bit, but in truth I knew she wouldn't miss the clutter and noise that came along with her son and teenage granddaughter as roommates. After my parents split and my mom first went to treatment, we needed somewhere to land, and she'd offered without a second thought. Never mind that I'd probably racked up enough of a bill in broken china and scuffed floors to cover my college tuition: Nana said she wouldn't have it any other way. Her home was a work of art filled with works of art, each detail from the carpets to the wall hangings curated and considered. Now it featured a banged-up bike in the entryway, as well as a huge wide-screen TV (Nana didn't watch television). After a renovation that would happen while she was floating down the Nile, she would get it back all to herself to do with as she chose. And I was glad.

I was happy for my dad as well. After the roller coaster of dealing with my mom, Tracy was the most welcome of changes. She didn't take more than she gave, or give nothing at all. She could be trusted to go to a work dinner and not embarrass him by drinking too much or telling a joke that had profanity or sex as part of the punch line. And if she said she'd be somewhere at a certain time, she was always there. It was this last thing that I think he appreciated most about her. I knew I did. After loving someone you couldn't depend on, you realize how important it is to trust someone will do what they say. It's such a simple thing, not to promise what you can't or won't deliver. But my mom had done that all the time.

In our new home in Lakeview, in the Arbors neighborhood, I would have my own suite with a big airy bedroom, as well as a bathroom and a small balcony that looked out over the rest of our street. It would be a change from our apartment, where I could look out at night and see city lights, and the noise from the street was muted but still always there: garbage trucks rumbling in the morning; drunk students walking home from the bars after midnight; sirens and car horns. I knew I would miss it, the way I'd miss my breakfasts with Nana, us splitting the newspaper—she took the cultural section, while I preferred the obituaries—and being able to step out of my house right into the world going on around me. But change was good, as Nana also said, especially the kind you were prepared for. And I was.

Before all that, though, my dad and Tracy would leave for their honeymoon to Greece. There, they were chartering a boat, just the two of them, indulging their shared love of sailing to tour the islands. It was a perfect culmination of their courtship, which, despite their shared profession, had not begun in a tooth-based setting. Instead, they'd met at a general interest meeting of the Lakeview Sailing Club, which gathered every other Sunday at Topper Lake to race dingys and knockabouts. I knew this because before Tracy, I'd had the unfortunate luck of being my dad's first mate.

I hated sailing. I know, I know. It was my *name*, for God's sake—Emma Saylor—chosen because my dad's passion for mainsheets and rudder boards had been what had brought my parents together at another lake all those years ago. My mom, however, had felt the same way about sailing as I did, which was why she'd insisted on spelling my name the way she had. And anyway, I was Emma for all intents and purposes. Emma, who hated sailing.

My dad tried. He'd signed me up for sailing camp one summer when I was ten. There, I was usually adrift, my centerboard usually having plunged into the lake below, as instructors tried to yell encouragement from a nearby motorboat. But sailing with other people was worse. More likely than not, they'd yell at you for not sitting in the right place or grabbing the wrong line under pressure. Even when my dad swore he was taking me out for a "nice, easy sail," there would be at least one moment when he got super stressed and was racing around trying to make the boat do something it wasn't wanting to do while, yes, yelling.

Tracy, however, didn't mind this. In fact, from the day they were assigned to a knockabout together at the sailing club, she yelled right back, which I believed was one of the things that made my dad fall in love with her.

So they would go to Greece, and holler at each other over

the gorgeous Aegean Sea, and I would stay with Bridget and her family. We'd spend the days babysitting her brothers, ages twelve, ten, and five, and going to her neighborhood pool, where we planned to work on our tans and the crushes we had on Sam and Steve Schroeder, the twins in our grade who lived at the end of her cul-de-sac.

But first, there was tonight and the wedding, here at the Lakeview Country Club, where the ballroom had been lined with twinkling lights and fluttering tulle and we, along with two hundred other guests, had just finished a sit-down dinner. Despite the lavishness of the celebration, the ceremony itself had been simple, with me as Tracy's maid of honor and Nana standing up with my dad as his "Best Gran." (One of the wedding planners, a dapper man named William, had come up with this moniker, and he was clearly very proud of it.) I'd been allowed to choose my own dress, which I was pretty sure was Tracy's way of trying to make it not a big deal but instead did the opposite, as who wants to make the wrong decision when you are one of only four people in the wedding party? Never mind that I was an anxious girl, always had been, and choices of any kind were my kryptonite. I'd ended up in such a panic I bought two dresses, then decided at the last minute. But even now, as I sat in my baby-blue sheath with the spaghetti straps, I was thinking of the pink gown with the full skirt at home, and wondering if I should have gone with it instead. I sighed, then reorganized my place setting, putting the silverware that remained squarely on my folded napkin and adjusting the angle of my water glass.

"You okay?" Ryan asked me. We'd been friends for so long, she knew my coping mechanisms almost better than I did. Perpetually messy herself, she'd often told me she wished she, too, had the urge to keep the world neat and tidy. But everything is welcome until you can't stop, and I'd been like this for longer than I cared to remember.

"Fine," I said, dropping my hand instead of lining up the flowers, glass jar of candy, and candle as I'd been about to do. "It's just a big night."

"Of course it is!" Bridget said. There was that optimism again. "Which is why I think we need to celebrate."

I raised my eyebrows at Ryan, who just shrugged, clearly not in on whatever Bridget was planning. Which, as it turned out, was turning to the table beside us, which had been full of young hygienists from my dad's office until they all hit the dance floor, and switching out the bottle of sparkling cider from our ice bucket for the champagne in theirs.

"Bridget," Ryan hissed. "You're going to get us so busted!"

"By who? They're already all tipsy, they won't even notice." She quickly filled our flutes before burying the bottle back in ice. Then she picked up her glass, gesturing for us to do the same. "To Dr. Payne and Dr. Feldman."

"To Dad and Tracy," I said.

"Bottoms up," added Ryan.

We clinked glasses, Bridget with a bit too much enthusiasm, champagne sloshing onto the table in front of her. I watched them both suck down big gulps—Ryan wincing—as I looked at my glass.

"It's good!" Bridget told me. "Even if you don't drink."

"My mom says it's bad luck to toast and not imbibe," Ryan added. "Just take a tiny sip."

I just looked at them. They knew I wasn't a drinker, just as they knew exactly why. Sighing, I picked up my flute and took a gulp. Immediately, my nose was tingling, prickles filling my brain. "Ugh," I said, chasing it with water right away. "How can you really enjoy that?"

"It's like drinking sparkles," Bridget replied, holding the glass up to the light just as Nana had, the bubbles drifting upward.

"Spoken like a true princess." Ryan tipped her glass back, finishing it, then gave herself a refill. "And my mom also says nobody really likes champagne. Only how it makes you feel."

"All I feel is that everything is changing," I said. Saying it aloud, it suddenly felt more true than ever.

"But in good ways!" Bridget said. "Right? New step-mom, new house, and before that, new summer full of potential . . ."

"For you two," Ryan grumbled. "I'll be stuck in the mountains with no internet, with only my dad and some drama nerds for company."

"You get to spend the entire summer at Windmill!

That's one of the best theater camps in the country—" Bridget replied.

"Where I'll be the camp director's kid, so everyone will automatically hate me," Ryan finished for her. "Except my dad."

"You *guys*." Bridget lifted out the bottle again, topping off our glasses. "It's going to be an amazing summer, for all of us. Just trust me, will you?"

Ryan shrugged, then took another sip. I looked at my own glass, then across the room at my dad, who was now leading Tracy back to their table. He looked flushed and happy, and watching him, I felt a rush of affection. He'd been through so much, with my mom and then the divorce, raising me basically as a single parent even before he really was one, all the while working nonstop. I *was* really happy for him, and excited. But the time that he'd be in Greece would be the longest we'd been apart in my memory, and I already knew I would miss him so much. Parents are always precious. But when you only have one, they become crucial.

I reached down, moving my dessert fork and coffee spoon a bit to the right. When Ryan looked over at me, I expected to be called out again, but instead, this time, she just gave me a smile. Then she turned her head away so I could arrange the vase, candy jar, and candle as well.

TWO

I'd heard a lot of words used to describe my mom both before and since her death five years ago. "Beautiful" was a big one, followed closely by "wild" or its kinder twin, "spirited." There were a few mentions each of "tragic," "sweet," and "full of life." But these were just words. My mom was bigger than any combination of letters.

She died in 2013, on the Monday of the first week after Thanksgiving. We'd actually spent it together: me, my mom, and my dad, even though they'd been split up at that point for almost five years. First love against the backdrop of a summer lake resort makes for a great movie plot or romance novel. As a working model for a relationship and parenthood, though, it left a bit to be desired. At least in their case.

I was so little when they split that I didn't remember the fighting, or how my dad was never around as he finished dental school, leaving my mom to take care of me alone. Also lost to my memory was an increase in my mom's drinking, which then blossomed into a painkiller addiction after she had wrist surgery and discovered Percocet. By the time my consciousness caught up with everything, my parents weren't together anymore and she'd already been to rehab once. The world, as I remembered it, was my post-divorce life, which was my dad and me living with Nana Payne in her apartment building in downtown Lakeview and my mom, well, anywhere and everywhere else.

Like the studio apartment in the basement of a suburban house, so small that when you fully opened the front door, it hit the bed. Or the ranch home she shared with three other women in various stages of recovery, where the sofa stank of cigarettes despite a NO SMOKING sign above it. And then there was the residential motel on the outskirts of town she landed in after her final stay at rehab, where the rooms were gross but the pool was clean. We'd race underwater across its length again and again that last summer, her beating me every time. I didn't know it was her final summer, of course. I thought we'd just go on like this forever.

That Thanksgiving, we ate around Nana's big table with the good china and the crystal goblets. My dad carved the turkey (sides were brought in from the country club), and my mother arrived with Pop Soda, her nonalcoholic drink of choice, and two plastic-wrapped pecan pies from the grocery store. Later, I'd comb over that afternoon again and again. How she had that healthy, post-treatment look, her skin clear, nails polished, not bitten to the quick. She'd been wearing jeans and a white button-down shirt with a lace collar, new white Keds on her feet, which were as small as a child's. And there was the way she kept touching me—smoothing my hair, kissing my temple, pulling me into her lap as I passed by—as if making up for the weeks we'd lost while she was away.

Finally, there was crackling chemistry between my parents, obvious even to a child. My dad, usually a measured, practical person, became lighter around my mother. That Thanksgiving, she'd teased him about his second and then third slice of pie, to which he'd responded by opening his full mouth and sticking out his tongue at her. It was stupid and silly and I loved it. She made him laugh in a way no one else could, bringing out a side of him that I coveted.

It was getting dark when I went down with her in the elevator to meet her ride. It bothered me for a long time that I never remembered this person's name, who picked her up in a nondescript American compact, gray in color. Outside the lobby door, my mom turned to face me, putting her hands on my shoulders. Then she squatted down, her signature black liner and mascara perfectly in place, as always, as she gazed into my eyes, blue like hers. People always said we looked alike.

"Saylor girl," she said, because she always called me Saylor, not Emma. "You know I love you, right?"

I nodded. "I love you too, Mama."

At this she smiled, pulling her thin jacket a bit more tightly around her. It was always windier by our building, the breeze working its way through the high-rises, racing at you. "Once I get more settled, we'll do a sleepover, okay? Movies and popcorn, just you and me."

I nodded again, wishing it was still warm enough to swim. I loved that motel pool.

"Come here," she said, pulling me into her arms, and I buried my face in her neck, breathing in her smell, body wash and hair spray and cold air, all mixed together. She hugged me back tightly, the way she always did, and I let myself relax into her. When she pulled away, she gave me a wink. My mom was a big winker. To this day, when anyone does it, I think of her. "Now go on, I'll make sure you get inside safe."

She stepped back and I took one last look at her, there on the sidewalk in those bright white sneakers. Nana had been in cocktail attire for dinner and insisted my dad wear a tie and me a dress, but my mom always followed her own rules.

"Bye," I called out as I turned, pulling the heavy glass lobby door open and stepping inside.

"Bye, baby," she replied. Then she slid her hands in her jacket pockets, taking a step back, and watched me walk to the elevator and hit the button. She was still there when I got in and raised a hand in a final wave just before the doors shut.

Later, I'd try to imagine what happened after that, from her walking to her friend's car to going back to the motel, where the pool was empty and her little room smelled of meals long ago prepared and eaten by other people. I'd see her on her bed, maybe reading the Big Book that was part of her program, or writing in one of the drugstore spiral notebooks where she was forever scribbling down lists of things to do. Lastly, I'd see her sleeping, curled up under a scratchy blanket as the light outside the door pushed in through the edges of the blinds and trucks roared past on the nearby interstate. I wanted to keep her safe in dreaming, and in my mind, even now, I slip and think of her that way. Like she's forever stayed there, in that beat between night-time and morning, when it feels like you only dozed off a minute but it's really been hours.

What really happened was that a couple of weeks later, as I was thinking of Christmas and presents and Santa, my mom skipped her nightly meeting and went to a bar with some friends. There, she drank a few beers, met a guy, and went back to his house, where they pooled their money to buy some heroin to keep the party going. She'd overdosed twice before, each one resulting in another rehab stint and a clean start. Not this time.

Some nights when I couldn't sleep, I tried to picture this part of the story, too. I wanted to see her through to the end, especially in those early days, when it didn't seem real or possible she was gone. But the settings were foreign and details unknown, so no matter how I envisioned those last weeks and hours, it was all imagination and conjecture. The last real thing I had was her standing on the sidewalk as I pushed the elevator button, her hand lifted. Goodbye.

THREE

Middle of the night phone calls are never good news. Never.

"Bridget?" I said, sitting up as I put my phone to my ear. "Is everything okay?"

"My grandpa," she managed to get out, her voice breaking. "He had a stroke."

"Oh, my God," I said, reaching to turn on the bedside lamp before remembering that it, like most of my other stuff, had already been packed. It had been a week since the wedding: Nana's flight was midmorning; my dad and Tracy were leaving that afternoon. The next day, the movers would come. All that was left was the bed itself, a couple of boxes, and the suitcase I'd packed to bring to Bridget's the following afternoon. I looked at the clock: it was four a.m. "Is he okay?"

"We don't know yet," she said, and now she was crying, the words lost in heavy breaths and tears. "Mom's taking all of us kids to Ohio to be with him and Grandma. I'm so sorry, Emma."

"It's fine," I said automatically, although now that I was

beginning to wake up, I realized this meant I had nowhere to stay once my dad and Tracy left for Greece. "What can we do for you guys?"

She took a shuddering inhale. "Nothing right now, I don't think. Mom's just in her total crisis mode, packing suitcases, and Dad's on hold with the airline trying to find a flight. The boys are still asleep."

"I can come over," I offered. "Help get the boys up and ready so you guys can pack."

"That's so n-n-ice." She took a breath. "But I think we're okay. I just wanted to let you know, so you can make other plans. Again, I'm really sorry we're bailing on you like this."

"That's the last thing you should be worrying about," I told her. "Just take care of yourself. Okay?"

"Okay." She took another shaky breath. "Thanks, Emma. Love you."

"Love you back," I replied. "Text me an update later?"

"I will."

We hung up, and I put my phone back on the floor, where it glowed another moment before going black. Outside, the sky was still dark, the only sound the central air whirring, stirring up the curtains at my window. The last thing I wanted to do was go down the hall to my dad's room, where he and Tracy would still be fast asleep, and throw this wrench into their honeymoon plans. So I didn't. It could wait until the morning.

* * *

"Well," my dad said, rubbing a hand over his face, "I guess we just reschedule?"

"No," I said immediately. "That's crazy. You guys have had this booked for over a year. You're going."

"And leaving you to stay here alone?" Tracy asked. "Emma. I appreciate what you're trying to do, but—"

"You're seventeen, and this place is about to be full of sawdust and subcontractors," my dad finished for her. "Not happening."

Nana, sitting at the table with a cup of tea, had been quiet for much of this debate. But I could tell she was mulling this. "Surely there must be someone we're not thinking of."

I sighed—I hated that I was the problem—but not before catching my dad rubbing his eyes again under his glasses. It was his tell of tells, the one way I could always be sure he was nervous or stressed. I said, "She's right. There has to be—"

"Who?" my dad interrupted me. "Bridget's leaving, Ryan is at camp, your grandmother is about to be on a cruise ship somewhere—"

"Egypt," I reminded him.

"Actually, Morocco," Nana said, sipping her tea. "Egypt is Thursday."

"Thank you," he said. He rubbed his face again, then snapped his fingers, pointing at Tracy. "What about your sister?"

She shook her head. "Leaving the day after tomorrow to

hike the Appalachian Trail. Remember?"

"Oh, right," he said, his shoulders sinking. "We only talked about it with her at length *three days ago*." As proof, he gestured at the stack of wedding gifts and cards, some opened, some not, that had been piled into some nearby boxes for the movers to take to the new place.

"It was a wedding," I told him. He looked so down I felt like I had to say something. "You talked to a million people."

This he waved off as Tracy, seated at the table, watched him, a cup of coffee balanced in her hands. In front of her, right where she'd left them the night before, were their passports, the boarding passes she'd printed out after checking in online to their flights—"just to be on the safe side," she said—and their itinerary. Doodling at some point since, she'd drawn a row of hearts across the top, right over the word DEPARTURE.

"This is crazy," I said, looking from it back to my dad. "It's your honeymoon. I'm not going to be the reason the dream trip gets canceled."

"No one is blaming you," he said.

"Certainly not," Nana seconded. "Things happen."

"Maybe not *now*," I said. "But just think of the long-term resentment. I mean, I have enough baggage, right?"

I thought this was funny, but my dad just shot me a tired look. He took my anxiety personally, as if he'd broken me or something. Which was nuts, because all he'd ever done was hold me together, even and especially when the rest of my world was falling apart.

"We reschedule," he said firmly. "I'll call the travel agent right now."

"What about Mimi Calvander?" Nana suggested.

Silence. Then Tracy said, "Who?"

Behind me, I could hear the clock over the stove, which I always forgot made noise at all except during moments like this, when it was loud enough to feel deafening. "Mimi?" my dad said finally. "Waverly's mom?"

It was always jarring when my mom's name came up unexpectedly, even when it wasn't early in the morning. Like she belonged both everywhere and nowhere at the same time.

Nana looked at my dad. "Well, she is family. North Lake isn't too far. And Emma's stayed with her before."

"I did?" I asked.

"A long time ago," my dad said. He'd stopped pacing: he was processing this. "When you were four or so. It was during the only trip your mom and I ever took alone. Vegas."

A beat. The clock was still ticking.

"Second honeymoon," he added softly. "It was a disaster, of course."

"Well, it's just an idea," Nana said, taking another measured sip.

"You have to go to Greece," I told my dad. "It's your honeymoon, for God's sake."

"And this is your *grandmother*," he replied, "who you haven't seen in years."

"I do know her, though," I said quickly. He looked at me,

25

doubtful. "I mean, not well. But I remember her. Vaguely."

"Okay, stop," my dad said. He rubbed his face again. "*Everyone* stop. Just let me think."

It was one of those moments when you can just see the future forking, like that road in the yellow wood, right before your eyes. I knew my dad. He'd give up Greece for me. After all he'd already sacrificed, a whole country was nothing at all. Which was why I spoke up, saying, "Mimi, at the lake. With the moss on the trees. There's porch swings on the dock. And an arcade down the street you can walk to. And the water is cold and clear."

He looked at me, sighing. "Emma. You were four."

"Mom talked about it," I told him. "All the time."

This, he couldn't dispute. Every now and then, he got to hear the bedtime stories, too. "You don't understand," he said. "Your mother's family is . . ."

He trailed off, all of us waiting for a word that never came.

"And the high tourist season is just getting started," he continued. "Which means Mimi is probably too busy to take on anything else."

"I don't know about that," Nana said. "It's been so long, I bet she'd love to see Emma."

"*Sometime*," my dad said. "Not today, this second."

"But we don't know that for sure," I told him. "If she's really anything like Mom, she's not much of a planner."

He looked at me again. "North Lake, Emma . . . it's . . .

26

different. They're different. It's not like here."

"I wouldn't be moving there," I told him. "It's three weeks."

More silence. More ticking. "You really want me to do this?"

What I wanted was for him to go to Greece and sail that boat across the water there, with Tracy beside him. So I knew what to say.

"Yes," I said as Nana caught my eye. "Call her."

All my life I'd thought my mom grew up so far away. But after an hour and a half, we were there.

"Anything look familiar?" my dad asked.

"Every single bit!" I said, my voice bright. "Especially this part right here, the exit ramp."

He shot me a look I knew had to be sharp, not that I could tell from behind his dark sunglasses. "Hey. Don't be a smartass. I was just asking a question."

Actually, what he wanted was reassurance that this would not turn out to be the worst idea in the history of ideas. But the truth was that it was all new to me, and I'd always been a bad liar.

"Wait a second," I said now as we approached a single red light, blinking, and came to a stop. "There are two lakes?"

He peered at the sign across from us, then smiled. "No," he said. "Only one."

It didn't make sense, though. If that was the case, why

was there an arrow pointing to the right that said NORTH LAKE (5 MILES) and another to the left indicating the way to LAKE NORTH (8 MILES). "I don't get it."

"What we have here, actually," he replied, "is one of the great idiosyncrasies of this area."

"Second only to you using the word *idiosyncrasies* while sitting at an exit ramp?"

He ignored me. "See, when this place was first settled, it was pretty rural. Working-class people both lived here year-round and came to vacation in the summers. But then, in the eighties, a billionaire from New York discovered it. He decided to build an upscale resort and bought up one whole side of the lakefront to do just that."

We were still sitting there at the light, but no one was behind us or coming from either direction. So he continued.

"They had a big grand opening for the first summer . . . and nobody came. As it turned out, the rich folks didn't want to spend big money to stay at North Lake, because it was so solidly known as a blue-collar vacation spot." He put on his blinker. "By the second summer, though, the developer figured this out, and incorporated his area as Lake North."

"Which was the same place."

"But it *sounded* like a different one," he said. "So the rich folks came and bought houses and joined the country club. And from then on, there were two towns. And one lake, that sounded like two, between them."

Still not a single car had passed or come up behind us at the light. Despite different economies, neither town seemed to have much going on, at least at the current moment. "Let me guess," I said. "When you came here with Nana in high school, you went left here, to Lake North."

"Smart girl," he replied. Then he put on his blinker, and we turned to the right.

It was a short trip. Four stoplights, to be exact, and then another turn onto a two-lane road, past a big sign with blue faded letters that said WELCOME TO NORTH LAKE: YOUR FAVORITE VACATION. Just past it, the motels began.

I lost count after six different establishments, each very similar in appearance. They were all one-story concrete buildings with grass driveways and parking lots, cars in diagonal spots lining the room doors. Most had an office, identified by a hand-lettered sign or an occasional one in neon proclaiming it as such, and many featured flower and rock gardens with yard art out in front. They had names like NORTH LAKE MOTOR INN and LIPSCOMB COURT and THE JACA-RANDA. Mixed in here and there were trailer parks, but not the kind with big double-wides. Instead, these were the small type you attached to a car and towed, some silver and stainless, others white or painted bright colors. There was so much to see, and all of it new, that even though we were going slowly, I couldn't process much but a glimpse at a time before the scenery turned to something else.

In fact, I was looking ahead at two mini-golf courses that

faced each other from opposite sides of the street—could an economy so small sustain this, I wondered?—when my dad slowed, turning into a drive on our right. It was another hotel, this one a single story of yellow painted concrete and bright blue doors, with a big scripted sign that said only CALVANDER'S. NO VACANCIES.

We pulled in, parking outside the office. As we climbed out of the car, I got my first glimpse of the water, blue and wide. Jutting out into it were a series of long wooden docks. On the one closest to us there were two porch swings hanging by chains, and in the quiet that followed the engine cutting off, I could distantly hear them clanking.

That was the first time I felt it, that twinge of recognition as something from my long-lost past reached out from my subconscious. Splinters, I thought as I looked at the docks again. But as quickly as the memory came, it was gone.

"Matthew? Is that you?"

A woman in shorts and a faded tie-dye T-shirt had come out of the office, the door in the process of shutting slowly behind her. She had white hair cut short, spiking up a bit at the top, and she was small in stature, but formidable in the way she carried herself, like she owned the place. Which, as it turned out, she did.

"Mimi," my dad said, breaking into a wide smile. "How are you?"

"Better than a woman my age has any right to be," she told him. As they embraced, I saw she really was very small,

30

with tiny feet, like my mom's. "You haven't changed one bit. How is that?"

"Look who's talking," my dad said, stepping back to look at her and taking her hands. "You Calvanders, I swear. You don't age."

"Tell that to my hips and my knees." Then she gave me a wink. "And this can't be Saylor. Can it?"

I suddenly felt shy, and concealed myself a bit more behind the car.

"Emma," my dad said, correcting my name kindly but clearly, "just turned seventeen. She'll be a senior this year."

"Unbelievable," Mimi said. She looked at me for a minute. "Well, girl, come give your grandma a hug. Lord knows I've missed a few."

I went, still feeling self-conscious as I approached her. As soon as I was close enough, she pulled me into her arms, her grasp surprisingly strong. I returned the hug, a bit less enthusiastically, while towering over her despite the fact that I am hardly a tall person.

After a moment, she released me, then stepped back to study my face, giving me a chance to look at her as well. Up close, I could see the effect of years of the dark tan she'd clearly cultivated in the leathery skin of her neck and face, as well as a penchant for gold braid jewelry (necklace, bracelet, knot earrings) that almost glowed against it. Most noteworthy, though, were her eyes, which were bright blue. Like mine, and my mom's.

"I'm so glad you came, Saylor," she told me, now squeezing both my arms. "It's about time."

"Emma and I," my dad said, trying again, "are both really grateful you agreed to let her come visit. We know it's literally last-minute."

"Nonsense," Mimi said. She winked at me again. "You're family. And you're not just coming. You're coming back."

A car drove by then, the first one other than our own we'd seen in ages. Actually, it was a truck, bright green, and when the driver beeped the horn as they passed, Mimi waved, not taking her eyes off me.

"Dad says I was here before, but I don't really remember," I told her, because it seemed like I should start at an honest place, considering. "When I was five?"

"Four," she replied.

"I guess I'll just have to take your word for it."

"I'm good as my word, so I'd welcome that." Then she turned back to the office door, pulling it open. "But just in case, come inside a second. I want to show you something."

As I followed her, stepping over the threshold, the temperature dropped about twenty degrees, thanks to the window A/C unit blasting cold air from across the room. I felt like my teeth would start chattering within seconds and saw my dad wrap his arms around himself, but Mimi was unfazed as she walked to the wooden counter, which was covered with a sheet of glass.

"We're almost out of room here, after so many summers,"

she said, leaning over it. "I'm thinking I may have to expand onto a bulletin board or something soon. Not that anybody prints pictures anymore, though, with all this digital this and USB that. Anyway, let me see . . . I used to know right where it was. . . ."

I stepped up beside her. Under the glass, I saw, were what had to be hundreds of pictures, from old black and whites to dingy Polaroids to, finally, color snapshots. Across them all, as the faces and clothing changed, the scenery and backgrounds remained the same. There was the water, of course, and those long docks, the swings beneath them. The rock garden under the Calvander's sign. And those yellow cinder blocks, broken up by blue doors. So many faces over so many years, both big group shots clearly taken for posterity and candids of people alone or in pairs. I leaned in closer, looking for my mom, the one face I might be able to pick out. But when Mimi found the snapshot she was looking for, tapping it with a long fingernail, all the people in it were strangers. Small ones.

"Now," she said, gesturing for me to come closer, "this was the Fourth of July, I believe. Let's see . . . there's Trinity, on the far left, she would have been, what, nine? And next to her is Bailey, she'd be four then also, and Roo and Jacky, who despite the age difference might as well have been twins . . ."

I wanted to be polite, but was so cold I was losing feeling in my extremities.

". . . and then there's you." She looked at me, then back at the picture. "Oh, I remember that cute bathing suit! You always did love giraffes. See?"

Me? I bent over the counter. Five little kids—three girls of varying ages and sizes, and two little towheaded boys—sat lined up on a wooden bench, the lake behind them. All held sparklers, although only a couple seemed to still be lit when the shutter clicked. The girl on the far left had on a bikini, her rounded, soft belly protruding; the younger one beside her, long blond hair and a one-piece with a tie-dye print. Then, the two boys, both in bathing suits, shirtless and white-blond, one of them squinting, as if the camera were the brightest of lights. And finally, me, in a brown suit with a green giraffe and the pigtails and home-cut bangs I recognized from other shots of the same period. I was the only one who was smiling.

It was the weirdest feeling, so foreign and familiar all at once, seeing my own face in a place I didn't recall. I knew the timeline, though. My parents' marriage was crumbling due to my mom's drinking and drug use, and by the coming winter, she would be in rehab and we'd move in with Nana. But sometime before all that, lost to my memory, was this trip. I'd clearly known these people well enough to be this comfortable and yet I'd still forgotten them.

"How long did I stay?" I asked Mimi.

"Two weeks, if I remember correctly," she replied. "It was supposed to be one, but your mama got sick and plans changed."

Sick, I thought, and only then did I remember my dad. I'd assumed he was listening to this. But he was standing

34

facing the big glass window, looking out at the road, and appeared to be lost in thought.

"Where are all these people now?" I asked Mimi, who was rubbing the glass counter with the edge of her T-shirt, taking out some thumbprints on a low corner.

"Oh, they're around," she said. "You'll see most of them, I'm sure, depending how long you're here."

"Three weeks at most," my dad said now, having at some point tuned back to us. He sounded apologetic. "No change of plans this time, I promise."

"You know I wouldn't mind it," Mimi said. "She can stay as long as she likes."

There was a creak behind us: the door opening again. With it came a rush of warm, humid air, and an older man in khaki shorts and a golf shirt, a newspaper under his arm, walked in.

"There's never been peace in that house in the morning, you'd think I'd—" He stopped talking when he saw me, then my dad, standing there. "Oh, sorry. Didn't realize we had guests checking in."

"They're not," Mimi said. "This is my granddaughter Saylor, Waverly's girl. And Matthew, remember, I told you about him?"

The man smiled politely, sticking out a hand to my dad. "I'm sure you did. I'm Oxford."

"My husband," Mimi explained. When my dad looked at her, surprised, she said, "Joe died back in two thousand fifteen."

"I'm sorry," my dad said automatically. He looked shocked, and I realized again how strange it was he'd lost touch with her entirely. "God, Mimi. I had no idea."

She waved her hand, batting his apology away. "Life gets busy when you're raising kids. He had cancer and went quick, honey. And he went here, looking out at the lake, which is just what he wanted."

We all stood there, taking a moment of silence for this person, whoever he was. Then Mimi looked at me. "Let's get you over and settled, okay? Then we can send your dad on his way."

I nodded, and she led us back outside. Oxford stayed behind, settling in an easy chair by the window with a sigh I could hear as he opened his paper.

"I can't get over how much it looks the same," my dad said as I went to the trunk to retrieve my suitcase and the small duffel I'd originally packed for Bridget's. "But the dock's new, or part of it, right?"

"Two years ago," Mimi said, shading her eyes with one hand. "Hurricane Richard came through here and left nothing there but a pile of sticks. I cried when I saw it."

"Really?" he asked. He looked at the dock again. "I figured this place was indestructible."

"I wish," she sighed. "A storm can change everything."

"But you had insurance?"

"Thank goodness," she said. "Joe always was one to prepare for the worst. So yes, we rebuilt. Luckily, the house and motel stood strong, although we lost a few trees and had flooding in some of the units. Nothing new carpet couldn't fix, though."

She started down the sidewalk that ran along the motel, and we fell in behind, first my dad, then me. There were seven units by my count, each with two plastic chairs parked outside, most of which were being used as drying racks for bathing suits or brightly colored towels. Every one had a window A/C unit going full strength as well.

A cleaning cart sat outside the last room, piled with folded towels, rolls of toilet paper, and little paper-wrapped soaps. I glanced inside: a dark-haired girl in shorts, quite pregnant, was wiping down a mirror. She glanced over as we passed before going back to what she was doing.

"We're filled up this week, which is great for so early in the season," Mimi was saying as we left the sidewalk and began across the grass to a nearby gray house with white trim. "The economy rules all, as Joe used to say, but most of our yearly bookings hung in even when everything went bust."

"A lot of these motels and houses are rented by the same people for the same week, every single year," my dad explained to me. "The reservations are handed down literally in wills, so they stay in the family. A lot of people have been coming here for generations."

"And thank goodness for that," Mimi added, starting up the front steps of the house, which had a wide porch, a couple of rocking chairs facing the water. "Joe used to say that it doesn't matter what you do, everyone needs a vacation. In this business, we just happen to count on it."

My dad followed her, taking the screen door she'd pulled open and holding it for me as she went inside. Once in the foyer, though, a cluttered living room to my right, I found myself stopping short. I was steps onto a shiny wooden floor that stretched down a long hallway before opening up to a wide room full of windows. Beyond them, there was only lake, the sun glittering off it.

"Emma?" my dad asked. "You okay?"

"Yeah," I said. I wasn't sure how to explain to him, or if I even could, how I knew that this floor would tilt up slightly as I walked across it, or that the room at the end of the hall was the kitchen, even though I could see nothing of it from where I stood. Outside, this house had felt new and unknown. But standing here now, I would have bet my life I'd walked down this same stretch many times before.

"Now, I've put you in the little bedroom, if that's okay," Mimi said over her shoulder as I finally moved forward, down the hallway to come into, yes, the kitchen. A big wooden table sat against the wall of windows facing the lake and everything smelled like toast. Also, the sink was stacked full of dirty dishes. Of course I noticed. "It's the only one free and I knew you'd want your privacy. The sheets are all clean and there's towels on the bed if you want to freshen up."

"Thanks," I said. "Is it . . ."

I trailed off as my dad climbed a nearby flight of stairs, carrying my suitcase with him, then went left on the landing. Clearly, he needed no directions.

"Right up there," Mimi said to me. "You'll find it."

I thanked her, then went up the stairs myself, the middle one creaking audibly beneath me. At the top, the carpet was beige and well worn, and I could see there were three bedrooms to the left, a bathroom to the right. Only the door on the end was open, so I headed that way.

"You know your way around this place," I said to my dad when I found him in a small bedroom with a single bed, a closet, and one window facing the lake.

"Spent some time here," he replied, his voice low. I'd been so focused on my own memories, I hadn't given much thought to what he'd been feeling. But it was definitely kicking up something. He'd put my suitcase in the closet, my duffel on the bed next to two stacked towels and a washcloth. They were white with a little pink rosebud pattern, and seeing them, I felt it again, that familiarity. "This was your mom's room, way back when."

"Really?" I walked around the end of the bed to look out the window. The roof below it slanted down at an angle, ending in what looked like a porch overhang. "She used to tell me stories about this."

"This room?"

"And this view." It was gorgeous, the pane of glass capturing the lake in a perfect frame. Straight out ahead I could see a floating platform, a motorboat tethered to it. To the right, there were the motels we'd passed, as well as more docks in front of small beaches where moss hung from the trees. And far to the left, what looked like a whole other town of large houses, hotels, and other newer construction. "And the boats. She talked about those, too."

"Yes, I'm actually glad you brought that up while we were, um, alone." He sat down on the bed. "I'd like a word with you about that."

"About what?" I asked.

He nodded at the window, where another boat had now appeared, zooming past. "Boating. One of the great pastimes of North Lake. Which I enjoyed about as much as you do sailing."

"Isn't it the same thing?"

"No," he said. "Sailing is about wind. With motorboats, it's speed, which means it can be very dangerous, even if the driver of the boat hasn't been drinking. And here, they often are."

"You know I won't drink, Dad," I said.

"Yes," he replied, "but I still want to say this. I don't want you to ever go out on the water with someone who has been drinking or plans to."

"Is this like a drug talk, but aquatic?"

"Emma." That tone was like a yellow light, just before red: a warning. "Just promise me, please. It's important."

I looked out the window again. The boat had circled around and was now going back the other way. "I'll be careful. I swear."

"Okay." He sat back, resting his palms on the nubby bedspread. "And you know, now that I think about it, this would be a great place to work on your driving. I'm sure Mimi has a car you could borrow."

"Dad," I said in *my* warning voice, "I'd rather talk about boats."

"I know, I know." He sighed. "And I'm trying to be understanding. But this is your driver's license! When I was your age, I was counting the days until I could get on the road—"

"Because it represented freedom, and independence, all things already available to me via public transportation and ride apps," I finished for him. "I don't need to drive. It's just not necessary."

"But don't you *want* to?" he asked.

"Frankly, no," I said. "I like walking."

"When we move, you won't be able to walk everywhere, like you do now."

"So I'll take the bus or use GetThere."

He sighed again. I felt like I understood my dad pretty well, a by-product of it just being us two for so long. But I didn't get why, ever since I'd turned fifteen, it was *so* freaking important to him that I get my license. He'd relentlessly pushed me to take driver's ed and get my permit, then made a big deal of me getting my provisional license, followed by my full one six months later. I stuck it in my wallet, intending to forget about it, but then he was always wanting us to go out driving together, when he'd spent the entire time I was behind the wheel gripping what Bridget's dad called the "oh shit" handle over his window and pounding an imaginary brake. The whole thing just amplified my anxiety, even before I'd backed into a neighbor's SUV in our underground parking deck, which had scared me so badly I'd burst into tears.

"Dad," I said now. "Maybe I'm just not meant to be a driver. Not everyone is. Think of the accident rate."

"Driving changed my life, though," he said. "Do you know I bought my first car, a used red Audi—"

"A4 with a sunroof and leather seats," I filled in for him. This story was as familiar as one of my mom's.

"—right before I came to Lake North to work my first summer?" He sighed once more, this time happily. "Stocked shelves at AllDrug nights and weekends my entire senior year to save up for it, and drove it off the lot and straight here to my job at the Club. Or, you know, there." He nodded at the left side of the window, and the lake. "I just don't want you to miss that feeling. That you can go anywhere. It opens up the world."

I rolled my eyes. "Dad, I'm about to spend three weeks in a place that for all intents and purposes I've never been to before. Gotta say, the world seems pretty wide right now."

"Yes," he said, "but with your license you'd be free to see even more of it. Like Lake North, for example."

"Where I'd probably back Mimi's car into another, more expensive SUV. Is that what you really want?"

This was a good point. I'd hit a Range Rover in that fender bender: it hadn't been cheap. "Okay, fine. But once I'm back, we discuss. Deal?"

"Deal."

That resolved, he got to his feet, coming over to join me where I was standing by the window. "So, look," he said, putting a hand on my shoulder. "Be honest: You okay with this arrangement? It's not too late to change your mind."

"I'm fine," I said, although now that his time left here was dwindling, I was feeling a slow simmer of anxiety I could only hope wouldn't reach full boil. Did I want to change my mind?

The panic, now hitting medium high, said yes. But I had learned, over time and with various therapists we'd consulted, that it did not get to speak for me. I could do this. And I would, for my dad and Tracy first and foremost, but also, in some small way, for my mom. I worried so much about forgetting her as the years passed. Maybe spending a month in the place she came from would help me remember.

We walked downstairs, back into the kitchen, which was now empty. Peering down the hallway, I could see Mimi outside, talking to the pregnant girl out by the cleaning cart over at the motel. As they conferred, a car zoomed past on the road, beeped, and she waved her hand.

"Still the same table," my dad marveled as we passed the big wooden one against the windows. I, of course, could only see all those dirty dishes, still untouched. "But that toaster's new."

"Toaster?"

He gestured at the corner of one counter, by the sink.

Sure enough, sitting there was a huge shiny silver toaster, the kind with multiple bread slots and various dials for settings. "In a place like this, you notice change," he said to me, starting down the hallway. Appliances, too, I thought, before following behind him.

"Leaving already, Matthew?" Mimi asked when we got back outside. "You just got here!"

"He has a plane to catch," I told her. "The honeymoon awaits."

She stepped forward, giving him a hug. "Have a wonderful time. And don't worry a thing about this girl, she'll be fine."

She said this so confidently, as if she knew me, as well as the future. The weird part was how much I wanted to believe she was right.

"Thanks, Mimi," he replied. "For everything."

She smiled at him, then gave me a wink before turning and pulling open the office door. I felt a blast of cold air before it closed behind her.

"Still feel weird about this," he said when it was just us again. "It's not the way I planned to be leaving you."

"I'll be fine," I told him. "Go. Sail. Honey that moon. I'll see you in three weeks."

He laughed. "Honey that moon?"

"Just go, would you?"

Finally, he got in the car and started the engine, backing out slowly as I stood there. I made a point to wave at him, smiling, as he pulled onto the main road. Then I turned around to face the house and the lake, taking a deep breath.

As I started walking, the pregnant girl was still outside the last unit, now sitting in one of the plastic chairs, looking at her phone. She didn't say anything, but I could feel her watching me, so I picked up my pace crossing the grass, as if I had a solid plan. No matter where you are, home or the strangest of places, everyone wants to look like they know where they're going.

FOUR

"Well, shit."

I opened my eyes at the sound of voices, the first I'd heard since crawling into my bed after my dad left and falling asleep. It had still been morning then: now the clock on the bureau, analog with tiny numbers, said 3:30. Whoops.

"Why is there no bread in this house?" a woman was saying in the kitchen, the question accompanied by the banging of cabinets. "I just brought a loaf over here two days ago."

"I'm not hungry," a voice that sounded like a child said. "I told you that."

"You'll eat something if I make it." Footsteps, then a door—the screen one downstairs, I was pretty sure—slamming. "Mama! What happened to all my bread?"

"Your what?" That was Mimi.

"My bread! I'm trying to make Gordon a sandwich."

"Honey, I don't know. If there's bread, it's in the regular place."

"But that's not my bread, that I bought with my money, for *my* family to eat," her daughter replied.

"I'm not hungry!" came again from downstairs.

"I'll remind you that we are all your family," Mimi hollered, "and if you want to get picky about it, then you can stop drinking all my Pop Soda and not replacing it."

Silence. But the heavy kind. Meanwhile, I thought of my mom, who was the only person I'd ever known who had heard of Pop Soda, much less drank it. It was like a generic Diet Coke, heavy on the syrup. It had been years since I'd had one, but I could still remember how it made my teeth hurt.

"Mama, all I am asking is where is the bread," the woman said, sounding tired. "If you have some other issue with me, let's get into it, by all means, the day hasn't yet been long enough."

Mimi responded, although at this point they were apparently close enough not to be yelling, so I couldn't hear it. But I was up now, so I grabbed my toothbrush and navigated the way to the tiny bathroom at the end of the hall. Once rid of nap breath, I finger combed my hair, took a deep breath, and went downstairs.

At first the kitchen looked completely empty. Only when I'd started to the cabinets for some water—again noting all those dirty dishes, how could you just leave them like that?—did I notice a little girl standing just inside the opening to the hallway. Until she reached up, adjusting the glasses on her face, she'd been so still I'd assumed she was part of the wall.

"Oh," I said, startled. "Hi."

She studied me, her face serious. While her appearance—dark hair in a ponytail, denim shorts and thick plastic clogs, a purple T-shirt that said #AWESOME—was young, the expression on her face reflected the world-weariness usually seen in a much older woman. "Hello," she replied.

I glanced down the hallway, to the screen door. "Are you looking for Mimi?"

"No," she said. "Are you?"

"No," I replied. "I was actually trying to find a glass for some water."

Another beat as she studied me. Then she turned, crossing into the kitchen and standing on tiptoe to open an upper cabinet. She pulled out a plastic tumbler with a gas station logo on it, holding it out in my direction. "If you want ice, it's in the bucket in the freezer."

"I'm good," I said, taking the glass. "Thank you, um . . ."

"Gordon," she said.

"Gordon," I repeated. "I'm Emma."

She nodded, as if this was acceptable. Then she watched as I went to the sink, filled my glass, and took a sip. "My real first name is Anna," she said after a moment. "But nobody with two names ever uses the first one."

"I do," I said.

This seemed to intrigue her. "Really?"

I nodded. "I'm Emma Saylor, technically."

"And you get to be just Emma?"

"Well, yeah."

She looked wistful for a second. "Lucky."

The door banged again, and I heard footsteps approaching. A moment later, a woman in jeans and a polyester uniform top that said CONROY MARKET entered the kitchen. She had long blond hair pulled back in a headband and wore tall wedge sandals of the sort Nana would call ankle breakers.

"Well, it looks like you're having a quesadilla, Gordon, despite the fact I just bought—"

She stopped talking when she saw me, her blue eyes, lashes thick with mascara, widening. I put my glass down on the counter, thinking I'd overstepped by helping myself.

"Oh, my God," she said softly, putting a hand to her chest. "You look just like . . . Waverly?"

Her voice broke on the word, and I saw now she was pale, like she literally had seen a ghost. "No," I said quickly. "I'm Emma. Her daughter."

"Emma?" she repeated.

"Saylor," Gordon offered. "That's her other name."

The woman moved her hand to her mouth, still staring at me. "I'm sorry," she managed finally. "I just . . . I just didn't expect you here."

"It was kind of last-minute," I told her. "My dad was leaving the country and I didn't have any other place—"

Before I could finish, she had crossed the short distance between us and was pulling me into probably the tightest hug I had ever experienced. It felt like she was squeezing the breath right out of me.

"Oh, my God," she said again. Over her shoulder, Gordon

observed our embrace, chewing a thumbnail. "You're her spitting image—I saw you there and it was like she was back for a second."

"I'm sorry," I said.

Now, finally, she pulled away, and I saw tears in her eyes. They were so blue, like Mimi's. Like my mom's. And mine. "Do you even remember me?"

I paused, not wanting to hurt her feelings. "I—"

"Celeste," she told me, putting her hand back on her chest. "I'm your aunt. Do you remember? And Gordon there, she's your cousin."

"Oh," I said, glancing at Gordon again, then back to her. "Right. Hi."

Celeste blinked, a tear running down her face. "Oh, God, you must think I'm a total psycho, look at me."

"You're fine," I said as she reached over to a roll of paper towels and ripped one off, dabbing at her eyes. "I'm sorry you weren't warned."

"Well, that's Mama for you," she said. She blew her nose with a honk. "We've only talked on the phone three times today already. Are you hungry? I was just about to make Gordon something."

"Oh," I told her, "you don't have to do that. I can just—"

"Sit," Celeste said, gesturing to the table. She handed me my water. "Now, let me find those tortillas . . ."

I went to a chair, doing as I was told as she opened the fridge and began taking things out. A moment later, Gordon joined me, bringing a thick paperback book along with her.

"What are you reading?" I asked.

"Oh, Lord," Celeste groaned. "Don't get her started about those damn gorillas."

"They are *chimpanzees*," Gordon said. From the annoyance in her voice, it was clear this was a common exchange.

"Can I see?" I asked, nodding at the book. She pushed it toward me and I flipped it over. *The Allies, Gathering Two: Justice Begins*, it said in thick raised print on the cover. The illustration was of, yes, a chimpanzee, but with very human features, staring into a red-and-yellow-streaked setting sun. "Oh, the Allies series. I remember these. There are, like, a million of them."

"Twenty in the first gathering, fourteen so far in the second," Gordon replied. "And that's not counting all the extra editions and compilations, plus the manga and graphic novels."

"It's like she's speaking another language," Celeste added from the stove, where she was now heating up a frying pan. "I gave up trying to follow years ago."

Gordon, unfazed, flipped the book back over and opened it to a bent-down page, then started to read. After a moment, she reached up, twirling a piece of hair around one finger.

"She's gone," Celeste told me, tossing a tortilla into the frying pan. "Gets lost when she reads. Thank God for it. I give her a hard time, but I was never good in school. She is."

"What grade is she in?"

"Starting fifth in the fall. She's in accelerated reading

and math," she replied, sounding proud. "Clearly not my child, but I will take some of the credit."

"Oh," I said. "I thought she was—"

Celeste looked over her shoulder at me. "What? Oh, no. Her mama's your cousin Amber, from my daddy's side. She lives in Florida right now."

Amber, I thought. The name was familiar, but only faintly so. "Was my mom close with her?"

"Thick as thieves," she replied, pushing the tortilla with a spatula. "But we all were, back then. Growing up here, family was everything. It had to be. We only ever had each other."

It occurred to me that at some point I would need to draw up a family tree to really understand my place in all this. But as long as I had Celeste here, it was worth getting started.

"So you have . . . how many kids?" I asked her.

"Three," she said, flipping the finished quesadilla onto a nearby plate and starting another one. "There's Trinity, who you may have seen earlier, she's pregnant right now. . . ."

I thought of the girl with the cleaning cart, eyeballing me as I passed. We were first cousins? So much for family being all you had. She'd acted like she hated me. "She works at the motel, right?"

"Yes," Celeste allowed with a sigh, "but only in the broadest definition of the word. Mostly she's on her phone complaining about how her feet hurt while Mama does both their jobs because she's a damn softie."

"Right," I said.

"Then there's my son, Jack, he's three years older than you," she continued, shaking the frying pan over the burner, "and finally Bailey, who is your age."

"She's seventeen?"

"Both your birthdays are in April. Your mama and I were pregnant at the same time, our due dates just weeks apart. We spent a lot of time on the phone complaining to each other, now that I think about it. I probably shouldn't be so hard on Trinity."

She finished up the second quesadilla, then brought both plates over to the table.

"Thank you," I said as she put one in front of me.

"You're very welcome," she replied. "Silverware and napkins are—"

Before she finished saying this, I was reaching like it was a reflex to the rattan basket across from me, pulling it closer to retrieve a fork, knife, and napkin. Huh.

"Well, never mind," she said with another smile. "Gordon. Put the book away and eat."

"I can eat and read," Gordon replied, picking up her quesadilla and taking a bite, her eyes still on the page.

Celeste rolled her eyes and went to the fridge, retrieving a can of Pop Soda. Then she sat down, opening the can before kicking off her shoes, first one, then the other. "What a day. It's only early season and I'm already exhausted."

"You work at a market?" I asked.

She looked surprised I knew this, then glanced down at

her uniform top. "I forgot I had this thing on! Usually take it off the second I get in the car. Yes, Conroy Market. Only grocery store in North Lake. I'm an assistant manager."

I took a big bite of the quesadilla: I hadn't realized how hungry I was until I'd begun eating. "This is really good," I told Celeste.

"You want another one?" She started to get to her feet. "It'll only take a second."

"Oh, no," I said quickly. "I'm fine. Thank you, though."

While I ate, I could tell she was trying not to stare at me, my presence still so surprising. Finally she got to her feet, taking my now-empty plate and Gordon's. "I can do those," I said as she started to run water into the sink, crammed with all those dishes.

"Oh, no," she said. "You're a guest."

"I want to," I said, wanting to add that it had been driving me crazy all day. "You cooked, I clean. That's the rule in our house. Please?"

Celeste looked at me for a second. "Okay," she said finally. "But know this: you start washing dishes in this house, you'll never stop."

In response, I stood up and walked over to the sink, pulling the faucet aside and turning it all the way hot before beginning to sort everything into categories. I knew I probably looked like the weirdo cousin, but as I added soap to the water, finding a scrub brush in the nearby dish rack, I felt more in control than I had since that call in the dark from Bridget twelve hours earlier. I was in a strange place, feeling strange even to myself, but this task was one I knew well, and I took comfort in it. So much so that when I finished, I turned to see both Celeste and Gordon had gone, leaving the Allies book and the lake as my only company.

I always did a lot of good thinking while washing dishes, and Mimi's sink had been slam full. By the time I was done, I'd decided to look at my time here at North Lake as a kind of organizing. So back up in my room, once I unpacked my suitcase and put my clothes away, I pulled out the one note-book I'd brought with me. MIMI + JOE, I wrote at the top of a blank page, with CELESTE and WAVERLY each under a vertical line beneath. From those, I drew more lines, add-ing in my dad beside my mom's name, and mine underneath it. Then I did the same with Trinity, Jack, and Bailey under Celeste's, realizing as I did so I had no idea who her husband was. I'd be here three weeks, though. I had a feeling I could fill in the gaps.

Just then there was a whirring sound from outside, dis-tant, and I turned to see a motorboat puttering from the shore to the floating platform I'd seen earlier. Then I saw another from the corner of my eye, followed by one more, all of them converging to the same spot from varying direc-tions. The first pulled up alongside, and a dark-haired girl in a yellow bikini top and shorts jumped out, her phone to one ear. As the others docked as well, more people joined her. Within moments, between the boats and those who had arrived on them, you couldn't see the raft at all.

Downstairs, the screen door slammed—this sound was

becoming familiar—and I heard someone come into the kitchen, then start up the stairs.

". . . told you, I was at work and couldn't answer," a guy, maybe my age by the sound of it, was saying. "Taylor. Don't start. Seriously."

The bathroom door closed, and I heard water running, along with more of this conversation, now muffled. As the screen door slammed again, I thought how much this place would have driven Nana crazy: she treated her house like it was fragile, with doors and drawers eased shut, gently. You slammed, you scrammed. That was a direct quote from my dad.

"Jacky?" Mimi yelled from the kitchen. "You here?"

"One sec," the guy yelled back from the bathroom.

"Jacky? Hello?"

"ONE SEC," he replied, louder. This time, she didn't say anything, but a moment later I heard the fridge opening. I looked back at my family tree, full of gaps, and went downstairs.

"There you are," Mimi said when she saw me. Still in her tie-dye, she'd ditched her sandals and put on fuzzy slippers in their place. A can of Pop Soda was in her hand. "I wondered where you got off to."

"I fell asleep after Dad left," I told her. "And then saw Celeste and Gordon."

"Oh, good," she said, turning back to the fridge. "You want a soda?"

"No, thanks," I said. As the kid of a dentist, they'd been

56

so forbidden in my early life that when I finally could have them, I'd lost interest.

"Oxford's holding down the office until dinner, so I was just getting ready to watch my shows," she said, grabbing a bag of potato chips from the top of the fridge. "Want to join me?"

Upstairs, Jacky—Jack?—was talking again. "Sure."

She started down the hallway, to the living room we'd passed on the way in. The walls were lined with long couches—one leather, one dark blue corduroy—and there was a huge TV set, surrounded by shelves of family pictures. Off the back side of the room was the screened-in porch I'd seen earlier from outside, separated by a door with a glass pane that had been covered with a tacked-up towel. The result was a dimness that would have made the room feel cold even if the A/C hadn't been going full blast, which of course, it was.

"Does it feel hot in here to you?" Mimi asked as I thought this. I was about to say no, and try not to do it vehemently, but then she was over at the A/C unit, adjusting it from 67 to 65. "That's better. I hate a warm house. Have a seat."

She was already doing just that, lowering herself onto the leather couch and putting her soda into the built-in cup holder on its arm. Even though the couch was huge, I didn't want to crowd her, so I moved to the blue one.

"Now, let's see," Mimi said, pulling up a list of recorded programs. "What are we in the mood for?"

As I looked at the screen, scanning the titles, it was clear

57

there was only one answer to this question: home improvement. Everything listed—*Fix and Flip*, *Contractor: You!*, *From Demo to Dream House*—shared this same subject. I said, "I take it you like renovation shows."

"They're my therapy," she replied, scrolling through the titles before picking an episode of something called *3 Flip Sisters*. "Have a hard day with everything breaking down all around you, then come and watch somebody else fix something up nice. I can't get enough."

She sighed contentedly, taking a sip of her soda as the show began. "One family," intoned the announcer as the screen showed a trio of blond women, all with long hair, wearing matching plaid shirts, "three opinions, one firm deadline. This is *3 Flip Sisters*."

Just then my phone beeped in my pocket, the first noise it had made since my dad texted from the airport an hour earlier to say he and Tracy were boarding their plane. This time, it was Ryan. She'd been incommunicado since arriving at Windmill a couple of days after the wedding.

Testing testing. Anyone out there?

I smiled, quickly typing a response. **Your phone works? I thought you were in the middle of nowhere.**

I am, she replied after a moment. **But if I climb this hill and stand on one foot, I have a signal. For now anyway. What are you and Bridget doing?**

I filled her in, as succinctly as I could, while the TV showed a montage of the sisters and Bill and Shelley looking at various properties. By the time I hit send, they'd settled on a ranch house with hideous green linoleum floor in the kitchen that Angie, the sister Realtor, said was priced to sell.

"They'll end up putting an arch in there someplace, mark my words," Mimi said as the TV cut to a commercial. "Paula loves an arch."

My phone beeped. **Holy crap. Is Bridget's grandpa okay?**

Haven't heard from her since she left, I wrote back. **So not sure.**

Are you okay? What's it like there? I've never even heard you mention having another grandmother.

Even though Mimi was on the other couch, a fair distance away, I tilted the screen to be sure she couldn't see it. The desire not to hurt her was that strong, even as I knew that I, too, could have claimed injured feelings, considering. Where had she been all this time? It was one thing if my mom had kept her at arm's length—notoriously private, she got even more so when she was using—but five years had passed since her death. Had my dad run interference, thinking Mimi and all the rest of the Calvanders would be too much for me to handle?

Plus, my mom had never talked much about her family. It was Nana—my grandfather died young in his forties— who was consistently there for holidays and birthdays. Other than the funeral, which was a blur, the only trip I'd ever taken to my mother's home was so long ago I didn't even remember it. Yes, I had the Lake Stories, but they were never about people as much as a place.

"Arch!" Mimi said, pointing at the TV. "What did I tell you?"

Sure enough, on the screen, Paula was gesturing at a small, cramped living room as a computer graphic showed what it would look like with that shape as an entryway. "You told me," I said.

She cackled, and I looked back down at my screen at Ryan's question. What *was* it like here?

Unclear, I told her. **Stay tuned.**

I heard thumping, then footsteps crossing the kitchen. A moment later, a tall, thin guy with red hair, a baseball hat, shorts, and a faded NORTH LAKE T-shirt passed by in the hallway, his phone to his ear.

"Jacky," Mimi called out, and he stopped, turning to peer in at her. "Didn't you hear me calling you before?"

"I was taking a shower," he said, sliding his phone into a back pocket.

"Well, say hello to your cousin Saylor." She nodded at me. "She's staying awhile."

It was a testament to the dimness of the room, and the dark blue couch I was on, that Jacky hadn't even seen me until she said this. He looked surprised as he lifted a hand. "Hey."

"Hi," I said. "It's Emma, actually."

"Oh, sorry," Mimi told me, her eyes on the TV, where I saw someone was now carrying a sledgehammer. "I keep forgetting you changed it."

But I didn't, I wanted to say. I'd always introduced myself

60

as Emma, even as a kid: my mom was the only one who called me Saylor. Could you literally be a different person to different people? I was pretty sure I was going to find out.

"I'm going out to the raft," Jacky told Mimi. "Back for dinner."

"We're having burgers," she replied. "I made the patties already."

"All right," he said, then started toward the door again, drawing his phone from his pocket.

"Jacky."

He stopped, exhaling visibly. "Yes?"

Mimi shifted in her seat. "Why don't you take her with you?"

"What?" he said.

"Saylor," she replied, nodding at me. "I mean, Emma. She's just got here, doesn't know anyone. You can introduce her around."

"Oh," I said quickly, mortified, "he doesn't have to—"

"They're all out at the raft this time of day," she explained, cutting me off. "Figuring out what kind of trouble to get into later."

"It's okay," I said. I had no sense of the rules here, but I did know enough to not want to be someone's burden. "I'm fine."

The TV went back to *3 Flip Sisters*. "Demo," Mimi said, nodding at the screen. "You can tell, because everyone's in goggles."

"Right," I said.

Jacky hesitated a moment more in the non-arch hallway opening, then started out the door. "Be back to grill," he called over his shoulder.

"Okay," Mimi said, taking a sip of her drink.

The door slammed, and I turned my attention back to the Flip Sisters. A moment later, though, he was back.

"Hey," he said to me. "You really want to watch that?"

I looked back at Mimi. It wasn't clear she'd heard him, but I didn't want to hurt her feelings, even if this had all been her idea.

But Jacky didn't seem worried. Instead, he just pushed the door back open, holding it for me. "Emma," he said. "Come on."

FIVE

The girl in the yellow bikini I'd seen from the window spotted me as we approached the raft. By the time I looked her way, she was already scowling.

I'd been preoccupied, smarting from various ways I had almost died of shame since leaving Mimi's house. The first involved the awkward silence as I followed Jacky across the grass and down the nearby dock to a white motorboat with red seats that was tied up to a row of cleats.

"Thanks for bringing me along, Jacky," I said finally.

He glanced up, then began loosening rope knots. "It's Jack, actually. Only Mimi calls me Jacky."

"Oh. Sorry," I said. "I understand. She's actually the only person who has called me—"

But this was lost as he turned his back again, jumping onto the boat and behind the wheel. The seats were aged and cracked, the floor covered with a few beat-up-looking life jackets. He turned a key and the engine rumbled, coming to life.

I was still standing on the dock, not sure what I was supposed to do, when he looked up at me and said, "You getting in?"

Right, I thought, my face reddening. I took a step onto the boat, but because the ropes were loose, it drifted out into the water, taking my leg with it. This led to a frantic effort not to fall in myself accompanied by, I hated to admit, a shriek. I ended up back on the dock, but just barely.

Jack observed all of this with a flat expression. Then he pulled the boat up to the dock so I could climb in. Once inside, I started to the back bench by the motor, but hit a slippery spot halfway there that resulted in me tumbling down onto the life jackets, arms flailing.

"Whoa," he said, in that same monotone. "Careful."

As we picked up speed and my embarrassment subsided—slightly—I was able to begin to appreciate the view of the lake. It was one thing to look at it from land, like a picture in a frame, another to be within it, wide and blue all around you. It's pretty here, I thought, and turned in my seat, looking back at Mimi's house to find the window to my mom's bedroom, which was growing smaller behind us.

The raft, in contrast, was larger than it had looked from shore. By the time we got there, about seven boats were tied up, either to the raft or each other, with people on them in groups, laughing and talking. As we got closer, a tall, skinny guy with white-blond hair, shirtless and in swim trunks, walked out to the back of a blue motorboat with white trim to meet us. When Jack slowed the motor and walked to the bow, throwing him a line, I saw the girl staring at me.

Short, and stout, with strong-looking arms and legs, she had a deep tan, all the better to set off her yellow bikini top, which she wore with cutoff shorts. Her hair was black and long, flowing down her back, a pair of sunglasses holding it back from her face. When our eyes met, she slowly crossed her arms over her chest, squaring her shoulders.

"This is Emma," Jack said, cutting the engine. "Help her out."

The boy with the white-blond hair—it stuck up in the back, a cowlick I somehow knew he was probably always messing with—extended a hand. Cautious after how I'd boarded, and feeling awkward grabbing ahold of someone I knew not at all, I nonetheless got to my feet and gripped his fingers, stepping onto the blue boat, then the raft.

"I'm Roo," the blond boy said. He had a small gap between his two front teeth, which took the smile he gave me to another level. Gesturing to the group behind him, he added, "This is . . . everyone."

No one said hello, or even acknowledged this introduction, too caught up in their own conversations. Except, of course, Yellow Bikini, who was now glaring at Jack as he finished tying up.

"Jack Blackwood," she said in a voice that was just sharp and loud enough to make everyone else pause their interactions before stopping talking entirely, "I know we're fighting, but did you seriously bring another girl out here *right in front* of me?"

"Uh-oh. Here we go," a tall, slim black girl with short braids in an East U Volleyball T-shirt said under her breath.

"I'd stay out of it if I were you, April," another guy with a fauxhawk and tattoos covering his arms said to her.

"Yeah, because *that* will end well," April replied.

The next thing I knew, Yellow Bikini had crossed the short distance between us to stand right in front of me. Meeting my eyes, her own narrowed, she said, "Look, this is a basic lake rule. You don't just show up with someone else's boyfriend, okay?"

"Taylor," April said. "Remember your calming meditations? Breathe in, then—"

"I'm breathing," Taylor told her. "I just want answers."

"I didn't—" I said, trying to sound as assertive as she did. Unfortunately, my voice was shaking. Meanwhile, I could hear footsteps approaching, the new arrivals now also an audience to this.

"*I didn't*," she repeated in a high voice. She whirled around, looking at Jack. "Seriously? Who the hell is this girl?"

"His cousin," another voice said, sounding as confident as I wished I had. "Mine, too. So will you get out of her face, please?"

All of a sudden, a girl was standing beside me. Even before I saw she was my height, with the same color blond hair and slightly upturned nose I'd always been self-conscious about, I didn't doubt for a second that we were related. This was

Bailey. I remembered. Again in a way I couldn't even begin to understand, especially at that moment, but I did.

"Your cousin?" Taylor looked at me again. "You're forgetting that I *know* all your cousins."

"Not this one. Hasn't been here since we were little kids." Now, Bailey addressed me. "Hi, by the way."

"Hi," I said. This time, my voice didn't crack.

She turned back to Taylor. "Are we done? If so, let's make a plan."

Taylor looked at me again. "Jack," she said to my face. "We need to talk."

"Oh, boy," the guy with the fauxhawk said. "Duck and cover, y'all."

As someone across the raft snorted, Taylor turned on her heel and walked across the raft to climb onto Jack's boat. Jack followed, slowly, looking tired. As soon as he was on board, she started talking, although her words were lost as someone else arrived, their engine chugging.

I was no expert, but even at first glance I could tell something about this boat was different. It was longer, for starters, with a third row of seats—not worn, but shiny and clean—and a larger motor. The guy behind the wheel, tall with dark hair, was in shorts and a white polo shirt with some kind of insignia that I felt like I'd seen before. He had on mirrored sunglasses, reflecting our faces back at us.

"What's up?" he called out. "Got a plan yet?"

"Oh, great," April said with a roll of her eyes. "Look who's here."

"Stop it," Bailey told her. "I told you, he's nice."

April did not look convinced, even as Bailey crossed the raft, jumping across two docked boats—gracefully, how?—to go talk to him. To me, April said, "She knows to watch out for those yacht club boys. Not that you can tell."

"Yacht club?" I asked.

April nodded across the lake, at the distant big houses. "Over at Lake North. Everything's bigger and better there, not that it stops them from coming to our side."

I realized, suddenly, why I'd recognized the boy's shirt. It was identical to the one my dad wore in the few pictures I'd seen from the summer he'd spent here teaching sailing when he met my mom. I looked at Bailey again, now scratching one foot with the other as she spoke to the boy, who was grinning up at her.

"That's her boyfriend?" I asked.

"No," the guy with the fauxhawk replied.

"Not *yet*," April corrected, smiling. "Summer just started."

"She'll come to her senses," he told her, rubbing his arm, where a tribal-patterned tattoo covered one bicep.

"And fall for you, Vincent?" she asked him. "Keep dreaming."

"My point is," he said, his face flushing, "I just don't see them together."

"Why not? He's totally her type."

"Which is what? Yacht club?" I asked.

"Rich boy with a dazzling smile," she said. "And a nice boat. What's your name again?"

"Emma," I said. "You're April?"

"And this is Vincent," she said, pointing to the guy. "You here for the summer?"

"Just three weeks," I said.

"How you kin to this lot?" When I just looked at her, not sure what this meant, she said, more slowly, "Are you a Calvander or a Blackwood?"

"Neither. I'm a Payne." Obviously this was confusing, so I added, "My mom was a Calvander, though. Waverly."

At the name, her eyes widened. "You're Waverly's daughter? Really?"

I nodded, suddenly aware of another set of eyes on me: Roo. He'd been over near another boat, coiling some ropes, but now he turned, looking at me as if for the first time. "Saylor?" he said.

"Her name's Emma," April told him. "Keep up, would you?"

"It is Emma Saylor, technically," I said. "But mostly Emma now."

I felt like I was apologizing. Maybe because of the way Roo was still looking at me, startled, as if maybe he remembered more of that summer from the group picture than I did. It must have been confusing, for someone to reappear all those years later with a different face and name. Like the past wasn't what you'd thought. I knew that feeling.

"Okay," Vincent said, shoving his phone into his pocket. "Godfrey's at eight, then Lucy Tate's place afterward, but only if we bring our own beer and don't criticize her music."

"Since when do we have conditions?" April said. "I'd rather hang out on the dock and do what I want."

"It's high season," Roo told her. "Docks are out until August."

"Oh, right. Stupid tourists," she grumbled.

"What's the plan?" Bailey called out from the other side of the raft.

"Don't tell her," April said. "She'll just invite all the golf shirts."

"Godfrey's, then Lucy Tate's," Vincent yelled back anyway.

This seemed to be a signal that things were finalized, as everyone began saying their goodbyes and splitting off to their respective boats. Within minutes, the hum of engines filled the air and I was one of the only ones left, along with April and Vincent, with Roo alongside us behind his own wheel, motor idling.

"Let's get," Vincent told April. He looked at me. "You need a ride back to Mimi's?"

I looked over at Jack, who was still sitting on one of those red benches, Taylor standing in front of him. She'd been talking this entire time, and didn't seem to have any plans to stop soon. Meanwhile, Bailey had jumped in with the guy in the golf shirt and was already puttering away toward shore.

"I don't know," I said, looking at Jack. I still felt like a burden, this time to people I wasn't even related to. "Maybe I should wait for—"

"I wouldn't," April said flatly. "No telling how long they'll be talking. They are *always* talking."

"Right," I said. "Well . . ."

"I'll take you, Saylor," Roo said. When I looked at him, he added quickly, "I mean, Emma. It's on my way."

"Great," Vincent said as April hopped into a nearby small skiff, settling in the stern with the outboard motor there. He untied it, then joined her, his weight wobbling it from side to side. "See you at Godfrey's."

Then they, too, were gone, calling out goodbyes to Jack and Taylor as they passed. She was still talking; only he lifted a hand, waving back.

I looked at Roo, who pulled on a faded blue T-shirt before putting his boat into gear. Before, with Jack, I'd waited for permission to get in, which was the wrong thing to do. Then again, I didn't want to just go for it and risk a repeat of my earlier experience boarding. How could a single step from one floating object to another be so difficult?

I was beginning to sink into an indecisive spiral when he backed the boat up right next to where I was standing, then used one hand to pull it up to the raft's edge, making it an easy step in to take a seat beside him. Easy was good. Easy, I could take. So I did.

Once we got home, dinner was served.

"All I am saying," Celeste said as she picked up her burger, "is that I want you to be careful."

71

"Mom," Bailey replied. "You don't have to give me this same lecture every summer."

"Apparently, I do. Because you're already hanging out with yacht club boys."

"They're not all alike, you know."

"They're alike enough," Celeste told her. Mimi, at the head of the table, shot her a look over the bowl of potato salad between them. "What? You know what I'm worried about. I mean, we all know what happened when Waver—"

There was the sound of a thump under the table, and Celeste winced. The sudden silence that followed was awkward, not only for the kick Mimi had just given her, but the fact that we all knew it was to protect my feelings.

This was actually the second time my mom had come up since I'd left the raft. The first had been when I was riding back with Roo. Unlike when I'd gone out with Jack, we were side by side. So I was able to get quick glimpses of him, taking in the way his white-blond hair stuck up a bit in the back, the tattoo on one calf that was a series of numbers, and the way that he waved at every boat we passed, flashing a big grin. For all my own glances, he wasn't looking at me at all, instead squinting ahead, the back of his T-shirt rippling in the strong wind coming off the water. When he finally spoke, it took me by surprise.

"I'm sorry about your mom."

Even though it had been five years and some days, I worried I'd moved on too much. And then there were times like this, when just a mention of her gave me a pinch in my heart.

"Thanks," I said. "I miss her."

Now he did look at me: I could see it out of the corner of my eye, even as I watched Mimi's dock—marked with a sign that said FOR USE BY CALVANDER'S GUESTS ONLY—approach. "She and my dad were friends in high school. Chris Price."

I nodded, as if I'd heard this name, even though I hadn't. "He still lives here?"

He looked at me for a second. "No, not anymore. I live with my mom." He pointed to a line of houses down the shore from Mimi's, each painted a different bright color—yellow, blue, pink, red, and green—and trimmed with white. "Ours is the green one."

"Who has the pink?"

"Renters, usually," he said. "Season just started, though."

"How many people live here year-round?" I asked.

He was slowing the engine now. "More than you'd think. A lot, like Celeste, have houses they rent out for summer."

"I thought she lived with Mimi," I said.

"Only from June to August," he replied. "The rest of the time they have a place up by Blackwood Station, right on the water."

"Blackwood Station," I said. "I feel like I've heard of that."

"You probably have. It's the only boatyard in town. Plus, the arcade is right there, and the public beach."

I looked in that direction, getting my bearings, then back up at Mimi's house, now right in front of us. As I did, I saw

Celeste, standing in the grass, one hand shading her eyes as she looked out at us. I couldn't make out her expression.

"And Celeste is a Blackwood, right?" I asked.

"She was. Her ex-husband, Silas, runs the boatyard and gas station. Been in his family for generations."

Now I had something else to add to my family tree. "But you're not a Blackwood or Calvander," I said, clarifying.

"Nope." He cut the engine, letting us drift up to the dock. "Silas, Celeste, my dad, my mom, and yours all went to high school together. There's only one, the same one we all go to now."

I tried to picture my own parents at my school, Jackson High, walking the same halls I did with Ryan and Bridget. I couldn't. Nana Payne and my dad lived in Massachusetts when he was in high school, and my mom was, well, here.

"It's a lot, all this new information," I said. "I'm honestly having some trouble keeping up."

"Well, then you need to start asking people their five sentences."

I raised my eyebrows. "Their what?"

"It's a lake thing," he explained. "The basic idea is that since you meet a ton of people at the beginning of every summer, everyone has to condense their bio down to the main ideas. Thus, five sentences."

"Right," I said slowly. "What's yours?"

He cleared his throat. "Born and bred here at North Lake. High school senior this fall. Work multiple jobs. Want to go to journalism school. Allergic to shellfish."

"Wow," I said. "Didn't see that shellfish part coming."

"An element of surprise and oddity is crucial with this," he told me. "Hit me with yours."

"I need five in all?"

"Start with one."

"Okay," I said, thinking it over. "Well, I'm from Lakeview. Also about to be a high school senior."

"Coming out strong," he said as we hit a wave, water splashing over the bow. "I like it. Go on."

"My mom grew up here at the lake," I continued, "but this is my first real visit. I came once as a kid, but I don't really remember."

"Nice," he said. "Facts *and* intrigue. Now you need something random and memorable."

I thought for a second. "People don't get my humor."

"Meaning?"

"I think I'm funny, but other people often don't laugh."

"I know that feeling," he said.

"You do?" I hadn't met anyone who could relate before.

"Yep," he said. "Okay, now for the strong finish. Your shellfish allergy, so to speak. What's it going to be?"

I had to admit, I was feeling the pressure. Especially as the seconds ticked by and nothing came. What could I say? I was nervous to the point of obsessive? I liked organizing things?

Roo did not rush me. He just waited.

Finally, I had it. "I read the obituaries every day."

His eyes widened. "Seriously?"

I nodded. "Yep."

"Okay, that is *good*," he said, then held his hand up for a high five. I slapped it. "You, in five sentences. Nicely done."

Me, in five sentences. All facts, some informative, some colorful. Not really all that different from the obits themselves, now that I thought of it. Only shorter, while you're living, and still have time to add more.

Roo slowed the engine, then stopped it entirely, and we drifted up to the dock. As he hopped off the boat, pulling the line with him, I heard the thump of footsteps coming down the dock. Looking up, I saw Trinity approaching, now in a flowing black maxi dress, her hair wet. She looked grumpy, but considering this had been a constant each time I'd crossed her path so far, maybe it was just her face.

"Hey," Roo called. "What's up?"

"Mimi says you should stay for dinner," she replied. "Since you brought her in, and everything."

Her was me. Apparently. While I was not sure what five sentences Trinity would pick, I was pretty sure one would cover the fact that she *really* didn't like me.

"You know Trinity, right?" Roo said to me.

"We haven't been reintroduced formally," I told him. To her I said, "Hi. I'm Emma."

"Hi," she said, her voice flat. She turned her attention back to Roo. "Where's Bailey? She's not answering her phone."

"Rode off with some yacht club guy," he replied. "Maybe up at the Station?"

"Of course she is." Trinity rubbed a hand over her belly.

"Like I have the energy to go all the way up there."

"I can go find her," I offered. "I need to learn my way around anyway."

"I'll walk you," Roo said. "If I'm coming for dinner, I should go home and change."

"Will you just drive me?" Trinity whined. "I need to go to the store and I can't reach the clutch anymore."

"Sure," he said agreeably. "Emma, you want to ride along?"

"She should go help with dinner," Trinity said. Now I was *She*. "Mimi said to tell her to."

Roo looked at me. "Oh. Right. Well, rain check."

"Sounds good," I said, making a point to act like it was no big deal. Still, as Trinity and Roo started down the dock without me, I felt another sting, this one a sort of shame. Despite all my mom had told me about the lake, none of it explained why so far at least half the females I'd met had disliked or outright hated me on sight.

Now, back at the table, I looked out the window to the sandy beach below the house, where Roo, Trinity, and Jack were sitting in lawn chairs, eating their own dinners. We'd all fixed our plates together, assembly-line style, but it was only after I'd sat down that I realized the table was too small for everyone, and this contingent was eating outside. Which left me with Celeste, Mimi, and Bailey, as Gordon was again lost in her Allies book.

"So," Mimi said to me. "You getting situated? Meet everyone out at the raft?"

I nodded, finishing my bite of potato salad before saying, "A few people, yeah."

"Taylor got up in her face," Bailey said, adjusting the tomato on her burger.

"What?" Mimi said. "Why?"

"Because she was with Jack, and Taylor's got major jealousy issues." She rolled her eyes. "Even when they're together, they're fighting."

"It's not easy to disconnect from someone totally in a place as small as this," Celeste pointed out.

"Says the woman who married and divorced the same man twice," Bailey said.

I blinked: this was news to me. Another thing to add to my family tree.

Mimi chuckled. "She's got you there, Celeste."

Celeste, hardly bothered, reached for the bowl of potato chips. "I've got to tell you, Saylor, when I saw you coming in with Roo, man, it brought back some memories. Wild to see you two together, after how close you were as kids."

"Wait, what?" I said. Now I felt even worse about our first meeting at the dock, when he'd looked so surprised. "We were?"

"You don't remember?" I shook my head. "Well, I guess maybe you wouldn't. You *were* babies. But yeah, that time you stayed here, you two were like frick and frack. Always together."

"Remember the best friend hug?" Mimi said, smiling.

"The what?" Bailey asked.

"Whenever Roo and Saylor had been together and then had to split up, they did their best friend hug. Just clung to each other. Lord, it was the cutest."

Bailey, bemused, glanced at me, and I was pretty sure I blushed. Evidently, embarrassment had no statute of limitations.

"It got me thinking about Waverly and Chris, which of course got me in the gut," Celeste said to Mimi. "Those two really were inseparable."

"He did mention that, actually," I said. "How my mom and his dad were friends."

"Those Prices. All such sweet boys," Mimi said, looking out the window. Roo was saying something to Jack, who was grinning, as Trinity, still sour-faced, looked on. "I just hate all Roo's been through, with his daddy and everything."

"He said his dad doesn't live here anymore," I said. "Where is he?"

There are all kinds of silences. Natural ones, when conversation just ebbs after a flow. Awkward, just after someone's said something they shouldn't. The worst, though, are shocked silences, when no one can speak at all. This was one of those.

"He died, honey," Mimi said finally. "Before you two were born. Boating accident."

I didn't know what to say. All I could do, in fact, was look at Roo again while running through my mind again the moment earlier when I'd asked if his dad was still local. There had been a silence then, too, but only the briefest one, like a song missing a beat. He hadn't wanted to make me feel bad for being so ignorant. The way I felt right now.

"Oh, my God." I put my hand to my mouth, horrified. "I had no idea. I'm such an idiot."

"It's okay," Mimi said. When I just sat there, blinking, she added, "Saylor. You didn't know."

Down below the house, Jack was now on his feet, his plate empty except for a crumpled napkin. Roo got up as well, then extended a hand to Trinity, pulling her to a standing position. For him, she smiled.

"So. Saylor," Mimi said. "You going out with the kids tonight?"

I looked at Bailey, who was back on her phone. She didn't say anything, and the last thing I wanted was to yet again be forced on anyone. "I'm pretty tired, actually."

"Well, in case you change your mind," Celeste said, "Bailey, give Emma your number."

Bailey sighed. "You guys. Seriously. This is getting ridiculous."

I felt my face blush again. Here I'd thought this cousin was the nice one, but clearly even she was sick of dealing with me. I said quickly, "She doesn't have—"

"I mean," Bailey continued, over me, "is it Emma or is it Saylor? Because so far I'm hearing both, interchangeably. It's super confusing."

Everyone looked at me. So it wasn't me that was annoying. Just my names. I said, "At home, I've always been Emma.

80

Except if my mom was talking to me."

"Which is why I keep calling you Saylor," Mimi said softly. "Sorry. But she loved that name."

I bit my lip, hearing this. It had been a long day indeed, if this was the thing that would make me cry.

"How about this," Bailey said to me. "You think about it and let me know. Whatever you say, it sticks. Officially. Deal?"

I nodded. In time, maybe I'd figure this out.

"And give me your phone," she added. "I'll put in my number."

I swallowed, trying to pull it together, as I took my phone out of my pocket, unlocking the screen and sliding it over. BAILEY, I watched her type, then the digits.

"There," she said, returning it to me. Across the table, Mimi was watching us, but I couldn't read her expression. Half-sad, half-happy, all hard to explain. Like she was seeing something I wouldn't have, even from the same vantage point. "We're leaving here at eight. Let me know if you change your mind."

"Okay," I said. "Thanks."

After dinner, I went to my room, where I opened my notebook again to the family tree I'd started. SILAS, I wrote, next to Celeste, then drew a line through it. Twice. (There had to be a story there.) I added Amber under Joe, with a question mark, and Anna Gordon below her. So many gaps still to fill, but I was getting there.

Downstairs, I could hear Bailey and Trinity as they got ready in the kitchen and then the screen porch that functioned as their bedroom. There were other noises, too. Mimi's TV, most certainly showing another fixer-upper show. Jack on his own phone on the other side of the wall, speaking quietly, maybe to Taylor. But as darkness fell and I found myself nodding off earlier than I had in ages, it was those who were not there that filled my mind. Roo first, and the secret, not so much a secret, that he'd kept from me. My mom, in this same room. And the frick to her frack, Chris, gone as well. The past was always present, in its way, and you can't help but remember. Even if you can't remember at all.

SIX

I woke to the smell of toast.

It was actually the second time I'd been up. The first had been at four a.m., when my dad, obviously so worried about how I was faring that he forgot about the seven-hour time difference, called me from Greece.

"Dad?" I answered, after fumbling for the phone in the dark for a moment. "Is everything okay?"

"What's not okay?" he replied.

"What?" I said.

"Did you say you're not okay?"

"No," I said. "I asked if *you* were okay, since you're calling me so early."

A pause. Then, "Oh, no. What time is it there? I'm all turned around."

"It doesn't matter," I assured him, even as I noticed the little clock on the dresser said 4:15 a.m. Which made this the second morning in a row I'd been awakened by a phone call at this hour, something I could only hope wasn't a trend. "How was the flight?"

"Good," he said. "Long. But we're here now, in a taxi on our way to the hotel."

"Hi, Emma!" Tracy called out.

"Tell her hi," I said to my dad.

He relayed the message. "The important thing is, how are you? Is it all right there?"

I looked at the clock again, weighing how to answer this. Of course I didn't want him to worry. I was fine, just a bit discombobulated. Also I had a lot of questions, most of which he probably couldn't answer. "It's good," I said. "I had dinner with Celeste and her kids."

"Great." Hearing the relief in his voice as he said this one word made it clear how worried he'd been, and I was glad I'd chosen carefully. "How is Celeste?"

"She's good," I told him. "Raising a cousin's kid, this ten-year-old named Gordon. Her mom is in Florida. I think her name is Amber?"

"Amber? No. She's, like, ten years old herself." A pause. "Or, she was the last time I saw her. Which I guess was about twenty years ago, now that I think of it. Keeping up with your mom's family always made my head hurt. Glad to know some things don't change."

"Guess not," I said. "Look, I'm fine. Go enjoy your trip."

"Honey that moon," he said, chuckling. "Call me when it's a decent hour there, okay? We're supposed to have service on the boat."

"Okay," I told him. "I love you."

"Love you too, Emma. Bye."

I put my phone back on the bedside table, rolling over to face the window. I could just see the surface of the water, the moon overhead. I looked at it, thinking of my dad and Tracy, speeding across a city I'd never seen and couldn't even picture, until I fell asleep.

And now it was eight a.m., and there was toast, or at least the smell of it. Also, possibly coffee. Hopeful, I got up, pulling on some shorts and a clean T-shirt, then brushed my teeth and went downstairs.

"Morning," a voice said as soon as my foot hit the bottom step. Startled, I jumped: Oxford, Mimi's husband, was sitting at the table, a newspaper open in front of him. Otherwise the kitchen was empty, although when I glanced at the toaster, I saw the indicator light shone bright red, signaling it was on.

"Good morning," I replied. I walked over to the counter, where, sure enough, I found a coffeemaker with half a pot left. Score. "Okay if I take some of this?"

"Help yourself." He turned a page of the paper. "Milk and cream are in the fridge, sugar's over here."

I found a mug, filled it, then came over to the table, finding a spoon and adding some sugar before taking a seat. As I did, the toaster binged cheerfully, six slices popping up. Oxford didn't seem to notice.

"You want some of the paper?" he asked me.

"Sure."

"What section?"

I took a sip from my mug. Perfect. "Do you have the obituaries?"

He didn't bat an eye, rifling through to pull out the local news. "One of my favorites. Always good to start the day making sure I'm not in there."

"I'll let you know," I said, smiling at him.

"Do that."

We sat there, reading in companionable silence, which was a strange thing to do with someone you'd only barely met. But reading the paper I *did* know, since Nana and I did it together every morning. After all the newness of the day before, it was nice to have something familiar. Of course, the moment I felt relaxed, Trinity showed up.

At first she was just shuffling footsteps, coming down the hallway. Then she appeared, looking half-asleep in sweatpants and an oversized tank top, her pregnant belly stretching it out. She did not look at or address either Oxford or myself, instead just walking to the toaster, where she retrieved the six pieces of toast, piling them on a paper towel, before going to the fridge for a tub of butter.

"If you take that, bring it back," Oxford said, still reading. She did not reply, instead just going back the way she'd come, leaving us alone again.

The obituary section in the *Bly County News*—North Lake was too small for its own paper, clearly—was much smaller than the one in the *Lakeview Observer*. Which I supposed made sense: fewer people, fewer deaths to report.

Today there were only two, starting with Marjorie McGuire, 82, who had gone to meet her Lord and Savior the previous week. In her picture, she had a beauty shop hairdo and was smiling.

The fact that I was interested in the obits made my dad uneasy. He worried it reflected my anxiety, fear of death, not dealing with my mom's passing, or the triple bonus, all three. But it wasn't about that. When Nana and I had first started our breakfast-and-paper tradition, I'd cared about comics and not much else. The obits were always there, though, on the opposite page, and at some point I'd started reading them as well. Then my mom died. She'd had no obit, for reasons I could never understand, so I got even more interested in how people chose to be, or were, remembered.

Most obituaries, I'd found, shared the same basics. The opening paragraphs rarely gave specifics, other than the person had passed "after a long illness" or "unexpectedly." Occasionally someone died "at home," which sounded like it might be a way of saying it was on purpose without using those exact words. The religious ones often contained scripture, if not a mention of where the deceased planned to go and who they hoped to see there. Next up was usually a summary of the life itself, with education, marriages, and children and a listing of career high points. The final paragraphs usually touched on a hobby dear to the person who had passed—travel was big, and volunteering for good causes—before providing funeral info and suggesting where to donate in lieu of flowers.

I always made a point to read each word of every obit. This would be the last way this person was remembered: Was I really too busy to take an extra three seconds to read about their commitment to the March of Dimes? Also, I felt reassured when all the day's listings were people like Mrs. Maguire, who had lived a good, full life. An obit for a younger person, like my dad's age, always made me sad. A teen or a child was heartbreaking. It just didn't fit, like a rule had been broken, and I'd find myself trying to piece together the part of the story that wasn't told.

When I'd first started reading the obits, they never mentioned overdoses or drugs as causes of death. In recent years, though, as more opioid crisis stories hit the front page, they made this section as well. Occasionally it was spelled out, with the deceased having "struggled with an addiction," or similar. More often, though, you had to read between the lines, finding the references to battling demons, pride in a previous period of sobriety, or a family request to donate to Narcotics Anonymous.

Would it have made a difference, having a clipping from a paper with my mom's name and dates, a recap of the things and people she loved, and those who were missing her? It would have been at least more closure than that night outside the building as the elevator doors closed. Maybe that was what I was looking for, all those mornings with Nana and now.

"Morning," I heard a voice say. I looked up to see Bailey come into the kitchen in shorts and a red T-shirt that said BLACKWOOD on it, her hair pulled back in a ponytail.

"Morning," Oxford said. "You working today?"

"At nine," she replied. She went over to the counter, where she opened a loaf of bread, taking out six slices and dropping them into the toaster before turning it on. "Why?"

"Mimi's knee is acting up," he replied, folding down the top part of the sports section.

"Oh, no." Bailey came over, sliding into the chair beside mine. "How bad is it?"

"Doc says he wants her off her feet for at least a week, but we all know that's not happening. You want any of the paper?"

"Horoscopes, please."

He handed her a section as I went back to my own reading about Wallace Camp, 78, who had passed surrounded by loved ones after a long illness. His photo was from his military days.

There was a thunk from upstairs, then the sound of a door opening. Jack yelled, "Can someone put in some toast for me?"

"On it," Bailey called back.

"Thanks." The door shut again.

"I can try to trade shifts with someone for tomorrow," Bailey said, running her finger down the horoscopes before landing on Aries, which was my sign as well. "But it's late notice for today."

"Don't worry about it. We'll work it out somehow."

The timer sounded—BING!—and she jumped up, taking a plate from the cupboard and bringing it over to the toaster. As she plucked the pieces out, one by one, the screen door slammed and Mimi came in. Gordon was behind her, in shorts over a bathing suit, a backpack over her shoulders.

"Oxford," Mimi said, dropping a cordless phone receiver on the table beside him. "Answer this if it rings. I've got to take Gordon to camp."

"Where's Celeste?"

"Early shift. She left at six." Mimi looked at me. "Emma, honey, did you eat breakfast?"

"Not yet. I'm fine, though."

"Let me make you some before the bread's all gone," she replied, crossing the kitchen to load the toaster up with slices again. "If the Sergeant's spending his money on this fancy thing, we should use it."

The toaster being idle couldn't have been an issue. By my count we were at eighteen slices now and counting. I asked, "The Sergeant?"

"Trinity's fiancé," Oxford explained, not looking up from his own section of the paper. "Deployed right now."

"Where's the butter?" Bailey, now peering into the fridge, asked.

"Your sister took it," Oxford told her.

Bailey sighed. "Trinity! Bring back the butter!"

"I'm getting dressed," her sister replied. "You can come get it."

"Honey, I've got to take Gordon to camp!" Mimi yelled in the direction of the hallway, starting the toaster again. "So you'll be starting on your own today."

"Are you *serious*?" Trinity replied. "I'm huge. I can't even bend down to get under the beds."

Mimi exhaled, looking at the ceiling. "We'll talk about it when I get back. Gordon, come on."

"Trinity!" Bailey yelled as they left, the door again slamming behind them. "I need the butter."

"I told you, I'm getting dressed. Damn!"

"You two stop yelling, before you chase me out of my own kitchen again," Oxford warned.

"Fine," Bailey said, ripping a paper towel off the roll and folding two slices up inside it. "I'll eat it dry on the way to work. If I choke to death on the way, you'll know who to blame."

With that, she was gone, the door banging again behind her. A beat later, the toaster popped up: BING! Oxford reached over, extracting the slices and dropping them on the plate Mimi had left for this purpose. Then he put it on the table between us, taking one before looking at me.

"You want butter?"

I smiled. "Nope."

"Wise move," he said, and went back to his paper.

The two obits read, I pulled over the horoscopes to read Aries for myself. Apparently, Bailey and I were both going to savor something delicious in the day ahead. My thoughts drifted back to Trinity, who was coming back down the hallway, dressed now in shorts and a tie-dye, carrying the butter. She went straight to the toaster, loading it up again with what I could not help but notice was the last of the bread. Suddenly Celeste's frustration the day before made sense.

"Here," she announced, dropping the butter in front of me, as if I'd been the one demanding it. I didn't say anything, instead just picking up my dry toast and taking a pointed bite. I was pretty sure she didn't notice. "Is Bailey going to come clean today?"

"She's got to work," Oxford replied.

Trinity's expression, already sour, grew more so. "Great. So it'll just be me turning over four rooms before check-in."

Oxford did not reply to this. I said, "I can help you, if you want."

"You?" She narrowed her eyes, as if I was so small she couldn't see me otherwise. "You're on vacation."

This stung, for some reason. "Not really."

"Well, tell it to Mimi. That's what she said."

Oxford glanced at her, then me. I thought he was about to say something, but was glad when he didn't.

BING! went the toaster, six slices popping up. Trinity retrieved them before bringing them to the table on a paper towel. She reached across me for a knife, which she then used to briskly butter each slice, the scraping sound hard to ignore.

"I'm late," Jack, also in a BLACKWOOD T-shirt, said as he came down the stairs. "Is there any—"

Wordlessly, Trinity picked up two pieces of buttered toast, holding them over her head. As Jack passed, he grabbed them. "Thanks."

"No problem."

"We're short a cleaner," Oxford said as he started for the door. "Mimi's knee. Ask Roo if he wants some hours."

"Will do," Jack said, heading for the door. "Thanks for the toast."

"Thank the Sergeant," she replied. "He's the one who bought that huge thing."

I looked at the toaster, remembering how my dad had remarked that it was new. Apparently, there was a military aspect to it as well. In this house, even the appliances were complicated.

"Trinity?" I heard Mimi yell from outside. "Best get started on those rooms."

In response, Trinity sighed loudly enough I literally felt a breeze from her direction. Then she pushed back her chair, grabbing a piece of toast. Oxford said, "Mimi's got no business cleaning. Her knee can't take it."

"I'm *pregnant*," she replied unnecessarily. But she got to her feet, yelling outside to Mimi, "Coming!"

As she left, I looked at the table. Only three pieces of toast remained. On the counter, the bread bag, defeated, was crumpled into a ball. The clock on the stove said 8:58 a.m.

I stood up, carrying my plate over to the sink, which was again full of dishes. They don't want your help, I told myself, even as the urge hit, then grew, to start washing them. But I rinsed only my cup, putting it on the (empty) dish rack as Oxford grabbed a final slice of toast and the phone, taking both with him as he left. After so much noise and commotion, the house felt so still suddenly, with only me in it and the whole day ahead. What do you do when no one wants you to do anything? I wasn't sure. But I did put the butter away.

* * *

It's so boring, oh my God. I mean, I'm happy Grandpa's ok. But I am so sick of hospital cafeteria food and trying to keep my brothers quiet.

It was late morning now, and I'd finally heard from Bridget. Her grandfather was recovering in the hospital, the boys were driving her nuts, and there was nothing to do in Ohio. These were the headlines.

I understand, I wrote back. **So glad he's getting better, though.**

Me too. What are you doing?

What *was* I doing? At the moment, sitting on the front steps of Mimi's house, wondering how to keep myself busy while everyone else was at work. So far, that had entailed reorganizing my already neat clothes, reading part of an Allies book Gordon had left in the living room—the sixth book from the second series, according to the back cover, but I'd had no trouble dropping right into the mythology—and, now, watching the hotel guests converge on the beach for the day.

Guests emerged with beach bags, wheeled coolers, and more children as they made their way down the plank walkway to the water. They set up camp on the covered part of the dock or the sand, spreading towels and dragging chairs into position as kids were wrangled, protesting the application of sunscreen.

The office of Calvander's, in the opposite direction, was the other center of activity. All morning long, people had been coming and going: Mimi, of course, even though she was supposed to be off her feet. Oxford, wiping down the glass door with Windex and weeding the sparse garden. I even glimpsed both Taylor and April popping in before they walked off down the street, out of sight. Between the constant activity of both the beach and the office, I felt even more frozen where I sat on the steps.

Getting used to this place, I finally wrote back to Bridget. **What's the boy situation?**

Immediately, I had a flash of Roo the day before, shirtless, holding out a hand to me at the raft. That gap in his teeth. Which was ridiculous, I knew.

All related to me. Or might as well be.

Seriously?

Just then, I saw Mimi coming down the motel sidewalk, pushing a cleaning cart. She now wore a Velcro brace on one knee and had the office phone between her ear and shoulder as she stopped by a door marked 7 and pulled a ring of keys from her pocket. She let herself in, and a moment later the front blinds were rising, revealing a streaky window.

I thought of how I'd offered help to Trinity earlier and the way she'd so easily grouped me with the guests now out on the beach. She'd said it was Mimi who made this clear, and possibly she had. But maybe sometimes you had to ask twice. I walked over.

"No kidding," I heard her saying as I approached the door to room seven. "In a perfect world, my body wouldn't be breaking down. But this is the world we're in."

The room was dim, and it took my eyes a second to

adjust. Once they did, I saw the walls were made of cinder block painted white, the carpet a dated flat orange. There were two double beds, both stripped, a rattan bedside table between them. The TV was one of those ancient kinds, huge and mounted up high on the wall, a bunch of cords snaking out of the back. Against the far wall was a small fridge and stovetop, a microwave and a sink, three skinny cabinets above. The only other furniture was two faded canvas chairs, and between them a low table with a flyswatter and an ashtray on it. Who even smoked inside anymore?

". . . okay, well, keep me posted," Mimi said as she stepped out of what had to be the bathroom. Her arms were full of towels, which she dumped onto a pile of sheets already under the TV. "I'd better run. We've got two check-ins today plus housekeeping. Okay. Bye."

She sighed as she hung up, still not seeing me. I didn't want to startle her, so I knocked on the door lightly. When she didn't hear me, I did it again.

"Oh, hey," she said, breaking into a smile. "You need something?"

"No," I replied. "I just . . . I heard you could use some help."

"I always need help," she said, starting toward the door. Her brace creaked with each step. "It's an ongoing condition in a resort town. But nothing you can do, I'm afraid."

I stepped aside as she came out to the cart, grabbing a stack of paper bath mats and a handful of individually wrapped soaps. "I can clean. I'm actually pretty good at it."

She looked at me. "Oh, honey. You don't want to do that. Motel work is gross."

As if to emphasize this point, Trinity emerged from room six, carrying a plunger. "Got out the clog, not that it was pretty. There's a damn sign saying not to flush anything other than toilet paper. Can't people read?"

"Shhh," Mimi told her.

"Nobody's listening to us." She leaned the plunger against the cart. "You have linens yet?"

"Nope," Mimi replied. "Grab some, would you? Get them for six too, we'll do all the beds at once."

Trinity nodded, then turned, walking to a nearby door that said STAFF ONLY and pushing it open. As she did, the smell of chlorine bleach filled the air, along with the banging of what sounded like a dryer.

Mimi turned back to me. "Why don't you walk down to the Station, see what's going on there? There's usually a group at the arcade or the snack bar."

She turned me down so easily; it was frustrating. "I can help you," I said, emphasizing the words this time. "Really."

"Honey, I don't *want* you to," she replied. I felt unexpectedly hurt, hearing this. Which must have shown on my face, because she added, quickly, "Saylor, you haven't been here in over ten years. I want you to enjoy it. That's what your mom would have wanted, too."

Trinity walked past me, carrying a stack of folded linens, and went into room seven, dropping them onto the bed closest to the door. On the cart the phone started to ring and

Mimi picked it up, just as a white van that said ARTHUR AND SONS WINDOWS pulled up to the office.

"Hello? Oh, hey, Tom. Yes, it's unit ten. Okay. Meet you there in five minutes." She glanced at the van, then sighed again. "Lord, and there's Artie coming for an estimate. Everything's happening at once today."

The man in question was climbing out of the van now, carrying a clipboard. He lifted a hand in our direction, and Mimi, looking stressed, waved back. As she started making her way to meet him, I opened my mouth to say something, then closed it. Three times might have been the charm, but it could also mean not taking a hint.

"Why do you really want to help?"

I turned around to face Trinity. "Why?"

"Come on," she said. "You're the spoiled rich cousin and everyone's been told to make sure you have fun here."

I'd been tiptoeing around her so much the flare of temper I felt, hearing this, was welcome. "Not by me," I said, an edge to my voice.

"Who cares? Why not just kick back and enjoy yourself? I would."

"Well, that's you," I told her. She raised her eyebrows. "Look, you don't have to like me or the fact I'm here. But don't pretend you know me. Mimi let me come stay here with zero notice. The very least I can do is help her out when *she* needs it."

"Yeah, but have you ever actually *held* a job?"

I'm only seventeen, I wanted to say. Just as I thought this, though, I realized she'd probably been working for years. Things were different here. Out loud I said, "I can help you, if you'll let me. It's up to you."

She looked at me for a second, and I leveled my gaze back at her. Finally she said, "Go by the office and tell Mimi you need the keys to room ten. Then go let Tom in. Don't give her a choice."

"Okay," I said, surprised at how victorious I felt. "Then what?"

"You need something else?"

"What I need is to not feel I'm just sitting around doing nothing while she's working on her bad knee," I told her. "That's something I'm pretty sure my mom wouldn't have wanted."

She glanced out the door, toward the office. "Okay. Come back here after. I'll show you how to do the beds."

I nodded, then started down the sidewalk. Of course she hadn't denied not liking me, not that I really expected her to. But I'd take her offer. Since arriving, I'd felt like not family and not a guest, the sole inhabitant of this weird place in between. It felt good to have a job and task at hand. Like the chaos that was this trip could actually get a bit more organized, and I might just find my place in it.

SEVEN

"You know, it's not exactly that I don't like you."

"No?" I asked Trinity, spraying down the mirror in front of me, then starting to wipe it from the center out, as she'd showed me earlier.

"Not really." She added two folded dish towels to the dish rack, hanging them just so. "It's more the *idea* of you."

I looked over at her. "That's supposed to make me feel better?"

"It's not supposed to make you feel anything," she replied. "It's just the truth."

"You called me the spoiled rich cousin," I pointed out.

"Okay, well, I can see how that might have seemed bitchy."

Might? I thought. But I stayed quiet, taking my annoyance out on a stubborn streak.

"But look at it from my point of view," she continued. "Here I am, hugely pregnant and uncomfortable—"

"Not my fault," I pointed out quietly.

"—and alone, because my fiancé is still deployed even though he was supposed to be back last month," she continued. "And I'm on my feet all day doing this incredibly physical job, because no one else but my grandmother wants to hire someone almost eight months along at the beginning of summer."

"Again, not my fault," I told her. "Also technically not legal."

"And then," she went on, spraying some cleaner with jabs of the bottle, "here you come, with your hot dad in a fancy car, just to chill out for a while and take it easy. And we're told that, specifically. That you are here to have a good time, like that's our responsibility."

I turned to look at her, surprised. "You think my dad's hot?"

She shrugged. "Yeah."

Ugh. I made a face, then turned back to the mirror. Behind me, she laughed—which also took me by surprise, as I'd hardly even seen her smile—then said, "My point is, I made up my mind about you based on the information I was given. That's not mean. It's science."

"Science?" I repeated.

"What?" she replied, running some water into the sink. "Lake girls can't be good in school?"

"Just didn't peg you as a science nerd," I said.

"I'm not." She turned off the faucet. "Math is my favorite. And half my double major."

"What's the other?"

"Education," she said, wiping a bit of something off the stove handle. "I want to teach middle school algebra. I mean, once the baby comes and I finish my degree."

Hearing this, I realized she wasn't the only one who had made assumptions. I was embarrassed—ashamed, really. "I bet you'll make a good teacher."

This seemed to please her. "Yeah?"

"After that cleaning tutorial you gave me earlier? You bet."

Now, she did smile—briefly—and we both went back to work. It had been like this all day, into the late afternoon. Us working together, talking sometimes, but just as often, letting silences fall.

After our standoff by room seven—as I had a feeling I'd be remembering it—I'd done as she said, going down to the office, where I found Mimi deep in discussion with the window guy. Not surprisingly, it was freezing.

"Saylor?" she said as the wind chimes hanging from the door handle clanked behind me. "You need something?"

I took a breath. "Trinity said I should get the keys to room ten to meet the A/C repair guy?"

Mimi looked at me a moment, then walked over behind the counter, grabbing a set of keys from the board hanging there. "Here," she said. "Tell him it's been blowing warm since last weekend."

I nodded, taking the keys. That was easy, I thought, as I left to help Tom access the A/C. When I returned to Trinity, she was shaking a clean sheet over one of the double beds. As it billowed out and the edges fluttered down, our eyes met across all that whiteness.

"Grab the other side and pull it tight," she instructed me. When I did, she said, "Tighter."

Thus began my course in motel room cleaning, which was short, harsh, and brutally to the point, much like Trinity herself. Luckily, she wasn't the only one who was a good student.

There were two types of room cleaning at Calvander's, she told me as we made those first beds. Housekeeping, which was for rooms with guests staying on another night, and turnover, for rooms that had been vacated and needed a full clean before being occupied again. Both included what I'd come to think of as the defaults: vacuuming, emptying trash cans, cleaning toilets and wiping down sinks, replacing towels, and so on. For turnover, you then added changing the bed linens, wiping down the kitchen, mirror, and shower, and putting away all dishes and silverware, plus cleaning out whatever was left in the small fridges provided for guests. Which, so far, had been mostly beer, soda, and, in one case, a to-go box with a piece of leftover something, coated with mold.

"Turnover is mandatory," Trinity said as we loaded fresh towels onto the racks in the bathroom. "New guests, clean room. Housekeeping, however, is a courtesy. But people always want it, as long as they're not inconvenienced. Like exhibit A over there."

This referred to a woman staying in room four, who had been sleeping when we knocked, then let ourselves in. She woke up yelling, keeping it up until we beat a quick retreat, Trinity cursing back under her own breath. An hour later, she found us and said the room was ready to be serviced, and not to forget extra towels and to vacuum under the beds. As she departed, she nicked a bunch of our soaps from our cart, something Trinity clearly viewed as an insult.

"People will steal anything from a motel room," she said, nodding at the woman retreating. "I mean, those soaps are tiny and cheap. She's driving a Cadillac. Really?"

I didn't say anything to this, because I'd already figured out I had two jobs here other than my actual one: listen to what my cousin said, and retain that information. The commentary—and there was lots, sprinkled throughout—was just a bonus.

"You *will* be disgusted, daily," she informed me as we stood in the open doorway of our first truly dirty bathroom. Towels were everywhere, the trash can overflowing, and the toilet itself full of something I wasn't going to look at unless I had to. "There are rubber gloves on the cart. Do not be afraid to use them."

"Right," I said, bending down to grab the towels as gingerly as possible. Already, it was unspoken that we'd divide and conquer, with me doing the low stuff and her reaching the higher things.

"Clorox, and all its forms, is your friend," she continued, spraying an arc from her own bottle—which said TRINITY on it in pink marker—into the room ahead of us. "Ditto for the blue goo."

"The what?"

She nodded at the toilet. "Flush that first."

I looked at it, and the contents, reminding myself I had been warned away from this job. The spoiled city cousin wouldn't do it. So I had to. I started to reach for the lever.

"Not with your HAND," she bellowed, and I jumped. "Use a foot."

"My foot?"

In response, she stepped past me, kicking out a leg so one beat-up sneaker hit the handle, flushing the contents. As it swirled away, she sprayed the Clorox again in its direction. "Blue goo," she continued, grabbing another bottle from the counter beside her, "is this toilet cleaner. Major disinfectant. Lift the seat—"

"With my foot?"

She nodded. I did. "Good. Now, line that bowl with this stuff. Don't be dainty, load it in there. Then we leave it to do the hard work for us before we come back with gloves on."

I followed these instructions, the bottle squirting loudly as I did so. When I was done, she handed me the bleach again. "Now, the shower."

And so it went, as we covered everything, from the stacking of soaps—"Two in two places, the holders built into the shower and sink"—to checking the toilet paper supply— "one on the roll, one extra if it runs out. Any more, they'll just get stolen."

"People steal toilet paper?"

"I told you, people steal everything," she said. "Aren't you paying attention?"

This continued throughout the day, with us covering the polishing of mirrors (newspaper worked best for streaks), using caution when cleaning under beds (always look before you reach for something you see, you have no idea what else is there). With turnover, it was all about being thorough but quick, as people usually showed up early, eager to begin their vacation.

Housekeeping, on the other hand, involved an added layer of conscious, careful awareness. When working around people's possessions and luggage, you were to treat them pretty much the same as toilets: don't touch unless you absolutely must, and then, do it quick.

"We are always the first to be accused," she explained, delicately moving a tablet aside to retrieve an empty box of tissues. "Something goes missing, we stole it. And God forbid it's medication. If you go into a bathroom and there's a bottle with pills falling out of it? Leave it as is. Even if it means missing a spot. Do you hear me?"

I nodded. "Look me in the eye," she said. I did. "Understood?"

"Understood," I repeated. When she kept looking at me, I added, "Never touch a pill or meds. Ever."

"Good girl."

Not for the first time that day, I thought of my own stays at hotels with my dad over the years. Had I left a big mess, toilet unflushed, something gross? I didn't recall doing so, and certainly hoped not. Nevertheless, I felt a wave of shame as I realized I'd never given much thought to the people who cleaned our rooms, even after seeing them or their carts in the hallways. It was just like magic: messy became clean. Except it wasn't.

While we cleaned, people continued to come in and out of the office, the clang of the wind chimes on the door marking each departure. But I wasn't really paying that much attention when someone knocked on room five. I was fighting with the vacuum, which had a frayed cord and cut off every time I moved it. When I turned, there was Roo. I literally jumped, I was so startled.

"Hey," he said. "Surprised to see you here."

"Let me guess," I said, sighing. "You were also told I'm the spoiled cousin who is on vacation."

He just looked at me for a moment. "No," he said finally. "Because Mimi asked me to clean this room, but you're already doing it."

Whoops. I pushed my hair out of my face, taking a breath. "Sorry," I said. "It's just been frustrating. Nobody has wanted my help."

"Really?" He stepped inside, picking up my spray bottle. "Weird. We always need an extra set of hands."

"Not mine, apparently. Until I forced the issue."

He sprayed the table by the window, then grabbed a clean rag, wiping it down. "Well, you're in it now. Once you start, you're one of us. No escape."

I smiled at this, starting up the vacuum again as he

dragged the smaller garbage can over to the bag I'd left by the door. For a moment we worked in silence, him emptying another can. Then I said, "Do you work here a lot?"

"I fill in as needed," he said. "Like everyone else."

There was a loud crackle, followed by a squeak. Then a girl's voice said, "Breaker breaker. Who's got their ears on?"

Roo reached to his back pocket, pulling out a beat-up walkie-talkie. He pushed a button as he put it to his mouth, then said, "You've got Rubber Duck and Saylor, go ahead."

I just looked at him. "Rubber Duck?"

He grinned. "That's my handle."

"Your—"

"Roo and *who*?" the girl's voice crackled over the handset again.

There was another buzz, followed by a different girl's voice. "Taylor, it's the girl you were so awful to yesterday. Did you already forget?"

I must have looked as confused as I felt, because Roo explained, "April and Taylor. They work at the mini-golf places down the block."

That explained why I'd seen them that morning. "And you guys communicate?"

"The power of the walkie. Works all the way up at the Station." He grinned, then pushed the button again. "So, yeah, Daffodil. You want to apologize to Saylor now or do it in person later?"

No reply. Finally April said, "Taylor. We can hear you breathing."

"I'm thinking!" Taylor said.

"I thought they worked at the same place?" I whispered to Roo.

He shook his head. "Nope. Both mini golf, but two different places, right across the street from each other."

There was another beep, and then I heard a voice say, flatly, "I am sorry for my behavior yesterday. I am working on my jealousy and anger issues and I hope you can accept my apology."

Roo looked at me, his eyebrows raised. Then, slowly, he pushed the handset's button, holding it out to me. I leaned toward it, clearing my throat. "I do. Thank you."

"See?" April said. "That wasn't so hard, was it? Now we're one big, happy family again!"

"Which should last for about five seconds," Roo added into the walkie. "Okay, everyone. Catch you later."

"Bye, y'all!" Taylor said. She sounded different when she wasn't so angry.

Roo shoved the handset back into his pocket and glanced around the room. "I should get back to the Station—they're short-staffed today too. You want me to come back when I'm off? Or you guys got this?"

"You should ask Trinity, but I think we're okay," I said as he bent down, picking up a crumpled piece of paper and chucking it in the trash can. "So you guys are all really close, huh?"

He shrugged. "Guess so. Sort of inevitable when there aren't that many of you."

"You're all the same age?"

"Nope," he replied, picking up the trash bag and shaking it. "Trinity's the oldest: she's five years ahead of me. Jack graduated two years ago, and April's a sophomore at East U. Me, Taylor, Vincent, and Bailey are all seniors this year."

"Is Jack in school, too?"

He looked at me, surprised. "No. He's running the Station with his dad. Family business, remember?"

I did. But in Lakeview, everyone at least tried to go to college. Once again, I'd assumed it was the same here. Just like a rich cousin would.

"Okay, so I'm going," he said. "See you later?"

I had no plans to cross paths with him again that day, as far as I knew. But I still said, "Yeah. See you later."

Now, it was four thirty, and Trinity and I were on the last room of the day. By my count, we'd been at it six and a half hours, with only a thirty-minute lunch break, when we made and ate quesadillas in Mimi's kitchen. My arms ached from reaching up to polish mirrors, the smell of bleach was seemingly lodged permanently in my nose, and I understood for the first time the expression "bone tired." I knew hanging with her to the end would surprise Trinity. What I didn't expect was that I'd be so proud of myself. Putting things in order, even other people's things, felt familiar and soothing. Like my anxiety had found a good place to land, too.

"Go all the way out the door," Trinity instructed me as I cleaned the carpet to the threshold, stepping myself onto the sidewalk outside. "Then unplug and we're done."

I yanked out the cord, pulling the vacuum over to my side, and shut the door. "Now what?" I said to Trinity, who was wiping a smudge off the outside of the window.

"We put the cart back, deal with laundry, and fill bleach bottles for tomorrow. Then we get the hell out of here before anyone asks for anything else."

She led the way back to the door that said STAFF ONLY, opening it. The room inside was narrow, with a row of washers and dryers tumbling the sheets and towels we'd collected earlier. I followed her to a small countertop, lined with spray bottles. All of them were labeled with names, some in recent marker, others faded almost to the point of being unreadable. ESTHER. DAWN. MARIKA. CARMEN. It made me aware, suddenly, that the one she'd given me off the cart said nothing.

"We're possessive about our bottles," she said, clearly having noticed this. She pulled a huge container of bleach off a shelf. "If you find one you really like, you have to claim it."

"Aren't they all the same?"

She screwed off the top of her own. "At a glance, yes. But there are subtle differences. Tautness of handle, for example. And some have an adjustable spray, but others don't."

Again, I looked at my own bottle, which I was still holding, and gave it a quick squirt. It did feel a little loose.

"You don't get your own for just one day," she told me, filling up her TRINITY-marked one with water. "They're earned, not given."

"It's a spray bottle," I pointed out.

"Not here," she replied. "Here, it's a badge of honor. Now hand that over so I can refill it."

I did, then watched as she filled it up with the same mix of water and bleach. Then she put it on the shelf with all the others before placing her TRINITY one beside it.

"How long have you been doing this?" I asked.

"Officially? Since June. But I started helping clean when I was Gordon's age," she replied. "Bailey and Jack, too. We didn't have a choice, same as with the Station."

Family business, again. My dad had his own practice, not that I'd ever worked a day there. I'd spent my summers at various camps and traveling with my father or Nana. None of my friends worked real jobs yet. But things were clearly different here.

"A lot of people have passed through, huh?" I said, again scanning the names.

"It's a lake town," she replied. "Nobody stays for long unless they have roots here."

We put in some more sheets, then folded a load of towels before she pronounced us finished for the day. As we walked down the sidewalk toward Mimi's, we passed a family of guests heading up from the dock. The dad was pulling a cooler stacked with beach toys, the mom carrying a beer in one of those foam insulated holders. Their kids trailed along behind them, bickering and smelling of sunscreen.

As they all disappeared into room six, which we'd left pristine, I wondered how long it would take for them to mess it up again. Already I was tired. But thinking about this made me exhausted.

I was too wiped out to go out to the raft that afternoon, even if someone had invited me. Which they didn't.

"Lake North Pavilion at eight, then over to Colin and Blake's," Bailey reported as she came down below the house with her plate, joining Trinity and me at the picnic table there. Mimi, also worn-out, had asked Oxford to pick up two buckets of fried chicken for dinner and was eating hers in front of the TV. There was no sign of Jack anywhere, at least not so far.

"That's the plan?" Trinity asked.

"It's what I said, isn't it?"

"Sounds more like *your* plan," her sister replied. "Lake North and yacht club boys."

"Anyone who doesn't like it doesn't have to come," Bailey said, putting her glass of milk down with a thunk. "Nobody's got a damn gun to their head."

"Let me guess," Trinity said. "You're snapping at me because I'm not the only one who expressed a lack of enthusiasm."

"I'm not snapping at you," Bailey replied. "I'm just tired of putting things together every night only to have people bitch and moan."

"Summer just started, Bay."

"Exactly. Too early to be so damn picky."

They were both silent for a moment, during which I took

a bite off my own plate, wondering if it was possible to have any meal in this house without some sort of friction. Finally I asked, "Did I meet Colin and Blake?"

"Not unless you're taking sailing lessons at the yacht club," Trinity said.

Bailey shot her a look. "Colin was out at the raft yesterday. He gave me a ride in. Blake's his roommate."

"Oh, right," I said.

"And they've been over here every night this week," Bailey said. "So it only seems fair that we reciprocate and go there for once."

"Or," Trinity said, picking up a biscuit from her plate, "we could just stick with our own kind the way nature intended."

"That is such bullshit," Bailey shot back. "You know as well as I do that the kids from both sides have hung out since this place was settled."

"I'm not saying they haven't. I'm saying maybe they *shouldn't*."

"Why? Because we're not exactly alike?"

"Because we have nothing in common with those rich kids! And even if you do find one you like, do you think it's actually going to end up being anything that lasts? Every time some girl we know gets tangled up with one of them, she gets dumped at the end of the summer. It's like clockwork."

"Not every time."

"Every time."

"My mom didn't," I said.

That shut them up. Which had not been my intention, really. I was just contributing, because for once I had something to add. Now that I'd done that, though, I realized this subject was a fraught one.

"She didn't?" Trinity said after a moment. "They got divorced."

"Trinity," her sister said, her voice like a warning shot.

"After seven years," I replied. "And it was a mutual decision, from what I've heard."

Again, silence. Down at the shore, some ducks quacked as they walked along the small waves breaking there.

Trinity sighed, then looked up at the sky overhead. "Saylor. I don't mean to insult you or your mom and dad."

"It's never your intention," Bailey grumbled. "You just do."

"I'm not insulted," I told her. And I wasn't. I just knew so little of the history around here: when something came up I could claim, I wanted it to be correct. "But for what it's worth, my dad's a good guy. Even if he was a yacht club boy once."

"Fine, they're all probably wonderful," Trinity said. "I still don't want to hang out with them. Which is a moot point anyway because the Sergeant and I are doing a HiThere! tonight."

"We just went through all that and you're not even going with us?" Bailey asked.

"You know I haven't gone out since I got huge." Trinity

swung her legs around, off the bench, then grunted as she got to her feet. "But Saylor is."

"I am?" I asked.

"You have to," she replied, starting up to the house. "Otherwise she's going alone, and cousins don't let cousins do that. Especially with yacht club boys."

With this, she started up the hill to the house. I looked at Bailey, who was angrily picking at her chicken leg again. "You don't have to include me," I said. "She's just being nice."

She looked up at me. "Trinity? Nice? Since when?"

"Since I worked with her today," I said. Hardly convinced, she went back to her food. "And maybe it's more like nice-ish. I don't think she hates me anymore, at any rate."

"You cleaned rooms?" she asked. "Wow. I'm surprised."

This again. In a tired voice, I said, "Because you thought I was the spoiled rich cousin just here to relax and hang out?"

She blinked, hearing this. "Well . . . that is kind of what Mimi said."

"Well," I said, "I'm not. At least, I don't want to be."

We were both quiet a moment. Up at the house, the screen door slammed.

I picked up my drink, taking a sip. "So tell me about these boys."

She smiled. The change in subject was like that in the weather, the equivalent of a sudden cool breeze. Everything just felt different. "They're nice. Roommates at East U, just finished their freshman year."

"How'd you meet them?"

She wiped her mouth with a paper towel. "Where I meet everyone: the Station."

"You work there every summer?"

"Since I was fourteen. That's how it goes with a family business. You pitch in as soon as you can," she replied. That sounded familiar. "Trinity only ever worked the arcade and the snack bar, which is why she's so narrow-minded about Lake North folks. But like I said, working the pumps is different. You meet everyone there."

I put down my fork. "When my mom used to talk about this place, she never mentioned there were basically two different lakes. I had no idea."

"Well, it probably wasn't a bad thing as far as she was concerned, right? I mean, she did meet your dad that way."

She stopped talking then, clearly not sure whether this topic was all right to return to or still needed to be avoided. Taking out the guesswork, I said, "Do people here hate him?"

She turned to face me. "No. I mean, I don't think so. Why would they?"

I shrugged. "Because he was a rich yacht club boy. And he took her from here, and then she died."

"Because she was an addict," she replied. Immediately, she put her hand over her mouth. "Oh, shit, Emma. I can't believe I just said that. I'm—"

"It's okay." I bit my lip, then took a breath. "She was. The truth hurts, but there it is. I just wondered if everyone thought that might be Dad's fault, too."

"No." She said this so flatly, so quickly, I immediately believed her. "Look, again, I don't mean offense or to dishonor anyone's memory. All I've ever heard was how much everyone loved Waverly. But they also know she had problems long before and after he came along. I mean, that night with Chris Price, your dad wasn't even here."

Chris Price. It took a minute. "Roo's dad," I said finally.

She nodded. "He was her best friend. And she was with him that night, you know, when the boat crashed."

I didn't know. For all the stories, she'd never told this one. "What happened?"

Just then, though, I heard it: boys' voices, coming from the lawn above us. When I looked up, there were Roo and Jack, climbing out of a beat-up VW that had pulled up by the back steps.

"Yo!" Jack yelled. "I hear there's no plan for tonight. What gives?"

Bailey, too annoyed to even answer, just sighed and went back to her dinner. As she did, I watched the boys disappear into the house before re-emerging in the bright kitchen above, where they grabbed plates and descended on the chicken that remained. Clearly, the moment had passed to get the answer to my question and the story I'd not yet heard. Now, I turned back to the lake, looking past the church and that big white cross, over to the other side. From the way Trinity acted, it was another world. But really, how different could it be?

EIGHT

"Moment of truth," Bailey said, tying the boat up tight. "Who are you tonight: Emma or Saylor?"

Emma was the logical choice, of course. It was the name I knew, the one I'd always answered to as long as my mom wasn't the one calling. And she'd been gone five years now, almost six. Maybe I could just say she took Saylor with her. At the same time, though, she had picked that name based on the summer here when she'd met my dad. So if I was going to go by it, this was the time and place. Emma was the rich cousin from Lakeview who organized things and worried. Saylor, well, she could be anyone.

Even and especially this girl I was tonight, arriving at a pavilion adjacent to a yacht club in a new-to-me outfit and more makeup than I'd worn, well, ever. That was Trinity's doing.

"I'm huge and can't wear anything," she'd said as she dragged me onto the back porch that was her and Bailey's bedroom. "Just indulge me."

What this meant, I discovered, was standing there in my normal, chosen outfit of cutoff shorts and a JACKSON TIGERS T-shirt while she assembled other options on the unmade bed. Apparently, she had quite the wardrobe, pre-pregnancy, as well as a signature look: just about everything she owned was short, had cutouts, or both.

"This is really not my style," I told her, after she'd badgered me into a silky blouse, run through with gold thread, over a tight black skirt. "I don't think I can even sit in this."

"Who has to sit?" she asked, stepping back to look at me. "You're going out, not to church."

Bailey, across the room brushing her hair, snorted. Sure, it was funny to her. She was wearing jeans and a tank top, of her own choosing.

"I'm not wearing this," I said, tugging off the skirt. "It's cutting off my circulation."

"Fine." She pushed a minidress at me in its place. "Try this one."

It had a deep scoop neck, plus sleeves that billowed open to reveal my wrists and upper arms. "No," I said flatly.

"Why? It's perfect!"

"If I was giving blood," I said.

This time, Bailey laughed out loud. "You're funny," she said. "Do people tell you that?"

"More often I'm told my humor isn't for everyone," I told her. "Or, you know, anyone."

"Let's try shoes," Trinity said, heading over to a box by the end of the bed. There were no closets, the only storage

120

a few suitcases and a couple of cardboard boxes. The bulk of their possessions were piled on the beds and other surfaces. I'd had to move a laptop, two bottles of shampoo, and a big hardback book called *Pregnancy and You* just to make enough room to sit down. "How do you feel about stilettos?"

"Strongly opposed," I told her.

"Trinity, we're taking the boat," Bailey told her. "Not going to prom."

"Well, never mind, they're not here anyway." She stood up, putting her hands on her lower back. "None of my good shoes are, now that I think of it. I left them all at the storage unit at the house when we were cleaning out for the renters. It wasn't like I was going to be wearing them."

"That's got to be weird," I said as, undeterred, she went back to picking through the piles of clothes on the bed. "Having to move house every summer."

She picked up a red blouse, squinting at it. "With the two divorces, we're used to moving around a lot. It's not so bad."

"I hate it," Bailey told me. "People we don't know living in our room, sleeping in my bed. It gives me the creeps."

"Also makes Mom money," Trinity pointed out.

"You can't put a price on peace of mind."

"I can. Eleven hundred a week."

To this, her sister rolled her eyes, turning back to the small mirror that was propped up on a nearby bookshelf. "Well, you don't even have to worry, since this is your last time doing it."

"Really?" I asked Trinity, who was now holding the red shirt up against me.

"Yep," she replied. "Once the Sergeant is back, he and the baby and I will have our own place over in Delaney, closer to the base. And start planning the wedding. I can't *wait*."

She sounded so happy, her voice a contrast to Bailey's expression in the mirror, which was hesitant, worried. Change is hard, I thought, thinking of Nana saying this to me. When Bailey saw me watching her, though, she looked away.

Now, back on the boat, I watched my feet carefully as I stepped up from the seating area to the deck. Even so, I felt unstable, miles away from the easy grace that Bailey and all those other lake girls possessed doing the same thing. Clearly, it wasn't a genetic trait.

"You can take off those shoes, if you want," Bailey said as I joined her on the dock. "I won't tell Trinity."

I looked down at the red wedge sandals her sister had picked out. They were espadrilles, with cork soles, a twist of leather fastened by a tiny gold hoop between the big toe and the rest. I had to admit, they were unlike anything I'd ever worn. But once on, with my own cutoffs and the peasant blouse with the gold threads, they worked.

"I'm good," I told her.

"Your feet, your funeral," she said with a shrug. "Come on. The Pavilion's over here."

I followed her down the dock to where it made a T into a small boardwalk, about a block or so long, dotted with shops and restaurants. WELCOME TO LAKE NORTH! said a big painted sign on one end, a graphic of a little wave beside it. At the other, built out over the water, was a covered area crisscrossed with string lights. Beneath it, a band made up of older men in tropical print shirts and khaki shorts was playing beach music.

The ride from Mimi's dock had taken ten minutes, maybe fifteen. But as we began walking toward the Pavilion, I felt more like we'd gone a million miles. It wasn't just the boardwalk itself, which was lined with planters sprouting perfectly landscaped flowers, expensive cars parked along it. Or the stores we passed, with names like Sprinkles (an ice cream parlor with a madras theme), Rosewater Boutique (offering fancy, flowing resort wear of the type Nana had packed for her cruise), and Au Jus (a dim steakhouse with leather booths, antique blown-glass lights hanging over them). Compared to what I'd seen of North Lake, everything seemed new and, well, expensive. And that was even before I got to the Tides.

Calvander's was a motel. This was a resort. Several stories high, it had been built to resemble a Spanish villa, with the walls a terra-cotta color, moss spreading across them. Now, it was lit up, illuminating the crowded open-air bar and restaurant below, as well as its own dock and private beach. No plastic floats or wheeling coolers dotted the sand, much less unattended children. Instead, there were rows of wooden beach chairs, each with a folded white towel on its seat.

"Crazy, right?" Bailey said, nodding at it. "I heard the

rooms have whirlpool baths and a menu for pillows. Can you even imagine?"

I shook my head, remembering the rooms I'd cleaned earlier, with their cool cinder-block walls and those tiny, thin soaps. "Can't be cheap to stay there."

"Three hundred a *night*," she replied. "And that's just a basic room. Who has that kind of money?"

The answer: these people all around us. Women in flower-print tailored dresses and diamond stud earrings, wearing what my grandmother called a "statement" watch and carrying purses I knew cost more than that single room rate, easily. An army of men in golf shirts in all colors and dress pants paired with loafers. Even the kids looked polished and effortless, as they ran past us to the Pavilion, their shoes thumping across the decking. I looked down at the wedges I was wearing, which now seemed too red in this place where understated made the biggest statement of all.

"And there's the yacht club," Bailey said. "Which used to be the fanciest place on this side of the lake, before the Tides came along."

She pointed at a long white building with columns, with a big deck and steps leading down to a large dock. Inside, it was brightly lit, and I could see people moving around, as well as seated at tables, each covered with a white cloth, on the outside patio. The beach below had two lifeguard stands, and rows of boats were moored at the dock and just beyond it out on the water.

"There they are," Bailey said now. Up ahead at the

Pavilion, two guys—the dark-haired one I recognized from the raft, as well as a redheaded friend who was taller and skinnier, both in shorts and T-shirts—waved from where they were standing against the rail, the water behind them. "You okay?"

"Fine," I said, even as I felt a little zing in my stomach. The truth was, for all Bridget's talk and enthusiasm, neither she, nor Ryan, nor I had actually gotten as far as dating someone yet, instead sticking to groups and packs when we went out. This was looking more like a double date, which I hadn't exactly planned on. Not that I could bail out now. Could I?

"Hey there," Colin, the guy from the raft, said with a wide smile as we came up to them. He had a red plastic cup in his hand. "Where's everyone else?"

"They'll be along eventually," Bailey answered, so smoothly I kind of believed her, even as I knew this was a lie. "Probably meet us at your place."

"Great," he replied. He looked at me. "Hi. I'm Colin."

I certainly didn't feel like the same old Emma, not right then. "Saylor," I said.

"My cousin," Bailey explained. To me she said, "And this is Blake."

The redhead had a shell necklace around his neck and a nice smile, as well as freckles that made him seem younger than he was. "Hey."

"Hi."

"How's the music?" Bailey asked Colin.

"Terrible," he replied. "Like it always is."

"The yacht club runs this whole boardwalk," she explained to me, "so the Pavilion bands are always selected for their demographic."

"Which means three types of music," Colin said. "Beach, beach, and swing."

"Not always," Blake pointed out. "Spinnerbait's playing for the Fourth."

"Seriously?" Colin asked.

"It's probably as a favor to someone in the band's grandmother," Blake said. "Since I've never seen that kind of music here. And I've been coming my whole life."

The song ended, and there was a smattering of applause. Bailey hopped up onto the rail beside Colin and he handed her his cup. She took a sip, tucking a piece of hair behind her ear with the other hand.

"You from around here?" Blake asked me.

I shook my head. "Just visiting. From Lakeview."

"Oh. You at the U?"

Before I could answer, the band started up again. "Everyone, let's SHAG!" the lead singer said into his mike. A few couples took to the floor, whooping as they twisted and turned to the music.

"I can't take it," Colin said to Bailey. "If everyone knows where the party is, let's just go."

She nodded, hopping down, then gestured for me to follow them as they cut through the crowd around the bandstand, then down the boardwalk until it ended. As we stepped onto the sand, Blake bent down, retrieving his own plastic cup from where he'd apparently left it hidden under the decking and taking a gulp.

"Gin and tonic," he said to me, holding it out. "Want some?"

I shook my head. "Nah, I'm okay."

He seemed hardly bothered by this, sipping again as we started toward a parking lot. LAKE NORTH YACHT CLUB said a large sign stuck in the grass. MEMBERS AND THEIR GUESTS ONLY.

"Saylor's dad worked here when he was in college," Bailey said to the guys.

"Yeah?" Colin asked. "What did he do?"

"Sailing lessons," I said.

"Did he live on Campus?" Colin said.

I blinked. "What?"

"Campus," Bailey repeated. "It's what they call the apartments they rent to the employees for the summer."

"I don't know," I said. My mom was the one who always talked about the lake. "If he did, he never mentioned it."

"Then he probably didn't," Blake said as we stopped at the side of a road, waiting for a BMW to turn into the Club entrance. "You don't forget Campus."

Once across the street, we approached an L-shaped building made up of several units. It actually kind of reminded me of Calvander's: plastic chairs outside the doors piled with swimsuits and towels, a full garbage can with a pizza box poking out of it. As Blake pushed open the door to the unit F1, though, I saw the inside was actually nicer than the rooms I'd cleaned all day, with more modern fixtures and a bigger kitchen area.

"Home sweet hovel," Colin said, kicking aside a plastic garbage bag as he crossed the threshold. "Who wants a beer?"

"Me," Bailey said, following him across to the kitchen area, where he bent down to open a small fridge. "Saylor?"

"I'm okay," I called out as Blake flopped down on one of the unmade beds, grabbing a nearby remote. The flat-screen TV flashed and came on, showing a baseball game. "Thanks, though."

Across the room, I heard Bailey laughing, and turned to see her leaning against the stovetop, now with Colin's arms around her waist. She looked perfectly at ease, while I couldn't figure out if I was supposed to join Blake on his bed or just stand there. I was still wondering when the door opened again.

"Is this the party?" a girl's voice asked, and the next moment two were entering. One was a tall brunette with long legs and cheekbones to die for. Her friend was a cute Asian girl with red lipstick and a high ponytail. They both had on black shorts and yacht club shirts, white sneakers on their feet. "Because we need one. Badly."

"*Very* badly," the second girl added, heading for the kitchen. "The monsters were in top form today. And by top,

I mean at their worst."

"Hannah," Blake said, nodding at the taller girl, "and Rachel's got the ponytail." Both girls looked at me and nodded. "They work at the kids' camp."

"I almost quit today," Hannah said, pulling a beer from the fridge as Rachel plopped down on the other bed, leaning back onto her elbows. "Between the vomit and the lice scare, it was almost too much."

"Did you say lice?" Blake asked, rearing back from her, even though she was across the room.

"False alarm," she replied. "Although my head is still itching."

"But the vomit was real?" Colin said, coming across the room with Bailey behind him.

"Sadly, yes." She sighed. "The make-your-own-sundae bar seemed like a good idea, except Braden Johnson is a total glutton."

"Put the whole container of gummy worms on his," Rachel added, then shuddered. "The puke was blue and slimy."

"See, this is why you guys need to be working at the docks," Blake said as Rachel took a seat on the end of his bed, crossing her legs. "No puke and people tip."

"And deal with the parents of these children?" Rachel asked, pulling out her phone. "No thanks. They're even worse."

Listening to this, I couldn't help but think of Trinity and the similar sentiments she'd expressed as we cleaned that day. Not that she'd ever think of herself as having something in common with this group. I barely knew her, but this I was sure of.

"Where's everyone else?" Hannah asked now, taking a sip of her beer.

Colin gave her a look. "Do you mean everyone, or just Roo?"

Roo? I thought. My Roo? But he wasn't mine.

"Everyone," Hannah replied, her pretty, angular face reddening a bit. "And Roo."

Bailey, sitting with Colin on his bed close enough that their legs were touching, pulled out her phone. After glancing at the screen, she said, "They should be here soon. I think work ran late."

"Then I have time to change," Hannah said, getting to her feet. "Rachel, you coming?"

They both got up and started for the door. "Back in five," Hannah said. "Don't let anything fun happen without us."

This didn't seem likely, especially considering that the moment they left, Colin and Bailey turned to each other and began talking in low voices. Their conversation was obviously private even before he reached out, smoothing her hair back with his hand, and she closed her eyes. Meanwhile, I was left with Blake and the baseball game, which had cut to a commercial.

"So," he said, jabbing the remote at the TV as he flipped channels. "So you said you go to the U?"

I shook my head. "No. Just live in Lakeview. I have

one more year of high school."

"High school," he said. "Wow. That brings back memories."

"You're a freshman, right?"

"Going into sophomore year," he corrected me. "*Big* difference from high school."

"I bet," I said, although privately, I wondered. "What's your major?"

He sat up a bit. "Business. Although I don't know if I'll actually stay long enough to get my degree. I'm going to do this startup, sooner rather than later."

"Like a company thing?"

"Yep," he said, taking another sip of his beer. "Me and two of my friends, we've got this great idea for an app. We've got backing and everything."

"Like an app for your phone?" I asked.

"You got it." He sat up suddenly: it was clear this subject energized him. "Want to hear the idea? You can't steal it to develop yourself. We've already applied for patenting."

This would never have occurred to me, but I said, "Sure."

He muted the TV, then held up both hands. "Okay. So you drive, right?"

Already, I wasn't thrilled with the turn this conversation had taken. "Um, yeah."

"And what's the one thing everyone told you a million times when you got your license?"

I thought for a moment. "Wear a seat belt."

"No," he said. "The other thing."

"Don't drink and drive," I said.

"No." He sighed. "The *other* other thing."

I was still clueless, which must have been obvious, because he pulled out his phone, holding it up.

"Don't text and drive?" I said.

"Exactly!" he replied. "It's, like, the most dangerous thing for any driver, but especially new ones. So imagine if there was a way to turn off that function anytime you were in a car. Not only *should* you not text: you *couldn't* even if you wanted to. That's the power of I'M DRIVING. Not only can your messages wait until you get from point A to point B: they will."

He sat back, clearly pleased with himself. I said, "Wow."

"Right? It's great. I mean, just imagine the market for parents, what they'd pay for that peace of mind. You can't even put a number on it, really."

"No?"

"Well, we're thinking four ninety-nine, actually," he admitted. He really did look like a little kid with those freckles. "Again, though, we're only in the early stages. It's going to take a lot of development, since it has to work with different operating systems and stuff. Luckily, we've got a programmer on our team."

"And you're funded already?"

"We had a connection," he explained. "Taz, my suitemate? He's the real driving force behind all this."

"So to speak," I quipped. Blake looked confused. "Never mind."

"Anyway," he went on, "his dad runs Hermandos Foods, which invented the Zapwich."

"Seriously?" Zapwiches, which were like frozen calzones, had been a staple of my childhood, when I'd been allowed them. "I love those things!"

"So does everyone. Which is why they are big money." He held up two fingers, rubbing them together. "We came up with I'M DRIVING in a programming class we took fall semester, me and Taz and our other friend Lucas. The assignment was to create an app that made something safer."

"Like driving," I said, as if I was a person who did this, and worried about such things, instead of, you know, driving itself.

"Got an A, of course," he continued. "But what we were really working toward was the pitch to Taz's dad over winter break. He loved it: totally in. So now, it's just a matter of development, getting it up and running. Our long-term plan, though, is to be bought out so that I'M DRIVING becomes standard on *all* phones."

This was more than he'd said to me all night, so I took a second to catch up. "Wow," I said again.

"I know." He leaned back into the pillow behind him, picking up the remote again. "It's kind of crazy, being nineteen and knowing you've probably already made your first million. Definitely makes college seem like less of a priority."

I didn't even know what to say to this. I mean, we were well-off, as was Nana Payne, from my grandfather, who, although not the inventor of an iconic frozen food item, had also been a successful businessman. Even so, though, we never talked about money this confidently, or at all, really. It made me uncomfortable, and not just because I'd spent the day cleaning motel rooms. Although that really made me aware of it.

"This game's done," Blake announced, glancing at the TV. "You up for some beer pong?"

"I'm not much of a drinker," I told him. "But I'll cheer you on if you play."

"Yeah?" He seemed surprised by this, even touched.

"Sure," I said.

He smiled, then got to his feet, picking up his cup. Before moving, though, he waved a hand in front of him, signaling I should go first. That's sweet, I thought. As was the touch of his hand, which I felt briefly on the small of my back as I started toward the kitchen. Was this what it really felt like to have a boy interested in you? Girl falling in love at the lake was my mom's story. But maybe it could still be mine as well.

"Great minds," Blake said, waving a hand between us. "It's hot as balls in there."

That wasn't exactly how I would have put it, but he wasn't wrong. Hannah and Rachel had returned, the beer pong game began, and I watched as Blake lost three rounds in a row. Meanwhile, a bunch of servers and waiters, off their shifts from the Club restaurant, began to show up, taking the room from crowded to outright packed. Unlike at

Mimi's, the A/C couldn't keep up. I'd basically had to leave before I melted.

Still, I hadn't expected Blake to follow me outside, as this was technically his party. Then again, he had downed several beers in a short period. He probably needed air even more than I did.

"Having fun?" he asked. "I mean, aside from the hot-as-balls part."

"Yeah," I said.

"You sure you don't want a beer? We have plenty."

I shook my head. "No thanks."

"Why not?"

"I'm sorry?"

He cleared his throat. "Sorry. It's just in college, when people are sober, there's usually a reason. Religion. A problem. Parents super strict. Or something."

"Nothing like that," I said, and he nodded. I thought maybe I should explain more, tell him about my mom. But something stopped me. "Just not my thing."

"Ah. Got it." He snapped his fingers. "Speaking of parents, I wanted to show you something."

"Is it *your* parents?" I asked in a deadpan voice. "Because if so, you might want a mint. And some coffee. And a chance to make better choices."

"What?" he said.

Again, I thought of Roo, nodding as I discussed my humor. Clearly, Blake was not of our people. "Never mind," I said. "Show me."

I followed him down the sidewalk. At the end of the row, there was a laundry room, a dryer inside banging loudly, as well as a bulletin board with the clearly ignored rules of NO PARTIES and NO GUESTS. After that, the walkway ended, but Blake kept going, hanging a left into the dark behind the building. We passed a row of shrubs before coming up on a blank bit of wall, a pair of floodlights shining down it.

"I give you," he said, "the Campus wall."

What I was looking at was a square expanse, maybe six feet by eight feet, weather-worn and streaked with dirt. It looked in need of a power washing, not our attention. "It's nice?" I ventured.

"Nice?" He sighed, then stepped closer, right up to it, gesturing for me to do the same. "It's history. Look."

I stepped up beside him. As I did, I saw what I'd thought was dirt and blotches were actually signatures, tons of them, stretching from one side to the other. KENT RAMENS KITCHEN WARRIOR! CLASS OF 1987. ELIZABETH WAS HERE '94. ALEX AND EVIE, 7/20/2000–4EVER. It reminded me of the pictures under glass in Mimi's office, all these memories, but in words, not images.

"When was your dad here?" Blake asked me now. "Do you know?"

I thought for a second. "The late nineties, I think."

He bent down to study something scribbled by one of the bushes. "I've seen some from then here for sure.

Unfortunately, they're not in any order. You just sign where you find a spot."

"Have you?" I asked.

"Yep. It's up there." I looked where he was indicating, scanning the scribbles above us to the left. Finally, I found it: BLAKE R., DOCKS Y'ALL! '18. Colin's signature was below.

"You do it every summer," I said, clarifying.

"At the *end* of summer. The bash on the last night. It's a ritual."

I looked back up at all those names and dates, wondering if my dad's really was up there someplace. It was weird, picturing him at Blake's age, maybe with my mom nearby. And now here I was, brought to this same place all these years later. It seemed crazy, and fated, hitting me all at once, so that I felt unsteady even before I turned to find Blake right there, his face close to mine.

"Hi," he said softly. Up close the freckles weren't so noticeable, which was weird.

"Hi," I replied. I could see a name in my side vision—MARY!—with a heart, but only for a second, because then I was closing my eyes and he was sliding his arms around my waist and kissing me.

I'd waited so long for this moment, my first real kiss, and envisioned it in a million different ways. None of them, however, involved a wall, the thought of my mom and dad, and then, just as I'd managed to push these things away, the sudden sound of someone yelling.

"Did you hear that?" he asked, pulling back from me.

"Yeah. What was it?"

We were both quiet. His arms were still around my waist. A beat later, I heard a girl's voice, distant but clear. "I always do what you want! The least you can do is return the favor *once*!"

"That sounds like Bailey," I said softly, not sure why I was whispering.

"You want me to let you drive the boat home when you've been drinking," a male voice replied.

"Goddammit, Jack. I didn't say that!"

Blake looked at me. "Her brother," I explained. "I should probably—"

"Yeah," he said, stepping back to wave me past him. "Let's go."

Quickly, I made my way around the building and into the light of the Campus. As my feet hit the sidewalk and I passed the bulletin board, I realized how loud their voices actually were.

"I set this whole thing up," Bailey was saying. "I told everyone you guys were going to be here, and then you finally show up and just want to take the boat—"

"Because you're not driving it," Jack shot back. "Look at you! You're slurring!"

"I am not slurring!" she shouted, and she wasn't, to my ears. "I'm pissed!"

Now, coming around the final corner to the row of

units, I could see a small group—Colin, Rachel, some of the servers—gathered around my cousins, who were face-to-face. I hurried over.

"Give me the keys to the motor," Jack said now, sticking out his hand.

"You couldn't just hang out for an hour," she said, and I thought of how she'd organized this from the start to bring both sides of the lake together, folding Colin in. "For me."

He wiggled his hand at her, impatient.

"You're an asshole," she said.

"Whoa, whoa." Colin stepped up beside her. "Let's take it down a notch."

Jack pointed at him. "You stay out of this. It's your fault she's drunk in the first place."

"Me?" Colin objected. "I didn't force anything on her."

"She's underage!" Jack said. "Still in high school. Did she tell you that?"

In response, Bailey surged forward, slapping both hands against his chest and pushing him backward. As he stumbled, then caught himself, I spotted Roo just behind him, watching all of this with a tense look on his face.

"Bailey," I said to her softly.

"Just get out of here," she told Jack, her voice cracking. "You don't want to be here, go."

He held out his hand again. "Give me the keys and I will."

She shoved a hand into her pocket, pulling out a key ring and winging it at him. "Fine. Here."

Even though she was upset, her aim was good enough that he had to shift right at the last minute to avoid getting hit. The keys hit the ground with a clank. He bent down, snatching them up, then turned and started to walk away.

"You'll thank me tomorrow," he said over his shoulder. "When you realize how close you came to doing something stupid."

"I wasn't going to drive home!" she replied. "We both know I wouldn't do that."

"What we know," he replied, "is that death is no joke. So stop fucking around."

Furious, Bailey started to charge at him again. I looked at Colin, who was beside me, but he just stood there, so I reached to grab her, pulling her back. She was shaking, an actual heat coming off her skin as I tightened my grip around her wrists. On Jack's other side, Roo was watching, too.

"Take a breath," I said into her ear. "Bailey."

After fighting me for another moment, she finally went limp. Jack was almost to the road now, his own pace brisk, but Roo remained where he'd been.

"I wasn't going to take the boat home," Bailey said to him, her voice tight. "Roo. I wasn't."

"Okay," he said quietly.

She exhaled a half sob, half breath, running her hands through her hair. I'd been so caught up on what was happening I hadn't noticed everyone else had gone back into Blake and Colin's place, leaving the three of us alone. I watched as Bailey saw this as well, processing what it may or may not have meant, before she spoke again.

"I'm leaving. Come on, Saylor."

I looked back at the guys' apartment, where the door was half-open, voices and music drifting out from inside. It seemed rude to just take off, especially since I'd been lip-locked with one of the hosts only moments earlier. And didn't she want to say goodbye to Colin?

Apparently, the answer was no. She was already halfway to the road.

I looked at Roo again. "What just happened?"

He was watching Bailey crossing the grass. Jack was long gone. "Depends on who you ask, I guess."

"I'm asking you," I said.

Now, he did meet my eyes. "She wanted him to stay. He wanted to go. And drinking and boats don't mix."

The accident. I blinked, it only just then hitting me that we were talking about his dad, and that night all those years ago, when my mom was with him.

I squinted through the dark, to the road. Bailey was about a block down now. "I should go, I guess." I kicked off Trinity's shoes, picking them up in one hand, then started across the grass.

"Hey," Roo called out. I turned. "See you later?"

I told myself it was just what they said here. And yet. "Yeah," I said. "See you."

I had to jog to catch up with Bailey, leaving me breathless. Finally I reached her, the lights of Campus dimmer now behind us. "Hey," I said. "You okay?"

"No," she replied, still walking. "Yes. Maybe. I don't know."

We walked in silence for a bit, passing the back of the Tides—PRIVATE! GUESTS ONLY! said several signs—as well as the boardwalk, which was pretty much deserted. It was clear that North Lake and Lake North had many differences, but neither was a late-night town.

"I wasn't going to take the boat home, just so you know," she said suddenly as a gated neighborhood called Bellewether came up on our left.

I didn't say anything.

"Seriously! I wasn't." She tucked a piece of hair behind her ear. "I figured Roo would bring them over, Jack would take our boat back, and we'd catch a ride with someone. It would have worked out fine if he'd just not been such a jerk. But lately he's always a jerk because my dad is putting all this pressure on him about taking over the Station."

A car was coming toward us now, moving slowly, headlights bright in my eyes. I started to move out of the road, but then it turned, leaving just us and the dark again.

"I'll be honest," I said. "I don't really understand what happened back there."

She sighed, shoving her hands in her pockets. "Jack's the oldest of all of us. He knows that what he does, everyone else will do. He's hung out with Rachel and Hannah before on our side. If he'd come over here in good faith, it would have been just like any other night. Only the setting is different."

"But he didn't do that," I said, clarifying.

"Of course not. He had a chip on his shoulder, the way he always does about guys from the yacht club, and everyone from Lake North, for that matter."

"And it probably doesn't help if they're into his little sister," I added.

She glanced at me. "That's irrelevant. He'd rather I date a certified douchebag from our side than a saint from over here."

"Is there really a verification process for that?"

She rolled her eyes. "Ha, ha."

I smiled. "So maybe he's biased. But it seems like what you were actually about to come to blows about was the whole drinking-on-the-boat thing."

"Because he knows that subject negates anything else!" she replied, loudly enough so I stopped walking for a second, startled. "Sorry. It's just we've heard about that accident our whole lives. It's the cautionary tale of all cautionary tales and had nothing to do with all this. And the fact that he brought it up in front of Roo just makes me look more like a jerk, because . . ."

She trailed off, her flip-flops slapping hard against the pavement as we passed a third gated neighborhood in a row, by my count, on this tiny deserted road. What were they keeping out? Civilization?

"Because it was his dad," I finished.

"Which, again," she shot back, "had nothing to do with Jack sabotaging my night and this thing I had going with Colin!"

"I know," I said carefully, holding up a hand. "I'm new here, remember? I'm just trying to catch up."

She ducked her head down, not saying anything for a minute. Up ahead, the road was widening as we approached an intersection, a single red blinking light above it.

"Your mom never talked about it?" she asked me finally.

"The accident?" She nodded. "No. She told a lot of stories, but not that one."

"Whereas my mom," Bailey said, "couldn't forget. Everything was a reminder. The summer starting, their group hanging out together, even the lake itself. It was like a ghost, haunting her."

"What happened?"

We were almost to the light now. Just beyond it, there was a sign: NORTH LAKE 3 MILES. An arrow pointed the way.

"You really want to hear it?" she asked.

"Yeah."

We passed under the light. Blink. Blink. Blink.

"All right," she said. "So it happened in July."

NINE

July 9, 2000, was my mom's twenty-first birthday. She'd been with Dad for a year by then, dating long-distance during the school months. By Christmas, they'd be engaged, and she'd be pregnant with me.

But in June, as summer began, she didn't know any of this. She was just missing her boyfriend, and more nervous than she wanted to admit about starting a new life almost two hours west. She dealt with it the way she did most things, back then. She tried to forget.

Most lake kids liked to party—in that small of a town, there weren't a lot of entertainment options—but even with this as the norm, my mom had always stood out. Whatever she liked to do, she did to excess. What she was best known for, though, was her disappearing act.

The gist was this: they'd all be out on the water at night, having a few beers at the raft, when someone would notice she was gone. The first time, of course, panic ensued, especially when despite zigzagging the water and yelling, she couldn't be found. Until Celeste, near hysteria, got back to the shore to call 911 and found my mom sitting there wrapped in a towel, sucking on a cold Pop Soda. She'd swum all the way back, in darkness, then sat and watched as they searched for her.

My dad hated the disappearing act. One time she did it while they were sailing with his friends on the Lake North side, and he was so angry he broke up with her as a result. It took a full week of profuse apologizing before she finally convinced him to change his mind.

Her birthday that year fell on a Sunday, but my mom planned to celebrate all weekend, starting with when my dad arrived on Friday from Lakeview, where he'd been taking summer classes for dental school. She'd been so looking forward to his visit, literally crossing the days off the calendar she kept on her bedroom wall. That morning, though, he called: the mandatory study group for one of his classes could only meet that weekend. He wasn't coming.

My mom, hurt and furious, screamed at him over the phone before slamming every door on her way out of the house to her car. The next time anyone saw her was the following afternoon, when she came home hungover, slept until noon the next day, then started up again to celebrate her first legal birthday in earnest.

Her party was being held at Celeste and Silas's new place. By then they'd been married two years and had Jack, who was just starting to walk. The house was small, but homey, and they'd planned a cookout and game night. There were stations for cornhole, pin the tail on the donkey, Texas

Hold'em, and others. Celeste wanted everything to be perfect.

My mom arrived at the party with Chris Price and an open beer in her hand, then proceeded to down some shots of tequila in quick succession. As her sister began to explain the protocol of game night, my mom heckled her. When she crumpled up her hand-printed scorecard and chucked it at her, Celeste threw her out.

Chris and Silas tried to negotiate a peace, but Calvander girls, stubborn as a rule, were not budging. So Celeste locked herself in her room, crying, while Waverly and Chris Price left together to go to Splinkey's, the only bar in town. They drank a pitcher of beer and played darts, cutting up, until the guy serving them told them to go home. Instead, they went to the lake.

At twenty-two, Chris was a year older than Waverly, and had a kid on the way with his on-and-off girlfriend, Stephanie. At that moment, they were split, having broken up after fighting about money, impending parenthood, and his own partying. Like Waverly, Chris was known for his love of a good time as well as a sense of humor that bordered on the annoying. Celeste said there were lots of reasons he and my mom were best friends, but a big one was that sometimes, no one else could stand to be around them.

They were alone, then, that night, as they climbed onto Chris's boat with a six-pack they'd grabbed from the market. It probably felt like old times, high school days, when they'd had nothing to worry about but curfew. But beyond that buzz, the real world was looming: Chris was going to be a dad, and my mom was moving away. Bailey said Celeste had always wondered what they talked about that night, alone on the raft in the dark. But Waverly had never said. She never talked about it at all.

What we did know was this. At some point, Waverly pulled her disappearing act, slipping into the dark water. When Chris realized she was gone, he started shouting for her, first half laughing, then angry. By the time he got into the boat to search, he was enraged and, as blood alcohol tests would later show, way over the legal limit. He had to be, everyone said, to forget the contours and landmarks of the lake he knew by heart, and run at full speed into the mooring that was a hundred feet from the Calvander dock. Chris wasn't in the boat as it began to sink. He'd been pitched into the water, breaking his neck. It might have all started with Waverly wanting to vanish, but in the end, he was the one who was gone.

Emma? You there?

I picked up my phone. It was early morning, the sun not even up, and I'd assumed it was my dad calling from Greece again across time zones. But it was Ryan.

Why are you awake right now? I asked.

Sunrise hike with cast and crew. Bonding experience. My legs are screaming.

I blinked. **Cast and crew?**

For the musical. South Pacific. I told you, right?

No. You're in a show? I'm impressed!

Downstairs, I heard a door slam. Even at this hour, someone was up. Probably making toast.

Well it is a drama camp, she wrote back. **Dad strongly suggested I stop moping in my room and get involved. Please never tell him I said this but it's actually kind of fun.**

So you're acting? I wrote back.

I'm not. Tech crew. Everyone's pretty cool, though.

There was a pause, and then two pictures popped up on the screen. One was of Ryan at a picnic table with a bunch of other campers, all of them making stupid faces for the camera. The next was of her standing over a lightboard, a girl with long black hair in an army cap beside her.

How's the mystery grandmother?

I'd only texted with Ryan a few days earlier, and this had been what we'd talked about. But already, North Lake felt like something bigger than just Mimi and me seeing each other again, or even me coming to stay. But I wasn't sure how to word it for myself yet, much less someone else.

Good, I wrote. **Learning my way around.**

Oh crap, we're going back down the mountain. Pray for me. Talk soon???

I sent her a thumbs-up. When she replied with a heart, I rolled over, closing my eyes again. Ryan was doing shows. I was cleaning rooms. When Bridget had predicted a different summer, she'd been onto something. Even if I'd never expected anything like this.

"Hungover?"

I looked at Trinity, who had just come in from the porch, still in her pajamas. "No," I said. "Why?"

"You and Bailey were out pretty late," she replied, picking up the bread from the counter.

"Jack came and took the boat," I explained. "We had to walk back."

"In my shoes?"

"I took them off first." I nodded at the steps, where I had left them neatly lined up. "My feet were filthy."

"Ugh. I bet." She loaded the toaster and pushed down the lever. Then she leaned against the counter, her belly poking out in front of her. "So how was it?"

I shrugged. "Fine. We just hung out until Jack showed up and wanted the boat. The guys were nice."

She scoffed at this, blowing her hair out of her face. "Let me guess. They're both rich and in college."

"Don't know about rich," I replied, although I didn't doubt it. "But yeah, they're roommates at East U."

Another snort, although this time she saved me the commentary. A moment later—BING!—the toast popped up. After she quickly moved the slices to a plate, cursing at the heat on them, she said, "You want to work this morning?"

"Sure," I replied.

She went to the fridge, collecting the butter, then came to the table to grab a knife. "We'll start at nine sharp. Meet you over there?"

"Sounds good."

She shuffled off, toast and butter balanced on the plate. I pulled over the paper Oxford had left behind and flipped to the obits. Just as I was about to start reading about Hazel Walker, aged 85, who had passed away surrounded by her loved ones, my phone beeped again. Blake.

At the docks today. You should come by.

So he'd gotten my number. Which meant that despite my nerves, I'd clearly made a good impression. Plus, he wasn't bad to look at, and the kiss (my first!) had been nice while it lasted. Maybe I just needed to give this a chance.

Have to work. Will try, I wrote back. A beat later, he sent me a smiley face. A redhead. Cute.

"Morning."

I jumped, startled to find myself there in my seat at the table, the obit for Hazel Walker still unread in front of me and Jack crossing the kitchen to the toaster.

"Hey," I said in return.

He loaded up some bread before coming over to sit. "Obituaries, huh?" he asked. "Kind of a morbid way to start the day, isn't it?"

"Death is no joke," I pointed out.

He smiled, a bit ruefully. "I did say that, didn't I?"

"Among other things."

A sigh, and then he ran a hand over his hair. "Well, it's the truth. I was in the right, whether she sees it that way or not."

To this I said nothing, focusing again on Hazel as I took another bite of my toast.

"Okay, fine." He sighed. "I was in the right but *might* have handled it a bit more diplomatically."

"A bit?" I asked.

"How pissed was she, really?"

I looked up at him. "On a scale of one to ten? Twelve."

BING! went the toaster. He got up, plucking out the slices and dropping them onto a plate, then went to the fridge. "Where's the butter?"

"Trinity took it." I pointed. "The porch."

He glanced down the hallway, then came back to the table. Picking up a piece of toast, he said, "What about you?"

I swallowed. "What about me?"

"How pissed are *you*?" he replied. "At me."

Surprised he'd care either way, I was nonetheless truthful. "Not at all. It was a nice walk."

"Except for Bailey being at a twelve."

"Well, there was that," I agreed. "She cooled down after a mile or so, though."

He sighed again. Then, nodding at the paper, he said, "One more question and I'll leave you to your death notices."

"Shoot."

"How much is she really into this yacht club guy?"

I thought of Bailey's face the night before, streaked with tears, as we made our way down the middle of the empty road that led home.

"I think it was pretty obvious," I said finally. "Don't you?"

Jack bit his lip, and for a second I could see just what

he must have looked like as a little kid, getting caught for something and instantly sorry. Just as quickly, though, he was getting to his feet, taking his breakfast to go. "Tell her the boat needs gas," he said over his shoulder as he dropped his glass in the sink. "Not sure she realizes."

I nodded, and then he was gone, down the hallway to the door. As he went to push it open, I saw him pause, glancing at the entryway to the living room and porch beyond where Bailey was still sleeping. I thought he might go to her or say something. No. He did, however, ease the door shut slowly behind him, so for once it didn't slam.

TEN

I was working in room three that morning, while Trinity tackled four, her vacuum banging against the wall separating us. I'd just started changing the sheets when Roo passed by, carrying a ladder.

The walkie-talkie was stuck in his back pocket again, and he was whistling cheerfully, as he passed room four, then five, before finally stopping in front of six to set up the ladder. I watched, silent, until he started to climb it. Then I couldn't help myself.

"Be careful!" I yelled, realizing too late I'd startled him. Whoops. "You need a ladder buddy."

He just looked at me. "A what?"

"A ladder buddy. So you don't fall." God, I was such a dork. I put down my spray bottle, walking toward him. "You know, to hold it. My dad . . . he has this rule."

That was putting it mildly. If my mom had been one to throw caution to the wind, my dad had always held it close and tight. We walked with scissors. At even the smallest intersection we looked both ways. Twice. And when it came to ladders, you never went up alone.

"Ladder buddy?" Roo repeated. He looked amused. "I have never heard of that in my life."

"Maybe it's a dentist thing," I suggested, assuming my normal position on the other side of the ladder, both hands gripping it tight. "Okay, you're good. Go ahead."

"You're going to stop me from falling?"

"No," I replied, a bit huffily, "but I will keep the ladder from collapsing underneath you, which would pitch you off to your death."

"Death?"

"I'm a Payne," I explained. "We're a careful people."

He considered this, and me, before saying, "Well, I'm a Price. We're mostly known for sticking our fingers into light sockets."

"All the more reason to make safety a habit," I said. He snorted. "Just climb, would you?"

He laughed. "Okay, buddy."

Up he went, while I, still gripping, contemplated when I'd escape the long shadow of my father's safety practices. Not yet, apparently. As Roo pulled his phone from his pocket, I said, "What are you doing, exactly?"

"Mimi needs some roof work done, so Silas sent me down to grab shots of what needs repairing," he replied, snapping one photo, then another. The ladder wobbled, and I gripped it harder.

"I thought Silas and Celeste were divorced," I said.

155

"Twice," he replied, lifting one foot to scratch it. "But he's still family to Mimi. They take care of each other."

"Both feet on the ladder, please," I said before I could even stop myself.

He turned, peering down at me again. "You really are nervous about this, aren't you?"

"I told you," I replied. "It's genetic."

"Maybe," he said, examining a shot he'd already taken on his screen, "but you are also part Calvander. And they leap off ladders. For fun."

"Are you done?"

"Not yet," he said cheerfully, turning the phone to landscape mode. He looked down at me. "Question: Does it make you nervous when I do this?"

Gingerly, he jumped on the ladder step once. Then twice. With both feet.

"You stop that," I said in my sternest voice.

"What about this?" He widened his eyes, then dangled one leg off entirely. "Oopsie!"

"Roo. Just—"

"Boy!" Oxford bellowed from the porch of the main house. I jumped where I was standing. "Don't you be acting a fool on that damn ladder, you want to crack your head open?"

Roo pulled all his limbs back on, quick, as I laughed out loud. Then he looked at me. "Some buddy you are," he said. "What happened to *support*?"

"I'm supporting!" I said. "You're the one acting a fool."

BEEP, went the walkie suddenly. "Rubber Duck! You got the keys to the prize case? Someone just hit the jackpot on the bonus tickets and they're getting antsy."

"On my way," Roo replied, taking his hands back. He signed off with a beep, then looked at me. "Duty calls. Thanks for the support, buddy."

"You're welcome," I said.

"Saylor!" I turned to see Trinity, in the doorway of room four with the vacuum. "Are we working or are we flirting?"

My face went red-hot, but Roo just laughed. "Some buddy you are," I said. "What happened to support?"

"I'm supporting," he said, folding up the ladder. "You're the one flirting." Then he grinned at me, stuck it under his arm, and started toward the office. Again my face was flushed. But for different reasons, now.

"Now, what I want us all to do is to breathe together," Kim, the leader of the birthing class, was saying from the front of the room. "Okay? Inhale on three. One, two, THREE."

I drew in a shallow breath, not sure how me doing this would actually help this process. Trinity, who was leaning back against me, sucked in enough for both our lungs, before letting it go when instructed with a whoosh that blew her bangs sideways. Impressive.

"When the baby comes," Kim was saying now, "there will be moments to push and moments to rest. But no matter what, you want to be breathing."

"Seems like a good rule for anytime, really," I muttered.

"Hush." Trinity shifted her position, elbowing me in my stomach in the process. "You're supposed to be the Sergeant, remember?"

"He doesn't make jokes?" I asked.

"Not stupid ones, no."

Originally it was Celeste who had been Trinity's partner, as the Sergeant's delayed homecoming meant he wasn't around when the birthing classes began in early June. But then Celeste's boss at the grocery had quit, so she'd had to take over running everything, and Mimi stepped in. With the season beginning and the hotel still down a housekeeper, though, soon she too had her hands full. The only other ones with free time were me and Oxford, who claimed he'd faint at even the mention of the word *uterus*, much less a whole class about its capabilities.

So here I was, in the partner position, breathing and reassuring and watching incredibly disturbing birth videos that I could not forget despite really, really trying. If all went well, the Sergeant would be home by the end of July, in time for the birth itself, if not the last few classes. I didn't know him at all, but I was still pretty sure he'd be better at it than I was.

Until then, though, it was my job to tote the nursing pillow, water bottle, and pad that Trinity used to jot down notes. She was so big it was all she could do just to drive us there and walk in, and that day, she'd decided maybe she couldn't even manage that.

"You drive," she'd said as we'd come out to Mimi's

Toyota, parked by the Calvander's office. "It's just too hard for me these days."

I hesitated. "I can't."

Already at the passenger door, she glanced over at me. "You don't have a license?"

Lie, I told myself. But out loud I said, "No, I do."

"Great," she said, starting to ease herself into the seat. It was a multiphase process: backing in her rear end first, then a pivot to a sitting position, followed by pulling in her legs. When she finished and I still hadn't moved, she said, "What's the problem?"

"I don't like to drive," I said, or rather blurted. "It makes me nervous."

"Nervous?" she repeated. "This is North Lake. We'll be lucky if we even pass another car."

"I know," I said. "But I've never liked it, and then I backed into a car in the parking deck—"

"That happens to everyone," she replied, shifting to get both feet more in the center of her floor mat. "Rite of passage. Now get in, we're going to be late."

She shut her door. I stayed where I was. A moment later, she rolled down the window. "Are you serious about this?"

"I don't like driving," I said again.

"Well, I don't like that my fiancé isn't here for birthing class, but I'm doing it anyway," she replied. "You have your license on you?"

"Yeah."

"Then come on." She tossed the keys into the driver's

seat. "If I can get in the goddamn car at my size, you can do this."

I wasn't sure what it was about Trinity, exactly, that caused me to find myself doing things I normally thought impossible. Maybe that it wasn't her faith in me as much as her frustration. She just had no time for my neurosis, which made me wonder if maybe that was an option for me, as well.

I walked over and pulled open the driver's-side door. "I'm going to be nervous."

"Great. You'll drive carefully. Let's go."

She pulled out her phone as I picked up the keys, and then I slid behind the wheel. It felt weird, and I wished I was in her seat, where the view was familiar. I was trying to figure out another way to get her to switch with me when she took a pointed view at the clock on the console.

It's North Lake, I thought. We'll be lucky if we even see another car. I put the key in and turned it.

She was partially right. After we turned out of Calvander's—a Payne, I looked left, right, then left again, and would have done another round of this if she hadn't sighed, loudly—we were the only ones on the road for a good ten minutes. Then, though, we came up on construction and a row of cars backed up as a bored flagman held up a sign that said STOP. With people suddenly ahead of and behind me, I felt my palms begin to sweat against the wheel.

"The thing is," Trinity, who'd spent the entire trip so far detailing various grudges she had with the army, her pregnant body, and the world in general, was saying, "this isn't the way I would have done this, given the chance. No one wants to be knocked up before the wedding, you know?"

I nodded, realizing I was clenching my teeth. The flag guy, bored, was looking at his phone.

"But it is what it is, and I am," she continued, rubbing a hand over her stomach. "And honestly, I just want the Sergeant here when the baby comes. Even if he shows up literally the night before my water breaks. It's one thing to be pregnant alone. I don't want to start my life as a parent that way, too."

Breathe, I told myself, as someone beeped behind us. It didn't work, so I went for another way to distract myself. "So how did you guys meet?"

At this, she smiled. It was a rare thing, as I'd noticed soon after meeting her, and happened mostly when the subject turned to her fiancé. "He and one of his buddies rented a room last summer for his twenty-first birthday. But really, it all started with toast."

I glanced in the rearview just in time to see the guy behind me shake a fist at the flagman. I said, "Toast?"

"Yep." She sat back, now with both hands on her belly. "The morning after they checked in, he was outside the unit when I went to work at the office. I had my two slices with butter, and they were burnt, because our toaster then was a fire hazard. He made a joke about it and we started talking. Been together ever since."

"That's cute," I said, because even in my anxious state, I had to admit it was.

"I know, right?" she replied. "We got engaged in the fall, and I found out about this one"— she patted her stomach— "a month later, about the same time he got his deployment orders. Right before he left, he bought me the toaster. It's a good thing, too, because I was so sick the first trimester, and bread was all I could eat."

I'd figured there was a story behind all this, and under any other circumstances I would have been glad to finally hear it. As it was, though, I couldn't focus because traffic was moving again, this time around the construction in the opposite lane. Trinity kept talking about the Sergeant, but I was too busy white-knuckling it until we were back on the right side of the road to really listen.

Now, back at birth class, I took a deep breath as I grappled with the fact that in less than a half hour, I would have to drive back. Normal people don't do this, I thought as Kim encouraged all the mamas to visualize an ocean with the contractions as waves. But I'd never been "normal," especially when it came to being in my head. Although other people's worries still seemed to be freeing me from my own a bit. Which was a nice surprise.

I also appeared to, maybe, have something going on with Blake. To find out, I'd turned to another expert.

"Tell me *everything*," Bridget had said when I finally got hold of her a few days after that first trip to the Campus. "And go *slowly*."

I glanced at my watch. I was sitting on Mimi's side steps, with thirty minutes for lunch before I had to go back to cleaning with Trinity, who was currently stretched out across a bed in an empty room eight, resting her feet. But Bridget could drag out a story like no one else: with her questions, follow-ups, and then follow-ups to the follow-ups, I could see this easily taking the entire afternoon.

Still, I did my best. By the time I was done, we still had ten minutes for analysis. She got right to it.

"Well, it's obvious he's into you," she said as I finally ripped open the pack of peanut butter crackers that was my lunch. "The wall, that kiss . . . it's like textbook. But what's happened *since* the kiss? That's important."

I thought for a second. There had been the texts that morning following the night at Blake's apartment. Also, the invite to come visit the docks, which didn't happen, as I'd instead ended up at my first birth class. Two nights later, however, I'd ridden out to the raft in the late afternoon with Jack. When Blake had shown up with Colin and a few other guys from the Club, he'd immediately climbed off the boat to come over to talk to me, in full view of everyone. Then, when we met up later at the Station, he'd again sought me out, issuing a challenge to a Skee-Ball tournament. I lost, but he let me choose the prize when we cashed in tickets. I picked a small stuffed bear wearing an even tinier pair of board shorts in a Hawaiian print, which he insisted I name Blake for its shock of red hair. Currently, it sat in my room by the clock, although we'd agreed to share custody from week to week.

"Okay," Bridget said when I finished detailing all this. "That's all three of the IFS. Total boyfriend behavior."

"The IFS?" I asked.

"Initiative, Future thinking, and Sweet," she replied. "It's the checklist. Initiative: he reached out first by text and came to find you. Twice. Future thinking: he's assuming you'll still be hanging out when it's time for the bear to go to him. And sweetness, because guys who are only wanting a quick fling or even less don't bother with that."

"Where did you hear this?"

"I didn't. It's my own invention." When I laughed, she said, "Hey, I'm being serious! I've watched just about every rom-com from the last twenty years, read all the great romances. . . . I've retained things. Studied patterns. There's a science to this."

I smiled. "You know, you should be the one sort of dating someone. Clearly, you're the expert."

"Right?" She sighed. "Unfortunately, I'm living here in a senior community in Ohio for the time being. There's plenty of shuffleboard, but not a lot of opportunity to test my theories."

"Summer's not over yet," I pointed out.

"At least Grandpa is doing better," she said, "which means I may get back home to pursue the twins solo before school starts. You have to admit, I will have earned it by then. But anyway, tell me again about the kiss. I feel like you're leaving things out."

I hadn't, not that I was aware of. It didn't matter anyway, because just then Trinity emerged from room eight, moving slowly and rubbing her eyes. When she started to push the cart down to the next room, I'd said goodbye to Bridget, grabbed my spray bottle, and went to join her. The first room we opened was a shambles. Just what I needed.

Since then, Bridget and I hadn't talked. If we had, though, I was sure she'd probably have another acronym, if not multiple theories, about how well things were developing between Blake and me.

Maybe it was just that I had high expectations, thanks to all the romantic movies and books I myself had consumed. But I'd always thought that if and when this finally happened, I would have that whooshing, tingly feeling, almost an out-of-body experience.

I wouldn't have been so aware of this if it wasn't for Bailey. After that night at Lake North when we'd walked home, I thought things would have cooled between her and Colin. I mean, he hadn't exactly stood up for her with Jack, and then went inside when things got really ugly between them. In her mind, however, he hadn't been a disappointment: she had.

"What could he do?" she asked me the next night, as we sat in her bedroom. "My brother shows up and the next thing Colin knows, we're outside screaming at each other. It's so embarrassing. I would have taken off, too."

"No, you wouldn't have," I said, thinking of her sticking up for me on the raft.

"And all those people were there!" She sighed, as if this was the worst part. "My dad always says if you want to really know someone, look at how they act when *no one's* watching. That's the true test of character."

I had to think about this a moment. "But that doesn't make sense. I mean, if you can see them, then someone's watching you. Right?"

"The point is," she continued, missing this or choosing not to hear it, "he did me a favor. The last thing I wanted was for him to see me get so upset. It's not who I am."

It made my head hurt, trying to follow this logic. But to her, it made sense. It had to, because the only other option was that Colin didn't care about her the way she did him, and that she wouldn't even consider.

As a result, her feelings for him had only grown more intense. If not at Campus or planning how to get there, she was on the phone with him, texting him or—more often—waiting for him to respond. At all other times she was visibly distracted, with any question posed to her needing to be repeated, often more than once. I'd never seen anything like it.

It wasn't like that with Blake. At least, not yet. But sometimes, you just need something to get you there. I was counting on Club Prom.

Around as old as the Club itself, it was held every year, just as the season was reaching full swing. The ballroom would be decorated according to a chosen theme, a band brought in, and everyone attending had to dress up in what was referred to as "resort finest." At the beginning, this had meant bathing suits with corsages, the whole thing more of a joke than anything else. But in the last ten years or so, it had become more of a real formal dance. It was a big deal to go, and if you weren't a Club member, you had to be asked.

I was well versed in all of this because lately, Bailey was obsessed, spending what free time she had looking for dresses at Bly County Thrift and the discount stores, as well as dog-earing pages with makeup looks in Trinity's fashion magazines. Colin hadn't yet formally asked her—nor Blake me—but she assured me repeatedly this didn't mean anything, since it was over two weeks away. When he did extend the invitation, she'd have everything ready along with her yes, and thought that I should, too.

"But what if he doesn't ask me?" I'd said the previous evening, after we'd ridden with Vincent, who I'd met that first night, out to the raft in late afternoon. "Then I have a dress and makeup and everything, and I'm pathetic."

"You're sharing custody of a stuffed animal," she said, squinting in the direction of the yacht club. "He's going to ask you."

"Stuffed animal?" Vincent said. "What kind of weird stuff are you into, Saylor?"

"Leave her alone," Bailey said. "It's romantic."

"Really weird stuff," I told him at the same time. "Would put hair on your chest."

"I could use that," he said, then laughed, hard enough that his sunglasses, which he kept parked on his head, slid off and hit the dock with a bang. "Damn, my shades!"

"You need one of those things to hang them around your neck," Bailey told him.

"You offering to buy me one?" he replied.

She rolled her eyes, but I saw her smiling. I thought back to that first night I'd been out to the raft, how Vincent's face flushed when April alluded to a possible crush. Maybe she was onto something.

"I cannot wait to see the Club at Prom," Bailey said to me.

"You've never been?" I asked.

"Nope. But this girl from the Station went last year, with a guy she was dating who was a valet over there." She sighed happily. "She said it was beautiful."

"Oh, please," Vincent said with a snort. "Who wants to dress up at the lake?"

"I do," she said, and he made a face. To me she added, "Just wait. You'll see. It's going to be great."

She, at least, was sure of things. I supposed it was good that one of us was.

Now, back at birth class, Trinity turned around, looking up at me. "Hey. Saylor. Are you breathing?"

I blinked, surprised to find myself with her and not with Vincent and Bailey. "Yes," I said quickly, blowing out some air as proof. "Of course I am."

"Well, you're the only one. So stop." She turned back around, elbowing me sharply in the stomach again as she did so. "The movie's about to start."

"Movie?" I looked at the front of the room, where, sure enough, Kim had rolled in a cart with a TV and DVD player on it. On the screen, a title page: STAGES OF LABOR AND DELIVERY. "Oh, God. Is it okay if I wait—"

"Nope," she said as the lights went dim overhead and the video began. The camera zeroed in on a woman in a hospital bed, hugely pregnant, her feet up in stirrups. She was smiling, as was her husband, sitting beside her.

I looked at the clock: there were twenty minutes left of class, and then I'd have to drive us home. When faced with two not-so-good options, there really isn't even a point in choosing between them. Still, I did cover my eyes.

ELEVEN

"Hey. Do you want to go to Club Prom with me?"

Every movement in the guys' apartment did not screech to a halt as Blake said this. It just felt that way.

"What?" I said, although I'd heard him. So had Bailey, who was now looking squarely at us from where she was sitting on the other bed with Colin.

"It's this dance," Blake said casually, taking a sip from his beer. "They have it every year at the Club. Kind of a joke, kind of not. It's usually fun."

I looked at Bailey again, feeling helpless. She'd talked about this so much, it seemed wrong that I'd get asked first, and I wanted to give Colin a chance to make his move. But when I looked at him, he was studying his phone, his eyes narrowed.

"Um," I finally said to Blake. "Yeah. Sure. I'd love to go."

"Cool," he said, so nonchalantly I wondered, briefly, what he would have done if I'd said no. "It's next Saturday, and you'll need something kind of formal, just FYI."

"That's fine," I said. "I'll figure something out."

"I have procured a date to Club Prom," Blake yelled toward Hannah and Rachel, who were by the doorway, huddled over their phones. "So you can stop nagging me."

"Thank God," Rachel said. "Nothing like waiting until the last minute."

"Last minute? It's Monday. The dance is next Saturday," Blake told them.

"We're girls," Hannah informed him. "We need time to prepare for things like this."

"Which is why," Rachel said, "we asked our guys ages ago."

At this, Colin got to his feet and walked back into the kitchen, where he opened the fridge, taking out another beer. He popped the tab, then just stood there, holding it and looking out the back door.

"You already have dates?" Bailey asked the girls now. "Who are you taking?"

Rachel shook the ice in her plastic cup. "These German exchange students from the kitchen."

"Who are super cute but don't speak English," Hannah said. "And we don't know German. Should be fun."

"You," Rachel said, "are just pissed because Roo said no. Don't take it out on Gunther and Konrad."

Bailey, surprised, said, "You asked Roo to Club Prom?"

Hannah blushed. "Oh, God. Yes. He shot me down, but at least he was nice about it. Said he had to work."

"He probably does," Bailey told her. "He has, like, four jobs."

"That's what he said," she replied. "Truthfully, though, I don't think he's into me. Which stinks, because he's totally my type."

"Your type," Rachel repeated. "What's that, blond and handsome?"

"And *nice*," Hannah added. "The other night at Lucy Tate's, I lost my shoes and he spent like a half hour helping me find them. What's not to like?"

Shoe buddy, I thought. It was hard not to wince.

Bailey stood then, walking back to the kitchen, where she said something to Colin I couldn't hear. He replied, his voice also low, and then they were going out the back door, the screen swinging shut behind them.

"Someone seems tense," Rachel said to me. "Everything okay with them?"

"As long as he's asking her to the Prom right now, yes," I said.

Hannah's eyes widened. "He hasn't asked her yet?"

"No," I said.

"Who else would he take?" she asked Blake.

He held up his hands. "Whoa. Don't look at me. I know nothing except I needed a date and now I have one."

I couldn't help but notice this was the second time I'd been referred to as his date, not by name. When everything comes easy, I guess you learn not to sweat the details.

"Boys are so weird," Rachel observed, shaking her drink again. To me she said, "Hey, you need a dress? We brought a few options that should fit."

This was a nice offer, I knew, extended in kindness. And maybe I'd been spending too much time with Trinity—okay, I was definitely spending too much time with Trinity—but I wondered about her motivation. I was a North Lake girl going to a Lake North Prom: of course they'd think I wouldn't have something suitable to wear. And the truth was, here, I didn't. But at home, my closet held a number of expensive dresses, most purchased by Nana for dinners at *her* club. Not that they'd know that, though. They only knew Saylor, not Emma.

The back door opened again then, and Bailey came in, followed after a beat by Colin. Now, she was smiling and so flushed that I guessed what had happened even before she plopped down beside me and said, "He asked me! Finally."

I looked at Colin, who was still in the kitchen, getting another beer, his face, unlike hers, neither relieved nor over-joyed.

"That's great," I said as Blake stood and also walked back to the kitchen.

"Better than great," she replied, taking my hand and squeezing it. "See? It's all coming together."

"Club Prom?" my dad asked. "Man. That brings back some memories."

It was seven thirty a.m., the time my dad had taken to calling me to check in. Which was great for him, because in Greece, it was midafternoon. I, however, was always only (barely) waking up.

"You went to Club Prom?" I asked him now.

"Oh, yeah." He was quiet for long enough for me to picture him on the boat, with a faraway look on his face, smiling. "Twice, actually. And both times with your mom."

"*Mom* went?" I asked. "She never mentioned that."

"Because it wasn't a great night," he replied with a sigh. "Either time."

"What happened?"

Another pause, but this one felt different, like he wasn't thinking as much as deciding how best to answer this. "Well, you know, she always felt out of place at the Club. Even though she knew a lot of people there. And when she was nervous, she . . ."

". . . drank too much?" I finished for him.

"Well," he said. "Yes."

Even after all this time, it was hard for my dad to talk about my mom's issues. He preferred to avoid the subject as much as possible, as if bringing it up did some disservice to her or her memory. This was in marked contrast to what I'd seen of Celeste, Mimi, and the rest of the family at the lake, for whom my mother's problems were as much a part of her story as, well, I was. There were lots of ways to love someone, I guessed, both by remembering and forgetting.

"I wish you'd taken pictures," I said now.

"I'm sure somebody did," he replied. "All I remember is that even barefoot in a borrowed dress, your mom was gorgeous."

"Until she got drunk," I said.

Another pause, this one to let me know I'd crossed a line. "Anyway," he said a moment later, "you must need something to wear. I left you a credit card, didn't I?"

He had, for emergencies: it was tucked in a spare pair of sneakers in my closet. "I should be able to borrow something from Bailey, I think."

"Well, if not, buy something," he replied. Then, quickly: "Within reason, of course."

"Of course," I agreed. How hard could that be?

"I just filled it up, so there's plenty of gas," Mimi said, handing me her keys. "Bly Corners is pretty much a straight shot once you get into Delaney. You can't miss it."

"Great," I said. "Thanks."

"Oh, I remember when Waverly and Matthew were going to that dance over at the Club," she said, somewhat wistful. "Ancient history, but it feels like yesterday."

Then she just stood there, clearly waiting for me to get behind the wheel. So with dread building in my gut, I did.

In a perfect world, driving Trinity to birth class would have been just what it took to get me over my fear of being behind the wheel. In reality, though, it just made everything worse.

Sure, I'd gotten us there and home alive. But between the traffic jam and near panic attack going, followed by having to slam on brakes to avoid hitting a car that stopped suddenly on the way home, I'd stepped out from behind the wheel swearing I'd never return. Which wouldn't be a big deal, I figured, because this was North Lake, a place small enough to get anywhere on foot. Except, as it turned out, a place to buy a dress for Club Prom.

It had all started innocently enough. That morning, I'd been minding my own business, having breakfast and reading the obits, when Bailey came down to go to work.

"It's dress day," she informed me as she loaded slices of bread into the toaster.

"Actually, it's Thursday," I replied, still reading about Daniel Polk, 74, who had left this earthly plane after a long illness.

"I just wish I didn't have to work," she said, ignoring this. "I'm worried about you picking out something at the mall on your own."

"Well, don't," I said, "because I'm not doing that. I'll just find something around here that will work."

She turned, looking at me. "Here? What are you going to wear, a Calvander's tie-dye? One of Trinity's maternity dresses?"

"Maybe." I felt her glare at me. "Look, you have your dress, so what are you worried about?"

"*Your* dress," she replied, as if I was stupid. "We're going together, remember? And this is a big deal."

"I'll find something," I said again.

"I know you will." BING! went the toaster, spitting out her slices. "Because I told Mimi you were borrowing her car to go to Bly Corners today."

This got my attention. "You what?"

She walked to the fridge, pulling it open. After scanning the contents, she sighed, then shut it. "I told her you needed to borrow her car to go buy a dress. She's fine with it. Said to come grab the keys whenever you're ready to go."

"Never," I said. "That's when I'll be ready."

"You don't like shopping?"

"It's not that," I said.

"Then what is it?"

I just sat there, not wanting to get into the whole driving thing with another Blackwood sister. "Well, I have to work, for starters."

"No, you don't." She took a crunchy bite. "Mimi says there's no turnover and only three rooms for housekeeping. Trinity can do it."

"She can't even bend over," I pointed out.

"So she'll do it standing up. You need a dress," she replied. I sighed. "Look, I'm not taking no for an answer, Saylor. Just go."

She made it sound so simple to get in the car and drive miles into a town I'd never been to before, all by myself. In practice, though, everything was more complicated.

"Have fun!" Mimi said now, stepping back from the car. "Can't wait to see what you come home with!"

I smiled, waving as I cranked the engine. Then, gripping the wheel and with her watching, I drove—slowly—out of the Calvander's lot. A block later, when I was sure I was fully out of sight, I pulled into a gas station. There, I cut the engine and wiped my sweaty palms against my shorts, trying to calm the thudding of my heart in my chest. Finally, I just leaned my head against the steering wheel, closing my eyes.

A few weeks earlier, I'd been planning a summer at Bridget's, every detail organized and in place. Now, here I was, at the lake with my mother's family, sort of dating a college boy and needing a formal dress. Also, driving, or trying to. Even with my imagination, I never would have pictured this.

Knock. Knock.

Startled, I jumped, my eyes springing open. There, standing on the other side of my closed window, was Roo Price.

"Hey," he said. He had on a green collared shirt and shorts and was squinting in at me, eyes narrowed. "You okay?"

I turned my key, then put down the window. "Do I not seem okay?"

"You're in a gas station parking lot collapsed over your steering wheel," he pointed out.

"I was resting my eyes," I replied.

He glanced around at the nearby pumps, the blinking neon sign out front that said COLD SODAS. "Interesting spot for a nap."

"Well, life is busy," I said, smiling. "Sometimes you have to take them where you can."

A car drove by and beeped. Roo raised his hand in a wave. Did everyone know everyone here? Lately I felt like the only stranger.

"What are you doing?" I asked. "I mean, other than policing people taking naps in public places."

"Just got off work," he said, bending down so he was level with the window.

"I hear you have a ton of jobs."

"Not really," he replied, running his fingers through his hair, which was short and the whitest of blond. When he was done, a single tuft stuck up, and it was all I could do not to fix it. "Just five."

"That's four more than most people," I pointed out. "I bet you could use a gas station nap."

"I prefer to grab my shut-eye at grocery stores," he replied.

"Different strokes for different folks," I said. "What are the jobs?"

"Well, there's the Station arcade. Fifteen hours a week." He held up four fingers, then folded one down. "Then I work the night desk at the Park Palms when they need someone to fill in."

"That's a hotel?"

"Nursing home," he said, folding down another finger. "The grocery store, with Celeste. That's another fifteen a week, usually."

"Okay if I rest my eyes again? I'm getting tired just hearing this."

"And finally," he continued, "there's the Yum truck."

"The Yum truck?"

Instead of replying, he turned, glancing behind him. There, parked only a few spaces away, was a white food truck, plastered with pictures of various frozen desserts. YUM! was painted across the hood in hot-pink letters. It was a testament to my level of distraction that I hadn't even noticed it.

"You drive an ice cream truck?" I asked. "Seriously?"

"It's the lake," he replied. "Ice cream is big business."

"Can I see?"

He stepped back, waving a hand. "Be my guest."

Suddenly energized, I got out of the car, following him over. "Are you selling right now?"

"Not a lot of takers at ten a.m.," he said. "The truth is my car broke down again, so I took this to work last night."

I raised an eyebrow. "You drove an ice cream truck to a nursing home?"

"I'm very popular with the residents," he said, flashing that gap in his teeth again.

"I bet you're popular with everyone."

"That's my charm, though," he corrected me. "Not my access to frozen desserts."

"Keep telling yourself that," I replied, patting his back.

"Oh, I will."

I was too busy laughing, at first, to realize how easily we'd fallen into this rapid-fire exchange. Like when I was with him, I wasn't a stranger after all.

"Why *do* you work so much?" I asked. "Are you saving for something?"

"College," he replied.

Of course. I felt my face get hot: I was always getting this wrong. "Oh, yeah. You mentioned journalism school in your five sentences."

"Yup," he said, pulling a hand through his hair again. "I'm the editor of the paper at school this year. It got me into it. There's a good program at the U, actually, if I stay in-state. Which I probably will. It's cheaper."

I was beginning to realize that not thinking about money was a luxury, and one I should have been appreciating more.

"With all these jobs," I said now, "how do you even remember where to be and at what time?"

He pulled his phone out of his pocket. "Alerts. Lots of them. If you hear a beep, it's probably me."

"Good to know," I said as he walked over, sliding open the door to the truck and stepping back.

"Watch your step," he said. "It's perennially sticky."

I climbed in, my footsteps clanking on the metal floor. "This is so cool."

"It is," he agreed. "Until you get mobbed by a bunch of damp kids all screaming for sugar. Then, not so much."

"Tell me there's a little song you turn on as you drive."

He smiled, pointing to a white box with some buttons installed above the driver's seat. "Four melodies total, with a choice of tempos."

"Can you play one now?"

"No, because someone will want ice cream and I'm not on the clock," he said.

I looked out the window. The lot was empty. "There's no one around."

"Doesn't matter. It's like a dog whistle. If you play it, they will come." He stepped around me, into the narrow walkway that led back into the truck. "You can have something, though, if you're an ice-cream-at-ten-a.m. person."

"Who isn't?"

"Well, me, for one. But again, different strokes." He bent over a built-in cooler, turning a handle and then pushing it open. "Pick your poison."

I stepped closer, peering inside at a huge selection of offerings, all individually wrapped and organized by category: frozen candy bars, push-ups, cookie sandwiches, Sundae in a Cup. Even if you didn't like ice cream—and I did—you'd have to be excited by such a selection, at ten a.m. or, really, anytime.

"This one," I said, pulling out a Choco-wich, two chocolate chip cookies with vanilla ice cream between them. It was cold in my hands. "Thank you."

"No problem," he replied, sliding the cooler shut. He leaned back, arms crossed over his chest, as I unwrapped it and took a bite.

"So you want to tell me what you were really doing collapsed over your steering wheel in a parking lot?"

"Waiting for the Yum truck," I replied, grinning. "And it came!"

He just looked at me.

"Fine." I swallowed. "The truth is, I'm supposed to be driving to Bly Corners."

"The mall?" I nodded. "So what's the problem?"

"I don't like to drive."

"You drove here," he pointed out.

"And I drove Trinity to birth class on Saturday," I said, sighing. "What I'm saying is I didn't *like* it."

"You went to birth class?" he asked. "Did Kim show one of those videos?"

"She did."

He shuddered. "See, now *that's* something to be scared of. You can handle a full dilation shot, you can handle anything."

"You went to birth class?"

"Filled in for Celeste once, when she had to work." He reached down, rubbing a smudge on the cooler top. "Fair to say it traumatized me."

I tried to picture Roo in that little room, Trinity elbowing his gut as she tried to practice her ocean breathing. It actually wasn't that hard. At this rate, we'd all be trained to help push when the baby came.

"See, that's me when it comes to driving," I said. "Like, I literally panic when I have to get behind the wheel."

"Since when?"

"Always. Although it got worse when I hit another car in a parking deck." Even as I cringed, saying this, I felt a sense of relief. The truth felt good. "I freaked."

"Understandable."

"Not to my dad." I took another bite of my Choco-wich. "He's always been so pushy about me getting my license, even when I was adamant I didn't want to. He won't let up. I don't get it."

Roo considered this for a second as I chewed. "Well, that

probably has more to do with your mom than you, though, don't you think?"

"My mom?"

"Because she didn't drive," he said. "She wouldn't. Right?"

It was like time just stopped, my breathing as well, as I stood there, the Choco-wich melting down onto my wrist. Could this be true? I'd been in a car with my mom behind the wheel. Hadn't I?

"Wait," I said. "She was afraid to drive? Are you sure?"

He opened his mouth, then quickly shut it before pulling a hand through his hair again, this time leaving a different tuft vertical. "That's just what Celeste said."

"Celeste," I repeated.

"I'm sorry," he said quickly. "Obviously, you know your mom better than—"

"I don't, though," I said. I heard the catch in my voice, and hoped he didn't. "That's what I'm realizing. I didn't really know her at all."

We just stood there for a second, the truck dark and cool all around us as a car drove by, beeping.

"I'm sorry," Roo said quietly. He looked back down at his hand, spread on the cooler. "And for what it's worth, I can relate to having more questions than answers. My dad died before I was born."

"That's harder," I pointed out. "At least I had her for a little while."

"Or, easier," he countered. "You can't miss what you never had."

I looked out the window at Mimi's Toyota, parked where I'd left it, in the perfect center of a space, no cars anywhere nearby. "I guess everyone's afraid of something."

"Yeah." He was quiet for a minute. "With me, it's clowns."

"Shut up," I said, hitting him.

"What? I thought we were having a moment."

"You," I said, "are not really afraid of clowns."

"I am. And before you mock, I'll remind you that clowns are much more avoidable than driving."

"Not if you work at the circus."

"Joke's on you. That's my fifth job."

We looked at each other, slightly breathless. Then, together, we cracked up, the sound amplified by all the metal surfaces around us. I laughed until I cried, harder than I had in years. Or maybe ever. There was something almost primal about it, this moment of near hysteria with a boy I'd just met and yet, again, felt like I knew.

It was hard to stop, taking some deep breaths, not making eye contact with Roo, and throwing away my mostly melted Choco-wich to get calmed down. Even then I was still sputtering a bit. "I should go," I said finally. "I'm not going to find a dress store within walking distance standing here in the Yum truck."

"You're not going to find one, period," he replied as I turned and started toward the seats up front. "Bly Corners is pretty much the only option."

I sighed as he reached around me, sliding the door open. Immediately, I felt the heat of the day, bouncing off the asphalt and thick with humidity, smack me in the face. "What's your real fifth job?"

"What if I said it was driving instructor?"

I just looked at him. "I'd say you were full of crap."

"And you would be right." He grinned, shutting the door with a bang. "It's actually landscaping with my uncle. That said, I would be happy to ride along with you for moral support, if you want. I'm told I have a very calming presence."

"Just as long as we don't see any clowns."

"Well, obviously," he said. "Then you're on your own."

I snorted, then looked over at Mimi's car again, remembering how happy she'd been waving at me as she left.

"How about this," I said. "You drive my car. I'll watch out for people in face paint wearing big shoes and spraying water bottles."

"How about *this*," he countered. "I drive there. You drive back. And we don't talk about the other thing."

"Clowns?"

"Watch it," he warned me. "You want to drive both ways?"

"Nope." I grabbed the keys, holding them out to him. "Let's go."

TWELVE

"I *love* it when boyfriends come to help pick out for formals," the salesgirl said with a sigh as I turned sideways in front of the mirror, trying to decide if I liked the long black sheath I had on. "It's the cutest."

I knew I should tell her that Roo, who was standing nearby examining a leather cuff with a quizzical expression, was not my boyfriend. That he was just being nice—"What's not to like?" I heard Hannah say, in my head—tagging along, not to mention driving me, at least halfway. But for some reason, I didn't correct her. He didn't, either. I couldn't help but notice.

"What's your feeling on feathers?" he asked me.

"Opposed," I replied. "Unless it's on a bird, in which case, fine. Why?"

"I'm intrigued by these shoes," he said, gesturing to a pair of green sandals that had, yes, feathers woven into the straps. "Do people really wear stuff like this?"

"Sure!" the salesgirl, a skinny redhead in a too-short minidress, said as she hurried over. "That's part of our new

Femme Tropicale line. It's all about being uninhibited and wild."

Roo looked into the mirror he was facing, right at me. "Hear that? Uninhibited and wild."

"Sounds exactly like Club Prom," I said. "Grab them before someone else does."

"What's your size?" the girl asked me.

"She's kidding," Roo told her.

"What?" She looked at me, confused. "You don't want the shoes?"

"No," I said, narrowing my eyes at my reflection again. "Or this dress, actually."

"Good call," Roo said. "I didn't want to say anything, but you kind of look like the Grim Reaper."

"You think I *literally* look like death, and you weren't going to mention it?" I said.

"Well," he replied. "Yeah. I mean, what's with the cape?"

"It's not a cape, actually," the girl told him cheerfully. "It's a detachable midi top to add flow to the piece."

I faced the mirror again, and they both looked at me. Roo said, "Looks like a cape."

I sighed. "This is, like, the millionth dress I've tried."

"Then I bet number million and one is the charm." He glanced at his watch, then added, "No pressure, but it kind of has to be. I'm supposed to be in the Yum truck doing the motel circuit by one at the latest."

I walked back into the dressing room. "You know what

would save us lots of time?" I yelled over the door. "If you drove back."

"About as likely as someone not thinking that's a cape," he said. "Nice try, though."

Standing there alone, in front of yet another mirror, I smiled at my reflection. Normally, two hours of shopping for anything would try my patience to a point of rage. This outing, however, had been different. It was actually fun.

First, there was the ride over, during which I got to relax in the passenger seat as Roo drove, entertaining me with stories about his interactions with the residents of Park Palms, the nursing home where he worked the night shift. Then, our arrival at Bly Corners, which was less a mall than three stores and a food court surrounded by a huge parking lot in which we were one of only four cars. I counted.

"Is this place even open?" I asked as he pulled right up to the main entrance, taking one of many empty spaces.

"Careful with the judgment, Big City," he replied. "For Delaney, this is mobbed."

As we got out of the car, the only sound was Roo shutting his door and, I kid you not, a pigeon I could hear cooing from atop a nearby light pole. "Seriously, how do they even stay open if no one comes here?"

"Selling overpriced dresses to desperate out-of-towners," he replied. "Now, watch your purse. Pickpockets thrive in crowded places."

I laughed as we walked to the main entrance, where he

pulled the door open for me. Nice, I thought again. This time, I heard it in my own voice, not Hannah's.

Our first stop was TOGS!, a narrow store blasting loud music where everything was neon and priced at twenty-five bucks or less.

"NO!" Roo said when I presented him with the only thing I'd even slightly liked, a royal-blue dress with a pink ruffle underneath. "You look radioactive. Next."

That was Claudia's Closet, a women's boutique that specialized in flowing, loose-waisted clothing for women of a certain age that was *not* seventeen. Still, I tried on a maroon dress with a full skirt that swished when I walked.

"Might look good with a high wind," Roo observed when I emerged from the fitting room. "But we can't count on that. Let's move on."

We had, to Douglas Arthur, the department store, where we'd been ever since. Everything was fun and games until you were out of time, though. And we almost were.

"All that is left is the green-and-white one," I reported, again over the door. "With the halter neck."

"You know how I feel about that," he said. "I told you when you picked it out."

"What did you say, again? That it makes me look like I'm—"

"Being strangled," he finished. "So that's a no. Try this."

I stepped back, startled, as a dress was flung over the top of the door, its hanger clanking. The top had thin, gauzy straps, the skirt ending in a series of layers, all of it a pale rose color.

"Pink?" I said.

"Don't be gender biased. Just try it."

I slipped out of the black one, then pulled the dress down, removing it from the hanger. Looking at it up close, I had more doubts: it was so simple as to be almost plain, the fabric delicate and thin.

"I don't think this is me," I said. "How strongly are you opposed to the cape?"

"I'm not answering that," he replied. "Put it on."

I did, turning my back to the mirror as I slid it over my head, easing the straps over my shoulders. When I looked down, all I saw was pink.

"This is a no," I reported.

"But we haven't seen it yet!" the salesgirl said. "And he picked it out himself!"

I sighed. At this point I'd leave with nothing to wear and Roo would have himself an actual girlfriend, not just a pretend one. Oh, well, I thought, and opened the door.

He was standing right outside, the salesgirl a few feet behind him, a grin on his face. When he saw me, however, he immediately stopped smiling.

I looked down at myself. Was there a cutout I had missed, exposing me? Could the entire thing be not just thin and delicate, but transparent?

A quick, panicked check confirmed neither of these was the case. But he was still staring at me. "What?" I said, crossing my arms over my chest anyway. "What's wrong with it?"

He blinked at me. "Nothing," he said. "It's—"

"Perfect," the salesgirl sighed. "You look incredible."

I did? I turned, facing the mirror on the dressing room door to see for myself. And while I wouldn't have said perfect—nothing was, in clothing or otherwise—I did have to admit that it worked. The color, which warmed up my skin and the beginnings of a tan I'd gotten since I'd been here. The cut, which emphasized my waist and made me look tall, even in bare feet. But there was something else, too, that had nothing to do with the dress itself. Roo had seen something in it, and recognized a part of me that matched. How could someone know you better than you knew yourself? Especially if they really didn't know you, not at all.

"I'm not convinced," I said after a moment. "The fact it's lacking a cape is kind of a deal breaker."

"You want a cape?" the salesgirl asked, dismayed. "Well . . . I guess we could look for something. . . ."

"She's kidding," Roo told her. Again. Like a translator I never knew I needed. To me he said, "Seriously, though, you should get that. You look great."

I felt my face flush, hearing this, and quickly turned back to the mirror. Which was stupid, because of course he was still there in the reflection, although he immediately turned his attention back to the shoe rack. What was happening here? We were friends. Not even that. Acquaintances whose parents had been closer than close. But relationships were not passed down like hair or eye color. Were they?

I looked down at the tag, hanging from my armpit. The dress was ninety bucks, which I knew was a lot more than Bailey had spent on hers from Bly County Thrift, even with the alterations it had needed. Nana Payne, though, would have plunked down three times that without hesitating, for herself or me. It's important to remember this, I told myself, whether I was here three weeks or always. Don't forget.

"Okay, I'll take it," I said. "But only because we have ice cream to sell."

"And you don't want a cape," the salesgirl said, clarifying.

"No," Roo and I replied in unison. Then he looked at me in the mirror again. And smiled.

After I paid, it was back to the parking lot, where we were still one of the only cars present. Which did not make me any less nervous about having to drive out of there.

"You know," I said as Roo slid into the passenger seat, "you can drive if you want."

"Not our deal," he reminded me, shutting his door. I stayed where I was, outside on the driver's side. A moment later he swung it open again. "Are you getting in?"

"Eventually," I replied.

"Can't drive from outside." Still, I didn't move. "Saylor. Come on."

"I'm nervous!"

Now he got out of the car, so we were both standing by our open doors. "About what?"

I thought for a second. "Crashing."

"What else?"

"That's not enough?"

"Planes crash. You still fly."

"You don't know that. For all you know, I've never even been on a plane."

He considered this. "Okay, fine. How about this: pedestrians get struck by cars. You still walk. And I know, because I have seen you."

"That is not the same."

"As the car thing or the plane?" he asked.

"Neither," I replied. A seagull flew by, cawing above us. "Look. I never wanted to drive. I was fine without it. Then my dad forced me, and I hit that car. It was traumatic."

"Trauma can be educational," he pointed out in that same maddeningly reasonable voice. "And even if you fail, at least you tried."

"Fail?" I said. "Do you think I can't do it?"

"You won't even get in the car," he said.

I slid behind the wheel, feeling like I'd show him. Until I realized that was probably exactly what he wanted. By then, though, I'd already shut my door. Crap.

"Okay. Put your foot on the brake." I did, and he reached over, turning the key I'd put in the ignition so the engine revved to life. Like one of Pavlov's dogs, just the sound made my heart jump. "Now, tell me what you're feeling."

I was too scared to go into more detail than "Terrified."

"Why?"

"Because I might kill someone."

Roo took an exaggerated look around the mostly empty parking lot. "Who?"

I tightened my grip on the wheel, right at the ten and two spots. "You. Me. Everyone."

"The only way to overcome a fear is to face it," he said. "You have to knock down the power it has over you."

"Have you done that with clowns? Because if not, I don't see why I have to do this."

"Because," he shot back loudly, over the A/C, which had just come on and begun blasting us, "as we discussed earlier, clowns are location-specific. I see them on TV or at the circus. My fear of them does not prevent me from fully living my life."

"I am living my life!"

"We've been sitting here for seven minutes," he said, poking a finger at the clock on the dashboard. "Seven minutes, spent in fear, that you won't get back."

Great. Now I was a failure *and* a waste of human energy. "You know, a lot of people don't drive. They are just happy and grateful passengers."

He sat back, looking at me. "Yes, but when you only ride, you're never in control. You get taken from point A to point B through no volition or work of your own. It's like drifting. If life is a journey, wouldn't you rather be the person behind the wheel than the one just being carried along?"

I bit my lip, looking out the window at the empty row of spaces beside us. Put like that, I couldn't help but think, again, of my mom. So willful, so strong in so many ways, and yet in the end she succumbed to something that drove her, so to speak, and not the other way around. I'd worried for so long about all the ways we were alike and what that meant for my own future. Here was a way to make one choice, at least, to be different.

"Fine," I said. And I turned the key.

Since the engine was already on, however, it made a loud, screeching noise, sending another nearby gull into sudden flight. Shit. My face flushed, bright red I was sure, and I felt tears in my eyes.

"Engine's on," Roo said cheerfully. He was not looking at me, but straight ahead. "Now let's just get into reverse so we can back out of here."

I did, swallowing a huge lump in my throat as I did so. Then I hit the gas, gently, moving out of the space in a very slow, wide arc.

"Tip number one," he said as I switched gears. "Never back up more than you have to."

I looked around the empty lot. "We're, like, the only ones here."

"True. But everything is practice. So you should do it right. Try again."

"Get back in the space, you mean?"

"Yep." He sat back, crossing one leg over the other. "I'll wait."

I pulled back in, then reversed out once more, this time keeping the car tightly between the empty spaces. "Better?"

"Great," he said. "Now: the road."

It wasn't easy. I got beeped at as I turned out of Bly Corners ("Not your fault, they're being an asshole," Roo said) as well as when I was merging onto the road home ("Okay, that one was your fault, watch your blind spot next time"). But unlike my dad, who did commentary on my driving between obviously clenched teeth, and Trinity, who ignored my panic while looking at her phone, Roo actually was, as he'd claimed, a calming presence. He watched everything, from what I was doing to the traffic around us, correcting and praising as necessary. Even when I froze as we approached a huge pothole—I drove right into it, almost taking Mimi's muffler off in the process—he just said lightly, "And *that's* why we steer around road hazards."

Even so, by the time I got him back to the Yum truck, I was soaked with sweat, my shirt sticking to my back and my nerves jangled. "I can't believe I did that," I said. "I think that's the farthest I've driven, like, ever."

"You still have to get back to Mimi's," he reminded me. I slumped a bit. "But hey! It's the perfect way to cap this off. Solo drive to celebrate. A win-win."

I just looked at him. "Are you always this positive about everything?"

"Me?" I nodded. "No. In fact, about a year ago, I went through a real doom-and-gloom phase. Wore black, sulked, shut myself in my room. Good times."

"I can't imagine that," I said, because I really couldn't.

"I was working through stuff. Thinking about my dad,

how I never knew him. You know, woe is me, et cetera." He pulled a hand through his hair, leaving a bit sticking up. Something I was already thinking of as his signature look. "But then I realized me being all down was really a drag, not just for me but for my mom. She's had enough darkness already. For her, at least, I figured I should at least try to look for the good in things."

"And it was that easy?" I said, doubtful.

"It was a process," he admitted. "I also got my license. That helped."

I gave him a look. "How convenient for this story."

"No, seriously!" he said. "Once I could drive, I could literally go places. This small town, my dad's accident . . . I could get out of it all. Even if it was just for a little while. Like a trip to Bly Corners."

I considered this. "You could also walk there to clear your head, though."

"You could," he agreed. "But the trip would take a *lot* longer."

I had to admit, he had me there. Not that I wanted to tell him this, so instead I said, "Can I ask you a question?"

"Sure."

"Why does everyone call you Roo?"

He sighed. "My real name is Christopher. When I was little, I was super into kangaroos. Some might say obsessed. I couldn't say the whole word for a while, so I called them roos. It stuck."

I smiled. "That's pretty cute."

"To everyone else," he agreed. "Now I have a question for you."

"Shoot."

"*Have* you ever been on a plane?"

I bit my lip. "Yeah. A bunch of times."

"I knew it!" He snapped his fingers. "I could tell."

"How can you tell something like that?"

He shrugged. "Dunno. Maybe you just look like you're going places."

It was so stupid and corny, but still, I laughed. And now, on the porch with Bailey and Trinity, I felt myself again begin to grin, remembering this, before I quickly rearranged my face into a neutral expression. This had kept happening over the last few days, my mind drifting to one exchange or another from the trip to Bly Corners even when I tried to stay focused. Stop it, I thought. Blake is the boy you're going to Club Prom with.

Right.

Celeste squinted into her camera, a Pop Soda dangling from her other hand. "Okay. Now let's take one of just the girls. Gordon, get in there."

"Mom," Bailey groaned. "I think you have enough pictures."

"What? I've barely taken any," Celeste said, gesturing for us to move in closer in front of the gardenia bush chosen as the backdrop for this documentation. "Gordon. Put down the gorilla book and get between them."

"It's *chimpanzees*," Gordon said, getting to her feet and coming over to join us. She brought the book with her.

"Whatever." Celeste peered at her camera again. "Now, hold on, I think I've been in portrait this whole time . . ."

"You need landscape," said Mimi, who was off to the side with a Pop Soda, observing. "Turn it sideways."

"Mama, I know."

Beside me, Bailey sighed loudly. "I just want the guys to get here. Where are they?"

"It's only seven fifteen," I told her.

"Yeah, but we said seven."

"You can't smile while you're talking!" Celeste said. "Now, everyone look here. Say cheese!"

We did, as she took several without a flash, some with, and then a few in portrait mode just to be on the safe side. "Perfect," she said as Gordon returned to the steps, reopening her book to her marked place. "Now we just need a few with the boys and we'll be set."

"No," Bailey said flatly. "We are *not* doing that."

Celeste looked up from her camera, where she'd been examining the shots she'd taken. "What do you mean? Of course we are. It's a formal dance, we need pictures with your dates."

"You don't, actually," Bailey replied. "Because I'm sure we'll take some once we're there, as a group. And anyway, we're running late. There's no time for anything else."

Celeste looked at Mimi, who shrugged. "Fine," she said. "But I want to meet these boys before you leave with them. Especially the famous Colin."

Bailey rolled her eyes. Then she pulled out her phone, quickly firing off another text. When I glanced at her screen and saw it was the fourth in a row with no response, I quickly messaged Blake, asking for an update.

Be there in ten, he wrote back immediately. **Meet me outside.**

"Look," I said, showing Bailey. "Everything's fine."

"Why does he want you to meet him outside, though?" she asked worriedly, squinting at the message.

"You're the one who just said they're running late," I pointed out. "Bailey. It's fine."

She did not look convinced, though, as Mimi and Celeste headed into the house, telling us to yell when the boys arrived. Gordon stayed on the steps. "I just want to get there," Bailey said, looking at the Club, which we could see, lit up across the water, from where we were standing. "I hate all this waiting."

"It's fifteen minutes," I assured her, but this she ignored, already checking her phone again.

A moment later, a car did turn into the Calvander's lot. It wasn't Colin and Blake, though, but Jack, returning from work at the Station with Roo in tow. As they made their way toward us, I suddenly felt shy, standing there in what he'd picked out for me. But when he saw me in it, he grinned.

"Really like the dress," he said, looking me up and down.

"But you know what it's missing?"

"A cape?" I asked.

He gave me a thumbs-up. "You got it."

I laughed, but Bailey just looked at him. "Shut up, Roo. She looks great."

"Whoa," he said, holding up a hand. "I was—"

"It's an inside joke," I explained.

"Yeah, I'm just kidding around, Bay," Roo told her.

"Well, don't," she told him. "You can't just show up when someone's done all this work to get ready and make fun of them. That's a jerk move."

"Nobody's making fun of anyone," Jack said to her. "What's wrong with you?"

"Nothing. I just don't know why you're here if you can't be nice."

"Because I live here?" He shook his head. "Man. Talk about self-centered. It's not just about you all the time, you know."

Bailey looked like she was about to respond to this—and hotly—but then another car slowed, turning into the lot. It was Blake, in a black Toyota, and the first thing I noticed was that he looked nice in his tux. The second was that he was alone.

"Where's Colin?" Bailey yelled at him, as soon as he parked. When he didn't hear her, or pretended not to, she started walking up the sloping grass toward him. Gordon, a finger now marking her place in her book, watched her go.

"What's her problem?" Jack asked me, but I didn't answer,

my eyes only on Bailey as Blake got out from behind the wheel. When she said something to him, he just shrugged, then waved at me.

"We're late," he called out. "Come on."

"Where's Colin?" I replied, but he didn't hear me over Bailey, who was now repeating this same question, but with more emotion. Enough, in fact, that he started to get back in the car, shooting me another look first.

"Something's up," Jack reported, his eyes on both of them. I started walking.

"Look, enough with the bullshit," Bailey was saying, her voice cracking slightly, when I came up. "Just tell me what's going on."

"I told you," Blake replied. Seeing me, he reached over, pushing open the passenger door. "I'm not part of all this."

"Actually, you are. You're his best friend."

"Saylor," Blake said to me across the empty seat. As if she wasn't even there, breathing hard, close to tears. "Let's go. We're meeting everyone there."

"I can't go with you," I said, and I did look at Bailey, who bit her lip. "Not without her."

"Well, fine. Then you can both stay here," he replied. "It's not worth all this trouble."

Trouble, to expect someone to do what they said they would. Then again, he was someone to whom things came easily, always: a job, a future, a girl. I said, "Yes or no: Is Colin coming?"

Blake, still avoiding looking anywhere near Bailey's

direction, closed his eyes for a second. "No," he said finally. "He's not."

I heard Bailey exhale, a shaky, long breath. Back by the steps, Jack and Roo were still watching us.

"Why not?" Bailey said to him now.

"I don't know," he replied, cranking the engine. To me he said, "Can we go, please?"

"Answer her question," I said.

"Because he's with the girl he asked a month ago!" Blake said. "His girlfriend, from school."

I was stunned. Bailey said, "Colin has a girlfriend?"

"Yeah," he said, as if we were stupid for not knowing it. "They have an understanding, just like he had with you."

Bailey was just standing there, eyes wide, her phone in her hands. She turned to me. "What does that even mean?"

"That he's an asshole," I replied.

"Enough about Colin, Jesus!" Blake said. He looked at me. "Are you getting in or not?"

I looked at my cousin, in the dress on which she'd spent so much time and effort, her makeup applied so carefully it was perfect. She didn't deserve this. Nobody did.

"Not," I told Blake.

In response, he threw up a hand, then hit the gas, spraying some gravel as he pulled away. I watched him turn out onto the road, cursing us, and kept my eyes on him until he was out of sight. Only then did I turn back to Bailey, who was now standing with her arms around herself, her face streaked with tears. What could I even say at this moment?

What words would even make any difference? I didn't know where, or how, to start. But as it turned out, I didn't have to.

"Bailey," Jack said. He was standing there, his own keys in hand. Roo was coming up the grass behind him. "Let's get out of here."

THIRTEEN

"I can't believe this," Bailey said. She turned around, her face tear-streaked, and looked at me. "Can you?"

I shook my head as, distantly, I heard her phone beep again. About five minutes earlier, Celeste had realized we'd left without saying goodbye. Seriously pissed, she was making her displeasure clear with a series of angry texts, none of which Bailey had responded to so far. All she had been capable of, really, was sitting in the passenger seat and crying while Jack drove us, well, someplace.

The phone beeped again. Bailey leaned her head against the window, closing her eyes. "I can't tell Mom what happened," she said. "It's so humiliating and she'll just say she told me so."

"No, she won't," Jack said, glancing in the rearview.

"Yeah, right. All she and Trinity have done all summer is say how Colin is going to break my heart. And now he has. They'll be thrilled."

"More likely, they'll want to kill him," Roo, who was

beside me in the back seat, said. "I'd be more worried about that. Trinity's temper these days is off the charts."

Bailey, reaching up to wipe her eyes, didn't smile at this comment, but I did. "He'll just need to stand still," I said, thinking of her struggling cleaning with her huge belly. "And not be on a low or high shelf."

Roo snorted, which made me laugh out loud, and then we were both cracking up. Bailey turned around to look at us again.

"You guys aren't funny," she informed us as we composed ourselves, or tried to. "And Saylor, you just got dumped as well, in case you didn't notice."

"Easy come, easy go." I couldn't think of a phrase that fit the situation more.

"I thought you liked Blake!" she said.

I shrugged. "It was fun and all, but . . . I think I'll be fine."

Her phone beeped. Then once more. If it could have screamed, it would have.

"Give me that," Roo said to Bailey, holding out his hand. "I'll explain to Celeste what happened."

She handed it over to him and he started typing a response. With him and Jack both on the same side of the car, dressed in shorts and T-shirts, and Bailey and me in our formal wear on the other, we looked like we were headed to very different evenings. Which made me think of something.

"Where are we even going?" I asked Jack. We'd turned left out of Calvander's, heading toward the main road, but at some point we had entered a neighborhood with narrow streets and trees strung with moss. Through my open window, I could smell the lake, but not see it.

"Green house," he said, as if I knew what this was.

O-kay, I thought. Bailey sniffled, wiping her nose with the back of her hand. "I can't believe I spent all this money and time on this dress. I'm so stupid."

"You're not," Roo said, still typing.

"He has a *girlfriend*." Her voice broke on the final syllable. "Why did he even ask me if he already had a date?"

I thought back to that night at the Campus apartment, how Colin had gotten up and left when the subject of Club Prom came up, only to finally invite her when they were outside. He probably figured he'd just dump her before the dance, so it wouldn't come back to bite him. And now he was at the Club, far away from the pain he'd caused.

Jack slowed the car, turning down a dirt driveway. It was long, and bumpy with tree roots, but as we came over a rise, I saw a little green house, the lake behind it. A skinny dock extended out into the water. April and Vincent stood on it, a cooler on a bench nearby. The sun was just going down.

"I can't do this," Bailey said as we parked behind a blue pickup. "It's so embarrassing."

"These are your friends," Jack told her. "Nobody gives a shit."

She sighed, but pushed her door open. Then she bent down, undoing the strappy sandals she'd been so excited to find almost new at Bly County Thrift. She left them on the floorboard as she climbed out, shutting the door behind her.

I kept my shoes on. "What is this place, again?" I asked.

Roo, a few steps ahead, turned back to look at me. "My house. Come on."

I raised a hand to cover my eyes just as Bailey started down to the dock, her dress flowing out a bit behind her. When she got to the end, April, who was standing there, looked up at her.

"Boys STINK," she announced, then opened her arms. Blinking fast, Bailey stepped into them. Vincent, standing just nearby with a beer in his hand, looked at them for a second, then out to the lake.

"Yacht club boys," Jack announced as the rest of us made our way out to the end. "Get it right, please."

"I'm so stupid," Bailey groaned, now resting her head on April's shoulder. "I thought he was a good guy."

"Because you are a trusting, wonderful person," April told her, patting her on the back. "Vincent, get this girl a beer. She needs it."

Vincent complied, kicking open the cooler and pulling out a dripping can. He wiped it on his shirt, then handed it to Bailey, saying, "I'm sorry. For what it's worth."

"Nothing," she replied, and he laughed. "But thanks anyway."

"Great dress," April said to me.

"Thanks."

"I picked it out," Roo said, helping himself to a beer. When he held one out to me, I shook my head.

"Really?" April cocked her head to the side. "Wow. Since when are you a stylist?"

"Sixth job," he said, popping the beer.

She looked at me. "Is he kidding? I can never tell if he's kidding."

Suddenly, I was the expert. I didn't mind. "I think so," I told her. "But again, I'm new here."

She smiled at me, then turned back to Bailey, who was now facing the water, looking at the yacht club in the distance. "Hey," she said, "don't torture yourself, all right? You're better off. When Dana went to Club Prom last year, she said everyone was super snooty and into themselves. Who wants to deal with that?"

"Me," Bailey said softly. "For just one night, anyway. And I couldn't even get that."

"There will be other dances," April said. "Trust me."

"What?" Bailey scoffed. "Prom in the gym with some guy I've known my whole life? Sorry, not the same."

Vincent, hearing this, turned and looked back up at the house, putting his own can to his lips. I caught his eye and smiled. A beat later, he smiled back, although his mind was clearly on other things.

"Then let's have a dance," April said.

"Where?" Jack asked.

"Here." When we all just looked at her, she sighed. "What? I'm on the party committee at my sorority. All we need is some lights and music."

"You want to throw a dance in my house?" Roo asked. "Have you forgotten how small it is inside?"

"We'll move the furniture," she told him.

"Where?" Jack asked again.

"Outside," she replied, sounding annoyed. "Look, our friend is sad and this will make her happy. Saylor, too."

"I'm not really sad," I pointed out.

"But you are all dressed up for a magical night, and you should get one," April told me. She clapped her hands, grinning. "Okay, I love this idea. It's perfect."

"Perfect would be us over there, where we're supposed to be," Bailey said morosely. "And anyway, I'm not in the mood."

"But you *are* in a dress," Jack said. "What else are you going to do?"

"Drink away my sorrows," she replied.

"You can still do that while you're pushing the couch outside," April told her. "Follow me."

When Taylor arrived a little later, I was nervous, considering our first face-to-face encounter had almost ended with her kicking my ass. But her apology had obviously been for real. So far, she was being perfectly nice.

"Okay, who needs a corsage?" she asked from the small kitchen table where she was sitting, bent over a bowl of gardenia blossoms and some stickpins. "If you don't look too closely, they're actually not bad."

"If this was a real dance—" April said.

211

"It's not," Bailey told her from the couch, which she'd only left long enough for the guys to move it outside to the front porch. The house was tiny, though, and the door open, so she might as well have been inside.

"—then we wouldn't be putting on our own corsages," April finished. "The boys would do it for us."

We all looked out at the deck, where Jack, Vincent, and Roo were still all gathered around the cooler. "I am not," Bailey said, "going to let my brother pin a corsage on me for this fake dance. It would be even more humiliating than anything else that's happened so far. Which is really saying something."

"Jack's with me, remember?" Taylor told her. "So you don't have to worry about that."

"Great." Bailey took a gulp of her beer. "Now I don't even have a fake date to the fake dance."

April raised an eyebrow. "Slow down with those beers over there. The night is young."

"This night sucks," Bailey replied.

Taylor, piercing a stem with a pin, sighed. "Fine. Be that way."

I actually felt kind of bad for her. "I'll take one," I said. "If that's okay."

She looked up at me. "Sure! Whichever you want, although the smaller ones are holding together better."

I went over to the table, where she had laid out three little bundles of gardenias and stems so far, each pierced with a pin. The tiny kitchen smelled of nothing but their scent.

I picked one from the middle, holding it up to the strap of my dress.

"Too small," Taylor said, handing me a larger one. "Try this."

"I wish I'd known I was going to a formal tonight," April said. "I would have worn something else."

"You could run home and change," Taylor suggested, bent over the flowers again.

"No, I like the DIY aspect of this. Making do with what we have." April, her hands on her hips, surveyed the room. "Okay, so we have the lights up—"

"It looks like Christmas," Bailey, continuing her role as the dark shadow of the evening, observed. "Which is also depressing."

"Bailey. Enough with the gloom and doom, okay?" April said.

"Yeah, listen to your party planner. They'll be great once we turn them on," Taylor said. Bailey, unconvinced, looked out at the water again. "Wasn't Roo supposed to be finding a power strip?"

"He was," April replied. She walked over to the open door. "Roo!"

Outside, he turned his head. "Yeah?"

"Power strip?"

"Oh. Right." He put down his beer on the bench. "Coming."

As he jogged up the dock, then came in the back door, brushing his feet on a mat, I took another look around me.

213

Where Mimi's house was big, airy, and full of windows, the place where Roo lived with his mom was small and cozy. The tiny kitchen, with its metal countertops and collection of sea glass lining the windowsill, opened into a bigger space, which held the couch (now outside) and a worn leather recliner, both facing a small TV. The table where Taylor sat, plain wood with four chairs, made up the only dining area somewhere in the middle.

Normally, small spaces made me anxious. But I felt different here. I had since the moment I'd stepped inside, following April with Bailey dragging along, complaining, behind me. There was just a comfort to it, even before I saw the fridge.

It wasn't the appliance itself, which was white with a few rust spots. What drew me were the pictures that were scattered among the receipts and lists also adhered to the surface. Unlike the counter in the Calvander's office, there were only a handful here, which made each of them seem that much more important.

The first I saw was a school picture of Roo, from what looked to be maybe second grade. Smaller and skinnier, he was still unmistakable, with that same white-blond hair, cut short and sticking up in the back. The grin on his face showed he was missing a top tooth, a gap in its place.

A little over from that one was a shot of who I assumed were his parents. Chris Price, shirtless and with the same blond hair and squinty smile, was sitting on a bench on the dock, a pretty girl with short red hair in cutoffs and a bathing suit top on his lap. He was looking right at the camera, while she had her head thrown back, caught in the middle of what looked like a big belly laugh.

Picture three, a little lower down, was of Roo and his mom, and more recent. Dressed in a gray EAST U sweatshirt, he was taller than her. She had on a black dress, her hair shorter now, one hand resting on his chest as she smiled proudly.

The last one was the oldest of the group, stuck high in one corner of the fridge door with thick brown tape. There are those pictures that are clearly posed, where the subjects were told to stop what they were doing and gather together. Then there were the ones when the photographer just aimed and shot. This had to be why Roo's dad, in shorts and a baggy T-shirt, was slightly blurred: he'd been in the process of moving. The girl in the picture, though, was still facing him, and in profile, one hand held up as if making a point. She had blond hair spilling down her back and blue eyes with long lashes. My mom.

I leaned in closer, startled and not sure why. She was everywhere at the lake so far, so why not here as well? Maybe because you never think, leaning into a snapshot in a stranger's kitchen, that you'll see the person who probably knew you better than anyone. Like she'd been waiting there for me all this time, and now here I was.

"That's one of my favorites," I heard someone say. "It's such a lousy picture, but so real."

I turned, facing Roo, who was now standing right behind me, a power strip in his hands. "That's your dad, right?"

"Yep." He squinted, leaning in a bit closer. "My mom

215

says it was at a cookout at someone's house. She'd just gotten into photography and was driving everyone crazy snapping pictures. That's why Waverly isn't even looking. She'd had enough."

I looked at my mom again. She had on white shorts and a blue halter top, drugstore flip-flops on her feet. "Mimi said they were inseparable, her and your dad."

"Yeah." I watched as his gaze flicked to the other pictures, then came back to the one of our parents. "But our moms were actually super close as well. When mine moved here senior year, Waverly was the first person she met. She introduced her to Chris."

"Where's your mom now?" I asked.

"In the bedroom," he said.

I looked at all the beers on the table in panic, not to mention the mess we'd made moving things around. "Seriously?"

"No." He grinned at me. "She's an ER nurse in Delaney and works nights. She'll be back in the morning."

"Ah," I said. I looked at the shot of Chris, the redhead in his lap. "It must have been hard for your mom, losing a husband and one of her closest friends."

"Yeah." He was quiet for a second. "It was."

I looked at the picture again. It seemed crazy that after all these years, I had never known about the accident until this summer. For so long I'd questioned why she was in such pain, what could have been so awful that haunted her. The answer, like this picture, had been here all along. I'd just had to come find it.

"You going to wear that?" Roo asked me now.

I blinked, unsure what he was talking about until he nodded at the corsage I was somehow still holding in my hand. "Well, it is a dance," I said.

"You don't put on your own corsage, though." He placed the power strip on the kitchen counter, then reached out, taking the gardenia bundle from me. "Stand super still so I don't stick you, though. I can't take the sight of blood."

"Blood?" I repeated, but he just smiled, gesturing for me to step closer. So I did.

And then he was reaching out to me, sliding a finger under my dress strap and putting the corsage flush against it. Then, with his other hand, he carefully removed the pin before sticking it into the stem and around it. It all happened so quickly, but I was aware of every single detail. His hand against my skin, the way his eyes narrowed, lashes lowering, as he concentrated on fixing it tight. In movies and in life whenever I'd seen this done, it had been awkward, but here, now, the action felt almost sacred in a way I couldn't explain. Which was maybe why I felt like I had to make a joke.

"Thanks, Corsage Buddy," I said.

"Safety first," he replied, his eyes right on mine.

I cleared my throat. "Thanks."

"No problem." He turned around, grabbing the power strip. To April he said, "Where do you want this?"

"Um," she said, looking at me, then him. "By the door."

"Got it," he said, walking over and bending down. He

got it set up, then started plugging in the lights one strand at a time. We stood there watching, the tiny dim room coming alive as they came on, soft and white and twinkling, all around us.

"It's beautiful," April sighed. "If I may say so myself."

"Looks great," Taylor agreed. "Clearly, you are learning something in college, party planner."

"You doubted that?" April replied, giving her an indignant look. "I'll remind you I've got a 3.9 this semester. I contain *multitudes*."

I glanced over at Bailey, still on the couch, her feet now tucked up underneath her. She looked at the decor but didn't say anything, instead taking a sip of her beer as she turned back to the water.

"How's the prep coming?" Jack asked as he came through the kitchen door, pitching a beer can into the bag for empties there.

"You mean the stuff you guys have been absolutely no part of?" Taylor said.

"Not true. We moved the couch," Vincent told her as he joined us. "And if you are lucky, I will bless you with one of my playlists."

"No!" Taylor and Jack said in unison. April snorted.

"What?" Vincent said, pulling out his phone. "It's a dance. I have great dance music."

"What you have," Jack told him, "is heavy hair metal. No one wants to dance to that."

"Heavy metal is great for dancing!" Vincent said. "It's

loud, there's a beat, and you can scream. What's not to love?"

"You scream while you dance?" Roo asked him.

"Sure," Vincent said easily. "Who doesn't?"

"Here's what I think we should do," April said. "Let's set up the room, then go outside and come in again."

"It will still be Roo's living room," Jack pointed out.

"Yes, but it will *feel* different," she told him. She reached down for a bag hanging off one of the chairs, digging around for a moment, then pulled out a bottle of liquor. "Especially if we take a shot first."

"Now, I'm in," Jack said.

"You're driving," Bailey said.

"Actually, I'm not," he told her. "I'm staying with Roo. But even if I wasn't, I could walk home. Just like you did the other night."

"That wasn't my choice," she said, glaring at him. "It was because you were being an—"

"And we're going outside!" Taylor announced in an enthusiastic voice, getting to her feet. She gathered up the corsages in her hands, holding them against her. "Everyone, follow me."

We all traipsed out the door and gathered around the couch, where Bailey still sat, her expression dark. Roo fetched some plastic cups, pouring a little bit from the bottle—rum, I saw now—into seven and lining them up on the porch rail. When everyone took one, only a single cup remained.

"Who are we missing?" April said, glancing around.

"Saylor doesn't drink," Jack told her.

"Oh. Sorry!" Taylor said. "I'll just—"

Before she could finish this thought, Bailey reached over and picked up the shot. Then, as we all watched, she threw it back, then tossed the cup over the rail.

Taylor raised her eyebrows. "O-kay then. What should the rest of us drink to?"

Roo handed me an empty cup, then held out his own shot to the middle of the circle. "To summer. And to us."

Even though I'd never been one to imbibe, I knew that normally, toasts were taken all at once. Here, though, like so much else, it was different. Lake rules.

"To summer," Jack repeated, pressing his own cup against Roo's. "And to us."

Slowly, we went around the circle to April, Vincent, and then Taylor, each of them following suit. Then it was Bailey's turn.

"Fine," she said, adding her own shot to the cups pressed together.

"Do it right or don't do it at all," Roo told her.

She sighed, rolling her eyes, then said, "To summer and to us."

Now, I was the only one. From where I was standing, through the nearby window, I could see the fridge and the picture of my mother, although the specifics were blurry at a distance. Still, I knew she was there, caught in that beat of time as I was in this one.

I held out my empty cup, putting it in the circle. "To summer, and to us."

Everyone drank. Then April put her hand on the door-knob. "Okay. Everyone ready?"

"Yes!" Taylor said.

"No," Bailey grumbled at the same time.

Ignoring her, April opened the door. "Welcome," she said, "to the first annual North Lake Prom."

She stepped back, waving an arm for the rest of us to enter: Jack and Taylor first, laughing, then Vincent, with Bailey, Roo, and me bringing up the rear.

"We were just in here," Bailey said. "How different can it really look?"

A lot, actually. Maybe it was really the change in scenery. Or the fact that I'd been busy examining the pictures and worrying about Bailey instead of watching April and Taylor work their decorating magic. But as I came in, Roo's living room seemed transformed.

There were the lights, of course, tiny and white and strung across all four walls, then meeting in the center of the ceiling, where they were bound with gardenias. The furniture had been pushed to the corners and covered with white sheets, leaving an empty stretch of hardwood floor. Off to one side was the kitchen table, which held a speaker, a punch bowl, and the rest of the corsages, laid out neatly in a row. To someone else, maybe it could have been a room where we'd just been. But I was new here, and could see it as something special. Because it was.

"Is this a punch bowl?" Jack asked, peering down at the table. "Seriously?"

"Formals always have punch!" April told him. "Take it from a party planner. It's like a rule."

"Right," he said as he picked up a corsage, holding it out to Taylor. She grinned, then stepped closer, watching as he affixed it to her tank top. "Hey, does this mean we can skip your prom this year now? Because that would be—"

"No," she replied flatly. She took his hand. "Dance with me."

"There's no music."

"I can fix that," Vincent, by the door with Bailey, offered.

"No!" Roo and April said together. Then she pulled out her phone and tapped it a few times. A moment later, as a pop song filled the room, Taylor stepped into the center of the floor, pulling Jack with her and grabbing April with her other hand. As she began to shimmy, grinning, and he clapped his hands, April let out a whoop.

I could feel my cheeks flushing as the small room got warmer and louder. Vincent slipped around me to the table, picking up a corsage, which he then brought back to Bailey, holding it out to her.

"You don't have to," she told him.

"I want to," he said. "Okay if I put it on?"

"Fine," she said.

Vincent carefully removed the pin, then attached the small bundle of flowers and stems to her dress as she watched. This was not the corsage she'd wanted, nor the place she'd planned to get it. Still, I hoped so much she could still see it for the sweet act it was.

"Wanna dance?" he asked her once he was done.

Bailey looked at her brother, who was spinning Taylor out as she tilted her head back and laughed. To Vincent she said, "Are you going to scream?"

"I'll try not to," he replied.

They joined the group, Vincent pumping his hands over his head while Bailey, less enthused, shifted from side to side. When April saw her and stuck out a hand, however, she took it, doing a little spin. When everyone else applauded, I saw her smile, but just barely.

Back against the wall, alone, I wished I could have captured this moment like those ones on the fridge. Posed, or spontaneous, I wouldn't have cared. I just wanted to remember it, every detail, long after this night was done.

"Saylor."

I looked up: Roo was standing in front of me. "Yeah?"

"Want to dance?"

I felt myself blink. Of course he'd think I'd want to be part of this: I was here, too. But all my life I'd felt more like an observer than an active participant. Beside the wheel, not behind. It was safer there, but could be lonely too, or so I was now realizing. Maybe there was a middle ground between living too hard and living at all. Maybe, here, I was finding it.

"Sure," I said. Then he stuck out his hand, I took it, and he pulled me in.

I danced. We all did, there in that small dark room lit with tiny white lights, spinning and bumping each other and laughing. We made our way through a couple of April's playlists, then one of Jack's, before finally Vincent was allowed to take over DJ duty. Two songs later, when my head was throbbing with happy screaming and my dress literally stuck to me with sweat, April threw open the door and announced we were going swimming. No one hesitated except for me.

"But you *can* swim," Roo said. "Right? Because if not, you should have told us that first night out at the raft. Strong lake rule, that one."

"Yes, I can swim," I told him. "I just haven't here. Yet."

And why was that? Because no one else had been swimming and invited me. Once again, it was all the actions of other people, like Bailey, that made my own life happen: Blake, my first kiss, even the prom I'd almost attended that night. I was like those pieces of litter I sometimes saw swept up on windy days and carried down entire streets. You just look up and there you are.

I watched now as Taylor took off her corsage, carefully laying it on a porch rail. "I'm going in," she announced before shaking her hair back and running down the grass to the dock. At the end, she leaped off with a shriek before disappearing into the dark water. We all cheered.

"My turn," April announced, kicking off her shoes. "Dare me to belly flop?"

"Don't do it," Vincent said. "Remember last time!"

"What happened last time?" I asked as she barreled down the dock before launching outward flat, arms outstretched, with a scream. A beat later, we heard the slap of skin against water.

"She'll feel that tomorrow," Roo said.

"She's not the only one," Jack said, turning to look behind him at Bailey, who was sound asleep on the couch, her dress tangled around her legs and bare feet dirty, flecked with sand. All the time and money she'd spent to make this night perfect, only to end it passed out, alone.

"She'll be okay when she sleeps it off," I said, to him as well as myself. Then I stepped inside the door, grabbing a blanket I'd seen earlier from a chair there. When I shook it out over Bailey, she slapped it away, muttering as she curled deeper into the cushions. I left it at her feet in case she changed her mind.

"Hey!" April called out from the water. "Y'all coming in or what?"

"On the way," Jack replied, then pulled off his shirt, dropping it to the grass. After a quick check on Bailey—I saw it, if no one else—Vincent did the same. Those already in increased their volume as Jack dove in sideways and Vincent did his own cannonball. Splash. And then there were two of us. Who were conscious, anyway.

"You know I was just giving you a hard time before, right?" Roo said as I watched Taylor splash Jack, and him dunk her in return. "I understand not wanting to swim in that dress."

I looked down at it, the corsage he'd pinned on now wilted, hanging feebly by its pin. Like it, my dress had lived the evening hard, the hem now dirty and one strap, loosened by a particularly enthusiastic conga line, hanging down over my shoulder. I pulled it back up; it fell again. This time, I just left it there.

"It's not the dress," I said, looking back at the water. "I think it's more that it's nighttime. I've never gone swimming in the dark."

"Some people might say night swims are a lake rite of passage," he pointed out.

"I guess." I crossed my arms. "But maybe my mom did it enough for both of us."

He bit his lip, ducking his head as he turned to look at the water, dark except for the moon and thrown light from the motels and houses along the shore. "Right," he said finally. "I wasn't even thinking about that. Didn't mean to make it awkward."

"You couldn't," I said, and smiled, to prove I meant it.

Behind us, Bailey shifted, talking in her sleep, but I couldn't make out what she was saying.

"You know," Roo said, once it was quiet again, "I'm really glad you came this summer."

"Yeah?"

He nodded. "I always wondered, you know? What happened to you. Because I remembered that time you came when we were kids."

"I wish *I* remembered," I said. "I lost a lot. Like, everything from this place."

"Wasn't lost," he said. "You just left it here. You know

what Mimi says: the lake keeps us."

"I've never heard that before."

"Sure you have," he replied. "Just now."

He smiled at me then, and as I felt myself smile back, I wondered if our parents, the best of friends, had ever stood in this same spot. There were so many stories here, like every moment had already been lived once before.

But then, Roo did something different. He reached forward with one hand, sliding my fallen strap back up on my shoulder. It was a simple gesture, but like earlier, with the corsage, I felt my heart catch in my chest. Once the strap was fixed, he left his hand there, fingers spread cool over my skin. Like a take two, second chance. The kind you don't get often.

Maybe this was why I stepped a little closer, lifting my chin as I looked up at him. His eyes widened a bit, but he stayed where he was.

"Hey!" someone yelled from the water. "What are you guys doing up there?"

We both jumped, him turning his head at the noise while I took a full step back, putting space between us again.

"One sec," he called back. Turning back to me, he said, "Look, I didn't mean to—"

"It's fine," I said quickly. I could feel my heart beating in my chest, as well as the weight of his hand on my shoulder, even though it was now gone.

"Roo! Get in here!" Jack yelled.

He reached up, tugging his own shirt off and tossing it

onto the grass with the others. Then, with a final look back at me, he jogged down the dock as everyone else whooped and clapped, and dove off.

"Shoulda done it."

Again startled, I looked over to the couch, where Bailey was now curled up on one side. "What?"

"Kissed him," she said, her voice muffled by her hair. Her eyes remained closed. "Had the perfect chance. Shoulda taken it."

"I panicked," I said, looking out at the water. Familiar story. "Why do I always do that?"

She didn't answer, as her breathing had steadied: she was asleep again.

Back inside, the room was still hot, one of the light strands had fallen down, and a leftover corsage lay flattened on the floor. No one had touched the punch. When I realized the speaker was buzzing steadily, not connected to anything, I went over and turned it off. That was when I heard my phone.

It was in my bag, which I'd left in the kitchen on the counter. By the time I went over and pulled it out, it had gone silent as well, although a message remained on the screen. My dad.

Just got off the boat. Great time but EXHAUSTED. See you Friday! Can't wait.

No way, I thought, rereading this a second time. But when I flipped over to my calendar, scanning the month of June into July, I saw it was true: my trip was almost over.

Before long, I'd be going back to Lakeview to move into our new house and begin another life. But what about this one?

I started down the steps, and when I felt grass beneath my feet, my instinct was to stop, stay where I was. Instead, I started moving faster, enough to blow my hair back and feel a breeze on my skin. I knew I must look ridiculous, a girl in a formal dress, running alone down the grass. But at least I was doing it myself, each step a choice as I got closer to the water.

"Saylor?" April called out, spotting me, but I didn't look for her, or anyone else, as I banged down the dock, gaining speed. I just had my eyes on the end, that leap to come, and in my mind I could see it as jumping past so many other things as well: the view behind the wheel, my neatly organized closet and room, Trinity's judging face. Blake leaning in for that kiss, then Roo fixing my strap so carefully while I stood by, frozen. You can make your life, or life can make you. Was it really that simple of a choice?

As I hit the dock's end and jumped, I wanted to see it, that change from passenger to driver, Emma to Saylor, watching to doing. So when I hit the cold lake and went under, I kept my eyes open.

FOURTEEN

Things move fast once you decide to get behind the wheel. Or maybe it just seems that way.

"Good. Now, wipe it with those newspapers. Rub in circles."

Gordon did as she was told, her skinny arm moving across the mirror as Trinity, stretched out across the bed with her feet up, watched. "Like this?"

"Yes," I said as I passed behind her with the bathroom trash can, then dumped it into the garbage bag by the unit's door. "Be sure to take all the dust to the edge and off. That way you don't leave any."

"Listen to you," Trinity said, turning a page in the magazine she was reading. "You sound like an expert."

"I had a good teacher," I said.

"Puh-leese," Bailey groaned from the bathroom, where she was scrubbing the shower. "Don't flatter her. She's already acting enough like a princess."

"I'm *pregnant*," Trinity pointed out, unnecessarily. Her

stomach was like a mountain when she was prone, blocking the view of her face from the end of the bed.

"And I'm working two jobs and we have Gordon on as child labor," her sister replied. "So everyone's suffering, not just you."

It was true. Not so much about the suffering, but the extra hands on deck. The morning after the first official North Lake Prom, Trinity had woken up with some light spotting, which prompted a panicky trip to the ER. She wasn't in labor, but they did put her on bed rest. That left only Mimi and me to clean rooms, so Bailey had been coming in afternoons after her shift at the Station as well as her days off, with Roo and Jack filling in as they could as well. When Gordon got strep throat and couldn't go to camp, she'd been recruited as well. Somehow, we were getting both turnover and housekeeping done, although with two beginners and one super-reluctant veteran, I wasn't exactly sure how.

The truth was, everything had been chaotic since that morning, and not just because of the bed rest and new workload. There was also the issue of my dad and Tracy's return from Greece, scheduled for late that evening. The plan had been for them to return to Nana's, who had just gotten home from her own trip, then come fetch me so we could all move over to the new house. But the "easy" remodel of Nana's condo had hit a permitting snag. With our new house also still needing some work to pass inspection, I was now the only one with someplace to stay.

"I mean, we can do a hotel," my dad had said the day

before, calling from Athens, where he was about to board his plane. "But your grandmother . . ."

He didn't finish this thought, not that he had to. Nana was used to a certain level of comfort. All she wanted to do was get back to her newly redone home, and now she couldn't even do that.

I, however, felt like I'd been given a break by the universe. If the house wasn't ready, I could just remain here for a while longer. When I floated this by my dad, though, he was not convinced.

"You've been there three weeks," he told me. "We don't want you to outstay your welcome."

"I'm helping," I pointed out. "They need me to clean rooms at the motel anyway."

"You're cleaning rooms at Calvander's?"

Whoops. I bit my lip, realizing I shouldn't have shared this. "Just because they're short-staffed. With the baby coming and everything."

"Baby?"

"Trinity. Celeste's daughter? She's having a baby really soon."

"Who?"

I sighed, switching my phone to my other ear. Downstairs, I could hear Oxford in the kitchen, making coffee and rustling around with the paper. Even though it hadn't been that long since I'd arrived, it was already hard to imagine a morning now that didn't start this way. "The point is, I'm happy to stay here and I'm sure it's okay with Mimi."

"But what if I don't want you to stay?" he replied.

"Why wouldn't you?"

I heard some friction on the line. "Because," he said, his voice quiet, "we're starting a new life in a new house, as a new family. It seems only right we do it together."

"But you just said the house wasn't ready."

"Well, it isn't."

"So how are we going to stay there?"

"Emma." Before, he'd sounded tired. Now, irritation was creeping in. "Just let Mimi know you'll be leaving by the end of the week."

"But—"

"Let her know," he repeated, as in the background, an announcement began. "That's our group. I'll call as soon as we're back in your time zone. Okay?"

"Okay," I replied. "Fly safe."

We hung up, and I flopped back against my pillow, looking at the ceiling above me. After sulking a bit, I went downstairs for toast and the obits, and when I saw Mimi, I told her nothing. My dad was in the air, over an ocean. I still had some time, and there were rooms to clean.

Now, I pulled out my spray bottle, pumping the handle until the small glass table I was standing over was covered with bleach solution. As I started to wipe it clean, Trinity said, "Who are you today, Saylor?"

I looked down at my bottle, where a name was written in pink Sharpie, surrounded by plump hearts. "Vicki," I said.

"Oh, right," she replied. "Big on pink, not so much on

233

working. I think she lasted one season."

"And a half," Bailey said, banging against something in the bathroom. Thump. Thump. "She took off with that trucker, remember?"

Trinity thought for a second. "God, you're right!"

"Of course I am," Bailey said. "I remember everything. All details, every story. You know that."

"Is this good?" Gordon, now at the edge of the mirror, her face red with exertion, asked.

"Missed a spot," Trinity told her, pointing to the left side.

As Gordon started rubbing again, I asked, "Is that true, Bailey? Do you really remember everything?"

Another thump. Then, "Yeah. It's like a gift. Or a curse."

"It's seriously creepy sometimes," Trinity added. "She remembers the stuff she wasn't even here for, because she's heard Mom tell *her* stories."

"Do you remember hearing about when I was here?" I asked Bailey as she threw a pile of towels out the bathroom door. "When we were four?"

"Yeah," she said. Her voice carried out as she added, "Your mom and dad were going on a trip and they left you with Mimi."

"Second honeymoon," I said, adding the pillowcases to my own pile. "That's what he said."

"They didn't seem like newlyweds," Bailey said. I could hear her own spray bottle. "Pretty tense, as I recall hearing. Your mom hadn't been here since Chris Price died, so there was that, too."

"She never came back, all those years?"

"Nope." More spritzing. "Mom said Mimi went to visit her, with Joe, when you were born and a couple of other times. But she was weird about this place. It was like there were—"

"Ghosts," I finished for her.

"Yeah." She came out, gathering the towels in her arms and crossing the room to add them to the pile of linens. "She just wasn't herself, according to my mom. And then when Steph came over, she kind of lost it."

"Steph?" I asked.

"Roo's mom," Bailey said. "It was the first time Waverly had seen her since the funeral. And she'd never met Roo."

"That, I remember," Trinity said, turning a page. "Waverly started crying, just standing there watching you and Roo together."

I plumped the pillow I was holding, then replaced it. "I wish I could remember."

"This was *your* mom, though, and she was really upset. Your mind is probably doing you a favor by forgetting."

"I'd rather remember," I said. "There are enough holes."

"But lots of pictures," Bailey said.

I looked over at her, now standing by the front door scraping what looked like gum off the carpet. "What did you say?"

"The pictures," she replied, not looking up. "Because of Steph."

I just looked at her.

"Because she was so into photography," she continued.

"She documented everything."

"Are you saying there are more pictures of that visit than the one in Mimi's office?"

"Which one is that?"

I told her about the snapshot I'd seen under the glass my first day, of all of us kids together on the steps. "Oh, yeah," she said. "Steph definitely took that. She lined us all up, too, while your mom was off to the side watching."

"Bribed us with candy," Trinity added, sniffing a perfume insert.

Hearing this, I sat down on the bed, the pillow I'd been about to cover in my arms. I wasn't sure what compelled me at that moment, but I heard myself say, "My dad wants me to come home."

It was quiet for a second. Even Gordon, wiping the TV, stopped in mid circle. Trinity said, "You just got here, though."

"It's been almost a month," I pointed out. "That was how long I was supposed to visit."

"Yeah, but that was when you were just here because you needed a place to stay," Bailey said, standing up and tossing a paper towel with the gum in it toward the trash bag.

"Isn't that why I'm here now?"

"No." She picked up her bottle from the windowsill, then looked at me. "You're learning your history. Before it was just a visit, yes. But now it's personal."

"Sounds like news to her," Trinity observed. "So maybe not *so* personal."

"My history," I repeated. "How do you figure?"

Bailey sighed, looking at the ceiling. "Hello, what were we just talking about? Filling in the holes in your memory. Getting the rest of the story about your mom. I mean, you didn't even know about the accident!"

"Bay, where are you going with this?" Trinity asked.

"I'm making a *point*." She looked at me again. "You were just saying how you don't have any memories of the lake before this summer. But you do, because we're helping you fill them in. Part of grieving is letting go of the past. But how can you let go if you never knew it in the first place?"

Outside, a man, a motel guest, walked by shirtless, his flip-flops thwacking. He glanced in at us, but only briefly, as he passed by.

"People should wear shirts if they're not *right* on the beach," Trinity said, once he was out of earshot. Gordon snickered.

"My mom's been gone five years," I said to Bailey, ignoring this. "I don't think I can claim to be grieving anymore."

"Of course you can!" She picked up the garbage bag, shaking it. "Look. Saylor. My mom still cries for yours at least once a week. No joke. It's not like you just snap your fingers and move on."

Now I felt even worse. I didn't cry that much anymore. In fact, I couldn't remember the last time. Which, as I thought about it, made me feel close to tears myself. "I don't want to leave yet," I said, swallowing. "I'm not sure it's for the reasons you're saying or something else. All I know is that

I wish some of these were *my* memories, not just everyone else's. Like there's more to the story, but I'm not there yet."

"You should ask to see the pictures."

Gordon spoke so softly, at first I wasn't even sure it was her who had said this. When we all looked at her, though, she blushed a deep red. "What did you say?" I asked.

She cleared her throat. "The pictures. That Roo's mom took. Bailey said there were tons of them. Maybe they'd help you remember."

Trinity and Bailey exchanged a look. Then Bailey said, "That is a great idea, actually."

Gordon, pleased, turned back to the TV and started dusting again.

"You think?" I asked Bailey as she headed back to the kitchen.

"It can't hurt," she said. "And neither can asking your dad again if you can have a little more time. For your mom, and her memory, if nothing else."

I wasn't so sure about that. My dad had always been selective about my mom's legacy, what we remembered and what we didn't. I truly believed he thought he was doing me a favor by keeping the bad stuff out.

"Just ask him," Bailey said, spraying down the stovetop. "The worst he can do is say no."

"No."

The answer came so quickly—mere moments after I'd gotten up the nerve to ask—that I wasn't even ready. "But you didn't even think about it!"

"Emma—"

"You asked me to come here so you could go on your honeymoon. I did," I said, pacing across the sand below Mimi's house, where I'd come to make this call while everyone else got dinner together. "And I'm learning a lot about Mom, and myself, and just don't understand why, if I have no place to stay, I can't—"

"Because you *do* have a place to stay," he finished over me. "And if you'd just let me talk for a second, I'll tell you about it."

I bit my lip, then sat down at the picnic table. Now that I'd pledged to try to take control of my life, the last thing I wanted was to hear more plans that had been made for me. Unfortunately, I didn't have a choice.

"What I was going to say, before you started in about this—" he began.

"It's my history," I blurted out. "My memories. I'm already here, I should be allowed to finish what I've started."

"Emma. Please just let me talk for a second." He sounded tired. "As you know, we are currently between residences, as is your grandmother. After some discussion, she's suggested a temporary solution that I think will work for all of us."

Whatever it was, I was sure I wouldn't like it. But I stayed quiet. For now.

"Nana has a friend with a resort in Lake North," he continued. "He's been offering her use of a suite of rooms for ages, and now seems like a good time to take him up on it."

It took me a second to process what he was saying. Finally I said, "Wait. You're coming *here*?"

"We," he replied, "will be spending two weeks at Lake North, all of us. Then we'll head home to our hopefully finished homes."

"You're coming to Lake North," I said again. "Great. So I'll just stay here. Everyone's happy."

"No. You've been with Mimi, and we're very grateful. But it's time to be together as a family now."

"This is my family, too."

"Emma." He sighed. "I know you're having fun. But I don't think these people are at the same level as Tracy, Nana, and myself."

"Why do there have to be levels?" I asked, getting to my feet again. "I went from a four-person unit to discovering all these cousins and aunts and uncles I never even knew I had. I don't want to just forget them now."

"No one is asking you to forget anyone."

"But why didn't we ever visit here, except for that one time before you and Mom split and the funeral? Why didn't she ever come back, with me or just by herself?"

He groaned. "Do we have to get into this now? I'm so jet-lagged I can barely think."

"I know about the accident," I told him. "What happened with Chris Price. But only because of Bailey. It makes me wonder how much else I don't know."

"You don't need to know everything," he said. Now there was an edge to his voice.

"Maybe I do," I replied. Silence. I pressed on. "Look, Dad. I know you want me to remember only the good stuff about Mom. But it's okay that she was human and flawed. You don't have to hide that fact from me."

"I couldn't even if I wanted to!" he said. He exhaled. "And that's just my point. Despite everything, *you* are okay. My one job is to protect you. I tried to do that by building our lives in Lakeview. There just wasn't room for anything else."

"You can protect me without keeping secrets," I said. "She was my mom. And this, here, it's part of my life. And you kept it from me."

"We both did," he replied, sounding frustrated. "Look, Emma. Your mom never went back to the lake because by then it meant nothing but tragedy to her. It was where her problems started, the drinking, the addictions. Her bad choices led to the death of her best friend. She never got over that."

"Then why did you guys bring me that summer?" I asked. "What was the point?"

"We were trying to save our marriage," he said. I could hear the fatigue now in his voice, although whether it was literal or just this subject was hard to say. "Nana couldn't help with you and we had no other options."

"Just like this time," I said. "So they're family when you need a babysitter, and strangers when you don't. That makes sense."

He was quiet for what felt like a long time. As for me, I felt sick: I rarely, if ever, argued with my dad. Finally, he spoke.

"It's not my intent to take you away from your family." He said this last word slowly, as if it was difficult to pronounce. "But if we're talking about what's fair, you've spent three weeks there with her experience. It doesn't seem wrong to ask you to do the same with mine."

"You?" I said. "You're not a lake kid."

"No," he agreed. "But I did spend summers working at the Club and met your mom there. It was a big part of my life, too."

Not the same, I thought. But I didn't say this aloud.

"How about this," he said now. "You agree to come stay at the Tides. But you can still visit Mimi's, as long as you make time for us as well. Get a bit of both worlds. Is that fair?"

"You're staying at the Tides?" I said, remembering the ritzy resort Bailey had pointed out to me on my first trip to Lake North.

"It's your grandmother," he said helplessly. "And it's not like we have a lot of choices."

So that's what it comes down to. Choices. Good and bad, right and wrong, yes and no. Like being behind the wheel, there are some that are instinctive, others you have to think about. It was only three miles to the other side, a distance I'd covered by foot already. Before I went back, though, there was one more trip to take. Luckily, it wasn't far.

FIFTEEN

When I got to Roo's, the Yum truck was parked outside, an extension cord stretching from it to the small garage. As I passed and heard the coolers humming, I thought of all that ice cream inside.

I went around the house to the screen door and peered in, but didn't see anyone. There was a pair of sneakers kicked off on the floor, though, as well as a phone and some keys on a nearby table. When I heard a shower running, distantly, I sat down on the steps to wait.

It had only been a day since the conversation with my dad, and the fact that I was going to be moving to Lake North was just beginning to sink in. Partly this was because I hadn't exactly told anyone about my dad's directive. Yet.

First, Gordon went back to the doctor, who said she needed another round of antibiotics, making day camp still off-limits. Since I was the only one without a full-time job who wasn't hugely pregnant, I'd offered to keep an eye on her. I hadn't imagined it being that big of a task, until she attached herself to me like a shadow. If I was cleaning rooms, Gordon, her own spray bottle in hand, was right there. At lunch, she waited for me to make her a quesadilla after my own, then sat beside me at the table, reading her Allies book until we were done, at which point she followed me back to the motel. In the evenings, while Bailey worked late at the Station—since the breakup with Colin, she'd focused on making money and not much else—Gordon sat next to me on the couch as I watched house remodeling shows with Mimi, cheering when the hard hats came out and demos began. The only time we parted ways was when she went to bed, and I was pretty sure she would have stayed in my room if I'd offered. Which I didn't.

"I think it's cute," Trinity had said that morning as we sat eating toast together in her room. In a rare moment, we were alone: Gordon had gone with Mimi to open up the office, although I knew she'd find me as soon as I started cleaning. "She looks up to you."

"Yeah, but why?" I asked. "She barely knows me."

Trinity shrugged, slathering butter onto one of the four pieces of toast I'd brought her. Her bed, which was basically her home until the baby came, was piled with magazines, dirty plates, and her laptop, which she used to alternately HiThere! with the Sergeant and watch *Big New York*, her favorite reality show. Although I'd managed to quell a lot of my organizing urges, I was dying to get her out of the room just long enough to do a deep clean.

"Well, think about it," she said. "Her mom's out of the picture. So is yours."

"My mom is dead, though."

"True. But if you're ten and live in another state from your only parent, it probably feels like a death, right?"

I thought about this. "What's Amber's story, anyway?"

She finished chewing. "Grew up here, followed some deadbeat guy to Florida, where she got hooked on pills. Social services was going to take Gordon until Mama and Mimi got involved."

I thought of Gordon, so small in her glasses. My heart just broke for her. "Sounds kind of familiar."

"You're more alike than you know," Trinity continued, shifting herself and rubbing a hip. "There's also the fact that you both have two names but only go by one."

"You think that bonds us?"

"It doesn't hurt."

I thought of that first day, when I'd told Gordon about my name and she'd called me lucky. It made me think maybe I should call her Anna once in a while. "I just don't think I'm much of a role model. It makes me nervous."

"Are you kidding?" she snorted. "You're a good student with a bright future who lives in a big house with a nice, normal family. Forget Gordon. *I* want to be like you."

It said something that this description, so easily put, did not describe me in my mind at all. "I'm also an anxious person with a dead mom who was an addict, trying to figure out what that means for me in my own life."

"In your big house with your normal family," she added, raising an eyebrow.

I made a face, just as over at the motel, Gordon came out of the office, shutting the door behind her. She had on shorts and an oversized Calvander's tie-dye, just like mine, her short hair gathered back in an identical ponytail. When she saw me on the porch, she immediately started over.

"If I were you," Trinity said, having observed this as well, "I'd enjoy it. You'll notice nobody is wanting to emulate me right now."

I smiled at her. "Pretty soon, you'll have someone who loves you best, though."

"Here's hoping." She put a hand on her belly. "I was so hard on my mom, though. Still am. With my luck, the payback is going to be *brutal*."

She'd started saying this kind of thing a lot lately, as the due date got closer and she grew increasingly nervous. And a couple of weeks earlier, I might have privately agreed that maybe she didn't have the most tender, motherly touch, though I never would have had the nerve to tell her to her face. Now, though, I'd caught enough glimpses of her good heart to know it was in there somewhere. A tough mom was better than none at all. Gordon and I, of all people, could vouch for that.

Now, sitting on Roo's steps, I heard whistling. When I turned around, he was walking into the living room, in shorts and bare feet and a Blackwood T-shirt. "Hey," he said. "How long have you been there?"

"Not long," I told him, getting to my feet. "Got a second?"

"Sure." He walked over, pushing open the screen door with a creak. "Come on in."

I did, feeling strangely nervous by this formality, plus the fact it was just us. Since the night of Club Prom, we'd barely seen each other, a result of my increased work schedule and his beginning a (yes) sixth job. Or was it seventh?

"How's work going?" I said, thinking this.

"You'll have to be more specific," he replied, gesturing for me to have a seat on the couch.

"The new one," I told him. "What was it again?"

"Driving for RideFly," he said.

"Is that like GetThere? A ride-sharing thing?"

"No, it's an airport shuttle," he said. "Fifty bucks round trip from Lake North or North Lake to the Bly County airport. Plus, you get a free water and some mints."

"There's an airport in Bly County?"

"And here you thought it was just a mecca for formal wear," he said, picking up his phone from the table and sliding it into a pocket. "Yes, there is an airport. It's about the size of a dentist's waiting room, but it exists."

"Wow," I said. "I had no idea."

"Don't feel bad. Nobody I know has ever flown out of it," he said, plopping down beside me. "It's mostly Lake North people who have money, and there aren't much of those unless there's a big event going on. This weekend it's a wedding. We're scooping up the out-of-towners."

"Sounds like you could do that in the Yum truck," I said.

"Is that an ice cream joke?"

"Couldn't resist," I said, and he laughed. As he sat back, stretching his feet out to rest on the buckled trunk that functioned as a coffee table, I said, "You know, it's funny you mention Lake North. I'm actually going there tomorrow."

"Are you attending the Janney-Sipowicz wedding?" he asked. "Because if so, I've already met the father of the groom. He likes jokes that start with someone walking into a bar."

"Sadly, no." I took a breath. "I'm actually moving over there. My dad and his new wife and my grandma are all coming down and we're staying at the Tides, together."

"The Tides? That place is super fancy. When are you coming back to stay at Mimi's?"

"I'm not."

He raised his eyebrows. "What? You're leaving for good?"

"I can still visit," I said. "For two weeks, anyway. After that, we all go back to Lakeview."

"Wow." He reached up, running a hand through the back of his hair. Another tuft sprang to attention, sideways. "I thought you were here all summer."

"Nope," I said. "Really, I was only supposed to be here until now. The Lake North thing just sort of happened because our house and Nana's are still under construction. So I guess I should be happy."

"Are you?"

"No," I answered, honestly. "I mean, a month ago I had no plans to come here. I didn't even think about this place. Now that I have to leave, I can't imagine not being here to help with Calvander's and see the baby come."

We were quiet for a second. Outside, on the water, I could hear a motorboat chugging by.

"So you came to say goodbye," he said. He looked at me. "That *sucks*."

Hearing this, I felt a pang I didn't expect. "Not goodbye yet. First I have a favor to ask."

"You want some complimentary RideFly mints? I've got a whole bag."

"No." I took a breath. "Bailey said your mom took a lot of pictures that week I was here, when I was a kid. Do you guys still have them?"

"I'm sure we do," he replied. "The tricky part will be finding them."

He got up, crossing the room quickly over to a low cabinet beneath a window. When he bent down, pulling open the doors, I saw it was jammed full of photo albums of all types, sizes, and colors.

"Like a needle in a haystack," he said, taking out a small flowered one that was wedged at the top and opening it. After scanning a page, he said, "Well, this one documents my awkward stage. So we can rule that out."

"Can I see?"

"No," he said flatly, putting it on the cabinet and taking out another one that was deep green, square, with an embossed cover. Opening it, he said, "Oh, here's a picture of Waverly. So at least we're getting closer."

He handed the album to me. Sure enough, in the right-hand corner was a snapshot of my mom, in rolled-up jeans and a Blackwood Station T-shirt, bent over one of the dock pumps. "I wonder when this was."

Roo, now rummaging through the rest of the cabinet, glanced over my shoulder. "Well, that's the old Pavilion. It got taken out by a hurricane in 1997, so it had to be before that."

"She met my dad in 1999," I said. "And I guess she left for Lakeview in—"

"2000," he finished for me. "That fall, after my dad died."

I looked at the picture again. In it, my mom would have been around the same age I was now, although she looked like much more of a grown-up than I felt. What was it about pictures that aged people?

"Okay," Roo said suddenly, putting another album, this one burgundy-colored, on the top of the cabinet and opening it. "I think we're getting somewhere. Look."

It was a picture of three little girls with blond hair, sitting at the picnic table below Mimi's. They were all in swimsuits, eating Popsicles, and turned in the same direction, as if they'd been told to look at whoever was taking the shot. I immediately picked out myself, in the red tank suit with a giraffe on it. It took a second of looking this time, but only that, to realize the other two were Bailey and Trinity.

"That's the summer," I said. "2005. My parents split up that fall."

"So we were four."

"Yep." I looked to the next picture, also of the beach area

at Mimi's, but this one was of a skinny little boy in a skiff, holding a set of oars. "Is that you?"

"Nope. Jack. He's always been skinnier and taller." He pointed to the row below. "That's me."

I leaned in closer, taking him in: towheaded and skinny as well, in baggy shorts and a T-shirt with a dinosaur on it. He was sitting on the hood of a car, feet balanced on the front bumper. Behind him, you could see the driver's-side door was open, an arm—thick and hairy—cut off by the frame.

"Who's that?" I asked, indicating the driver.

"Some boyfriend of my mom's," he said with a shrug. "There was a string of them for a while there. Then she went back to school and didn't have time to date."

"Did she ever remarry?"

"Nope." He squinted down at the shot again. "I think I remember that car, actually. It was huge. The guy was small. Probably compensating."

I looked again as well, but you couldn't really tell much by just an arm. "My dad was the opposite. Didn't date anyone for years, just threw himself into work. Tracy was the first woman he brought home, and now they're married."

"You like her?"

I nodded. "She's nice. She makes him happy. Plus, she likes to sail, which I hate."

"Ticks every box," Roo said.

"Exactly." I picked up the album. "Okay if I look at this one over on the couch?"

"Sure. I'll keep digging, see if there's another one."

251

I got through two full pages before I saw something that brought me to tears. Weirdly, it was not the shot of Bailey and Jack with my parents in the background, my dad with his arm over my mom's shoulders. Or the one of Celeste and my mom, posing together in front of what I was pretty sure was the same gardenia bush where we'd taken our pictures before Club Prom. Instead, it was a picture I'd almost passed over. It was of an older woman in a lawn chair, taken from behind, and the composition was weird, everything in the picture over to one side and just empty lake on the other. It was only when I looked more closely that I saw she had a child in her lap, blond-headed, and that they were holding hands. You could see a gold bracelet, braided and thick, on the woman's wrist. The child held a stuffed giraffe in her arms. Me, Mimi, and George.

By this point I'd seen my own face and that of my parents, cousins, aunt, and grandmother repeated in square after square of snapshots. But there was something about seeing my beloved giraffe there as well that made this one picture feel like the ultimate proof that the trip really happened. When things were hard between my parents, and later, when my mom moved out, he was the one I cried to most, burying my face in the soft, nubby fur of his neck. He'd stayed on my bed all the way up until high school before I'd moved him across the room to a shelf, where he remained close enough for me to see before I fell asleep every night. Even now, I knew exactly where he was: in the final box I'd packed up from my room at Nana's, with my books and favorite pictures. It would be the first one I would unpack in the new house, once I got there.

"I think that's the only album you'd want," Roo said now. I swallowed over the lump in my throat, turning the page as he walked over and sat down again. "Although you're welcome to keep looking. My dad's albums are someplace as well. Probably tons of shots of your mom there."

"This is great, actually," I said, studying a shot of Celeste, my dad and mom, and another man, with Jack's same nose and slim frame—Silas, I assumed—sitting at the picnic table. "These are all new to me."

"Really?" he said. "That's crazy. I've probably looked at them all a thousand times."

"Yeah?"

He crossed one leg over the other. "I had a lot of questions about my dad when I was old enough to finally ask. My mom usually just showed me these for her answers. That's why I was kind of freaked out that first day Jack brought you out to the lake."

I thought back. "I'm sorry."

"Don't be. It was just when I heard your name," he said, shifting slightly. His shoulder bumped mine. I didn't move, even as he did to add space again. "It was like you were actually real. Or something."

"I'll take that as a compliment, I guess," I said with a laugh.

"Okay, maybe that's the wrong word." He turned, looking at me. "It was just, you know, those pictures were part of a narrative for me. So you were, as well. Does that make sense?"

I wanted to say yes. It wasn't like I hadn't spent a fair amount of time lately thinking about stories, the ones we told and those we didn't. But the truth was, it didn't exactly track.

My face must has shown this, because he said, "Okay. So when I was nine or ten, I started to get really interested in my dad. I wanted to hear all about him, what he was like, all the time. It wore my mom out, so she'd often just give me these albums and tell me to go nuts. But of course, when I dug through them, I had other questions. Like who you were, and what happened to you."

"Why me?"

"Because, like him, you were in all these pictures. Until you weren't. Here, I'll show you." He pulled the album over into his lap. "See, this one of you with Bailey and Trinity at the table? That was the day your parents brought you. You just appear, after all these books filled with other faces I still knew. A stranger."

I looked down at myself, the Popsicle gripped in one hand. "You didn't remember me."

"I sort of did," he said. "But we were four. Like I said, I was in a thing. I had questions."

I felt my face get a little warm, suddenly, knowing I'd been discussed. It was the same finding that shot of my mom on the fridge: like I, too, had been here all along, even if I hadn't known it.

"And then," he went on, turning a page, "this was the first time we met, which was probably a few minutes later. She literally got the exact moment."

I looked at the picture. It was of the shoreline, littered then as it was now with various floats and beach toys. I was standing at the water's edge in the same bathing suit, holding a plastic flowerpot, as Roo, crouched in the sand, gripped a shovel and looked up into my face. Behind us, a white boat was sliding past, out of frame.

"I look skeptical," I said.

"You had good instincts. I was shady."

I laughed, glad for the release. This felt heavy in a way I couldn't explain. "Are there more?"

He turned another page, pointing to the bottom corner and a shot taken on a bumper car. The two of us were side by side, me behind the fake wheel while he had his arms up in the air, a gleeful look on his face. "Well, here we have evidence that you used to drive just fine."

"Maybe that's where I got traumatized," I suggested.

"Entirely possible." Another page turn. "I think we did better off four wheels. Look."

I did, following his finger to a picture of him and me in the grassy stretch behind Mimi's house, Calvander's office in the distant background. I had to look more closely to make out that it was bubbles, tons of them, floating up over us as we stood together. I had one arm looped around his neck, my eyes cast downward while he looked straight ahead.

"Wow," I said softly.

"I know." He leaned in a little bit more: now our shoulders touched again. "I've always really liked this shot, for some reason. It just looks—"

"Magical," I finished for him. As soon as I said the word, I felt silly. But that was what had come to mind.

"Yeah." He turned his head, smiling at me, and I wished more than anything, right then, that I did remember. That day, that shot, those bubbles. But especially him.

"Anyway," he said, "there are others, too. But those are the ones I remember. As well as that group shot, the one you already saw. Which is . . . here."

He turned a few more pages until it appeared, this time blown up bigger: me, Roo, Jack, Bailey, and Trinity, all on the bench, side by side. The day I had arrived and seen it beneath the glass in Mimi's office, every other face had been a stranger. Now, looking at them, I could see things I immediately recognized: the recognizable wry annoyance of Trinity's expression, how Bailey looked so serious, sitting with elbows propped on knees, framing her own face with her fists. Jack, the oldest, already focused on what would come after the shutter clicked, while Roo's grin was the same. I looked at myself last, thinking there would be no surprises there, at least. But this time, I did see something different. It was the way I was sitting, leaning against Roo, our knees bumping each other: the ease and comfortableness that comes with familiarity. It was, actually, much like we were sitting now.

"After that," he said, "you just vanish, never to be seen again. Poof. You can see why I was confused."

Like I was the ghost, I thought. "Did you think I was dead, too?"

"I was a kid, so it wasn't that cut and dry. It was more . . ." He sat back again, thinking. "I wondered about you. But it had been a while. And then you show up, at the dock, and you're Emma but really Saylor, and you don't know me. . . ."

"I'm sorry," I said instantly.

"Not your fault." He turned to look at me. "Look, the point is . . . I'm glad you came this summer. To see you again."

I stared back at him, feeling a tug in my chest. "I'm real now," I said.

"Yeah," he said, smiling. We were so close, I could see him breathing. "You are."

It was perfect, that kind of moment when time just stops. Until my phone, in my pocket, buzzed suddenly. When I pulled it out, I had a text from Bailey.

Where are you? Come find me. It's important.

Of course it was.

"Everything okay?" Roo asked.

"Think so." I shut the book. "I should go. Thanks for letting me look at this."

"You can take it, if you want," he offered.

"Really?"

"Sure," he said with a smile. "I know where to find you."

Lake North, I thought. The Tides. Sighing, I stood up, pressing the book to my chest. "Thank you. Really. You have no idea . . ." I trailed off, not sure how to put this. "It means a lot."

"No problem." He stood up. "You want a ride? I've got the Yum truck. I can play the music."

I shook my head. "Thanks. But I want to walk. Soak up the ambience while I can."

"At this hour, it's more likely to be mosquitoes."

"I'll be okay."

"It's your skin," he said amiably, pulling out his keys. I stepped out on the porch, with him behind me. "But we'll catch up later, right?"

He always said this, and I loved it. But later, like so much else, was now in shorter supply. I held the album closer to my chest, picturing us in all those bubbles. Magic. "Absolutely," I told him. "We will."

When I reached Mimi's dock, it was early evening, some guests from the motel gathered on the swings, while others cooked something on a grill, the smell of charcoal in the air. Just another summer night, to be followed by another, and one more after that. By then, though, I'd be at the Tides, a vantage point from which all of this would look much different, because it was.

I walked up to the house, stepping around a rather rowdy-sounding game of cornhole—"YESSSSS!" someone yelled as I passed—on the way. Gordon was on the steps with her book, alone. She wasn't reading, just holding it shut on her lap.

"Hey," I called out as I approached. It was prime home-improvement viewing hour, so I was surprised to see her. "What's going on?"

She looked up at me. "You're leaving."

I just stood there, not sure what to say. Finally I asked, "Who told you that?"

"Mimi," she replied, reaching down to scratch a violently red bug bite on one knee. "She said your dad says he's coming to get you."

I wasn't sure why I'd just assumed my dad would let me break this news by myself. Maybe because it was, well, mine? Clearly, though, he'd suspected I might not mention it, so calls had been made.

"It's true." I moved over to sit beside her. "I'm leaving tomorrow."

It wasn't until she rubbed a fist over her eyes, then looked away from me, that I realized she was crying. And as I looked at her, so small in her pink shorts and T-shirt with a unicorn on it, glasses smudged, her beat-up Allies book in her lap, I felt like I might, too.

"Hey," I said, reaching out for her, but she quickly moved, out of reach. "You'll still see me. I'm only going to Lake North."

"That's the whole other side," she said, and sniffled.

"It's not that far."

"It's not *here*."

She was right about that. I sat back, stretching out my legs, elbows on the step behind me. Inside, I could hear Mimi and Celeste talking, the TV on low behind them. "You know, I wasn't even supposed to come this summer," I told her finally. "I feel really lucky I got to meet you, and spend time with Bailey and Trinity and everyone else. It's been great."

"So you're not sad you're leaving?"

"Of course I am," I replied, reaching out to her again. This time, she let me slide an arm over her shoulder. "But I'll be back."

"When?"

It occurred to me there was no real way to answer this question. But I had to try.

"I don't know for sure," I said. She slumped a bit. "But listen. It's just like the Allies. There is always the rest of the story, right? Even if you don't know right now what it is."

She looked down at the book she was holding. "Twenty volumes in this series."

"See? And that's just a book!" I said. "In real life, the chapters go on forever. Or a long time, anyway."

I watched her face as she considered this. Then, out of nowhere, she said, "Do you miss your mom?"

I didn't know why this question hit me like a gut punch. Maybe because it was unexpected, or since she was young, closer to the age I'd been when my mom died than I was now. "Yes, very much," I said. "Do you miss yours?"

She nodded, silent. "Do you think I'll have to leave here, too?"

So that was what this was really about. Not me, but her fear that someone might take her away unexpectedly as well. "Is that what you want?"

"No," she said, reaching down to run a finger over the face of the chimp on the book's cover. "I like it here."

"I know that feeling," I said. She shifted a bit, my arm still over her shoulder. When I went to move it, though, she surprised me by leaning in closer, resting her head against my chest. "But you know what Mimi says. Even if you do have to go someday, the lake keeps you."

To this she said nothing. I could feel her warm face against my shirt, accompanied by that little-kid feral smell of sunscreen and dirt. After a moment she said, "What's that book?"

I'd forgotten about the album, which I'd set on the step beside me. Picking it up, I said, "It's photos from the first time I came here. Want to see?"

She nodded, sitting up again, and pulled the book into my lap, opening it up. "That's Mimi," she said, pointing to one of the first shots.

"Yep," I said. We looked at it quietly for a moment. "You said the pictures might help me remember. So I borrowed this from Roo."

Hearing this, she looked pleased. "Are there a lot of them?" she asked as I turned the page.

"Not really," I said. "But there are enough."

Now we were on the page with the shot of me with Trinity and Bailey with our Popsicles, as well as Jack in the boat and Roo on the car. "That's you," she said, putting a finger right in the center of my swimsuit. "Right?"

"Yep, that's the first one," I said. "Now we just need to find the others."

As she leaned in a little closer, squinting, I heard footsteps behind us in the hallway. When I looked through the screen, Mimi was standing there, watching us. I'd have to talk to her now about leaving, and how grateful I was for the time I'd spent here. There were other things I wanted to say, too. But for now, I turned back to Gordon, who was flipping a page with one finger, her eyes scanning the photos there. Everything changes tomorrow, I thought, but then again, that was always the case.

I wanted to tell Gordon this, share with her the things I was learning, these rules for us outliers. Instead, I got settled, the album square in my lap, and searched with her for my own face among the others that now, I finally recognized. But it was she who spoke first.

"Look," she said softly. "There's another one."

SIXTEEN

The day I was leaving, I woke up before the sun and everyone else. Or so I thought.

"Well, look who it is," Mimi said as I came into the kitchen. She was at the table, a mug in front of her. The paper was there as well, but still rolled up, waiting for Oxford, I assumed. "Isn't this a nice surprise."

"Didn't sleep well," I told her. "Are you always up this early?"

"Oh, honey, I've never been much of a sleeper." She picked up her drink, taking a sip. "Plus I love having the house and lake all to myself. I'm selfish that way."

"You're anything but selfish," I told her, crossing to the cupboard to take out a glass. At the sink, I filled it with water, then went to join her.

"I don't know about that." She smiled at me. "I'm wishing you could stay here awhile longer when I know your daddy is more than ready to have you back."

"I wish I could stay, too," I said with a sigh. "I feel like I'm just starting to figure things out."

"Things?"

I sat back in my chair, pulling a leg up underneath me. "I never really understood what this place meant to me. I mean, I knew my mom loved it, because she talked about it. A lot."

"I'm sure that's true," she said. "What did she say?"

"It was mostly stories." I looked out the big window in front of me at the water, which was still and quiet, the sky streaked with pink above it. "About a girl who lived at a lake and hated the winter. But in the summer, she was happy."

"Sounds like Waverly," she said. Her face looked sad, and again I wondered if I shouldn't have gone into detail. "She had a complicated relationship with this place. And a lot of things."

"My dad never wants to talk about her problems," I said, surprising myself. "It's like he feels like he has to present this sanitized version of her life for my sake. I mean, I never even knew about the accident with Chris Price until Bailey told me."

"Don't be too hard on your dad," she said. "Everyone grieves differently."

"Part of grieving is remembering," I pointed out. "He just wants to forget."

"I don't think that's true," she replied. She looked down at her mug. "If it was, you wouldn't know anything about her, and it sounds like you do."

"But it's selective, only what he chose to share." I looked

at my fingers, spread out on the table in front of me. "I feel like I missed so much. Like knowing you, and Celeste and her kids, and the lake. All the stuff I only found here, in these last three weeks."

Mimi slid her hand, tan and knotted with veins and sunspots, across to cover mine. "We never stopped thinking about you, honey. I hope you know that."

"That's just the thing, though," I said. "I wasn't thinking about *you*. Because I didn't know to."

"But now you do. So you will."

I swallowed, hard, and she gave my hand a squeeze. Finally I said, "Thank you for having me. I don't know how to repay you."

"By coming back," she said, and smiled. "And when you do, we'll be waiting."

Tears filled my eyes, and I blinked, just as Oxford came downstairs, whistling softly as he did so. Seeing us, he said, "What's everyone doing up so early?"

"I'm always up at this time, you know that," Mimi told him, getting to her feet. "You hungry?"

"Wouldn't say no to some toast," he replied. As he reached for the paper, he said to me, "You want the obits?"

"I will," I said as he shook out the main section, glancing at the front page. "But first I have something to do."

Mimi glanced at the clock over the stove. "You know it's only six a.m., right?"

"Yeah. I'll be back soon."

I pushed back my chair and took my glass to the sink,

which still had dishes in it from the night before. Had they even noticed the times I'd washed everything and put it away? Maybe not. But it had made me feel good. Like I was part of all this, in my own fashion.

"You want to borrow the car?" Mimi asked when I came downstairs after grabbing my shoes and wallet and pulling a brush through my hair. "I can get the keys."

"No, I'm good to walk," I told her. Then I waved and started down the hallway before she could ask any more questions or, God forbid, insist I drive.

At Calvander's, all the guest-room doors were closed, the beach empty. When I got to the road, instead of going left, I turned the other way. About a block ahead, just beyond a sign that said LAKE NORTH, 3 MILES, I could see Conroy Market, brightly lit and open. It wasn't a long way, but enough to at least try to clear my head, which I needed, especially after what had happened between Bailey and me the night before.

"Where have you *been*?" she'd demanded when she appeared in my room after I got back with the album. "I sent you a text. We need to talk."

"I went to see Roo," I told her. "What's going on?"

She shut the door behind her, then came over, climbing up to sit opposite me. "Colin called."

I just looked at her. "And?"

"And," she said slowly, tucking a piece of hair behind her ear, "we talked."

266

"Talked?" I repeated. "About what? The fact that he's a jerk?"

Clearly, the answer to this was no: instead of replying, she scooted a bit closer, lowering her voice. "Look. What he did was awful. But he did explain."

"You can't explain blowing someone off for a formal dance," I said, surprised at how angry I was getting. "It's horrible."

She looked doubtful, as if this was in question. "Well—"

"Bailey. He had a girlfriend the *whole time* you guys were hanging out."

"It's more complicated than that," she protested. "See, they were basically on a break for the summer, except that he'd mentioned Club Prom to her months ago, and she wanted to come see the lake, so . . ."

"He asked *you* to go with him," I said.

"Because he didn't think she'd actually follow through and come! But then, you know, she did. And he was stuck."

"Huh," I said.

"I know!" she said quickly, encouraged, as if I'd agreed with her, which I hadn't. "He's not a bad guy, Saylor. He just screwed up. And he's really sorry."

"Bailey." I narrowed my eyes at her. "You're not going to get back together with him, are you? Because that's—"

"We're *talking*," she said again. I already hated this phrase. "And he invited us over tonight, because they're having a Campus party. Will you come?"

"No," I said.

She blinked. "You didn't even think about it!"

"I don't have to," I said. "I don't want anything to do with those guys."

"Saylor," she groaned, adding syllables to my name to draw it out. "If you don't come, I have to go alone. Is that what you want?"

"What I want," I replied, "is for you to realize that you deserve better than someone who would stand you up when you are all dressed up for an event *to which they invited you* and then not apologize for, like, days."

"Saylor."

"I'm not going," I said, and she sighed, rolling her eyes. "Besides, this is my last night. I want to spend it here."

She looked at me, surprised. "Your last night? What do you mean?"

"I'm leaving tomorrow," I said, gesturing at my barely packed bag, which sat on the only chair in the room, symbolizing my ambivalence. "My dad's coming and we're going to stay at the Tides."

Now she was shocked silent, at least for a moment. "Are you serious?"

I nodded. "I found out a few days ago, but now it's really—"

"This is great!" She sat up straighter, suddenly energized. "You'll be over there right by the Club, so you can be my eyes and ears. You can tell me if he's serious about wanting to get back together."

Forget denial: this was delusional. "Did you hear me say I'm leaving?"

"For the Tides, though!" she said. "You can't be upset about that, it's like a dream."

Of course she'd see it that way. "I just want to stay where I am."

"God, why?" she said. "Saylor, you're going to hang out in the nicest hotel in the area."

Who cares? I wanted to shout. Out loud I said, "I like it here."

"Only because you don't know any better." She sighed wistfully. "God. You are *so* lucky."

I could admit to already being emotional. But something about her using that word, at that moment, made my temper flare. "*Lucky?*" I repeated. "Just because I'm going to stay someplace nice?"

"Well . . . yeah. I mean, Saylor, come on. It's kind of a first-world problem. If it's a problem at all."

"You've had the lake your whole life," I said, my voice rising a bit. "You take it for granted. I only had three weeks to meet you, and Trinity, and—"

"We're not going anywhere," she said. "You can come back anytime. But the Tides? That's, like, special. Can't you see that?"

Always about the place. Never about me. "What I see is that you don't care at all that I'm upset," I said. "When you aren't telling me I'm spoiled for feeling that way."

"You are spoiled!" she shot back. Then, immediately, she said, "I mean—"

I swallowed, hard. "Yeah. What *do* you mean?"

"You don't know what it's like to live here! How dead it is all winter, nobody around. And then summer comes and yeah, it's nicer, but most of us have to work all the time, because that's when you make money. For you it's a fun getaway, discovering your history or whatever. The rest of us don't get that luxury. Nobody does except for you."

I thought back to the first days I'd been here, when I'd found out Mimi had said I was on vacation and that everyone should let me relax. Since then I'd worked my butt off cleaning rooms, not to mention being Bailey's wing person as she made one bad choice after another. Clearly, though, it made no difference. I was the rich spoiled cousin then, and the rich spoiled cousin now.

"I need to pack," I said flatly, sliding off the bed. "Are we done here?"

"Are you coming to Campus?"

I just looked at her. "You just called me spoiled! Why would I go anywhere with you?"

"Saylor." She exhaled softly. "I didn't—"

"Yeah, you did," I told her. I walked over to the door, opening it. "Have fun. Maybe you can find someone else to date Blake this time."

She looked at the door, but didn't budge. "Okay, I think

things have gotten a little twisted. All I said was—"

"I know what you said," I told her. Then I walked over to my bureau, pulling open a drawer, and started to pack again.

For a while she just sat there, watching me. Waiting for me to say something, or reverse this. By the time I moved on to my closet, though, she'd gotten to her feet and started over to the door.

"Hey," she said. "Look. I'm sorry."

"Me too," I said. But I didn't turn around. "I'll see you around."

She stayed there another minute, waiting for me to look at her again, but I didn't. I was just so hurt, and frustrated, so close to crying I could feel the sobs in my chest. That first day, knowing me from no one, it was Bailey who'd stood up for me to Taylor, claiming family trumped everything. Back then, I hadn't expected such loyalty and had been touched. When I really needed it, however, she could only think of herself. I was putting the album in my bag when I heard her leave and go down the stairs.

Now, walking the silent block to Conroy's, I thought of Bailey and not much else. How we'd covered this same distance, but going the other way, on our own walk home together. We'd talked the entire time. Now it seemed entirely possible, if not likely, that I'd leave without even saying goodbye to her. It wasn't like we were sisters, only cousins. But it still made me sad.

When I reached the market, I crossed the parking lot

and pushed open the door. Immediately, I was hit with a blast of A/C like a wind gust, sending goose bumps springing up on my bare arms.

"Welcome to Conroy's," a distant female voice said in a monotone. I looked over to see Celeste behind the register, flipping through a sheaf of papers on a clipboard.

"Good morning," I said.

"Good—" That was as far as she got before she finally looked up. "Saylor! Sorry, I was focused on my BOGO."

"BOGO?" I asked.

"Daily discounted item," she replied. "Which today is . . . sticky buns."

Indeed, there was a display across from the register: they were buy one, get one, fifty cents each. "That's a bargain."

"I guess, if you like sticky buns." She sighed, putting down the clipboard. "What brings you in so early?"

"Couldn't sleep," I said. "I'm leaving today."

"I heard." She cocked her head to the side, smiling. "But at least you aren't going far. Thank goodness. I don't think Bailey could take it if you were going home for good."

That answered the question of whether she'd been told about our argument. "I wasn't sure I'd see you," I said. "I wanted to come say goodbye."

"Goodbye?" She came out from behind the counter, adjusting her CONROY MARKET apron. Beneath it, she was wearing jean shorts and, again, platform wedges with a thick heel, showcasing her bright toenails. "You're only going to the other side of the lake, though, right?"

"Yeah," I replied. "But it won't be the same."

"Oh, honey." She reached out, pulling me in for a hug. Her grip was still strong, but this time I leaned into it, holding on tightly as well. "Even if you were going all the way back to Lakeview, you couldn't get rid of us that easily. You're stuck with us now. You know that, right?"

I nodded, worried that a verbal response might get me teary again. "I'm sorry, Celeste."

She loosened her grip, holding me out away from her and looking at my face. "Sorry? Whatever for?"

"For never coming here before," I said. "All those years since my mom died. I didn't realize . . . what I was missing."

"How could you have?" She shook her head. "Honey. I know all you kids think you are long grown, but you are still children, for the most part. Which means adults make the decisions. The road runs both ways. We could have come to you."

"But you didn't," I said, and as she opened her mouth to protest, I added, "because of my dad, and how he probably would have reacted. He could have brought me here, too."

She gave one of my arms a hard squeeze. "Now, now. Family is complicated. You factor in a loss that's particularly hard to bear and it just makes it more so. I'm sure it wasn't your dad's intent to keep you from us. Being a parent is tough. Being a single parent, sometimes impossible. He was just doing the best he could."

"Which now is two weeks at the Tides," I said.

"Hard punishment." She smiled. "And, as we said, three

miles from here and a place we all are dying to see in person. Good luck keeping us away. You can't."

"Bailey was excited when I told her," I said.

"That child and the other side of the lake. It's like your mom, all over again. I couldn't keep her here even if I wanted. And I do, especially after what happened with that boy."

There was a chime as the front door opened and a tall, slouching guy with a nose piercing came in. "Morning," he mumbled, more into his collar than to us.

"Morning, Edgar," Celeste replied. Once he ambled past us behind the counter, she added, "Bless his heart. I've never seen anyone move so slowly. It's like a glacier or something."

Just then, somewhere, a phone began to ring. Edgar didn't seem to notice.

"I've got to take this, hold on a sec," Celeste said with a sigh.

"I should go," I told her. "I have packing to do."

"All right, then." She pulled me in for another hug, the phone still ringing. "You come back anytime, you hear? To Mimi's or the Station or even here. We'll be waiting."

"Thank you," I said. The phone was starting to make me nervous, but she squeezed me again before walking to the door marked EMPLOYEES ONLY and disappearing inside.

Which left just Edgar and me. Outside, a truck pulled in, a bunch of guys in orange T-shirts saying DOT piling out. I was going to slip out as they came in, but right by the door I saw a shelf lined with loaves of bread, which gave me an idea.

I grabbed three of them, then crossed to the coolers lining the wall, scanning the groceries there until I found the tubs of butter. I took one and then, after thinking about it, another, adding them to what was already in my arms as I walked over to the register to pay. When I got home, I'd put it all where everyone at Mimi's could find it. Like the dishes, they'd notice or wouldn't. But either way, there would be plenty of toast for a while. Maybe it was the best way to say goodbye.

Gordon swung her feet back and forth on the bench where we both sat, by the Calvander's office. It was eight thirty a.m. and my dad would be here any minute.

Back at the house, everyone else would be finally waking up and eating breakfast, maybe even breaking into the loaves I'd bought at Conroy's earlier. I'd had enough of farewells for one day, though, so I'd taken my duffel and the rest of my stuff up here to wait. If it was true what Celeste and Mimi had both said, I wasn't really leaving anyway, just changing locations. Even so, I hadn't wanted to deal with seeing Bailey after our argument, preferring to leave as I'd arrived, basically alone. But then Gordon showed up.

She moved silently, like a cat: I hadn't even realized she was approaching until she was right beside me. She was in a purple terry-cloth romper, her pink plastic jelly sandals on her feet. In her hand she carried an Allies book.

"What are you doing?" she asked, once I'd gotten over being startled.

"Waiting."

She slid onto the bench beside me, putting the book squarely in her lap. "I will too, then."

Behind me, I heard the familiar sound of Mimi's screen door banging shut. I tensed, sure it was Bailey, but when I looked, I saw Jack instead, crossing the grass to his car. A moment later, he pulled up next to us.

"What are you two doing?" he asked.

"Waiting," Gordon told him.

"For what?"

"My dad," I said. "I'm leaving today."

"Leaving?" He raised his eyebrows. "You're going home?"

"No." Another car drove by, an older VW, the muffler sputtering. "To Lake North."

He considered this as Gordon picked up her book. "But you'll come back to visit, right? I mean, it's only three miles."

The was true. But sometimes even the shortest distance can be impossible to navigate, whether you went road or shore or some other route. In all her recovery attempts, my mom had never lived far from us. But sometimes, when someone's not right there, they might as well be a million miles away.

"I'll be back at some point," I said to Jack. "You'll see me before I leave for good."

"Let's make sure of it," he told me. "Come to Taylor's birthday party. We're planning it as we speak."

"Am I invited?" Gordon asked.

"No. Sorry." She slumped, disappointed. To me he said, "It'll be at April's this weekend. Bailey will give you the details."

"I'm not sure I'll see her," I said as the A/C unit cut off. Just like that, I was shouting. I lowered my voice. "We had an argument."

"You're cousins. It happens," he said, sounding hardly bothered. "Ask Trinity. Or Roo. Or anyone, really. No gifts, but beer is welcome." He looked at Gordon. "You didn't hear that."

"Hear what?" she said. I couldn't tell if she was being clever or just hadn't been listening that closely.

"And you," Jack said, turning to me. "Don't be a stranger, because you aren't. You hear?"

Hear what, I wanted to say to be funny, but this was so unexpectedly sweet I found myself instead just nodding.

"And don't stay in Lake North too long," he added, starting to roll forward. "It's different over there."

I thought of that first night I'd crossed the lake with Bailey. The world changed in those three miles, for sure. Would I?

"I'll be careful," I promised him. "Thanks, Jack."

He smiled, then gave me a salute with two fingers, stuck his tongue out at Gordon, and pulled away. As he started to accelerate, he beeped, and I waved. Finally, not a stranger anymore.

I was watching him disappear around a curve, thinking this, when I saw my dad's silver Audi approaching. Even though I'd missed him, and was excited to see Tracy, I felt my heart sink a bit.

"Is that them?" Gordon asked.

"Yep."

A moment later, they were pulling in and parking, so I picked up my bag and purse and got to my feet. Gordon did the same, carrying her book, and we walked over together.

"Emma!" Tracy called out, jumping out and rushing over to give me a big hug. She had on a white sundress, all the better to emphasize a deep tan. "I missed you!"

"I missed you, too," I said, meaning it. "How was the trip?"

"An adventure," she replied. "I can't wait to tell you all about it."

"And if you're worried about her not having enough pictures, don't," my dad said as he walked over to join us. "The entirety of Greece was fully and thoroughly documented."

"Oh, stop," Tracy said as he gave me a once-over—did I look as different as I felt?—before pulling me in for a hug. "Everyone takes pictures on vacation."

"True," he said, smoothing a hand over my head, "but not everyone chooses to spend the entire trip seeing things solely through the camera lens. Who's this?"

I'd temporarily forgotten Gordon, who was still right beside me. "Dad, meet Anna Gordon. My cousin."

Hearing this, Gordon looked pleased. But I knew the name you used first was the one people remembered.

"Well, hello, Anna Gordon," my dad said, extending a

hand. She took it, shyly, not meeting his eyes. "It's nice to meet you. Is Celeste your mom?"

"No," I said. "Amber. From Joe's side."

"Amber," he repeated, still shaking Gordon's small hand. "Right. I remember her."

"And this is Tracy," I said to Gordon. "My . . . stepmom."

At this, Tracy and I both looked at each other. "Wow," she said with a smile. "That's the first time I've heard that. I like it."

"Me too," I said.

She bent down a bit. "So, Anna Gordon. What are you reading?"

Gordon held out her book. "It's the Allies series."

"That's the chimpanzees, right?" Tracy took the book, flipping it over. "I have patients who are nuts for these books."

Gordon looked at me. "Tracy and Dad are both dentists," I explained.

Instantly, she looked worried, biting her mouth shut.

"But not for another two weeks," Tracy said quickly, handing the book back. She took a look around. "Wow, it's great to finally see this place. It's gorgeous, just like your dad said!"

"Well, we're not going to be here," I pointed out. "Lake North is different."

"Not that much," my dad said. To Tracy he explained, "It's three miles down the road, with more new construction, bigger houses. But basically it's all the same no matter where you are on the lake."

It wasn't, though, and he'd been the first one to tell me so, when we first pulled up to the sign with two opposite arrows. But I chose not to point this out. "It's too bad we aren't staying here," Tracy said, looking at the Calvander's office, with its rock garden and blinking VACANCY sign. "It's charming."

"You could," I offered quickly. "There are rooms available."

"But Nana made her own plans," my dad said. "We'll come visit, though, when it's a more decent hour. Is Mimi up yet? I'd love to thank her in person."

"She went to Delaney," Gordon informed him. "Room ten needed new screens."

"Well, we'll definitely be back to visit," my dad said, looking at Tracy. "But for now, we should probably—"

"Yes," she agreed. "I'm sure your mother is wondering where we are."

And just like that, it was time to go. My dad took my bag, opening the trunk, while Tracy shaded her eyes with her hand, again looking at the big trees along the water.

"Anna Gordon, it was very nice to meet you," he said as the hatch closed with a click. "We'll see you soon, I'm sure."

I squatted down so I was at her level, then said, "You take care of everyone for me, okay? I'll be back before you know it."

"Promise?"

I nodded and she stepped forward, hugging my neck so

tightly I almost lost my balance, her book bumping my back.

"Bye, Saylor," Gordon said.

"Bye, Anna Gordon."

Tracy waved and started over to the car. I smiled, lifting a hand myself as I followed. When I climbed inside, the car was cool and smelled of leather, the seat sinking beneath me.

"She called you Saylor," my dad said as he started the engine and began pulling out of the drive. "Why is that?"

There was no traffic, but we stopped anyway, long enough for me to glimpse Mimi's house one more time in the side mirror, where it already was starting to look far away.

"Because it's my name," I said, and I saw them exchange looks as we turned onto the road. The sign said Lake North was three miles. A passenger again, I settled in for the ride.

SEVENTEEN

"Welcome to the Tides!"

The staff said this every time you walked through the main door, even if you'd only stepped out moments earlier. I'd been there less than twenty-four hours, and already I was sick of it.

Still, I nodded and smiled as I crossed the lobby, the copy of the *Bly County News* I'd just picked up under one arm. At the hotel restaurant, the Channel Marker, they offered a variety of newspapers at breakfast: *New York Times, Washington Post, Wall Street Journal.* For the local news—which was to say, obits—I had to walk across the street to the Larder, a glorified convenience store that sold gas and ice cream but also expensive wine and packages of cheese straws that cost six bucks each. I was a long way from BOGO sticky buns, not that I didn't realize this already.

That first morning, as Dad and Tracy and I drove away from Mimi's, I kept telling myself the same things, on repeat: it's only three miles. Not that different. But even as I did,

I was aware of the visible transition happening outside my window. After we passed Conroy Market, the squat concrete motels began disappearing, replaced by bigger neighborhoods. North Lake Estates, Fernwood Cove, the Sunset. And that was before we even pulled into the hotel itself.

"Welcome to the Tides," the young, cute valet—he looked familiar, making me think I might have seen him at one of the Campus parties—said as he opened my door. Two others, also both in white golf shirts and black shorts, were already helping my dad and Tracy out and getting the luggage. "We're glad to have you."

"Um, thanks," I mumbled, sliding out of my seat. He immediately shut the door behind me, then jogged back to help one of the other guys as they unloaded the hatch.

"Wow, this is nice," my dad said, looking around. "How long has this place been here?"

"The Tides opened in two thousand sixteen," another one of the valets, who had dark, shoulder-length hair, told him. "It's the vision of the Delhomme family, owners of the Lake North Yacht Club. They saw a need for a place where members could stay that allowed the same level of service. That's our goal."

He said this so easily I assumed the answer was company-dictated. "Well," Tracy said, "it's lovely. Although I guess I shouldn't have expected any less, since it *is* Grace who planned all this."

That would be Nana, who was already up in our suite, having been brought straight from the airport late the night before. She didn't drive either, but with her declining eyesight, she at least had a good excuse.

"Welcome to the Tides," the woman behind the desk said as we approached. "Checking in?"

"Yes," my dad said. "The last name is Payne. I believe my mother is already here."

"I can't wait to go for a swim," Tracy said to me. "And eat something. Are you hungry?"

I was, although I hadn't been aware of this until right at that moment. "Yeah, actually. I am."

"The Channel Marker, our restaurant, is open for breakfast, lunch, and dinner," the woman said, sliding some cards to my dad. "The hours are here on your keys. And room service is available twenty-four hours a day."

"Room service it is," my dad said, and Tracy grinned. He turned to face us. "Ready to go up?"

In the elevator, there was a screen showing a video, on repeat, of the highlights of the Tides. Here was the pool, blue and empty. The beach, with a clearly posed photo of a single child digging in the sand with a bucket. Even the lake, which I'd seen every day for weeks now, looked different in the sunset picture that appeared.

"Floor five," the voice announced as the doors slid open. Like "Lake North," it was all in the order you said it.

"Five fourteen," my dad said, glancing at the key card in his hand. "So that's—oh. Right here."

It wasn't hard to spot, as the door marked with these numbers was the only one on the short hallway where we were standing. On the other side of the elevators was 515. So we basically had half of an entire floor? Was that even possible?

My dad waved his card at the door, which clicked, and he pushed it open, standing back to hold it for Tracy and myself. "Hello?" Tracy called out as she stepped inside.

"In here," I heard Nana say. At the sound of her voice, I smiled.

I loved my grandmother. With her, everything was always, effortlessly, Just So, from the thin teacup she drank her coffee from every morning—in a matching robe and slipper set, hair combed perfectly—to the simple, but perfect, bouquet of seasonal flowers that always stood on her dining room table. Everything outside Nana's apartment might have felt fragile and already falling apart, but with her, there was always a sense that things were as they should be.

"Emma," she said when she saw me, holding open her arms. After all the foot dragging of the morning, now I felt like I couldn't move fast enough. "You are a sight for these sore eyes! How are you?"

"Good," I said, giving her a tight squeeze before she gestured for me to sit in the chair next to hers. "How was the cruise?"

"Oh, it was wonderful," she sighed. "The pyramids must be seen to be believed. Are you hungry? I have a few things here, but we can easily order more."

This was an understatement: I saw a pot of coffee and a plate stacked with pastries, as well as fresh fruit and berries, arranged beautifully in a bowl. There was toast, too, four pieces perfectly browned, balls of butter dotted with salt beside them.

"Have some," Nana said, seeing me notice this. She picked up the plate, putting it closer to me. "You look hungry."

"Thanks," I replied, reaching for a piece and putting it on the plate in front of me.

"It looks delicious," Tracy said after also greeting Nana. "This place is amazing."

"It's lovely, I agree," Nana said, looking around the room. Like the lobby, the floor was white tile, the room open, with a small kitchen tucked away in a corner and a living area to the right of where we were sitting. The real centerpiece, though, were the sliding doors, open now to let in the breeze, that framed both a patio and a gorgeous, wide view of the lake. "So," she said. "How are Mimi and the rest of the family?"

"Good," I said. "It was nice to get to know everyone. I just wish I'd had longer there."

"I told her she's only a couple of miles away," my dad said. "Easy to visit while we're here."

"And we'll have to have them, as well," Nana said, picking up a piece of toast and putting in on her plate. "Matthew, let's plan on that. A thank-you dinner. I'll talk to the desk about booking a table at the Club."

"Oh, you don't have to do that," I said quickly. While Bailey would lose her mind at the prospect, I could only imagine everyone else would be less than enthused.

"I think it's the least we can do since they took such good

286

care of you. Ask Mimi what night is good, will you? And how many will be coming. The more the merrier."

My phone beeped, the sound distant in my purse, which was on the back of my chair. Nana, who hated screens at the table, gave it a pointed look, making it clear I should not check it. So I didn't.

"I'll talk to her," I said instead. "But she's really busy with the motel and everything."

"All the more reason for a nice dinner out," Nana replied as, outside, a large boat puttered across the water, pulling a float behind it. "Now, what's the plan for today? Pool? Lake? A nap?"

"I vote pool," Tracy said. "Although once I eat, I have a feeling a nap might win out."

"They both sound good to me," I said. "I'll get settled and then decide."

"Perfect. Your room is the one at the end of the hall, with the twin bed."

I smiled, thanking her again, then grabbed my purse and headed that way. My room was small, but immaculate, everything white—walls, floor, sheets, and comforter. A fan turned slowly overhead. I walked around the bed, to the sheer white curtain, pulling it aside to reveal yet another sliding glass door with the patio beyond it. Another room with a view of the lake. If it was all the same, really, why did it feel so different?

It was a question I was still asking myself, these two days later, as the elevator opened again, depositing me in the empty hallway outside our room. My dad, Tracy, and Nana had easily moved into vacation mode and a schedule of late breakfast, pool, naps, and dinners at the hotel restaurant, but I was still getting adjusted. It didn't help that out every window was the lake, and the other side: from this height, through the big hallway window, I could actually sort of make out Mimi's house if I squinted. And I did, every morning.

I waved my key at the door, heard the click, and then pushed it open. Nana had not emerged from her room, and my dad and Tracy, swearing they needed to work off all the great Greek food they ate on their honeymoon, had gone out for a morning run. The quiet made my phone sound even louder as it signaled a new message.

Without even looking, I knew it was Bailey. Despite the fact that we hadn't exactly left things on the best note, she'd texted me at least five times since I'd left Mimi's. Our fight was still on my mind, but she had apparently gotten over it.

Promised I'd take Gordon tubing early afternoon. You in?

As coercion went, this was next-level. It was one thing to claim to want to hang out with me: another, entirely, to bring Gordon into it. As she intended, though, it gave me pause, especially after the conversation I'd had with Trinity the day before.

"You've got to come over here and see Gordon," she'd announced in lieu of a hello. "She's driving me nuts."

"Trinity?" I asked.

"I mean, if she could go back to camp, it would be different," she continued. "But instead she's home and sulking around. I'm a sitting target because I am literally bed-bound. You need to do something."

"Me?" I said. "I'm on the other side of the lake."

"It's three miles," she pointed out. "Also, can you take me to birth class this afternoon? Everyone else is working."

"I don't know," I said slowly. "I'm kind of stuck here with my family."

"I am *also* your family," she said. "Remember?"

I sighed. "I'll see what I can do."

Which had turned out to be not much, as my dad was determined to use the time we had together to bond us as a new family. While Nana stayed in the A/C of the room, reading, he was busy organizing activities to the point that I was, honestly, kind of exhausted. We'd done mini golf, attended a Pavilion concert (beach music, surprise!), and taken part in a low-country boil the Tides staff arranged on the beach for all the guests. But today was what I'd been dreading.

"An easy morning on the water," my dad had said the night before, presenting this idea as we sat on the wooden beach chairs, our plates of shrimp, potatoes, and sausage on our laps. "I reserved a day sailer and a picnic lunch from the kitchen. We'll just tool around, then find a beach to pull up to for a bit to swim and eat."

"Wait," I said, "are we all doing this or just you guys?"

"All of us," he replied, wiping his mouth with a napkin. "I mean, we three. Not Nana. She's never been a boat person."

"Neither have I," I pointed out.

"You said before you were out on boats all the time with

your cousins these last few weeks," he reminded me.

"Motorboats," I corrected him. "And that was just trans-portation. Sailing is different."

"Yes, because it's great," he replied. Tracy, beside him, smiled. "Emma, just be open-minded. You might actually really like it."

I doubted this. But it did give me a good reason to tell Bailey no to her invitation, which I did now, explaining I already had plans for the water. She wrote back right away, probably because it was the first time I'd responded so far.

Later today, then?

I sighed. All these invitations and requests, but not one from the person I really wanted to see.

I missed Roo. Which was weird, I knew, because with his multiple jobs and my work at Calvander's, it wasn't like we'd spent that much time together even when we'd been on the same side. But when we were hanging out, there had just been that ease, a shorthand, not to mention that moment with my dress strap that might have led to something else. But didn't, I reminded myself.

There was still Taylor's birthday party, that evening. April had texted me the details, and I'd told Jack I'd be there. It was one thing to say this, however, and another to actually find my way there, to a house I'd never been to, and walk in alone. Knowing Roo would be there was an incentive, but the truth was, I'd feel better if I was with Bailey. So maybe I had my own selfish reasons for making up as well.

Maybe, I wrote back to her now. A single word, without

weight in either direction. Immediately, she texted back a thumbs-up.

"Emma?" My dad was outside, his voice clear through the thin door. "Are you in there?"

"Yes," I called out, sliding my newspaper under a pillow. "Coming."

When I opened the door, he was standing there, in an ATHENS T-shirt and swim trunks. Sunscreen streaked his face. "Ready to sail?"

"No," I replied.

"Great," he said easily, too happily distracted to notice this. "The boat is ready for us. Tracy went to grab the cooler from the Club. Walk down with me?"

Clearly, I wasn't getting out of this. I took my stuff and followed him.

"Breakfast?" Nana asked as we passed by, gesturing to the expanse of room service plates that sat before her. "Sailing requires energy."

"No time," my dad said, plucking a muffin from a tray of pastries. "We're headed out right now."

I kissed her cheek as I passed her, taking a doughnut after she told me again to help myself. Once out in the hallway, as my dad pushed the button for the elevator, I wrapped it in a tissue, stuffing it deep in my bag.

"I think you'll really like this," he said as the doors slid open and we got in. "Going down," the voice informed us. "It won't be like those days at Topper Lake back at home, so choppy. Just an easy sail."

"I can't stay out long," I told him. "Bailey wants me to do something with her later, and then there's this party."

"Party?" he asked. "When?"

"Tonight," I said. "I told you, my friend Taylor. It's her birthday."

"I don't know," he said. "We're supposed to eat with the Delhommes tonight."

I'd forgotten. Nana's friends, who owned the Tides, had invited us to dinner at the Club. "I don't have to be there, though, right? It'll be all you guys drinking wine and talking."

"I think it's the least we can do to thank them for this vacation," he replied as we reached the lobby. "Plus, they're expecting you."

"Dad," I said. Before, I hadn't been that into going to Taylor's party. Now that it seemed I might not be allowed to do so, it felt imperative. "I'm going sailing. You have to let me do something I like today. It's my vacation, too."

He looked at me. "Emma. You've already spent a month with your friends. I think you can miss one party."

"But it's her birthday!"

"Maybe," he said, and having this same word as my answer felt like payback after all of Bailey's pleadings that I'd ignored. "We'll see. For now, let's just have a good time, okay?"

Sure. Because that was what *always* happened when we went sailing. I bit this thought back, though, as we stepped outside. The heat was like a thick wall, even with the chill of the A/C still on my skin, and I immediately dug in my bag for the baseball hat I'd brought, pulling it down to shade my face.

"Great day to be on the water," he announced, leading me down a side set of stairs to the pool area. The beach was just beyond, a girl in a white Club shirt sitting in the lifeguard chair, swinging a whistle on a chain. The sand was dotted with beachgoers, some with their chairs in groups, kids digging with shovels and pails nearby, others alone, soaking up the sun. A waiter moved through them with a tray in hand, taking orders. "The dock is just this way, I think . . . yes. Look, that's ours!"

I followed his finger, which was pointing at a small sailboat bobbing just off to one side. Staring at it, I felt a nervousness not unlike what I felt when I had to drive, a mix of dread and fear.

"Great," I said as another white-shirted Club worker came around from behind the sail, wiping his hands on his shorts. It was Blake, not that I had time to react, as in the next moment my dad was walking right up him.

"I think that's for us," he said, nodding at the boat. "Payne?"

"That's right," Blake replied, hopping onto the dock. "All ready for you as promised. Do you need a quick lesson?"

"No, no," my dad said as I pulled my hat down a bit farther. "I know what I'm doing. Actually taught sailing here when I was your age."

"Really?" Blake asked. "That's cool. Did you live on Campus?"

"Room fourteen," my dad told him proudly. "All four

years. Could still find my name on the wall, I bet, if I looked. Matthew Payne."

"Nice to meet you. I'm Blake." He stuck out his hand and they shook while I stood off to one side, willing myself to be invisible. "I've left a card with our number here at the docks and a backup Club one, just in case you run into any trouble."

"Hopefully not," my dad said. "We're just doing an easy sail. My daughter, Emma, here isn't exactly a fan."

Blake gave me a quick glance, nodding, then turned back to the boat. A beat later, though, he looked at me again. My hat had covered my face some, but not enough. Damn. "Saylor? Is that you?"

My dad, surprised, looked at me as well. "You guys know each other?"

Silence as neither one of us confirmed or denied this. Finally I said, "He's friends with Bailey."

"Oh, right," my dad said, as if I'd mentioned this before, which I hadn't. "Small world. Oh, there's Tracy."

With that, he was walking down the dock to the Club, where I could now see my stepmother emerging, a basket hooked over one arm. Blake and I both watched him go, if only to not look at each other.

"So," he said finally. "Um . . . how have you been?"

"You mean since you guys ditched us for Club Prom?"

He sighed. "Hey, *I* showed up. Remember?"

"Did you really expect me to leave Bailey, too, and come with you?"

"I don't know!" He lowered his voice, stepping closer to me. "Look, what Colin does is his thing. Don't hold it against me. What was I supposed to do?"

"Well," I said as a motorboat approached, puttering, "you could have been honest with me so I could be honest with her. That would have been a start."

"He's my best friend," he said. "And it was a crap situation. I'm sorry. What can I do to make it up to you?"

"Tell him to leave Bailey alone. It's not cool that he's calling her."

"I know." He slid his hands in his pockets. "But again, that's him. Anything else?"

I considered this, looking at the boat beside us, sails still fluttering. "Declare this thing unseaworthy so I don't have to go sailing?"

He cocked his head to the side. "It's a lake, though. Not a sea."

"Unlakeworthy, then," I said, giving him a smile. "Help a girl out."

"The thing is, I'm kind of here to help the guests get *on* the water, not hinder them," he said. "Sorry."

I shrugged. "It's okay."

"What about dinner?" he asked. "Tonight. Wherever you want, on me."

Suddenly I'd gone from no plans to being in high demand. But again, he was not the person I was hoping would be doing the asking. "I can't," I said. "I have a party to go to."

"For that girl Taylor?"

"You know about that?"

He nodded. "Rachel and Hannah are invited, too. Said we could come along."

"Bailey will be there," I warned him.

"I know. So does Colin. I think that's why he's going." He sighed again. "Let me give you a ride, at least?"

I bit my lip a second, considering this. Blake wasn't inherently a bad guy. As he'd said, *he* had showed up for Club Prom.

"Okay," I said, and he grinned so quickly I was immediately angry at myself for making yet another thing simple for him. "A ride. But if Colin's along, I'm out."

"He won't be," he promised. "He's covering the last couple of hours of a valet shift as a favor to someone. I'll text you when I get off work?"

I nodded, just as my dad and Tracy stepped back onto the dock, now carrying the basket. "Okay."

"Great," he said. "And have fun out there. Just remember the first rule of sailing: duck when they tell you to."

"Sounds like good advice for life in general," I cracked.

"You're funny," he told me, as if he'd forgotten this. He turned to Tracy, holding out a hand. "Ready to board?"

She climbed on, stepping down by the rudder, and I followed without an assist. My dad handed over the basket, which Tracy took and put in the small covered cargo area while he jumped on as well.

"Feels so small after weeks on *Artemis*," he said, gathering up the mainsheet as I found a seat on one of the flat cushioned areas. To me he added, "That was the boat we had in Athens. Forty-two-footer, slept six."

"This is nice, too, though," Tracy said, as if the boat might be offended. "Shall I go raise the front sail?"

"Yep," my dad replied, busy futzing with the rudder. "I'll get this one."

With that, they were in motion, her jumping up to walk down the boat's deck to the bow while he pulled the mainsail the rest of the way up. All around me, things were luffing, lines clanking, the side of the boat thumping against the dock with the waves. Even worse, over it all, I could hear my dad muttering, something he always did while sailing. I pulled my legs to my chest, trying to get small and out of the way, and looked out on the water.

"About ready?" Blake, up on the dock, asked.

"One second," my dad said from the center of the sunken part of the deck, right in front of me. "I'm having trouble with this centerboard."

"You just pull straight up and push down."

"I'm doing that," my dad replied. "But it won't—"

"Let me try," Tracy suggested, jumping down from the upper deck to where he was. "I think you just—"

"I've got it," he said, but she reached in anyway, and then he was grumbling again, both their hands on it, before it fell into the slot with a bang. "See? I had it. You have to let me do things if I say I am doing them."

"I would have," Tracy replied cheerfully, "but it seemed like you needed another pair of hands."

My dad grumbled again. Then to Blake he said, "Okay,

push us off. We're ready."

"Yes sir," Blake said, handing the line to Tracy, who shot me a smile. At least one of us was having fun. "Enjoy the lake!"

And with that, we were drifting toward the swimming area, the sails still ruffling, as my dad got himself by the rudder. Blake, on the dock, gave us an enthusiastic wave.

"All right," my dad said as we came close to bumping a float shaped like a huge toucan. He grabbed the mainsheet, pulling it tight, pushing the rudder over at the same time. "Ready about, hard a lee!"

Tracy bent her head down. I did not until the boom came swinging right for my face. We were now moving away from the shore at a fast clip, the sails suddenly full and creaking.

"Oh, yeah," my dad said, nodding up at the mast. "Feel that speed?"

"Watch out for the buoys," Tracy called out. "There's one right up here to starboard."

"I see it." My dad eased the rudder a bit to the right. To me he said, "Great, right? You can go up to the bowsprit if you want a better view."

"No thanks," I said.

"Keep the buoy on your right," Tracy told him. "There's a red one to port, about a hundred feet."

As we passed it, though, the traffic of swimmers and other boats began to clear out, leaving us an open path ahead. The water was glittering, sun bouncing off it, and

I let a hand dangle in as waves peeled off the sides. I had to admit it was nice, if you liked that sort of thing.

My dad pulled the mainsheet even tighter, leaning back as my side of the boat lifted up a bit. "Now we're cooking with grease! Emma, pull up that centerboard."

"What?" I asked.

"The centerboard." He pointed. "Grab it with both hands and pull straight up."

I scrambled over, grabbing for the centerboard handle. It didn't budge. Meanwhile, we were now moving what felt like even faster, the wind whipping in my ears.

"Pull straight up," he repeated.

"I am!" I replied, doing just that. Tracy got to her feet, coming over to join me. "It's stuck!"

"She's right," Tracy reported, after trying herself. "Maybe if we wiggle it again . . ."

"Emma, take the rudder and this mainsheet," he directed me. Which was even worse. Now I was steering?

"But—" I said.

"Take it." He stood, holding it out to me, and I grabbed it, moving into the spot where he'd been sitting, the mainsheet clutched in one hand. "Just steer us toward the other side, keeping all buoys on your left."

"Or right, if it's red," Tracy added.

"Is this thing broken?" my dad asked, his face flushed from his efforts to budge the centerboard. Tracy, trying to help him, pulled from the other side. Meanwhile, we were flying across the water, the sails I was holding full to the point of straining. It was scary enough even before I saw the Sunfish.

It was small, with an orange sail that had a smiley face on it. A guy and a kid, both in life vests, were sitting on it, staring at us openmouthed as we raced toward them.

"Um, Dad?" I said.

"Just keep us pointed in the direction I told you."

"But—"

Then, Tracy saw the Sunfish. "Emma! Come about!"

"What?" I said. On the Sunfish, the kid's eyes were wide, his dad now scrambling to get out of the way.

"Wait, what?" my dad said quizzically. Then he looked up. "COME ABOUT!"

But I didn't know how to do that. I didn't even really know what the centerboard was. And now we were almost at the Sunfish.

"Move!" my dad yelled. I did, jumping out of the way as he grabbed the rudder, pushing it away from us, hard. There was a jerk and the boom came swinging around: this time, I ducked. The mainsheet, caught on a knob between my dad and the mast, was pulled so tight I could see it straining. As I watched, helpless, as my dad tried to loosen it, we dipped even farther to the side, then farther still.

We're capsizing, I thought, panicked, but it was all happening so slowly it was surreal: the boat tilting, scooping up water, the sails all flapping, their lines thwacking.

"MAYDAY!" screamed the kid on the Sunfish, which

didn't really help anything.

"Hold on!" my dad yelled. "I'm getting her upright. Find life jackets!"

Tracy dove into the cargo hold, returning seconds later with three orange life preservers. As she handed me one, my dad cursing behind her, she said evenly, "Everything's fine."

Fine, I repeated to myself as I pulled it over my head, tightening the straps. We were upright again, although water was inside the boat now, rushing over my feet. That couldn't be good.

"Matthew?" Tracy asked. "Should I call someone?"

"Just give me a second," he said, wiggling the center-board, which finally came loose. "There. Okay. Now, let me just—shit, did we take in all this water?"

That wasn't encouraging. Trying not to panic, I turned, orienting myself with the shore by finding Mimi's again. There it was. There was the boat. And there were Bailey and Gordon, walking down the dock toward it. I didn't even think. I just yelled.

"BAILEY!"

At the sound of my voice, she turned her head, scanning the lake, then put a hand over her eyes.

"OVER HERE!" I yelled. "HELP!"

"Emma," my dad said sternly. "You never yell that on a boat unless it's an emergency."

"Matthew," Tracy said delicately, "there is quite a bit of water here."

She was right. What I'd thought had only been a bit

splashing around my toes was now up to my ankles. And we had a broken centerboard. But sure, yes, let's take our time asking for a hand.

Bailey was still looking in our direction, although clearly not sure what we needed. So I put my hands over my head, waving them wildly, the international sign for WE NEED RESCUING. She jumped into the boat, Gordon climbing in after her, and started the outboard.

"This is ridiculous," my dad said, kicking around the water at his feet as he went back to the rudder. "Who puts a useless knob right where it will catch the mainsheet?"

"Someone," Tracy said, still so calm. I don't know what we would have done without her. "I'm going to call the Club."

"You don't have to," I said. "Bailey's coming."

"Who?" my dad asked.

I pointed to where she was right then pulling away from the dock, already coming toward us. Gordon was in the bow.

"What happened?" she yelled once closer. Gordon waved excitedly.

"Just took in a little water," my dad replied.

"And broke the centerboard," Tracy added.

"Everyone have a life jacket?" Bailey asked, circling now to come up our other side. I gave her a thumbs-up. "Good. You want a tow back to the Club?"

"Just to that raft," Tracy replied as my dad grumbled something. "If you don't mind."

"Sure," she said. "Saylor. Throw me that."

She did another pass, coming up close, and I tossed her the line. Quickly, she tied it to the back of her motorboat, tugging to make sure it was tight.

"If you can pull up the centerboard, do it," she hollered as she took the motor again. "Less resistance. It'll be slow no matter what, though."

Personally, I didn't care. We could have been barely moving at all and it still would have been an improvement on the outing so far. My dad, however, looked glum as she started to the raft, tugging us slowly behind.

"We really could have just bailed out the boat on our own," he told Tracy. "We were fine."

"I know." She reached out, patting his leg. "But Emma was scared. This is better."

"I'm going to try to get you as close as I can!" Bailey yelled then from the motorboat. "Then I'll untie you so you can drift up alongside."

"Great," Tracy said. "Thank you!"

Bailey nodded, then turned back to face forward as we approached the raft. She and Gordon went just a bit past it, then cut the engine. A moment later, we floated right up. Tracy grabbed hold, jumping out, as Bailey undid our line, throwing it to her. Within seconds she had us tied up to a post, safe now. Scrambling down off the bow, I was never happier to feel deck planks beneath my feet. My dad, however, stayed on the boat, beginning to bail with a scoop he'd found in the cargo hold.

"Whew," Tracy said as Bailey came back around, pulling up to the other side. "That was exciting."

"That's one word for it," I said.

As soon as she could, Gordon hopped out as well, running over to give me a hug. I could feel her glasses poking my stomach.

"Hey," I said, smoothing a hand over her head. "How are you?"

"Good," she replied, into my shirt. "When are you coming back to Mimi's?"

This I didn't answer, although I saw Tracy heard it as well. Bailey, having tied up her own boat, now joined us. "What happened out there?"

"Combination of factors," Tracy told her. "You are a godsend, by the way. I'm Tracy."

"My stepmother," I said to Bailey. "Tracy, this is Bailey. And that's my dad."

"Hi," Bailey called out.

My dad lifted a hand in a wave, nodding at her. He looked sheepish, almost embarrassed, and I found myself both angry and sorry for him at the same time. God, I hated sailing.

"So," Bailey said as Tracy went over to join my dad. "Now you have to go to that party with me, right?"

"Because you gave us a tow?"

"Because I *saved* you. You owe me your life now." I just looked at her. "What? That's how this works!"

"I subscribe to none of these boat rules," I told her. "That said, I do thank you for the help. But I'd say that we're

304

actually even. You owed me, and now you paid up."

"I owed you? How do you figure?"

"Because you didn't even care I was leaving!" I said. "It was all about Colin this, and Colin that, and how you could use me to get to him. You didn't even say goodbye."

"You snuck out before the sun was even up!"

"Not true," I said flatly, and she sighed, rolling her eyes. "You could have found me. We're supposed to be friends."

"No," she said. "We're cousins."

Now I was exasperated. "That's different?"

"Of course it is!" She pushed her hair back from her face. "Look, Saylor. The first time we met, neither of us remembered. The second, you were about to get your ass kicked. We never had formalities, you and I. We're blood. It's messy. But we don't need goodbyes, because we're going to be stuck with each other forever. That's what family is."

This made me well up. And when I spoke, I actually started to cry.

"You hurt my feelings," I said, my voice breaking.

"I'm sorry." She bit her lip, then tucked a piece of hair behind her ear, lowering her voice. "Look, I know I've been stupid and crazy. I'm lucky that you've stuck with me. But you just don't understand what it's like to be really into someone so much that you make terrible choices. It's like . . . beyond my control, or something."

"He's going to hurt you again," I told her as my dad chucked the bailer into the cargo hold and hoisted himself onto the raft.

"Maybe," she said. "But this time, I'll only have myself to blame."

This was not altogether encouraging. I mean, why go into anything if you think there's a decent chance you'll get your heart broken? You don't risk what you don't want to, I supposed. Not that I could get into it, as my dad and Tracy were now joining us. She had the picnic basket over her arm.

"Who's hungry?" she asked.

"Me!" Gordon said. When Bailey shot her a look, she added, "I mean, only a little."

"You can have whatever you want from here," Tracy said, putting the basket down and opening it. "It's the least we can do since you saved us."

"We weren't in danger," my dad said. "It was just a little water."

Instead of responding, Tracy pulled out a bottle of wine, glistening with ice, fetching an opener from a side pocket. Deftly and quickly, she got out the cork and poured them each a plastic glass full before handing out thick bottled sodas to the rest of us.

"Wow," Gordon said, taking the bottle she handed her. "Is this a cola?"

"It's not Pop Soda," Bailey said, examining her own. She tipped it up, taking a taste. "Oh, my God. This is incredible. Where did you get it?"

"The Club made the basket for us," Tracy replied, digging farther in. "We have a cheese plate, too, as well as some sandwiches. Why don't I get everything out and we'll have a picnic?"

"Here?" my dad said. "I was hoping to get us to a beach spot away from everything."

"Well, we have the second part," Tracy said. "And I think we're better off not sailing the boat anymore today. I'll call the Club and have them tow it in."

"Oh, don't do that," Bailey said automatically, as I knew she would. "I can just pull you back."

"We're getting to go to the Club?" Gordon asked. "Can we see your hotel room?"

"No," Bailey told her. "We'll just get them safely to the dock. Then we need to get home to take Trinity to the doctor."

I turned to look at her. "Is everything okay?"

She nodded. "They just want to see her every week now, to check if she's dilated."

"What's *dilated*?" Gordon asked.

"Ready to have the baby," I explained. Then I looked up to see Dad and Tracy staring at me. I said, "She's due in like, a month."

"Who is this, again?" my dad asked, taking a cracker from the tray Tracy had unwrapped.

"My sister," Bailey told him. To me she said, "You can come back with us, come along to the appointment, and then we'll go to the party."

"Party?" my dad said.

"Our friend's birthday is tonight," Bailey explained. To me she said, "You can stay over with me, if you want. That way you don't have to get all the way back."

Already, she had a plan. I supposed I shouldn't have been surprised.

"Sounds great, but Emma is supposed to eat with us and our friends this evening," my dad said.

To me, this might as well have been a brick wall: my dad said no, end of topic. But I'd again forgotten about Bailey and the power of persuasion. Or cousinhood. Or something.

"Point taken," she said. "But the thing is, Saylor didn't really get to say goodbye, you know, when she moved over to be with you guys. It was just like, poof! And she was gone. Everyone's asking where she is. So can she come to something, you know, just for closure?"

"She's here for two weeks," my dad pointed out.

"I know! But it's already been a minute and we haven't heard from her. I mean, until now. Which was not the best of circumstances." Bailey smiled at Tracy, who immediately smiled back. "The longer she's at the Tides, the less inclined she'll be to make the trip all the way over to our side. I mean, the boys are *really* cute there."

Now my dad looked at me. I kept my face impassive, not wanting to get my hopes up, although it was hard not to show my relief when he said, "Okay, I suppose that's fine. But I want you to stay at the hotel, with us."

"Great! The party is at April's, which is just down from the Station," Bailey told him. "It starts at around seven. And we'll have Roo drive her back. He's got to leave early too, for work."

Okay. Now I *really* wanted to go.

"Roo?" my dad said. "Is that a person?"

"His real name is Christopher," I explained. "He's Chris Price's son."

"Price," my dad repeated. "Wait. Chris Price?"

"Yes," I said. Tracy raised her eyebrows, not following, and I added, "He was a friend of my mom's."

"Really." She smiled at me. "Well, I'm sure Matthew will agree, if he's a good driver and—"

"I don't know," my dad said. "Maybe it's not the best night for you to go out."

Roo was the deal breaker? That wasn't fair. "You just said it was okay," I protested.

He snapped his fingers. "Hey, I know. Why don't we go back during the day, when I can take you. Or we can drive together! Get in some practice. I'd like to see Mimi anyway."

"Mr. Payne," Bailey said, still in her best-behavior voice, "Roo's really reliable, if that's what you're worried about. He works for my mom doing night stocking at Conroy Market, and he has to be there at midnight. So he won't be drinking or anything."

I winced. Crap.

"Well, I would hope not," my dad said. "You are all underage, last I checked. Are you saying there will be beer at this party?"

"No," I said quickly. "But even if there was—"

"Saylor doesn't drink," Bailey finished for me. "Like, at all. You know that, right?"

Now, my dad looked at me. "She's not supposed to. She's seventeen."

"Dad, I can't control what other people do!" I said.

"If there's beer there, you're not going." When I opened my mouth, he repeated, "That's it. End of discussion."

There was that wall again, but this time, I could see it, not just sense its presence. Bailey, however, was not giving up that easily.

"It's your call, of course," she told my dad as Tracy, choosing wisely to stay out of this, bent back over the cooler and began to unpack sandwiches. "And we'll miss her. But for what it's worth, Saylor's a good girl, Mr. Payne. The kind of girl my mom wishes I was, if I'm honest."

"Her name is Emma," my dad told her.

I knew, in my rational mind, that he was just correcting her. I was Emma to him, I always had been. But as I heard him say this with such certainty, I could feel my temper rising. He could keep me from the other side of the lake. From Roo. But I would not let him take the weeks I'd already had, and the girl I'd been then, as well.

"It's Emma Saylor," I corrected him. "And I told you. They know me here as Saylor."

My dad looked surprised, although whether by this statement or my tone was hard to tell. For a moment we just looked at each other, both of us silent. "Why don't we have lunch," he said finally. "I'm starving."

I felt tears spring to my eyes as I turned, walking across to the other side of the raft so my dad wouldn't see. A moment later, Bailey stepped up beside me.

"You can always say you're going to the Pavilion and then come over," she said in a low voice. "We'll get someone to pick you up."

"Blake already offered me a ride," I said.

"Really?" Realizing she'd almost yelped this, she lowered her voice, shooting my dad a glance. "He's coming?"

"Taylor invited Rachel and Hannah, and they invited him," I told her.

A pause. Her unasked question boomed between us, loud to the point of deafening. I sighed.

"Colin, too," I added. Her face lit up. "But he's showing up later. I said I wouldn't ride with him, because I still hate him."

"Well, sure," she said easily, waving this off with one hand. "But seriously, now you really *have* to get there. I need you! It'll be the first time we've seen each other since Club Prom, and you know Jack and Roo will be all shitty to him, and—"

"Bailey?"

She stopped, mid-sentence. "Yes?"

"Do you remember when I said it seemed you only cared about Colin and not about me and my problems at all?"

"Oh, right." She exhaled. "Sorry. But look, if you want to go to the party, you can absolutely do it. Just tell them you're doing something else, take up Blake on the ride, and make it back before they check. No one is the wiser."

"This already sounds like a bad idea," I said.

"Why?" Which is what the planners of bad ideas always say. "Look. There's a movie outside on the beach at eight. Tell them you're going to that. It'll give you till at least ten. Oh, and make sure you mention the crappy reception on the Lake North side, so if he does demand you come home, you can say the message took a while to come through."

"How do you even know all this?"

She shrugged. "I like the Club. I may absorb any and all facts about it for that reason."

I looked back at my dad, who was now sitting with Tracy, eating as he sipped his wine. I turned back to the water. "What if he comes looking for me?"

"He's still jet-lagged, right? He probably won't even make it to ten."

This was clever, I had to admit: the last two evenings my dad and Tracy had both been out cold long before I turned in. "I'll try it," I said as my stomach grumbled. Turned out I was hungry after all. "But if I am coming, it's for me. Not for you and Colin."

"I know, I know," she said quickly. "Hey, do you think I can really have something to eat? I'm starving."

I nodded, getting to my feet and walking over to the basket, which Tracy pushed toward me, saying, "Help yourself. There are six sandwiches in there—I thought we might want extra."

I dug around a bit, finally finding two turkey and roasted red peppers as described by the custom, handwritten labels with the Club insignia. "Gordon," I called out. "Want a sandwich?"

"She doesn't like anything," Bailey warned me, taking one.

"We have turkey with red pepper," I told Gordon anyway. When she made a face, I turned to Tracy. "Are there chips or anything?"

"Um . . ." She dug around a bit. "No, just crackers and cheese, I'm afraid. But—"

Then I remembered something. "Hold on," I told Gordon, walking over to the sailboat and my bag, which I'd left on the seat. I pulled out the doughnut I'd taken from Nana's breakfast table, still wrapped in a napkin. "How about this?"

She looked over, expectations clearly low. Seeing the pastry, she brightened instantly. "You don't want it?"

I handed it to her. "All yours."

Grinning, she immediately took a bite, getting chocolate on her face. Chewing, she said, "Are you coming back to our side?"

With kids, you never wanted to make promises you couldn't keep. I'd learned that early, when my dad was often the bad guy, reining my mom in from her pie-in-the-sky promises. He wanted to protect me, I knew, and Emma would have let him. But Saylor, with her Calvander blood, had other ideas.

"Yeah," I told Gordon as we sat there. "I am."

EIGHTEEN

I met someone.

When my phone first beeped with this text, waking me from an afternoon nap, I just assumed it was from Bridget. Only she could declare a place hopelessly boring one day, only to find a dreamy summer romance the next. When I rubbed my eyes and looked at it again, I saw it wasn't her, but Ryan. My eyes widened.

What? How? Who is he?

She didn't respond for a bit, and it made me wonder if she'd already left that one spot where she had reception on the mountaintop. But then, finally, this.

Not he. A she.

I rubbed my eyes again, wanting to make sure I was reading this correctly. Even though these were only four words, and small ones at that, the message was big. I sat up, shaking my head to clear it. What I said now was important.

That's awesome. Details?

This time, she answered right away.

314

Her name is Liz. She's from Maine. Drama geek. But I think I might be too now?

This was almost as surprising as the fact she was crushing on a girl. **You?**

The tech stuff is actually really fun! Getting a crash course in a bunch of things, but I might want to do it at home, too? Anyway, she's the lead.

Wow, I wrote. **Picture?**

A pause. Then, with a beep, a shot of Ryan and the same girl with the olive skin and long, curly dark hair who'd had the army cap on in the shot she'd sent earlier. This time, though, it was just the two of them making faces, goofing for the camera, but even so, I could see something in my long-time friend that was different. A happiness, almost a glow.

She's pretty! You have a type, clearly, I wrote.

????

I laughed out loud. **Ry, she looks like Jasmine!**

A beep. Then another.

I am laughing so hard right now

Omg you're right!

Beep.

I didn't even make the connection!

Good thing you have me, I replied.

A pause. I tried to picture her on some steep hill, surrounded by scrub brush, away from camp to share this with someone. And she'd picked me, which felt like a gift.

I'm glad we're cool, she said now.

I am very cool, I agreed.

Not really, she replied. **But about this, yes.**

Then: **Don't tell Bridget, okay? I want to.**

Of course.

How about you? she wrote. **Found a prince (or princess) yet?**

I knew I should tell her about Blake, the prom, and everything else. But as she said this, I only thought of Roo.

Not yet, I typed back.

Beep. **Okay, I need to get off the mountain. Dress is tonight. Talk soon?**

Definitely.

A row of smiley faces appeared on the screen, followed by a bright red heart. I smiled, putting my phone back on the floor before stretching back out across the bed with a yawn. I couldn't say I was totally surprised by Ryan's news, as she'd always had a lack of interest when it came to Bridget's incessant chatter about boys. As one of her two closest friends, though, maybe I should have asked a few more questions. Instead, I'd just assumed she was straight because I was. What kind of a friend did that? I picked up my phone again and started a new text to her.

Hey I'm sorry

No, that wasn't right.

I didn't realize, I should have

Even worse.

The cursor just sat there, blinking. I looked out at the water outside my window. There was still time to come up with the right words, and probably better to say them face-to-face anyway. So I just sent her a heart back, and left it at that.

"So you'll be a senior this year," Mrs. Delhomme said to me as the waiter refilled her wineglass. A woman about Nana's age, she was deeply tan, with short white hair she wore so spiky it resembled plumage. "Do you have college plans?"

"We've taken a couple of tours while traveling," my dad said from my other side. "But she hasn't narrowed down a real list, have you, Emma?"

"Not yet," I said. "I want to keep my options open."

At this, my dad smiled. I'd never been great with other kids, but I could hang at any adult dinner party. The gift and curse of the only child.

"Options are good," Mrs. Delhomme said. "It's how we ended up with the Tides. The land went up for sale when Wilton was in college, and his dad snapped it up for what he called 'a rainy day.' Which is so funny, because I swear it never rains here! One reason why it's such a great place to get away."

I'd realized, over three courses and now dessert, that Mrs. Delhomme, like my grandmother, had a story for everything.

"Well, it's absolutely stunning," Nana said now from her seat, next to Tracy. "We're having just the best time. I can't thank you enough."

"Nonsense," said Mr. Delhomme, who was on my dad's other side. His wife was the talker of the two of them, while he spent most of the meal on the phone. "We're thrilled you finally came down to see us."

"And you're here for two weeks?" Mrs. Delhomme asked me.

I nodded, scooping up the last of my vanilla ice cream with chocolate sauce. "I was over in North Lake before this, with my mom's family."

"Really?" She smiled. "I didn't know she was from this area. Where do they live?"

"Her grandmother owns a motel called Calvander's," my dad replied before I could answer. "Just over the line."

"Such a lovely community, North Lake," she told him. "There's just so much history there, those families that have been coming for generations." She took a sip of her wine, leaving a lipstick mark on the glass. "It's what we really aspired to when we developed Lake North. That sense of tradition."

"That said, it's not someplace I'd want to spend my vacation," Mr. Delhomme added. "I'm a fan of modern comforts. The places there are a bit . . . antiquated."

I was pretty sure this was a burn. I couldn't help but say, "I think for some people it's just what they want."

My dad shot me a look. I pretended I didn't see.

"Coffee?" asked a voice right behind me. I turned to see a girl with two long braids I sort of recognized from a Campus party, holding a pot.

"No, thanks," I said, and she nodded, moving on.

"Are you going to the Pavilion this evening?" Mrs. Delhomme asked me. "I hear there is a great band playing.

Swing music, I believe. Sadly, my dancing days are behind me since my hip operation, but it might be fun for you."

Hearing this, I glanced at my dad, but now he was leaning into a conversation with Nana, nodding.

"I actually heard there might be a movie?" I said, a bit louder than necessary. "A friend mentioned it."

"Well, let's find out." She turned to the girl with the coffeepot. "Mila? Do you know anything about a movie here tonight?"

Mila smiled politely. "Absolutely. They do it on the beach. There's popcorn and everything. It's great."

"Oh, good," Mrs. Delhomme said. "You'll have a wonderful time."

"Did you say eight?" I asked Mila, making a show of checking my phone. "Because I don't want to be late."

"Go, go," Mrs. Delhomme, who probably needed coffee but was still downing her wine, said to me. "Grace, I'm giving your granddaughter permission to be excused. She's put up with our chatter all evening and wants to be with some people her own age."

"Oh, not at all," I told her. "I'm fine to stay."

"No, you go," Tracy said to me. When my dad looked at her, she said to him, "I mean, of course it's up to you, I just feel like she's been here all night with us . . ."

"Where is this movie, again?" he asked me.

"On the beach," I said, pointing out the back doors. "It will be over at ten."

"I'd go," Tracy said, stifling a yawn, "but this jet lag

is killing me. I'll be lucky to make it home without falling asleep on the way."

Bailey was good. I had to give her that.

My dad, however, was still thinking. Or pretending to, if only to torture me. Finally he said, "Okay, fine. But I want you home by midnight. And answer your phone if I call."

"Will do," I said, getting to my feet before he could give me any other addendums. "My reception isn't great on the beach, though, just so you know."

"Oh, it's horrible everywhere on this side," Mrs. Delhomme said to the table. "We're working on a tower. If we can get the permits."

A good time to make my escape. "Thank you so much for dinner," I said to the Delhommes, then walked over and kissed Nana's cheek before waving at Dad and Tracy and heading for the door. Outside in the hallway, I checked my phone. I had three messages from Bailey.

I'm here.

Where are you?

Remember to mention the bad reception!!!

I couldn't handle the nagging, so I turned it off again. Then I went into the bathroom, which had neatly stacked real hand towels, as well as complimentary lotion and perfume dispensers (ALL PRODUCTS AVAILABLE AT CLUB GIFT SHOP!). Five minutes later, smelling like honeysuckle rose, I brushed my hair, put on some lipstick, and took a deep breath. I was going to do this, consequences be damned. Although if I chose to believe Bailey, there might not be any at all. But how often was she right?

Just as I went to push the door open, it swung back the other way. I stepped back just as Mila, she of the coffeepot and braids, came in, bumping right into me.

"Oh, sorry!" she said, jumping back as the door shut behind her with a quiet swish. "I totally wasn't looking where I was going."

"It's fine," I said, stepping to the side so she could get around me and to a stall. As she stepped inside one, I reached to push the door open again, but then I heard her voice.

"You're friends with Blake and Hannah, right?"

"Um . . . yeah," I said. "I am."

"Then you should go to the party in North Lake tonight instead of the movie. It will just be all families there anyway."

"Oh," I said. "You think?"

The toilet flushed. A moment later, she emerged, walking to the sink. "Totally. Anyway, everyone's going to this party either now or when they get off work. I can give you the address, if you want. I know that guy Hannah's all into is going to be there."

"Hannah has a boyfriend?" I asked.

"Well, they're not there yet, but that's her goal," she said, turning off the faucet and picking up a hand towel. "He's cool. And really cute. His name's Roo."

Hearing this, I felt like I'd been punched. I'd only been gone two days: How had this happened? "I know Roo," I said quietly. "I didn't realize they were talking."

"Like I said, it's early days." She glanced at me through

the mirror. "She and Rachel are going over there pretty soon. Maybe text them and grab a ride? You won't regret missing the movie. I promise."

"Maybe I'll do that," I said, inching slowly toward the door again. "Thanks for the heads-up."

"Anytime," she replied. "See you over there!"

Back out in the Club lobby, I suddenly felt tired, the weight of the whole day—arguing with my dad, the sail— hitting me. Did I really now want to go all the way to North Lake, risking serious punishment, just to see Roo with another girl? Sure, I'd always have Bailey, but if things went her way, she'd be caught up with Colin. Maybe it was just better to take this enforced separation as a sign.

"Saylor! Over here."

I turned to see Blake just inside the doors of the Club, waving at me. On the other side of the glass door behind him was his car. Hannah was in the front seat, looking effortlessly gorgeous as usual, Rachel in the back. Great.

"Hey," I said, walking over to him. "What's going on?"

"You mean, other than assuming you'd bailed on me?" When I just looked at him, he added, "You didn't answer any of my texts."

Whoops. I pulled my phone out, powering up, then was immediately hit with a series of alerts. "Huh," I said. "According to this, you'll pick me up at eight just outside the lobby."

"Really?" he said. "Imagine that."

I smiled. "Sorry. Long day. So long, in fact, that I'm

322

thinking maybe—"

"Nope," he said flatly.

Stopped in mid-sentence, I paused before trying to speak again. "It's just, we were out on the water today, I'm really—"

"Nope."

"Nope what?"

"Nope," he said, "you're not going to bail on me right in front of my face. This ride, and party, is my apology. You accepted it. Therefore, you have to come."

I looked out at the car again. Hannah had the mirror visor down and was checking her lipstick, while Rachel laughed at something in the back seat. "I don't know," I said. "I'm not sure it's my thing."

"It's your *side*," he said. "Come on."

Sighing, I went, following him through the doors, which swung open automatically, and outside, where the valets were running around as cars came and went. When Rachel saw me, she squealed.

"Oh, good, you're coming!" she yelled. "Let's go!"

This enthusiasm was seconded by Hannah, who reached around for me once I was in the back seat and gave me a sloppy hug that smelled like beer. "*So* glad you're here," she said, her voice hot in my ear. "This is the night it all happens. I'm sure of it!"

She sounded so excited. But if she meant her getting with Roo, I wasn't.

Blake slid behind the wheel, starting the engine, then beeped at the valets as we pulled around the circle in front of the Club. Just as we pulled out on the main road, I caught a quick glimpse of a white screen set up on the beach beyond the pool. This is probably a bad idea, I thought. But then we were accelerating, the wind picking up through the windows, and it was done.

"This neighborhood is like a maze," Blake complained as we crept down yet another street, looking for house numbers. "And all the houses are so *tiny*."

Hearing this, I felt a flare of annoyance. They weren't that small, actually. I guess it just depended what you were comparing them to.

"Roo says it's a white house with a carport," Hannah said, reading off her phone's screen. "And that he'll come out so we can see him if necessary."

This was the fifth time she'd mentioned his name in the short trip over. And yes, I'd been counting.

"I swear, we've already been down this road," Blake muttered as we turned onto another dark stretch. "Unless it's at the very—"

"Roo!" Hannah yelled. Six. "There he is."

It was indeed him, standing at the end of a cul-de-sac right by a wooden staircase, waving at us. He had on jeans and a white T-shirt that said NORTH LAKE TIGERS, and seeing him, I felt my stomach drop. He couldn't really be into Hannah. Could he?

"Where should I park?" Blake yelled out his window.

"Anywhere up here's fine," he replied. "The driveway's already packed."

Blake pulled up next to a mailbox. He hadn't even cut the engine before Hannah was out of the car, slamming her door behind her.

"*So* ready to blow off some steam," she said to Roo, and I watched his face for signs he was equally enamored with her. He *was* smiling, but then he always smiled. "We brought beer."

"Great," he said as she gave him a hug. Don't, don't, I thought, surprising myself with how much I really did not want him to return this gesture, even as he gave her what seemed to be a quick, friendly squeeze in return. "I wish I could drink it. But I'm sure someone will be happy to."

"Do you really have to work?" Hannah said, cocking her head to the side.

"Money won't make itself," he replied cheerfully as Blake got out of the car, followed by Rachel. I was dragging my feet, enjoying being hidden in the dark of the back seat, like as long as I stayed put, this whole scene wasn't happening. Then Blake was popping the trunk, though, so Roo came over, lifting out the cases of beer there. Just as he was about to shut it again with a bang, he looked through the window and saw me. His eyes widened.

"Saylor?" he asked.

"Hi," I said, opening my door and getting out. "How are—"

This was as far as I got, however, before it happened: Blake, who'd been just off to my side, came over and took my hand, easily sliding his palm against mine and intertwining our fingers. And for some stupid reason, I didn't stop him. I just stood there, like on the boat earlier, watching it happen like I was helpless against it, too.

Roo noticed. It was clear in the way his eyes narrowed on our now-joined hands, quickly processing what this meant. Then, the beers in his arms, he turned back to Hannah. "Let's go," he said. "It's this way."

They started down a wooden staircase that led off the cul-de-sac, with Rachel right behind them. Down below, I could see people were crowded on the small porch, the steps, and the dock, their voices rising up to us. I suddenly remembered Blake was holding my hand.

"What are you doing?" I asked, finally coming to my senses and pulling it back. "This is an apology. Not a date."

"Oh, come on," he said. I just looked at him. "Fine. Kill me for trying. I had a chance, I took it."

"Well, we're not like that anymore," I told him. "Understood?"

"Yeah, sure. You just wanted a ride. I get it."

"That's what you offered!"

"Because I was trying to get back with you!"

I stopped walking, halfway down the stairs. Roo, Rachel, and Hannah had already gotten to the porch, their arrival (or that of the beer) celebrated with a burst of applause. "Why?"

He just looked at me. "What do you mean?"

"Why?" I repeated. Like his "nope" earlier, I wasn't backing down. "*Why* do you want to be with me?"

"I don't know," he replied, frustrated. "Why wouldn't I want to be with you?"

"You can't answer my question with a question. Try again."

He sighed, leaning back against the rail behind him. "What do you want me to say?"

"I want you to explain why you want to hold my hand. Why you want to date me. Why this"—here, I ran a hand through the air between us, to him, me, then back to him again—"is appealing to you."

"Well, right now, it's not," he said. I made a face. "What? Look, I'm an assertive person, okay? I go with the flow. And the flow treats me well. So what's not to like?"

I could not even begin to understand this. Yes, I'd been a person who'd benefited also from the actions of others: because of my dad and his hard work, I lived in a nice house and basically wanted for nothing. But people weren't things you just came across. They had to mean more.

"Colin liked Bailey. Bailey brought me along. And you dated me because I was there," I said to Blake. "This isn't a relationship, it's a coincidence."

"Who wants a relationship?" he asked.

Me, I thought, surprising myself. But not with someone who's been given everything. How could you value something if you never fought for it?

But what had *I* fought for, before this summer? All the

things I didn't want to do, a battle of prevention: driving, thinking too much about my mom, keeping the world as I knew it small, safe, and organized. Then I'd come here, where I was thrown in with little notice and no manual, forced to figure it out on my own. North Lake had changed me. And I wasn't sure I wanted to change back.

And then, of course, there was Roo. Who'd recognized me when I felt surrounded by strangers that first day. Who'd picked a dress that made me feel beautiful, made me laugh and think and, most of all, remember. He was right there in that house below us, nearby once again, and I should have been able to make this my moment to return the favor, find him and say everything I hadn't that night of Club Prom. *Shoulda done it*, Bailey had said. And for every moment since, I'd known she was right.

"I don't want to be part of your flow," I said to Blake now. When he opened his mouth to reply, I continued, "And you shouldn't want that either. Life is big and huge and scary. But you have to go and take your part of it. There's a reason the saying is 'Seize the day,' not 'Wait for it to come along at some point.'"

"Hold on, so you want me to seize you? I just did! I took your hand."

"But I'm not the one for you!" I said, exasperated. "I'm just the one who's right here."

He was quiet for a second. "So . . . are you saying you don't even want to walk in with me? You want, you know, me to wait out here until you go in?"

"No," I said. "We walk in together, as friends. Because we are. Right?"

"I hope so," he said quietly, and I could tell he meant it. Then he gestured for me to go ahead on the stairs, and I did, hearing him follow in the next beat behind me.

April's house was right on the water, with a great view of the lake. As we approached, I could see her through the window, adjusting some twinkling lights in the kitchen. The party planner at work.

"It's my BIRTHDAY!" Taylor, who was sitting on a cooler by the house's front door, wearing a light-up crown with feathers that said PRINCESS—slightly crooked—and only one shoe, said when she saw us.

"I heard," I told her, bending down to give her a hug. "Happy birthday."

"Thank YOU!" She looked at Blake. "Who's this?"

"Blake," I said, stepping back so he could say hello. "He works over at the Club."

"Blake from the Club," she said cheerfully. "You want a beer?"

"Sure," he replied. She slid off the cooler, opening it and taking out a can, which she handed him. Then she looked at me. "Saylor?"

We weren't even in the party proper yet, still outside. But through the screen door ahead of me, I could see Vincent, messing with a speaker up on the fireplace mantel. Two girls dancing together, laughing. And in the kitchen, Hannah sitting on the counter, Roo right in front of her. She was saying something, gesturing widely, as he listened, a smile on his face.

"Sure," I said, keeping my eyes on them. "I'll take one."

"You don't drink," Blake said as Taylor handed me a dripping can as well.

"Not usually," I said, popping the tab. "But it's her birthday."

"Hell YEAH it is!" Taylor yelled, hopping up and holding out her own beer to tap mine. "Let's drink to THAT."

She did, and I followed suit, even as I felt Blake's eyes on me. While the beer was cold, it still tasted awful, making me wince as I swallowed it down. Still, with a last look at Roo and Hannah—or what I hoped would be—I forced another one. Then one more.

"We should dance," I said to Taylor.

"Um, YEAH," she replied, keeping up the streak of shouting every few words. "I have a playlist I made just for this moment. Seriously! Let me just—hey, Vincent! Don't you dare pair your phone with that speaker. I'm not kidding!"

With that, she was opening the door to cross the floor to the fireplace, pulling her own phone from her pocket as she did so. Vincent, busted, slipped out the back door, leaving what I was pretty sure was, yep, heavy metal blasting behind him.

"Hey," Blake said to me as we came inside. "I know I'm not your boyfriend, but watch it with the beer. It can hit you fast when you're not used to it."

"I'll be fine," I said, taking another sip. "I'm only having this one."

And that was the plan. Just a few sips to loosen me up and take my mind off Roo and Hannah, as well as my dad. But as the alcohol began to hit, blurring the edges of this stressful day, and Taylor, after cursing Vincent loudly for a moment, put on a song with a whirly, pumping beat that Ryan, Bridget, and I loved, I was already thinking how another one would have to make me feel better. This would probably be the last party I'd attend on this side this summer. Or ever. I might as well make it one to remember.

"Isn't this AWESOME?" Taylor shouted in my ear a little while later. We'd started dancing just by ourselves, then pulled in the other two girls who'd been moving solo as well as April, who was now doing the bump with vigor. The room suddenly felt packed with sweaty, moving bodies, the music barely audible, even though the speaker was right there.

I nodded—it was too hot to speak—taking a swig from my third (fourth?) beer before pressing it to my temple. The taste wasn't bothering me anymore: really, nothing was. There was just the music and Taylor swaying in front of me, barefoot now, her own hair sweaty and sticking to her neck. I closed my eyes, thinking of my dad on the boat that day, shouting out orders to me when he knew I hated sailing. Telling Bailey my name was Emma, not Saylor.

"Whoa," I heard someone say, just as I realized I was stumbling and had bumped into the person behind me. I opened my eyes, but still felt dizzy as I stopped where I was to get my bearings. So hot. So loud. I pressed my can against my face again, but it was warm. And empty.

"There you are," said another voice from behind me, but this one was familiar. That said, I didn't realize it was Bailey specifically until I turned around to see her there. She had on a black maxidress, her hair pulled back, silver hoops hanging from her ears. "I've been looking all over!"

"We're dancing," I said, grabbing her hand. I went to spin, still holding it, feeling a flush creep up my neck—it was so hot—but then got tangled as she just stood there, elbow rigid, looking at me. "What?"

"Are you drunk?" she asked.

"No," I said automatically. "I just had one. Or two."

"Still two more than I've ever seen you drink," she replied as I dropped her hand, moving into a shimmy as Taylor did the same beside me. "Let's go get some air."

"I'm fine," I said, making a point to e-nun-ci-ate this carefully. "I'm just having fun, like you have basically every time we've gone out."

"Yes, but that's me," she said, eyeing me as I stumbled. Wait, *was* I drunk? Suddenly I wasn't so sure. "Saylor. Come on. Now."

She sounded strict, like a mother. Although not my mother. If anyone could understand blowing off a little necessary steam, it was Waverly. "I'm fine," I told her. "Since when are you the party police?"

"Since I found you drunk for the first time, like, ever,"

she said. And then, without another word, she grabbed my wrist and started to literally drag me toward the back door. Immediately, I resisted, surprising myself, yanking my arm from her. A bit too hard, as it turned out, because it flung back behind me, whacking Taylor, who was doing some low-down twist move, right in the face. I felt her eyebrows.

"OUCH!" she yelled, over the music and all the noise.

"Oh, sorry," I said, "I didn't mean—"

"Saylor." Bailey had me again, this time so tightly I knew there was no point in fighting her. "Let's go."

I went, although I told myself it was my choice. When we neared the kitchen, where Roo and Hannah were, I tried to stop, wanting to collect myself. But the momentum worked against me, suddenly and surprisingly, and just like that, I was down.

"Oh, shit," Bailey said as I hit the floor. In the next beat, a wave of dizziness hit me, just as I was trying to get up again. Maybe better to stay where I was, I thought. The tile was actually kind of cool. Above me, I heard Bailey say, "Can I get a little help here?"

"What's wrong?" a boy's voice said. Roo. I needed to get up. Off the floor. I was on the floor, right?

"Drunk," Bailey said flatly. "Help me get her outside."

After all of Bailey's dragging me and literal arm twisting, what happened next was smooth and quick: I felt hands beneath my arms, and then I was on my feet. But only briefly, because they didn't seem to want to hold me. Luckily, I collapsed into someone's side. Oh, right. Roo.

"Careful there," he said, locking an arm around my waist. "One foot in front of the other."

"I'm fine," I said.

"I know." Then, loudly, he said, "Make way, you guys! Coming through!"

Somehow, we got to the back door. I wasn't sure of the specifics because I kept my eyes closed, due to the fact that this was super humiliating. Also, I was suddenly feeling a tiny bit sick. I just need air, I told myself, and a second later, like a wish granted, I felt myself surrounded by it.

"Where are we going?" Roo asked before pausing briefly to scoop up my legs so he was carrying me outright. "Just on the porch?"

"Let's go down to the dock," I heard Bailey say. She sounded far away. "Just so we have some space to think."

At first when I got outside, I could hear voices and music, the party still close by. Now, though, we were moving away, all of it condensing to a distant hum beyond Roo's footsteps. Finally, he put me down.

"Ah," I said, spying the water nearby and reaching out to dip my hand in. Again, though, I misjudged my own weight and felt myself starting to tumble, until someone grabbed me by my hair. "Hey, OUCH that hurts!"

"Too bad," Bailey said, pushing me into a sitting position. Then she bent down in front of me. "What are you trying to do? Drown while we watch?"

"I'm hot," I moaned.

In response, she dumped the cup she was holding,

scooping up some water, and flung it on me. I went from sweaty to soaked in seconds.

"Hey!"

"Sober up," she commanded. "I don't like you this way."

"Bailey, come on," Roo said, and from the sound and direction of his voice, I realized what I was leaning against was actually his legs. I turned, looking at them in the light thrown from the house, as he said, "She can't help it. She won't even remember this."

"She will, because I won't let her forget."

"How many times have I pulled you out of parties?" he asked her. "Have a little compassion."

"I'm compassionate," she said, sounding just about anything but. "I just don't understand how she got like this."

"I'm guessing it was the beer," he told her, deadpan. "How many have *you* had?"

"Yes, but," she replied, "I'm not lying on the dock on my back, staring at your calves."

I laughed. Oh, wait, she meant me. I said, "What are these, anyway?"

A pause. Then Bailey said, sounding exhausted, "What's what, Saylor?"

"These," I said, pointing at the numbers on the back of Roo's leg. "I saw them the first day, on the boat. And I've been wondering ever since."

"Nautical coordinates," he told me.

"For what?"

"For the lake's center," he said.

I looked at the numbers again, which were blurring slightly. "So you can find it, always."

Roo gazed down at me. "That's right."

"Oh, Jesus," Bailey said. "I'm going to get her some water."

I heard her walking away, the deck bouncing with each step. And then it was just Roo and me and the lake, gurgling under the dock between us.

"She's mad," I observed.

"More like worried," he said as he took a seat. "Funny thing about always being the one out of control. You tend not to like it when other people are."

"I am not out of control," I stated. "I just had a few beers."

"Right," he said. "Of course."

Sitting there, though, I suddenly felt very fuzzy-headed, not to mention tired. And, apparently, honest, as I heard myself say, "Do you know that, at home, I always have to organize everything? My closet, the mail on the counter, even my toothbrush and toothpaste on the shelf. It doesn't matter what it is. It's, like, I can't control it. I've done it for as long as I remember. I was doing it when I first got here."

When he answered, he didn't sound like he found this weird or notable, just saying, "Really."

I nodded. "But then I started cleaning rooms, and hanging out with you guys, and I don't have to do it so much anymore. It's like this place is changing me."

He looked over. "That's good, right?'

"I guess. But now I'm gone and everything's different.

It's just going to come back."

"You're not gone," he said. In the dark, behind my closed eyes, his voice was all I could hear, like a lifeline I was still gripping, keeping me conscious. "It's just the other side of the lake."

"It's so different," I murmured, curling into him. "I miss you."

I mean, I miss it here, I thought, realizing too late what I'd said instead. But then it was fading, too, and I couldn't reach it to take it back.

"It's okay, Saylor," he said, smoothing a hand over my head. "Just rest."

But with this touch, this contact, I suddenly wanted to say something else, even as I knew I was fading. "I didn't know you were into Hannah. I wish—"

A pause, but maybe just my sense of time. Then he said, "You and Blake were holding hands."

"That was all him," I said. "I had no idea. I came here to see you."

It felt good, I realized, being this honest. At least now, whatever else happened, he would know. That day at his house, he'd said I'd always been part of his story. Now he would know that whatever happened from here, he, too, was in mine.

The dock was bouncing again as someone approached. So tired, I thought, closing my eyes. I was just about to drift off, leaning into his shoulder, when I heard Bailey speak.

"Okay. So we have a problem."

NINETEEN

"Just do me a favor. Don't puke again."

I blinked. I was in an enclosed space, and moving, by the feel of it. Also sitting on something very cold. But how did I get here?

"I threw up?" I managed to say. The thought of doing it was bad enough, but not realizing? I was horrified.

"Yep," Bailey said. She was beside me, one hand thrown across my midsection like a makeshift seat belt. "Luckily, Roo gave me that bucket, so you didn't make a mess."

I looked down at my lap: there was a plastic sand pail between my legs, the word TIPS APPRECIATED written on it in black marker. Inside was a bit of liquid I chose not to examine closely, instead turning again to my surroundings. White. Metal. Rattling and in motion. And my ass was *freezing*.

"Wait," I said. "Are we in the Yum truck?"

"Yep," I heard Roo say, from somewhere to my right. "And on our way to the Tides."

The Tides? Oh, shit. My dad. "What time is it?"

"Eleven," Bailey said, handing me my phone. "Which would be an hour after your father first texted asking you how the movie was."

Movie? Oh, right. I grabbed the phone from her, then opened up my texts. My dad had sent his first message at 9:58.

How's the movie? Want company? Can't sleep!

Then, at 10:05.

Hello? Are you getting this? Let me know please.

I was starting to panic now. I gave a sideways look at the TIPS APPRECIATED pail, swallowing down a bad taste in my mouth. 10:21.

Concerned. Coming down to find you.

"Oh, shit," I said. I thought I might puke again.

"No joke," Bailey replied, craning her neck to look ahead, out the windshield. "Where are we now? I can't see anything from back here."

"Still in North Lake," a girl replied. "But we're getting close to the line."

Oh, that's Hannah, I thought as I recognized her voice. A beat. Then I remembered. Everything. Oh, God. Shame went over me like a wave.

It's so different, I'd said. I miss you, I'd said. I wish, I'd said.

Panicked, I made myself turn my head and look at Roo, who was bent over the steering wheel, squinting in the headlights of an oncoming car. How could I take it all back, now, after the fact? I'd been drunk, I didn't know what I was saying.

But I did. And I'd meant every word.

"Okay," Bailey said, pulling me back from this crisis to the other one at hand. "Now, the key is what you say to him first. It sets the precedent for the entire incident."

"Incident?" I said.

"Well, he is pissed and, to use his word, concerned," she said, gesturing to my phone. "Which means that once he sees you are safe, he's just going to be pissed."

"I'll tell him I didn't have reception."

"And that might work," she agreed, "if he does not see you arrive in this ice cream truck but instead finds you somewhere on the beach, ostensibly just finishing the movie."

"Movie's been over for an hour, though," Hannah added from the front seat. I felt surprised by the rush of anger I felt toward her. What was wrong with me? "So you might want another plan."

"How about this," Bailey said as we went over a pothole, the entire truck rattling. "You were at the movie, then you bumped into Hannah and went to her place for a bit, where you had one beer, immediately regretted it, and returned to the Club, but the movie was over, so you just sat down on the beach to contemplate your bad choices."

"This sounds like something we'd watch in health class," Roo observed.

"Then come up with something better!" she barked at him.

340

"Okay, you don't have to—" Roo stopped talking, suddenly, and I saw him look out his window. "Oh, crap. Pit stop ahead, at the market."

"What?" Bailey asked. "We don't have time for that!"

"We also don't have a choice," he replied, slowing down now and starting to take a left turn, widely, which almost threw both Bailey and me off the cooler and onto the truck floor. "It's your mom with Gordon. She's waving us over."

"My mom?"

We stopped with a jerk. The lights in the back of the truck immediately came on, bright all around me, and I caught a glimpse of the contents of that bucket for real. Ugh.

"Thank goodness!" I heard Celeste say. She had to be standing outside in the lot. "My arm's about to fall off from waving."

"I'm coming right back to work," Roo explained. "Just have to drop someone off. Everything okay?"

"Oh, yeah," Celeste said. Beside me, Bailey opened her own purse, pulling out some breath mints and tossing a handful into her mouth. Suddenly everything smelled like wintergreen. "I just saw you coming and Gordon really needs a YumPop."

"What's Gordon doing up this late?" Bailey hissed to me, cracking her mints in her teeth.

"She's up late," Roo noted to Celeste.

"Joe and Mimi went to Bly County for the night and Trinity's too grumpy to be around anyone," Celeste explained. "Poor Gordon, she's tired and bored. I've been

341

texting Bailey and Jack, but of course neither of them are answering their phones."

"Can you turn this light off?" Bailey whisper-hissed from beside me. Roo, still focused on Celeste, shook his head almost imperceptibly.

"I think we can manage a YumPop," he said, pulling the truck's brake and getting up. "What flavor, Gordon?"

My head was hurting now, and I was pretty sure I had never in my life been so thirsty. Gordon's voice sounded very small as she replied, "Chocolate?"

"Move," Bailey said to me, giving me a shove as Roo came toward us, pointing at the cooler. I started to slide down, then fell instead, landing with a bang on the floor. Ouch.

"What was that?" I heard Celeste say.

"Just some junk falling," Roo told her, shooting me an apologetic look. "Chocolate, you said?"

"Oh, crap," I heard Celeste say. "That's the store phone. Can you just give it to her, and I'll see you when you get back? And if you hear from Bailey, tell her to call me and that she's in trouble."

"What?" Bailey whispered. "What did I do?"

"You're hiding from her," I pointed out from the floor. She ignored me.

"Chocolate!" Roo announced, pulling a wrapped cone from the cooler. "I'll bring it to—"

Before he could finish this thought, however, his driver's-side door creaked open and Gordon stuck her head in, looking down into the truck at us. "Saylor? Are you okay?"

"She's fine," Bailey told her. "And keep it down. You didn't see us, you hear?"

Solemnly, Gordon nodded. She was still looking at me. "Are you sick?"

I shook my head, but even as I did so, I felt it: shame, thick and hot, creeping up from my chest to my face. Here I was, in front of the only person who probably would ever think I was perennially awesome, drunk and sprawled on the floor of an ice cream truck with what I was realizing was probably vomit on my shirt. It was a horrible impression to make on anyone, but especially a kid. They were supposed to be protected from things like this, their world consisting only of chocolate YumPops, swimming, and a warm, safe place to sleep at night. Not this. I knew how scary it could be. Because I'd been that kid.

"I'm fine," I said to her, but even to my ears my voice sounded rough, uneven. "I'm just not feeling great right this second."

"Now take your ice cream and go act like you never saw us," Bailey added as Roo walked back up to the front, handing it to her. "Can you do that?"

"Yes," Gordon said. She was still watching me.

"Good girl," Roo told her. "See you when I get back, okay?"

Gordon nodded as Roo took his seat, cranking the engine again. The lights went out. But I could still see her, the market lit up behind, as we drove away.

"What's the over-under of her telling Celeste everything

anyway?" Roo asked as we pulled out onto the main road.

"About even," Bailey told him, hopping up on the cooler again. "But either way, she'll wait until she's done with the ice cream. So step on it."

He did, the engine rattling as we accelerated. From the floor, I watched the Lake North sign approach in the windshield, then disappear over us. I couldn't get Gordon's face out of my mind. Luckily, Bailey was not so distracted.

"So we'll drop you at the Pavilion," she was saying. "From there, you go back to the Tides and say you've just been out enjoying walking and thinking and had no reception. Okay?"

"Right," I said. I sat up, locating my purse, then dug through until I found my hairbrush and an elastic. My head was pounding as I pulled my hair up in a high ponytail, securing it, then accepted the mints that Bailey was already holding out to me.

"Don't make any rookie mistakes," she said. "I'm sensing this is your first time doing this."

"What? Being drunk in an ice cream truck?" I asked.

"Trying to explain yourself out of a punishment," she corrected me. "The most common screw-up is giving too much detail or information. Stick to facts in simple statements."

"Like five sentences," I said.

She looked at me. "What?"

"Five sentences," I explained. She still looked clueless. "What you say to introduce yourself, you boiled down to the basics. It's a lake thing."

"Says who?"

"Roo," I told her.

"It's true," he said from the front seat.

"I have *never* heard of that," Bailey said. "But sure, great. Five sentences. Keep it short and sweet. Like, 'I went to the movie. I saw a friend. We had a beer. I felt bad about it. So I've been out here thinking.'"

"Wow," Roo said, and I looked at the rearview mirror just as he did, our eyes meeting. To me he said, "She's a natural."

"Went to a movie, saw a friend, had a beer, felt bad, been thinking," I repeated. "Got it."

"Tears are helpful, too," Hannah added. "I always cry when I get busted. Sometimes the sympathy vote is all you have going for you."

"Not *too* many tears, though," Bailey warned me. "If you're blubbering, it just pisses them off more. Or it does Celeste. I don't know your dad, though."

When it came to this sort of thing, I didn't really know him either: I hadn't ever had to lie to him about where I'd been or what I was doing. There'd been no need to until now. Which was probably just what he would say, I was sure, if none of this worked.

"Getting close," Roo reported, slowing for a stop sign. He looked at Hannah. "You want to hop off at Campus?"

"Can you come back by and hang out before you go to work?" she asked. "We can watch a movie or something."

He glanced at the clock on the console. "Probably not. Sorry."

She bit her lip, clearly unhappy. "I thought we were

hanging out tonight. I mean, you invited me to this party—"

"Everyone was invited," Bailey said under her breath. But I could hear her. "Not just you."

"—and then, when I get there, all you do is take care of Saylor and leave early." She sighed. "I just don't understand."

"Hannah." Roo looked at her. "She was in over her head and we're friends. What do you want me to do?"

"Let someone else take over," she replied, nodding at Bailey.

"I'm kind of in this, now," he pointed out.

"Yeah, but you don't have to be," she said. "I mean, you don't have to save everyone just because you lost your dad."

Silence. Except for the truck rattling, the sound of which also seemed quieter after this statement.

"This is not about my dad," he said evenly. "Just trying to help out."

"Almost there," Bailey reported, and I looked up to see she was right: the Tides and the Club were lit up brightly just ahead. "You want to hop out, Hannah?"

"Fine," she said, sounding like she didn't. She looked at Roo. "Stop by for a second on your way back, okay? Just to talk."

"I have to work," he said.

"You always have to work!" she said as she jumped out, her feet hitting the ground with a slap. "God. What happened to summer being about having fun?"

Apparently, this was a rhetorical question, as she was walking away. As Roo watched her, Bailey said, "It's called real life. She should look into it."

"Let's go," Roo said, pulling away from the curb. "The Pavilion is just up here."

He was right: I could see it approaching, all the lights on, although there was no longer anyone there. How late was it now?

"We'll just pull up and you hop out," Bailey told me as Roo took a turn that sent me sliding toward the other side of the truck. "Then start walking toward the hotel. Remember to look regretful and contemplative."

"Right," I said, feeling a shot of adrenaline wake me up. I could do this. Five sentences. The truck suddenly slowed considerably.

"Wait, this isn't the Pavilion," Bailey said, squinting out the back window. "This is . . . Roo, what are you doing?"

"Stopping," he replied.

"Why?"

But then, we spotted the red and blue lights. LAKE NORTH SECURITY, it said on the car parked just a few hundred feet ahead, a man in uniform standing beside it. Next to him, phone to his ear, was my dad. I broke into a sweat.

"Oh, shit," Bailey said, which didn't help.

"Is that the police?" I asked.

"Worse," she replied. "It's Later Gator."

"What?"

"Crocodile Security Company," she said, taking a quick glance out the back windows. "They're the police at the

Club, the Tides, and around these parts. But everyone calls them Later Gator, because if you don't run and they catch you, you're screwed."

"Great," I said. "What do we do now?"

"I don't know," Bailey said, and while her endless instructions this evening had been wearing on my nerves, hearing this was worse. "But the thing is, I'm not supposed to be here."

I turned. She was looking out the back door again. "Where?"

"Lake North," she replied, as if it was perfectly normal to be banned from an entire town. "Since I got busted drinking at the Pavilion last year, I'm kind of, um, banned from city limits."

"But you've been coming here the entire time I've been visiting," I pointed out.

"Well, yes," she agreed. "But very stealthily! You'll notice we never came across security once."

"This is insane," I announced. We were now close enough to the Gator that the lights were bathing us in blue and red, and Roo had dropped the speed to where I was pretty sure we were just getting pushed along by the wind off the water. "Are we both going to get arrested?"

"You're not. You're just late and irresponsible." She kicked off her shoes, stuffing them in her purse, then strapped it over her chest, cross-body style. "I, however, need to get out of here. Think you can handle this like we discussed?"

"Out of here?" I repeated. "Where are you going?"

"Five sentences," she said, shooting Roo a look in the rearview. He nodded, slowing even more. "You were tired of his rules. You went to the party. You had a beer and it made you feel even worse. You feel awful now. You're sorry."

As she said this, she was sliding the lock open on the double doors, one hand moving slowly down to the handle.

"Are you jumping out of the truck?" I asked. "Seriously?"

"Shh," she said, easing the left-side door open. It creaked, but only barely audibly. Then she looked at me. "Text me when it's over, whatever happens. I'm sorry I have to go like this. But you can handle it. You're a Calvander."

But my dad, a Payne, was now standing right on the other side of the windshield, still holding his phone, eyes narrowed on Roo. The man in uniform, Later Gator, unnecessarily held up a hand to signal we should stop.

"Now, Bailey," Roo said under his breath, his lips barely moving as he started to roll down his window, Gator approaching from the other side.

It happened fast: one second she was there, perched by the half-open door, and then she was jumping out, noiselessly, into the dark behind us. I scrambled over, pulling the door shut again as Roo finally covered the last few inches between now and whatever was about to happen.

"Evening," Later Gator said through the open window. He had a slim flashlight in his hand, the beam of which he pointed in the truck, moving it around. "License and registration, please."

"It's me you want," I said, getting to my feet. I had one

hell of a head rush as I started walking, but pushed through anyway. "Let him go."

"Whoa," Later Gator said, aiming the light at me. "How many people are back there? Don't make another move. Understood?"

I nodded, standing there as his light shone bright in my face. "I'm Emma Payne," I said. "It's just me. That's my dad right there."

"Emma Payne?" he repeated.

Hearing this, my dad let his phone drop, coming up to the window as well. "Emma? Are you okay?"

"I'm fine," I said. "Can I please get out so I can explain?"

Later Gator nodded, gesturing toward the passenger-side door. To Roo he said, "You stay where you are and give me those documents. And keep your hands where I can see them."

"He didn't do anything," I protested. "He's just driving me home."

"Saylor, it's okay," Roo told me, digging into his pocket for his wallet before reaching across to pop open the glove box. To Gator he said, "The registration is in here somewhere. This isn't my truck—I've never had to find it before."

"Not your truck?" Gator said suspiciously. "Then whose is it?"

"It's an ice cream truck," I said. "He's a teenager. Of course it doesn't belong to him!"

"Emma," my dad barked through the window. "Get out. Now."

Gator gave him a look. "Sir, I'll ask you to step back so I can handle this."

My dad, annoyed, took a tiny step backward. Gator, satisfied, turned back to Roo, taking his documents. After studying the license for what felt like a long time, he said, "Christopher Price. You're from North Lake?"

"Yes, sir," Roo said. God, I hated that I'd gotten him into this.

"Anything in the truck I should know about?"

"Other than Emma?" Roo asked. Gator nodded, humorlessly. "Just ice cream, sir."

"Christopher Price?" my dad said. He looked at Roo, then me. "You're the one who's responsible for my daughter not being where she said she would be?"

"No," I said. The bright light, still shining at both of us, was making my eyes water. "I left of my own accord, with someone else. He just brought me back."

"You went to that party?" my dad demanded, now right back beside Gator despite his previous warning. "After I specifically told you not to?"

"I was upset," I said, thinking of Bailey for the first time since she'd jumped ship. I hoped for her sake she was halfway to the town line by now. "I saw some people who offered me a ride. I went. I drank a beer. I regretted—"

Roo winced, biting his lip. Oh, shit. I'd just made things worse without even trying.

"You've been *drinking*?" my dad said. Now he wasn't just

351

mad: he was furious. "What are you even thinking?"

"I'm sorry!" I cried out, my voice breaking. Six sentences. But who was counting? "I was angry and stupid."

Gator flipped the flashlight back so it was squarely on Roo. "Have you been drinking, Mr. Price?"

"No sir. I have to be at work at midnight. I was the DD tonight."

"And if I have to call the mobile unit for a Breathalyzer, it will confirm that?"

"He hasn't been drinking!" I protested. "He's just driving me home. It's me who screwed up—I'm the reason you're all here—just let him go!"

"Emma," my dad said. "Be quiet and let the officer do his job."

"But Roo isn't part of this!"

"Miss." Gator turned the flashlight back to me. "Calm down and be quiet or you'll have another problem. Understood?"

Roo glanced at me. I nodded and said, "Yes, sir."

Gator looked back down at the license and registration in his hand. "Now, Mr. Price, you say you're headed to work. Where is that?"

"Conroy Market, in North Lake. My boss is Celeste Blackwood. She's there right now."

"And where are *your* parents?"

I saw Roo swallow. "My mom is at work at the Bly County hospital. And my dad is deceased."

Gator nodded, then looked at the registration again. "Okay. Sit tight. I'll be right back."

With that, he turned, walking over to his cruiser and sliding behind the wheel. My dad came back up to the window, pointing a finger at Roo.

"You have a minor under the influence in your car," he told him, his voice thick with anger. "I don't care if you're sober or not, I'll still be pressing charges."

"For what?" I demanded.

"Saylor—" Roo said.

"Her name is Emma!" my dad exploded. His face was inches from Roo now: I could see spit flying from his mouth when he spoke. "And she doesn't go to parties and drink, or at least she didn't until she came here and started hanging out with all of you."

"Dad, stop it!"

"Look, I know what goes on with lake kids," he continued. "I married a lake kid, for Christ's sake. And I watched her destroy herself. I won't do it again."

Roo, my dad's finger inches from his nose, didn't say a word. He just sat there, taking this, and that was the worst thing of all.

"Mr. Price checks out," Gator announced to my dad, coming back from his car and sticking Roo's documents through the window. "Ms. Blackwood says she's expecting him at midnight and that he's a good kid. Said I should let him go."

"He gave my daughter beer!"

"No, he didn't!" I said. "God, are you even listening to me?"

"I don't have evidence of that," Gator explained to my dad. "Not much I can do."

"Go bust the party! Then you'll have your proof!"

"Well," Gator said, considering this, "the problem is it's in North Lake. And I only police Lake North. So—"

"Do not tell me this is out of your jurisdiction," my dad warned him. "This entire place is six miles long."

"Sir, I'll ask you to lower your voice," Gator replied.

"All he did was drive me home," I said. "Look, I understand you're pissed and you want to punish me—"

"You're damn right," my dad replied, but he was glaring at Roo as he said this.

"But leave Roo out of it," I finished. "Dad. *Please.*"

My dad didn't say anything for a moment. When he did speak, it was very quietly and very clearly. "Fine. But hear me when I say this: I do not want you around my daughter ever again. Whatever has been going on, it's over as of tonight. Are we clear?"

"Dad," I said. "You can't just decide—"

"Actually, I can." He pointed at me. "Get out of that truck. Right now."

I glanced at Gator, thinking he might step in, but no. He just stood there with his stupid entirely too bright flashlight, watching along with the rest of us.

"I'm sorry," I said to Roo. But he didn't respond, the beam still bright in his face. Of all the ways I thought the night would end, I never could have guessed this. There had always been invisible lines between the two sides and the two communities. But my dad had drawn another, his own. And even though I was right next to Roo, I could feel it between us.

"I'm sorry," I said softly to him. "I—"

"It's okay," he replied, still looking straight ahead. "Just go."

I nodded, feeling a lump rise in my throat. Then I got up and walked to the passenger door, pushing it open to step out onto the road. It was late, almost midnight, and thankfully, most of Lake North was asleep. But I thought of all those windows at the Tides, each with a person or people on the other side. How did I look, leaving this truck with a cop car, lights spinning, beside it? Maybe, like Waverly herself.

My dad was coming around the front bumper now, and I heard the Yum truck start as we began to walk back toward the hotel together. I wanted to turn and watch it, get this last glimpse of Roo to last me until . . . well, I wasn't even sure. But just as I was about to, I realized I couldn't bear it. It was easier, somehow, to just walk toward those doors already opening to reveal the night desk clerk, cheerful and oblivious.

"Welcome to the Tides!"

Neither of us responded as we walked to the elevator, where my dad pushed the button for our floor. The elevator chimed. We went in, the doors sliding shut behind us.

TWENTY

My summer had come to a full stop. But Bridget's was finally beginning.

"So then," she was saying, "Sam asks if I'm going to the pool fireworks. And I'm like, yeah, I should be there. And Steve says, 'What about Emma? Will she be home then?'"

Silence. Too late, I realized she'd paused for maximum dramatic effect. "Wow," I said quickly.

"I know!" She sighed happily. "I mean, granted, the first part of this summer did not go as I planned with Pop Pop's stroke and our detour to Ohio. But then to come back, and have this happen within days . . . it's like fate. It's what we've always wanted!"

She was right. And five weeks ago I would have been just as excited. Now, though: not so much.

"I hate that I'm not there," I said to her. "Although I'd probably be grounded anyway."

"Yeah, about that," she replied. "I have to admit, I'm kind

of impressed. The Emma I know won't even take a drink. Now you're getting pulled over by the police."

"It was security," I corrected her. "Which is *really* not the same thing."

"Still, very exciting," she told me. "The part about your cousin jumping out of the back of the truck . . . I mean, who does that?"

Calvanders, I thought, getting off my bed and walking over to the window. "I'm so stupid," I said. "If I just hadn't drunk . . ."

"He still would have freaked out, Emma," she said. "I mean, come on. Think about it. You weren't answering his calls or where you said you'd be."

"It made it worse, though," I said, thinking of Roo, his face in that bright light of Gator's flashlight.

She was quiet for a second. Then she said, "Have you heard from him at all? How did you guys leave things?"

Bridget was one of my two best friends for lots of reasons. But I especially loved that she knew what I was thinking, even when I didn't say it out loud.

"Not good," I said. "I know I should text him, but I'm so embarrassed. He must hate me."

"He doesn't hate you," she said automatically.

"Bridget. I almost got him arrested."

"*Almost*," she said, like this was hardly anything of note. "Not the same thing."

I watched a motorboat pass by, a girl with long hair

gripping the float as it bounced over a wake. Fun in the sun, all summer long. I sat back down on my made bed.

"Anyway," Bridget said now, "have you talked to Ryan? I can't get through to her except an occasional text. All she's thinking about is that show! And the *girl* in that show."

So there it was. "She told you," I said.

"After telling me she called you first!" She sighed again. "This is HUGE. And as the romance expert among us, it stings a little bit that I'm the last to know."

"Sorry," I said.

"I'll get over it. What's important," she continued, "is that she told us. I just hope this girl's good enough for her. If she's not, she'll hear from me."

I laughed. "I think Ryan can take care of herself."

"True." She thought for a moment. "Really, it's ironic. I was the one who was so sure this summer was going to be fabulous, full of amazing potential. And now you guys have romance for real, while I'm left standing, unkissed."

"I have a feeling you'll be fine in that department, though."

"Well, yes," she agreed. "But it better happen soon!"

I laughed. "I'm so happy for Ryan, though," I said, thinking of how she looked in the pictures she'd sent. "She's, like, giddy."

"No kidding. God, I feel so bad about all the times I dragged her along, trying to meet up with the twins. Assuming she'd want that."

"I feel the same way," I said. "Like we should have known or something."

"Ryan's always been private, until she decides not to be. And she told us when she was ready, which is all that matters."

It was true. I'd had two more top-of-mountain texts from her, and they were all about dress rehearsals and tech runs. There'd been a couple more pictures as well, of her hanging at camp with her castmates. Liz was beside her in every single one.

"Do you think they'll stay together when she's home?" I asked her.

"Long-distance? Oh, man. I don't know. Does that ever work?" she replied. "I mean, in the movies, summer romance tends to be location-specific."

I had a flash of Roo, then immediately pushed this thought away. We didn't have a relationship. And now, thanks to me, we never would. "My mom and dad remained a couple during the year," I pointed out.

"Yes, but they were only two hours apart. Ryan's dealing with entire states between her and Liz. It'll be a challenge." She was quiet for a minute. "But if it's meant to be, it will be. Things work out, that's what I'm saying. Look at Sam and me!"

"True," I said, choosing not to mention that right now what she had was an invitation, not a relationship. Which was still more than I could claim at the moment.

"Just promise," she said, "that even with all these new cousins and boys and everything else, you won't forget about me. When my time comes, you guys have to listen and be excited."

"I can't wait," I said. "I'll scream from the rooftops."

"Okay, that might be a bit much," she said, laughing.

"You think?"

"I'll let you know."

When I hung up, I looked at the digital clock on the bedside table: it was only ten a.m. Then again, I'd been awake since six, tossing and turning as I went over the events of the previous days. Normally I would have just slipped downstairs to walk over to the Larder for a copy of the *Bly County News* and a muffin. But I wasn't even allowed to do that. Because now, there were rules.

My dad had been clear: from now on, I couldn't go to North Lake. I couldn't go to the raft. Really, all I was allowed was to sit in the hotel room, which got boring quick. Which was why I'd found myself reorganizing my sparse belongings: folding and stacking shirts in my drawers, lining up my two pairs of shoes in the mostly empty closet, and making my bed the way Trinity had taught me, sheets pulled so tightly I could barely wedge myself beneath them.

It was in the midst of this routine—now repeated a few times—that I'd found the family tree I had begun my first day at Mimi's. I'd immediately sat down, flipping it open to read over the names that had once sounded like strangers, but were now as real to me as my own face. Now, I looked at those Calvanders, neatly organized on the page, then at my shoes, lined up against the wall, and shut the notebook again.

Suddenly there was a soft tapping on the other side of my

closed door. When I opened it, Nana was there, a *Bly County News* in her hand.

"Come have some food," she said, giving it to me. "I want to talk to you."

When I nodded, grateful, she smiled, pulling her lavender robe a bit more tightly around herself as she made her way down the hallway. There, on the table by the window, was her daily breakfast—already delivered and arranged by a Tides employee—as well as a plate of toast and butter for me. Lately it was all I'd been eating each morning, and of course she noticed.

"Thank you," I said, sliding into the chair beside her.

"You're more than welcome," she said. "I just feel like we haven't had a proper catch-up since . . . everything happened."

She was right: after the night of Taylor's party, I'd only left my room a handful of times, and each one I'd been so concerned about how my dad would react—not speaking to me, as it turned out—I hadn't had time to think about anyone else. Nana and Tracy had basically been tiptoeing together in the spaces between us, shooting me sympathetic looks he couldn't see. This also meant I hadn't formally apologized to her for causing all this trouble and tension, something I wanted to remedy now.

"I'm sorry," I told her as she poured coffee into a mug. "I know you hate conflict and seeing Dad upset. So this must be your worst nightmare."

She reached over, giving my hand a squeeze. "Don't you

worry about me, I'm fine. And your dad will be, too. He's just adapting. It's what we parents have to do, even when we aren't feeling up to it."

"I shouldn't have had those beers," I said, feeling embarrassed even saying these words in front of her. But I knew she was aware of the whole story. "I really let him down."

"Your father loves you so much," she said, pushing the plate of toast over to me. "He's always been overprotective because of what he went through with your mom. But you aren't Waverly, and he knows that. You just gave him a scare, is all."

This was classic Nana, the ability to break down anything to simple phrases that made sense and helped you feel better. She was like the original five sentences.

"I feel like I messed everything up," I said. "If I'd just waited a bit, he probably would have let me go back to Mimi's whenever I wanted."

"Maybe," she agreed. "But I think you're aware now that how your dad sees North Lake and how you do are very different things. For him, it was always just about your mother, her family, and her problems. He couldn't separate them. But you've had your own experience now, and redefined it accordingly. He's still looking with the same eyes. You have to remember that."

"So, what?" I asked. "I should try to show him it's not what he thinks?"

"Ideally, yes, that would be good," she said. "But I think we both know he might not be so fully open to it. Which is why even before this happened, I was thinking of ways to ease him into it."

I chewed my toast, which was delicious, as I tried to follow this. Then it hit me. "Oh, the dinner? Is that what you mean?"

She pointed at me, smiling. "Yes. It was my hope that by bringing Mimi and the rest over here to thank them for their hospitality, we could maybe begin a dialogue about something other than Waverly. A fresh start, as it were."

"And then I screwed it up," I said glumly. "I'm so stupid."

"Now, now." She dabbed at her mouth with her napkin, then folded it and put it back in her lap. "It's not too late."

I put down my toast. "You're going to invite them all over here, still? Really?"

"Well, yes," she said. "The planning will just require a bit more finesse, as we have to get your dad on board."

Immediately, I felt the wind go out of every sail in this plan. So to speak. "Yeah, well. Good luck with that. He hates them."

"Nonsense." There was an edge to her voice as she said this. "Your father doesn't hate anyone. He's just worried and frustrated."

"You're right," I said quietly.

"So," she continued, "what I'm thinking is we give him a bit of time. We could all use that, I think. So I've been looking at July thirteenth. Next Friday."

I raised my eyebrows. "Friday the thirteenth? Seriously?"

"Oh, now, don't be superstitious," she said. "By then

enough time will have passed since what happened between you and your dad for clearer heads to prevail. I've already spoken to the concierge about getting a table at the Club."

I wasn't surprised that Nana had thought things through to this extent. Her attention to detail was legendary. But it was one thing to design a good plan, another for everything to come together to make it work. Factor in several different people and personalities—and a dinner at the Club, no less—and disaster seemed even more possible, if not likely. But what was the other option? Sitting here in this suite stewing and angry until it was time to go home?

"I'm in," I said. "What can I do?"

She smiled. "For now, follow your dad's rules. Can you do that?"

"Yes." I nodded. "Thank you, Nana."

"Of course." She pointed at the *Bly County News*, which was next to my plate. "Now, tell me what you love so much about that paper. I glanced at your copy the other day and it seems to be nothing but ads and classified listings for boats."

"It's the obits, really," I said. "In the paper at home, there are at least eight to ten obituaries every day. Here, because it's smaller, usually they only run one or two. But they do a *lot* more In Memoriams, I've noticed."

"In Memoriams?"

I opened the paper. "They run on what would have been the person's birthday, or the anniversary of the day they died. They talk about how much they're missed and loved and all that. Like a letter to the beyond, but in the paper."

"Interesting," Nana said. "It's similar to lawsuit settlements, when you're often required to post terms in the classifieds. If it's in the public record, everyone sees it."

"Even the dead," I said.

"Even them."

As we sat there together, eating and reading in companionable silence, I thought of Mimi's kitchen, far across that water just outside the window, and my mornings there. It was possible I'd never get to wake up again to the smell of toast, arguments over butter, and a day of housekeeping ahead of me. But maybe I would. Even with all that had been taken from me, I still had time.

TWENTY-ONE

The one good thing about being in the same place all the time is that you're easy to find. Or, you know, call.

"How bad is it?" Bailey asked, skipping a hello. She'd been texting me nonstop since the night of Taylor's party, but I hadn't had the heart or energy to reply, so she'd been forced to reach out to me with an actual call. Which she hated. I was kind of touched, to be honest.

"Well, I'm grounded," I said. "I can't go anywhere."

"At least it's a nice place," she replied. "What else?"

"My dad is pissed. He's not talking to me. Still."

"Did you cry?"

"Yes. Didn't help."

"Damn." She sighed. "How long are you punished for?"

"He didn't say," I told her. Another loud exhale. "Is that bad?"

"Well, it's not good," she said. "Personally I prefer a date range for all my punishments at the time they are given. Otherwise extensions get tacked on again and again for even the smallest thing, and the next thing you know, you have no life whatsoever."

That was encouraging. I said, "My grandmother is trying to help, though. She wants to have you all over for dinner."

"Who's all of us?" she asked, sounding suspicious.

"Well," I said, "Mimi and Oxford, I guess, and you and Trinity. Celeste and Gordon and Jack."

"Is she thinking, like, a restaurant or something?"

"The Club, actually. She's looking at next Friday."

"The Club?" Now, I had her full attention. "Are you serious?"

"Yep," I said. "Do you think you all will come?"

"I'll be there," she said automatically. "Are you kidding? I've always wanted to eat at the Club. I hear they have specific forks just for oysters. Have you seen those yet?"

"I don't like oysters."

"Who cares? They're specific little forks just for ONE FOOD. I mean, what is that?" She laughed. "Oh, God, and what will I *wear*? And will we come by boat, or drive? Because if we come by boat, then I might see Colin, and—"

Hearing this name, I realized I'd been so caught up with my experience at Taylor's party I hadn't even thought of hers. Who was selfish now? "What's happening with Colin? Did you see him at the party?"

"Briefly," she replied, her voice coy. "I mean, it was kind of hard for us to talk with my drunk cousin about to be busted by her dad, but—"

"I'm sorry," I said.

"It's okay. I think me being busy was actually a good move. He, like, won't stop texting me."

"You're welcome."

She snorted. "I'm still mad at you for drinking. It's one thing for me to be messed up, but I didn't like seeing you that way. I need you compos mentis."

"You need me what, now?"

"Compos mentis," she repeated. "It's Latin. Means of sound mind."

"You took Latin?"

"Yeah, one semester," she said.

"Wow," I said, surprised.

"What? It's not easy for lake kids to get into a good college. We need all the credits we can get." So she was going to school, even if she never talked about it. I hated I'd just assumed otherwise. "Anyway, the point is you're not a party girl, Saylor. It doesn't suit you."

"No kidding." Just the thought of alcohol brought back a wave of shame that was hot and awful. "I've learned my lesson, don't worry. From now on I'll be the DD, every time."

"But first you have to, like, drive," she pointed out.

"Well, yes." By now, even getting behind the wheel sounded appealing compared to drinking. "I'm working on that. Or I was, before all this."

There was a chime sound, distant. "Oh, crap. That's Mimi, telling me to come do turnover. With you gone, I'm the last one standing. Or cleaning."

"I'd love to be doing that," I said wistfully. "I miss it."

"Are you crazy? You're at the Tides, for God's sake!"

"*Grounded* at the Tides," I reminded her.

"Which is still a million times better than wiping pubic hairs off a motel sink."

I cringed. "That was quite the visual."

"I know." Another chime. "God, I'm coming. I'll text you later. Reply this time, you hear? You know I hate talking on the phone." Then she hung up, again without a goodbye.

It was now two thirty, which gave me three hours until dinner. I was contemplating a nap, just to help the time pass, when my phone lit up again. This time, it was a HiThere! from a number I didn't recognize. Normally I would have ignored it, but what else was I doing? I hit ACCEPT.

There was that signature swooshing sound, and then a picture appeared. It was Trinity. Her belly, huge and rounded, took up all of the foreground.

"What is this I hear about you drinking?" she demanded. Did none of these Blackwood girls believe in greetings? "Are you crazy?"

"I made a mistake," I said, sighing.

"Damn right you did," she replied. "I expected more from you, honestly."

I wasn't sure if I should be flattered or ashamed by this scolding, considering not so long ago, she couldn't stand me. "I'm paying the price, believe me. I'm grounded until further notice."

"At the Tides," she said. "Boo-hoo. I'm here on the

porch, a million weeks pregnant with a fan on me and still sweating."

"What's the latest on the Sergeant?" I asked, wanting to get away from this tit-for-tat topic.

"Supposedly," she said, shifting slightly so that her belly eclipsed the entire screen, momentarily, "he is getting home on the eighteenth. Which is a week before my due date."

"That's great, Trinity," I told her.

"I'll believe it when I see it." She fanned her face with one hand. "At this point I honestly just want him here when the baby comes, even if he walks in the door when it's coming out of me."

I winced. "He'll be there."

"I hope you're right." She shifted again. "In the meantime, you need to come visit me. I need someone to paint my toenails."

"I'm grounded," I reminded her. "Maybe ask Gordon?"

She groaned. "Oh, God. No thanks. She's terrible with polish. Gets it everywhere. Besides, all she's doing is moping around since you left anyway. She's so pathetic Roo had her holding a ladder for him the other day."

I blinked. "A what?"

"I looked out there," she said, "and he's got her supporting the ladder while he climbs, like she's going to keep it steady or something. As if! She's ten. But you should have seen her face. You would have thought he'd trusted her with the world."

Ladder buddy, I thought, smiling. And in the next beat,

what Bailey had said: if you really want to know someone, look at what they do when they don't know you're watching. Oh, Gordon.

"She saw me," I said, remembering all over again. "When I was drunk. I feel awful about that."

"Yeah, well." Weirdly, I appreciated that she didn't tell me I shouldn't, or that it was okay. It wasn't. "It won't happen again."

"No," I said. "It won't."

We were both quiet for a moment, the only sounds the distant puttering of a motorboat and some kid shrieking from the beach.

"Just get back over here," Trinity said suddenly. "Okay? We need you. Or, my toenails do."

"I will," I promised. "And thanks."

"For what?"

Even though I'd been the one to say it, now I wasn't so sure how to answer this question. "Just being there."

"I'm bedridden," she reminded me. "Where else would I be?"

After hanging up, I walked back to the window. It was now three p.m., and the beach was crowded, almost every chair taken. Earlier, Tracy had invited me to go for a late afternoon swim with her at the pool, something I supposed she'd cleared with my dad. At the time, I'd said no. But Trinity and Bailey were right: this wasn't a bad place to be stuck at all. I went to look for my swimsuit.

I'd just put it on, and tied my hair back, when my phone

buzzed again. It was another number I didn't recognize, so at first I just ignored it, assuming it was a spam call. As it kept ringing, though, I got curious and answered it.

"Hello?"

"Good afternoon! My name is Chris and I'm calling from Defender Storm Shutter Solutions. How confident are you in your window protection?"

Nope, I thought, moving my finger to the END button. Just as I was about to push it, though, he spoke again, much more softly this time.

"Saylor. It's me."

I blinked, startled. "Who?"

"Roo."

Roo? I almost dropped the phone. "Oh, my gosh," I finally managed. "How are—"

He cleared his throat, then said loudly and confidently, "Well, then it's a good thing I called! For just a moment of your time, I can tell you why Defender Storm Shutters are the best choice for your home."

Slowly, I was starting to understand. "Hold on. You're selling storm shutters now?"

"Yes!" he said in that same loud, cheerful voice.

"What are you up to, now? Six jobs?"

In his normal voice, he said, "Actually, I'm back to four. Had to give up the airport job when they realized I'm not twenty-one. And then the Park Palms hired someone on salary for the overnight shift. I was panicking until I saw this open up."

Of course he was. "So now it's the Station, Conroy Market, Storm Shutters—"

"And the Yum truck," he finished for me. The next beat, he was back to his booming salesperson voice, saying, "Well, then, let me tell you about our in-house financing! With our easy payments and credit offer, you can focus on safety, not paying bills."

"Am I supposed to respond?" I asked.

"No," he said loudly. Then he added, in his normal voice, "I've been here since nine and have cold-called the entire list Juan gave me. Not one nibble. I think I suck at this?"

"Nobody buys anything over the phone," I told him.

"Clearly." I heard someone in the background, distant, say something. Returning to his big voice, Roo said, "Oh, no, ma'am, installation is simple! We do all the work so you can rest easy, knowing you and your home are protected."

"Let me guess," I said. "You're being watched."

"Yes!" he boomed. A pause. Then, in a normal tone, "Juan's a great guy. And he's paying me by the hour to sit here. He just passes through every now and—well, ma'am, of course! Our bonded installers will arrive at your home, do the work, and leave everything as they found it. No stress for you. Just peace of mind!"

"Sounds great," I said, trying to play along. "Unfortunately, I kind of live in a hotel now. So—"

"I heard you're grounded," he said, back to his regular voice.

"News travels fast."

"Well, I asked Bailey for your number," he explained. "I was worried about you."

Hearing this gave me a little twinge in my chest. He wasn't mad. He'd been thinking about me. "I'm so sorry," I said to him now. "I never meant to get you into trouble."

"You didn't," he replied, then added, "That's right, ma'am! I can easily run a credit check to find out if you qualify for our winter payoff plan. Get the shutters now, rest easy all year long!"

"You got pulled over by the police," I pointed out to him, once he'd finished.

"By Later Gator," he corrected me. "And I was sober as a judge. You, on the other hand, had reason to be worried. Your dad was *pissed*."

"No kidding. He's not speaking to me."

"Still?" He gave a low whistle. "Ouch."

"I know." Trying again, I said, "Seriously, though. I feel really bad. About you having to help take care of me, and Hannah getting upset—"

"It's not necessary!" he said, so loudly I had to pull the phone away from my ear. "We handle all removal and recycling, if pertinent, of your old shutters!"

"It's necessary for me," I continued, finally getting a rhythm between these two very different conversations. "You never signed up to be my caretaker."

"There was a sign-up period?" he asked, back to normal. All I could do was hope Juan would stay away for a bit, if only for my sanity. When I sighed, he said, "Look, Saylor. We're

374

ladder and corsage buddies, remember? We help each other out."

"I didn't exactly help *you*."

"Well, I'll tell you what comes next!" Here we went again. "First, we'll set up a time convenient for you to have one of our trained sales teams come to your home for an estimate."

I waited.

"And at that time, we can also discuss the current specials we are running." His voice faded out on this last part, then he was back, speaking normally again. "You're helping me now. I have two hours of this left to go and I'm here all week, until Kenyatta comes back from Barbados."

"What?" All this back-and-forth, now with detail, was making my head swim.

"She's the normal cold caller," he explained. "I'm just filling in, which stinks because this is an inside job, in A/C, where I get to sit down all day. It's the best."

"Except for the whole selling window protection over the phone thing."

"Ma'am, I am glad you asked!" he replied. "All of our shutters are American-made, guaranteed, and come with a ten-year warranty."

I felt like at some point, I should play along. "Do you take checks?"

"No, we do not!" he boomed back in reply. "But your credit card or bank draft is more than welcome, and again, we do offer our Winter Payment Plan, for ease of mind. Okay, we're clear. Sorry about that."

The switch was so quick this time I almost didn't notice. I was still waiting for more details about the installment plan. "He's gone?"

"Went to the bank. Which gives us about ten minutes to talk about things other than shutters."

So here it was. I'd apologized—or tried to, he certainly hadn't made it easy, or accepted it—and now we had time, uninterrupted, to get out everything else that had been on my mind. Maybe, if I was really brave, I'd tell him I'd been missing him, and how often I replayed that moment on the night of Club Prom, when we'd almost gone from friends to something more. But when I spoke next, I was surprised to find it wasn't about any of these things.

"I miss the other side so much; I was only there three weeks," I said. "I can't imagine my mom just swearing it all off when her whole *life* was here. Why didn't she ever come back, except that once?"

He was quiet for a moment, considering this. Finally he said, "Well, I've heard a lot of theories over the years. But I think it had to do with the accident. I mean, would you come back?"

"Probably not," I said, looking again at the lake, so pretty and blue with the sun glinting off it. But the water had moods and moments, like everything else. I could understand how after something like that happened, you'd never see it the same way again. "I just don't know what's worse. Not having any idea of any of these stories or history before last month, or only learning some to have them taken away."

"The stories haven't gone anywhere," he pointed out. "They, like me, remain in convenient central North Lake."

I smiled. "True. So maybe I should ask you to tell the rest to me."

"What? Your mom's history?"

"Yeah." According to the clock, it was now three thirty: I was going swimming with Tracy at four. "Or at least, some of them. I mean, I have the album you lent me, but—"

"Pictures only tell half," he finished. "I had my mom to tell me the rest, what was going on in the pictures."

"Maybe I should talk to your mom."

"Maybe. Or, you could just talk to me. I mean, I do know that album by heart. At bedtime it was that and *Goodnight Moon*. Which I can also remember perfectly."

"Really," I said, getting up and walking over to my bureau, where I'd left the album in the back of a top drawer. I reached in, pulling it out, then sat down on the carpet. "So what's the first picture?"

"Shot of my dad as a kid in footie pajamas," he replied. "They have yellow ducks on them."

I opened the album to look: he was right. He and his dad had the same face, those blue eyes and white-blond hair. "And the story?"

"My dad was an only child," he said. "Grandparents had him late in life, after they thought they could never have kids. And he was *wild*, full of energy, always keeping them running. See that guy in the background, on the plaid sofa?"

I hadn't before, too focused on the cute baby to notice.

Now, I looked, saying, "Yeah."

"That's my grandfather. He was about fifty in that picture."

I studied it again. The man had white hair, his face tired. "Really? He looks much older."

"Exactly. Takeaway: my dad aged people, he was so exhausting."

"*That's* how the album of stories begins?"

"Yep. I guess it was both history and, for me, a subtle warning." He laughed. "Now, see, after that there are, I think, a bunch more of my dad as a kid. School pictures, holding up a fish, at Halloween dressed like a Ninja Turtle . . ."

I was following along as he spoke, running a finger over each of these. "Impressive."

". . . until finally, on the top of page two," he said, "we have the arrival of Waverly Calvander. They met at summer day camp at Church of the Lamb, just after kindergarten."

I turned to that page, finding the picture. Chris and my mom were in the center of a group of about six kids standing on a dock. Everyone was wearing LAMB CAMP T-shirts, and he and a few others were smiling. My mom, however, held her mouth in a thin line, clearly displeased.

"She looks mad," I observed.

"She hated camp," he told me. "Too many rules. I don't think she even lasted the summer."

I zeroed in more closely, taking in every feature I could. My mom's bangs, blowing slightly sideways. The rope bracelet around one wrist. How adult she seemed, in comparison with the rest of the kids, like she'd discovered something they wouldn't for many years. And without Roo's voice in my ear, that would have been me, as well: I'd have the image, but as he said, that was only half. And I'd had enough of bits and pieces.

"Okay, so below that," he said now, "like, two or three rows and to the right? That's them on the Fourth of July with Celeste. It was my dad's first time over to Mimi's: she's the one who took the picture."

My mom wasn't smiling in this shot, but she didn't look openly hostile, either. She had on a jumper and sandals with little block heels, one arm thrown around Celeste, who was looking off to one side, her mouth open as she was saying something. Chris, excited, was holding a lit sparkler out to the camera, sparks falling off it. I recognized that same clump of gardenia bushes behind them.

"Your dad looks fiendish with that sparkler," I said.

"Good catch. He loved blowing things up and the Fourth. Later it was him who organized the fireworks out at the raft every year," he replied. "In fact, if you turn to the next page, on the right—yes, ma'am, that's correct! We're based in convenient North Lake, a quick trip to all of Bly County, and we offer a wide variety and price range of both hurricane and storm shutters."

Juan was back. I looked back at the picture, the goofy way my mom hung on her sister, hamming it up. I'd never known her to be silly. I guess by the time I came along, there was a lot less to laugh about.

Outside in the suite, I could now hear voices: my dad and Tracy were back from whatever outing they'd taken, and soon enough I'd need to go on that swim. But for now, with Roo still reciting his cold-call points in my ear, I studied the other shots on the page. My mom and Chris on the back of a tube, in life jackets. At the table at Mimi's, eating hot dogs with Celeste and another boy around the same age whose features looked a lot like Trinity, Bailey, and Jack.

". . . of course, I'd be happy to follow up with some more information when it's more convenient to talk," Roo was saying now. "I'll just take down your info and be back in touch. Will that work?"

Yes, I thought, although I stayed silent. At least until he stopped talking in that voice, his normal tone filling my ear. "You still there?" he asked.

"For a minute," I said. Which I hoped was long enough. "Can you tell me another one?"

That was how it started. The calls, and the stories. Before I knew it, I'd gone from watching the clock all day to watching my phone. Because every time it rang, there was a chance for a bit more connection with Roo, as well as everything I'd left on the other side. His voice was the conduit. All I had to do was listen.

"Top of page, three or four over," he said that evening, after I'd slipped out early from dinner at the Tides restaurant and come home while my parents and Nana shared a nightcap. "Middle school dance. Also known as the only time your mom and my dad ever tried to be more than friends."

Everything about the picture screamed awkward. First, there was the stiff button-down Chris Price was wearing that made him look like a kid playing dress-up. My mom, in a periwinkle dress with spaghetti straps, her hair loose over her shoulders, seemed years older and, solely by the twisty smile on her face, like she might be trouble. They were standing side by side outside of Mimi's house, not touching.

"It looks like a date."

"Mom always said my dad called it the worst one ever," he replied. He was in the arcade at Blackwood Station: in the background, I heard a siren, which meant someone had won from the bonus ticket machine. "Picture it. Eighth grade. Since Celeste and Silas had paired up the year before, they thought maybe they were meant to do the same. But it felt weird and they bickered all night except for one kiss, which was disappointing for everyone involved. So that was that."

"Makes me wonder if you ever thought about dating Bailey," I said. I couldn't imagine it, but I also didn't want to.

"No." He replied so quickly, and flatly, I was reassured. "Her brother would have killed me. Also, there's Vincent. Who has been hooked on her since middle school."

So it was true. "I *thought* he was into her!"

"He's obsessed." I heard a cash register beep: he'd told me his main job was making change for the arcade. "Unfortunately, he's also too scared to let her know or make a move. It's like watching paint dry, but more frustrating."

"I bet he'd be a great boyfriend," I said.

"Yeah? Maybe you should date him."

Hearing this, I had to think how to respond. Was he kidding? Trying to find out more information? Finally I said, "He's sweet. But not my type."

"No?" he asked. The siren went off again. "And what's that, exactly? Yacht club guys?"

"No," I said. "I got set up with Blake because of Bailey. Left to my own devices, I'd choose differently."

"You would? Like how?"

"I can't say exactly," I said, running my finger around the edge of the picture we'd been talking about. "But when you know, you know."

"Well, that's frustratingly vague," he replied.

I grinned, sitting back against my bedroom door with my legs stretched out in front of me. "But it's like my mom and dad, right? She didn't know what her type was until he showed up. We're not to that part of the album yet."

"But there aren't any pictures of her with your dad in there," he pointed out. "I know it by heart, remember?"

"True. I'm speaking of it in a larger sense."

"The big album in the sky," he said, clarifying.

"No," I said, stifling a snort, "just that, like history, it's ongoing. Just because the pictures stop doesn't mean the story does."

He was quiet, long enough that I wondered if we'd been cut off. Then he said, "You're right. I guess we all have those invisible pages, so to speak."

"Exactly," I said. "Like, say, for you, there will be shots

from in college, you working on the paper there, thanks to all those hours working at Defender and every other place in town."

I swore, I could hear him smile at this. "You think?"

"Sure," I said. "And Bailey's pictures will have her, like, running the Tides or something after college. And Trinity pushing her baby across a different campus, when *she* gets back to school."

"You've thought about this," he observed.

"It just makes sense, right?" I said. "A life isn't just the pages you know, it's everything. We just can't see what's happened yet."

Somewhere near him at the Station, there was a burst of laughter, loud and sudden. When it died down, he said, "Okay, then. What's your picture?"

"Of what?"

"The future," he replied. "What's the rest of your story?"

I thought for a second. What did I see, or want to see, ahead? "Something having to do with this place," I said finally. "Proof that it's not over, that I'll come back. That's what I want."

He was quiet again. But this time I could hear him, just there on the other end of the line. "Well, for what it's worth, nobody here's forgetting you."

I felt my face flush. It wasn't nobody I was worried about. "I hope you're right," I said. "Now, tell me more about this picture and that terrible kiss."

Just as he was about to launch into the story, though, I

heard a knock on my door. I scooted aside so it could open and my dad stuck his head in. "Hey," he said. "You busy?"

"Um," I said, gesturing at the phone at my ear. "Kind of. What do you need?"

"Just thought we could take a walk," he replied. "Five minutes?"

I nodded. "Sure."

He gave me a thumbs-up, then shut the door again. Slightly stunned, I said, "My dad wants to take a walk."

"So he's talking to you now?"

"Apparently," I said, still wary. "I wonder what he wants to discuss."

"Talking is good either way," he said. "But mark our place, okay? Up next is some good stuff, including but not limited to when your mom and my dad became obsessed with the California look and tried to lighten his hair."

I couldn't help it: I flipped ahead until I found a shot of Chris sitting in a chair, a towel around his neck and his head over the sink while my mom was shaking up a plastic bottle. I recognized a framed needlepoint by the sink that CLEAN UP AFTER YOURSELF: it was still in Mimi's bathroom. "Was it bad?"

"Awful," he told me. "You'll love it. Bye, Saylor."

"Bye," I said. But even after he hung up, I kept my phone where it was for another second of connection between us. Then I put it down, turning back to the album.

I grabbed all the pages that were left, turning them all in one motion to the back cover opposite that final one. If there was more room, how would this story go on?

In that moment, I hoped to see my dad and me together, side by side, talking. Beyond that, who knew. I closed the book and went to find him.

At first, it was awkward. So we started walking.

"I've been meaning to explore around here a bit," my dad said as we left the front entrance of the Tides and started toward the main road. "I bet a lot has changed in nineteen years."

"It's been that long?" I asked.

"Since I was on this side, yes," he replied as a BMW with tinted windows drove past us, barely making a sound. "When we came back with you that summer, we only went to Mimi's. And left quickly, as I remember."

This seemed like an opening. "The second honeymoon didn't take, right?"

"Nope," he said, wiping his brow. Even though it was dark, it was still hot. "Truthfully, I think we both knew things weren't salvageable at that point."

"But you went to Vegas anyway?"

He shrugged. "Well, yeah. I mean, I loved your mom so much. I wanted it to work. It just . . . didn't."

"Roo's been telling me some stories," I said quietly, hoping it wasn't too risky to mention his name. "About Mom and his dad, growing up here."

"Hmm," he said. I wasn't sure what that meant. "They were very close."

"You met him, right?" I asked. "Chris Price?"

"Oh, yeah," he replied. We were across from the Tides now, heading toward Campus, which I could see up ahead. "We all met the same night, actually. At a party on the raft."

"Our raft?" I said.

He looked at me, amused. "Well, we considered it *ours*, but yes. The very same."

"You guys had parties out there?"

"Yep," he said, nodding. "It was the gathering place back then too, especially in the evenings. Tons of boats, tied together, and everyone moving between them."

I would have bet the rest of my grounding there was beer there, too. Not that I felt I could say this out loud.

"How did you guys meet?" I asked.

He gave me a sideways look. "We didn't come here to talk about your mom and me."

"I don't know why we came here," I replied. "You're the one who invited me."

"True," he said mildly. We walked a little farther, until Campus, its low block buildings dotted with chairs heaped with towels, was right beside us. He stopped, looking at it, then said, "My unit was around back. Should we try to find it?"

I looked at the buildings, wondering who I might run into. Then again, it was better than being in the suite. "Sure."

He stepped up onto the grass and I followed him, crossing over to the first building. The door to Blake and Colin's place was closed, but Hannah and Rachel's was ajar, and I could see someone's feet up on the bed as we passed by. Then my dad turned down the short hall by the laundry and bulletin board where Blake had taken me all those nights ago.

"See, the back rooms were better," he explained as we popped out on that side and started passing doors. "More shade, so they weren't as hot."

"There's A/C now, though," I said, pointing at one.

"Ha! These kids don't know how good they have it," he said. "We melted all summer, every summer. Let's see . . . here it is. Fourteen."

It was the last door of the building, no chair or towels marking it. Just a single-bulb light, bugs circling it, and the strong sound of peepers coming from the nearby woods. This close up, they were deafening.

"Guess a tour is out of the question," my dad said, peering in the one, dark window. "But man, do you hear those frogs? Those first few nights, I couldn't sleep it was so loud. By the end of the summer, though, I didn't even notice them. It's funny what you can get used to."

"It is," I agreed, just as I heard footsteps on the other end of the walkway. By the time I looked, though, a door was just shutting, whoever it was having slipped inside.

"There used to be a wall," he said, glancing back down the way we'd come. "Everyone signed it, every summer. I wonder—"

"It's over here," I told him, walking around the corner.

"You know about the wall?" he asked.

Whoops. "Um, Bailey had to run over here one time for work. I rode along and she showed me."

He followed me until he was facing the wall himself. "Wow," he said, looking up at all the names. "Now it really doesn't feel like nineteen years."

There was a sudden hiss, followed by a popping sound, from somewhere in the neighborhood to our right. Fire-works. The Fourth wasn't until the next day, but everyone always started early.

"Did you—" I began to ask, but already he'd stepped up closer to the cinder block, squinting at all the names there. After a moment, he moved his hand over to the right, and down a bit, holding his finger to one small spot.

"Right here." He pushed his glasses up, squinting through them. "Your mom signed right below, even though she technically wasn't supposed to."

I moved closer as well, and he stepped aside, making room, his finger still holding the place. MATT PAYNE, SUMMER 1999, it said in black Sharpie in the same neat, block printing he still used for shopping lists and the notes he left for me. Underneath, smaller and scrawled: just WAVERLY, a chubby heart with an arrow through it right above. Both looked so clear in front of my eyes, but I knew I never would have found them alone.

"It must have been a lot of fun, working here," I said.

"It was." He dropped his hand, but kept looking at the spot. Then, suddenly, he said, "Emma, I'm not trying to ruin your life, even if you think I am. You know that, right?"

"Yeah," I said. "I do."

He turned, facing me. "Do you know how much you

scared me the other night? When I was calling and couldn't find you? It just brought so much back, all those nights with your mom when she disappeared. . . ."

"I didn't know that! I wasn't here in nineteen ninety-nine; I don't know all these stories."

"But you *did* know your mom, and are old enough to remember what she put us through when she was using."

"I had a couple of beers!" I cried, frustrated. "It's not the same."

"It's how it starts!" he shot back. Then, lowering his voice, he said, "Look, Emma. You have to be vigilant. We both do. There's a history there."

"I'm not going to do what she did, though."

"You don't know that!" he said. "You're seventeen. We don't know anything except what's already happened. The only thing we can do is prevent it from happening again."

"You make it sound like it's inevitable," I replied. "Maybe I'm different."

"Oh, honey." He looked so pained, stepping closer to me and taking hold of both my arms. "You are different. So different. But being here, especially on the other side, hanging out with those kids . . . we can't tempt fate. It's too dangerous."

"Roo's nice, Dad."

"I'm sure he is." He dropped his hands. "I just . . . I feel like you've been through so much. The divorce, then losing your mom. And you're great, you're perfect. I just want to be sure you stay that way."

"I'm not perfect, though. Nobody is." That would be true even if I'd never laid a foot in North Lake again. "And anyway, what about you? Were *you* perfect back then? Did you make all the right choices?"

"Me? God, no." He sighed. "I was young and stupid. But I didn't have a parent who was an addict. You do. It's an added responsibility."

"One I don't want," I grumbled. We were quiet for a second. Then I said, "So what did you do?"

"When?" he asked.

"When you were young and stupid."

He looked at me as if I was kidding. When it was clear I wasn't, he said, "We don't really need to get into that, do we?"

I shrugged. "I don't know. Stories help sometimes. That's something I've learned this summer."

"You want to hear my irresponsible stories," he said.

"I want to know what you went through," I said. "I know all about Mom. But not you."

There was another pop. We both looked up to see a firework shooting up above the trees, then split into a shower of sparks. Somewhere, a dog started barking.

"Give me some time, okay?" he said finally. "I'll work up to it. Or try to. Is that fair?"

I nodded. "Yeah."

Now, he smiled. Would this really happen? Time would tell. "We should probably get out of here," he said. "Don't want Later Gator to show up because someone reported a couple of prowlers."

I looked at him, surprised. "*You* know they call him Later Gator?"

He gave me a grin. "I'll explain another time."

Back out at the road, it was fully dark now, the Tides all lit up as well as the Club beside it. I could hear another pop as we crossed the street, but this time I didn't turn around to look. "Fourth is tomorrow," he observed. "The Club's having a cookout on the beach, followed by fireworks. You up for going?"

"Can I?"

"Tracy and I are," he said. "I think Nana will probably watch from the room."

"I'd love it," I told him.

He looked at me then, seeming surprised. "Great. I'll let the Club know. We'll have a nice family evening."

I nodded, just as we approached the main doors of the hotel. "Welcome to the Tides!" someone yelled as we came inside, the A/C feeling freezing after the humid night. Glimpsing the lake out the windows, I looked for the raft, trying to picture my mom and dad, just a little older than me, riding out on a similar night to meet cute on the water. I never had gotten the whole story out of him, but I knew how it ended. Us together, two instead of three, stepping into another elevator on a different night, this one.

TWENTY-TWO

"More toast?" Nana asked me, breaking the silence that we'd sat in together for the last half hour or so with our respective breakfasts and papers.

"I'm fine," I told her. "But thanks."

She dabbed her mouth with her napkin, moving her coffee cup to one side. "I heard you and your dad come in last night. It sounded like you were actually talking."

I nodded. "Yeah. We went for a walk and worked some stuff out."

"I'm glad to hear it," she said, giving me a smile. "In other news, the dinner is coming together nicely. I've got us a reservation at the Club for next Friday at six p.m. Large table, so we can invite whoever we like."

"It's really happening?" I asked, surprised.

"What's happening?" I heard my dad say as he came down the hallway from his suite in his trunks, carrying his goggles. An all-state swimmer in college, he'd begun starting every day with a dive off the dock, followed by a quick mile, before breakfast.

I looked at Nana, who said, "Oh, well, Emma and I were just talking about this dinner I want to plan with the Calvanders."

My dad, who had started to peel his banana, now stopped, looking at her. "The Calvanders? You mean Mimi and Joe?"

"Joe died," I reminded him. "Oxford is her husband now."

Nana said, "I was thinking Mimi and her husband, yes, and Celeste and hers, and then the kids. Maybe one or two of Emma's other friends, too, if they were free."

"Mother." He was still holding the banana. "Emma is grounded."

"And this is happening Friday, at which point I was thinking you may have revisited that issue." She picked up a napkin, holding it out to him, even though from what I could tell, the banana was barely messy. Nice touch. "Of course, if you feel strongly, then I can cancel the reservation. I just thought that after they had Emma all that time, it would be a good gesture."

"It is," he agreed. "But I'm not sure a Club dinner is the best way to express our gratitude. It might make them . . . uncomfortable."

"Not Bailey," I said. I couldn't help myself. "She's already excited about the oyster forks."

They both looked at me. Dad said, "Excuse me?"

"She's always wanted to eat at the Club. It's, like, her dream."

"Well." Nana smiled. "Now we're making dreams come true. That's nice!"

"Mother, maybe you and I should discuss this privately," my dad said, putting the napkin back on the table. "We certainly don't want to invite someone to something that will be stressful for them."

"The girl is excited about the forks," Nana pointed out.

"Maybe it would be better if I offered to do something at their place," my dad said. "On the beach, say. I could find a caterer, and—"

"Or," Nana said, "we could leave it all to the Club and just show up. That sounds easier, doesn't it?"

My dad did not look convinced. But instead of saying so, he looked at me. "So. Think you'll be leaving the suite today?"

I was confused. "I'm grounded."

"Yes, but that doesn't mean you have to sit in your room all day long," he said. "Tracy says there's a band you might like playing at the Pavilion for the Fourth."

More confusion. "I can go to the Pavilion?"

"Yes," he said, and while it was all I could do not to get to my feet right that second, before he changed his mind, I resisted. "But there are ground rules. Number one, you will stay on Tides or Club property. And if at any point I can't reach you, then you *will* be inside until we leave. Are we clear?"

"Crystal," I said. Across the table, Nana had her eyes on me. "Thanks, Dad."

He nodded, and then I did get up, thanking Nana as well as I pushed in my chair, then headed back to my room. The last thing I saw before going inside was him sitting down, then speaking in a lowered voice to my grandmother, who said something quietly in return. Probably better I wasn't there anyway. Nana worked best on her own.

In my room, I put on my bathing suit, then a sundress, before digging my flip-flops out from the closet. Through the window, I could see the Club attendants down on the sand, distributing towels to the chairs. It was only just after eight a.m., but I figured I should go while I had the chance, as there was no telling when my dad might change his mind.

Both he and Nana were gone when I came back through the living room, their plates being cleared by a woman in a Tides Golf shirt and a black skirt. "Happy Fourth of July," she said as I slipped past to the door.

"To you, too," I told her. Outside, a cleaning cart was parked by the elevators, and I looked it over, thinking of the rickety ones back at Calvander's, which usually sported at least one loose, wobbling wheel. This one might as well have been a sports car, chrome and sleek. Linens were folded below, toiletries and room supplies above, everything separated into neat, labeled categories. The spray bottles had Tides logos, but no names.

Downstairs, out on the back patio, I slipped on my sunglasses, then looked around, getting my bearings, before starting out to the pool. I was scoping out the perfect chair when I heard someone call my name. I turned around to see Colin and Blake heading down to the Club dock via a walkway that was right behind me. Great.

"Heard you were staying here," Colin said, clearly oblivious to the fact that I outright disliked him. Blake, behind him, remained silent, making me think he was still annoyed from the night of the party.

"Yep," I said mildly. All I wanted was to get away from them.

"Well, Fourth of July means it's going to be nuts. And that's not even counting the fireworks tonight. You going to the cookout?" Colin asked.

I nodded. "I got sprung, finally. Been grounded in the room for the last few days."

"Well, we're having a door party at Campus after the fireworks, if you want to come. Kind of a tradition."

"What's a door party?"

"Like bar golf, but with rooms, basically," he replied. "Different drinks in each room. There's a scorecard. Hit them all, get a prize."

"What's the prize?"

"Being wasted," Blake said, finally joining in the conversation. "And bragging rights."

"Yeah, I can't see that happening," I said as a man in madras shorts and a pink shirt passed by, talking into his phone in an irritated voice. "Drinking and parties is what got me grounded in the first place. I kind of have to lay low."

"Oh, right," Colin said. "Well, there's also this great band at the Pavilion midday. Spinnerbait. Should be fun. You heard of them?"

I shook my head. "Nope. My stepmother mentioned it, though."

"They play all the time at East U. You'll like them." He said this so confidently, like he knew me well, that I decided right then that I wouldn't. "You know if Bailey's coming?"

I just looked at him. So that explained the friendliness. "No."

"Well, if she does, you guys should come by the docks," he said. "Say hello."

"Better hop," Blake said to Colin, nodding at a motorboat that was approaching the docks. "We were supposed to be on two minutes ago."

"Right," he replied. To me he said, "Good seeing you, Saylor."

"You, too."

Blake didn't say anything as they headed down the walkway, now at a faster clip, to meet the boat that had just arrived. Jerks, I thought, just as my phone rang. It was the toll-free number I'd come to recognize, and I smiled before I even answered it.

"Good morning, ma'am! My name is Chris and I'm calling to talk about your home's defense against the coming storm season. Do you have a moment?"

"I do," I said, settling into a beach chair I'd picked and stretching out my legs. "Go right ahead."

"Perfect! Well, I'll begin by telling you a little bit about . . . okay, sorry about that. We're only open for a half day today for the holiday, but Juan still thinks someone sitting home feeling patriotic might bite."

"Could happen," I said, pulling some sunblock out of my bag. "So only half a day, huh? Are you off too, or just going to another job?"

"Driving the Yum truck around all the beaches until five," he said. "Then I promised Silas I'd come by the Station for backup in case he needs it before the fireworks start. But *then*, I am free and clear."

"Which will be when? Like, ten or so?"

"Probably," he said, and I laughed. "But still, it's something. Which is good because everyone knows the Fourth is my favorite holiday."

"Just like your dad, huh?"

"You remembered," he said. I remember everything, I wanted to say. "Yeah. My mom always talked about how much he loved the fireworks. The Fourth was one of the times we always remembered him, with the whole sparkler thing."

"What sparkler thing?"

"You haven't heard about that?" he asked. Then, before I could reply, he said, "Well, I guess you wouldn't have. It's kind of a lake thing."

So many lake things. Even if I'd had a whole summer, I was pretty sure I wouldn't learn them all.

"When my dad died, my grandparents planned the

whole funeral," Roo explained as I hoped against hope Juan was gone on a long errand this time. I wanted to hear this. "Church service, very formal and sad. But my mom felt like it didn't capture him as he really was, you know. So that evening, she had a service of her own."

"With sparklers?"

"Hundreds of them," he said. "She, Silas, Celeste, and Waverly bought every box they could find in the entire county. When people arrived, they got a handful and some matches. Then, after everyone said what they wanted to, they lit them all at the same time."

"Wow."

"I know." He was quiet a second: I could hear buzzing on the phone line between us. "The thing about sparklers? They're cool but quick. You light them, they go like crazy, and then it's all over. So it always seemed fitting to me, you know, that they did that for my dad. A big life lived, gone too soon. That sort of thing."

I was quiet for a moment. Then I said, "Like my mom, too."

"Well . . . yeah," he said. "After she passed, they did it again. Same beach, same crowd. And every Fourth since, that I can remember anyway."

"Sparklers."

"Yep. All year we buy them up wherever we see them. It's one of our few family traditions."

Out by the pool, the sun was growing stronger, people arriving to the chairs around me with their beach bags and floats. "I was already sad I was missing the fireworks with you guys," I said quietly. "Now I'd give anything to be there."

"You will be, in spirit," he said. "And if you're watching from the Tides, you'll probably see it. Hard to miss, especially if you know when to look."

"Which is . . ."

"At the very end, when the last big blasts are over," he finished for me.

I pulled my legs up to my chest. "I'll be watching," I told him. "And Roo?"

"Yeah?"

"Thanks."

"For what?" he asked.

"For the stories. And the album. And just calling."

"Don't thank me, it's mutual," he said. "I'd go nuts if this was seriously about windows all day long."

I smiled. "I will listen anytime."

"I appreciate that," he said. We were both quiet a second. "So, look. When you're free to come and go as you please—"

"If," I corrected him.

"When," he repeated, "do you think you might want to . . . well, I'm glad you asked! Once we run the credit check, we'll go ahead and set you up for a visit by one of our knowledgeable, bonded technicians. They'll take measurements, then discuss the best options for protection of your home, at which point . . ."

He kept talking, but I couldn't think about windows. I couldn't think about anything but those words he had been saying, leading to what I thought was a question, now unasked. Would I what? Want to buy storm protection? Light sparklers together? Or something else?

Just then, there was a burst of feedback from the Pavilion and Tracy appeared, now in her own swimsuit, to take the beach chair next to me. In between covering my ears and greeting her, I lost Roo. Sadly, with this job he could only call out. I'd have to wait. And I knew I would.

It was around six, as I walked across the lobby with Tracy and Dad, headed to the cookout on the beach, when the concierge called out to us. "Mr. Payne?"

My dad stopped, looking over at the desk. "Yes?"

"Something was left for you earlier," he said, reaching under the counter to pull out a small brown bag. "Or, for Saylor?"

"Emma?" he said.

The concierge looked at the bag, then back at us. "Perhaps I misunderstood? This says Saylor Payne, but . . ."

"That's me," I told him, stepping forward.

He handed me the bag. "Have a wonderful evening."

I thanked him, taking it, then carefully opened the flap. Inside was a box of sparklers and a pack of matches. I smiled.

"What is it?" Tracy asked. My dad, suspicious, was watching me, too.

"Nothing," I told them, dropping it into my purse. "Let's go."

We did, out to our reserved spot on the sand, where three chairs, an ice bucket with beverages, and a full view of the lake awaited us. As we sat and ate, I tried to focus on my dad, happily devouring a burger and fries from the plate on his lap, and Tracy, who was telling a series of honeymoon sailing stories.

Finally, after the ice cream sandwiches were served and the anthem played, the fireworks began. Set off from a Tides boat anchored near the raft, they were gorgeous and loud, with color exploding across the dark sky and reflecting in the water. All around me, people oohed and aahed, waiting for the next big burst. After the extended, no-holds-barred finale, everyone applauded.

But as my dad gathered up our trash, and people began dragging their tired, sugar-filled kids back to the hotel, I walked the other way, down the shoreline until I could see, distantly, Mimi's dock and beach.

"Emma? You coming?" my dad called out.

"I'll be there in a sec," I replied, then pulled out my box and the matches, getting a sparkler ready. I was worried the wind would blow out the flame, or it wouldn't catch at all. But as I saw the lights appear on that beach, shimmering and sudden, I dipped the tip of my own offering into the flame and watched it spark for all those big lives lived, gone too soon, and all the unanswered questions. I let it burn all the way down.

TWENTY-THREE

Finally, it was the day of the Club dinner. I was nervous and excited, but all anyone could talk about was the tropical storm that was supposed to hit the coast that evening before heading our way. While what it would do then was anyone's guess, everyone had an opinion.

There was the *Bly County News*, which ran pictures of destruction and damage from other storms, including Richard, which had taken out Mimi's dock two years earlier. The TV anchors had gone from occasionally breaking into programming to taking over the air entirely with footage and discussion of preparations, even though nothing had even happened yet. At the Tides, though, no one seemed concerned.

"There's absolutely no need to worry," I overhead the concierge saying to a woman in a brightly colored caftan and a straw hat that morning. "The Tides was built with more storm protection than any other structure on the lake. You could not be in a safer place."

This was the party line, clearly, as I heard it repeated multiple times before breakfast, including from my dad, who had talked to the hotel's general manager on his way back from his daily swim.

"Some tracking models have it not even coming this way," he assured us. "The dinner should go on as scheduled, no problem."

"Well, that's good," Nana replied, turning a page of her *Times*. "With all the planning for the menu and coordinating schedules, I'd hate for the weather to force us to cancel."

"You won't be able to keep Bailey away even if the Club is the only thing left standing," I told her. "She won't miss those forks for *anything*."

"Good," she replied, sipping her coffee. "Because I had them put oysters on our menu just for her."

This I couldn't wait to share. Did Bailey even like oysters? Did it really matter?

"Speaking of the dinner," Nana continued as I perused the day's obits, which consisted of one passing (Marlene Ficus, 55, after a brave fight against ovarian cancer) as well as an In Memoriam (John Davers, gone now five years, and missed greatly since he's been up in heaven), "I'm confirming the numbers this morning at nine. Did you hear from your friend?"

That would be Roo, who she'd told me to invite after asking who I'd been chatting with on the phone so regularly. Nana had never been one to miss much, but I was really glad this time she'd been paying attention.

"He says he'll be there," I said.

"Who's this?" my dad, chewing, asked.

I paused, hesitant. "Roo Price."

"Wait, he's coming to the dinner? After what happened at the party?"

"That was not his fault, remember?" I said.

"I thought this was a dinner for Mimi and her family."

"To thank them for all they've done for Emma this summer, yes," Nana said. "It sounded like this boy was part of that, so I said to include him. Is that a problem?"

Instead of answering her, my dad looked at me as if I was up to something. Which was so not fair, because I had followed his rules completely, not leaving the Tides except for short nearby outings, usually with him or Tracy. In fact, the only contact I'd had with the other side of the lake, other than my calls with Roo, hadn't even really been contact at all.

It had been a couple of days earlier when, after a particularly slow shift at Defender, Roo and I finally made our way through the entire photo album. Even though we'd been through so many pictures and stories from the first page to the last, I'd gotten used to there being another one to turn, one more reason for us to keep talking. I wanted it to keep going, like that big album in the sky we'd discussed. The final picture was him at the Station by the pumps, grinning, in a Blackwood T-shirt. The end.

"And now you're all caught up," he said as I sat there with the album on the bed in front of me. Outside, I could hear kids in the pool, playing Marco Polo. "You know as much as I do."

Which did not explain why I felt such a loss. I swallowed, then said, "I need to return it to you. Although I'm not sure how to get it over there."

"Don't even think about it," he said. "The last thing I need is you in trouble again because of me. Just bring it to the dinner."

The album meant so much to me, though: I could only imagine he felt the same way, even if he knew it by heart. Also, I didn't want to have to explain it to my dad or anyone else. "How about this. I'll leave it at the desk, like you did with the sparklers."

"Saylor. You really don't have to do that."

"I want to," I said. "I'll take it down right now. And then when you pick it up—"

"I will grab it and run before I bump into your dad," he finished for me.

"I was going to say I'd meet you in the lobby."

"No way." He was firm. "I'll see you at the dinner, when it's authorized. Until then, it's just the—Yes, ma'am, we do offer a ten-year guarantee on any work we do as well as all windows!"

And that was that. Now that the storm was building, suddenly people were very interested in home window protection. The phones were ringing so constantly that Roo was kept on even after Kenyatta returned from Barbados. He'd been so busy, in fact, that we'd barely talked other than him letting me know he got the album and confirming the dinner that night. But all that mattered was that I would finally see him.

"Well, it should be a nice evening," my dad said now as I got up, folding my paper. "Six, right?"

"That's right," Nana said. "We'll have a lovely time."

I hoped she was right. I had so much riding on this dinner, if only as a way to bring these two sides of the family, and the lake, together. Would drinks, appetizers, a salad, entrees, then dessert and coffee be enough to start to mend the tear of my mom's problems, the divorce, and the past? Maybe with oysters, and special forks, the answer was yes.

"I don't know," Bailey said about an hour later, as I put on my bathing suit to go down to the pool with Tracy. "I have a bad feeling."

"What?" Everyone on my end had been so positive, I was surprised. "Why?"

"This storm is a *lot* like Richard," she replied. "Same path in the Atlantic, same general size, same place it's supposed to come in. And it almost leveled us."

"But here at the Tides, they're saying it's nothing."

"They don't know anything!" She sighed. "That place was still under construction two years ago, and most of the people there aren't from the lake anyway. I've been watching my dad, and he's worried. So I'm really worried."

I got chill bumps suddenly, springing up along my arms. "Really?"

"Yep." She was quiet for a moment. "Listen to me, okay? Don't wait for them to tell you guys to take cover. Do it when the sky starts to darken. Get low and inside and away from doorways and windows."

I looked outside again. It was sunny and bright, with a breeze that was ruffling the awnings of the restaurant downstairs. Motorboats dotted the water.

"If it comes, I'll be careful," I told Bailey. "Although it's gorgeous now, so I'm pretty sure I'll be seeing you and everyone else at six."

"Hopefully," she replied, sounding anything but. "But for now, I've got to go help put plywood over the windows and drag in all the outside furniture."

Now I sighed. "I wish I could help."

"Don't. Wish for the storm to miss us. And then wish it again."

She sounded so serious. "Okay. I will. See you later?"

"Yeah." A pause. "Be careful, Saylor."

After hanging up, I sat there a second, then turned on the small TV in my room, flipping from an infomercial for a slow cooker to the local news. A guy in a windbreaker was reporting from Colby, a beach town about two hours to the southeast, where it was also still sunny, although the waves were starting to build behind him in the live shot. When a bullet list of Smart Storm Prep appeared, I turned it off.

As Tracy and I headed to the pool, there was little to no sign of any weather concerns other than a pile of sandbags that had appeared on the back patio. When I eyed them, a girl behind the outdoor bar in a Tides Golf shirt was quick to reassure us.

"Standard operating procedure," she said. "The Tides is more prepared for this storm than any other place on the lake, if it even comes. For now, can I get you a cool beverage?"

I declined, taking my bag to two chairs over by the far corner of the pool. When Tracy joined me a moment later, she had a tall pink drink in a frosted glass, a little yellow umbrella poking out of it. "To the storm," she said, holding it up. I did the same with my bottled water. "Let it stay far away."

"Amen," I said. We clinked, then drank.

About an hour later, my phone rang, the Defender Windows' familiar toll-free number popping up on the screen. I answered, readying myself for whatever pitch I would get this time. But when Roo spoke, it wasn't to some fake customer about credit checks. Just me.

"Saylor?"

"Hi," I said. "How's work? Still really busy with the—"

"Are they prepping over there? Do you have a place to go when the storm comes?"

I looked around again at the pool: a group of kids in goggles were wrestling in the shallow end, while the bar was already packed, even though it wasn't noon yet. "No . . . I mean, it's still gorgeous here."

Behind him, I could hear a phone ringing. "Which doesn't mean anything if you look at the forecast. They should already have told you where to go when it starts to get bad—it's Storm 101."

"According to them, this place is hurricane-proof. All

409

I've seen are a few sandbags."

"And they haven't said anything about shelter?"

"Well . . ." I looked at the bar again. "No. Not yet."

"Get low," he said. "Bottom floor, ideally a room with no windows if you can find it. Stay away from all glass. Bring your valuables and medication. And if you haven't charged your phone, do it now. Tell your dad and Tracy, too."

"Okay," I said, "but seriously, maybe they're watching a different forecast track over here, because they're really not worried."

"Then they're stupid," he replied. "Look, get ready and then hopefully it will all be for nothing. But if it isn't . . ."

He let this thought trail off, even as I waited for him to finish. Finally I said, "Are you scared?"

"I'm concerned," he said. Another phone rang. "And busy, so I should go, even though only morons think they can get storm windows put in before this afternoon. I just wanted to make sure you were safe. I'll call again later, okay?"

"Yeah," I said. "And you'll be at the dinner, right? At six?"

"Sure," he assured me, but he sounded so distracted I wondered if he'd even heard my question. "Talk to you soon."

When I hung up, Tracy turned her head, looking at me over her sunglasses. "Everything okay?"

I nodded. "Roo's just worried about the storm."

She tilted her head back, looking up at the blue sky, white clouds drifting across it. "It hardly looks like hurricane weather, though, does it?"

When I shook my head, she stretched out, then lowered

her sunglasses again. But the truth was, behind the Tides, over the trees, I could now see a row of darker clouds, shorter and squatter, piling up on the horizon. As I lay back, I called on my imagination to picture us all at dinner that night, with oyster forks and candles, Mimi and Nana and Bailey and Roo. But when I closed my eyes, all I could see were those clouds. By the time we left the pool an hour later, there were even more of them.

At four p.m., I was sitting at the table with Nana, looking out at the sky. By then, it was dark as dusk.

"Looks ominous," she observed mildly. She turned to my dad, who was watching the TV, now all storm coverage. "Should we double-check with the hotel that dinner is still going to happen?"

"They're saying they'll be fine no matter what the weather does," he replied, not taking his eyes off the screen, where the reporter in the windbreaker from earlier was being thrashed by rain and wind as he tried to describe the conditions. "But I'm wondering if we should have a shelter plan, just to be safe."

"Roo says so," I told him as I yet again tried Roo's number, only to have it ring and ring before going to voicemail. It was the same with Bailey. "We need to be downstairs, away from windows."

"You'd think they'd set up *something*," my dad muttered, walking over to the phone in the kitchen. "I'll call down, see what's happening."

"It's going to be okay," Nana told me. "If the dinner gets canceled, we'll reschedule."

But for the last few hours, I hadn't been thinking about the dinner anymore. It was Mimi's house and Calvander's that were on my mind: that big kitchen, with the shiny toaster. The gardenia bushes by the door. Each of those rooms I'd learned to clean, the tiny fold on the toilet paper at the beginning of a roll. I'd just gotten it all back. What if it was lost for good?

My phone rang then, startling me after so long of not being able to reach anyone. I jumped on it like it was alive. "Hello?"

"Can you get over here? Do you have a car?"

Trinity. She sounded like she was moving, her voice coming in and out. "What's wrong?"

"I just want to be at the hospital," she said, her voice breaking. "If this baby decides to come during the storm, I swear to God I will clamp my legs SHUT. I want my fucking epidural!"

Nana glanced over at me. Whoops. I stood up, putting some distance between us before saying, "Are you having contractions?"

"No," she said, "but I'm so uncomfortable and I can feel the barometric pressure dropping. Storms make weird things happen, and I do not want my kid to be one of them."

I looked at my dad, who was on hold with the front desk, still watching the TV. Outside, I could see several Tides employees in white golf shirts hurriedly folding up the chairs on the beach.

"I have a car," I said. "But I don't think—"

At first, I didn't recognize the sound she made in response to this. Then I realized it was a sob. "I just can't do this, I'm already alone without the Sergeant and everyone's freaking out here. Even if I just sit in the hospital parking lot, I'll feel better, I swear to God, I'll walk there if I have to. . . ."

"Can you call Roo?" I asked, turning my back to Nana and my dad. "Or Vincent?"

"Everyone's at the Station," she wailed. Good God. "Mimi and Oxford boarded up the hotel windows and went to help down there—it always needs a ton of storm prep. So it's just me and Gordon here, and she was all nervous, so I yelled at her, and now she's God knows where feeling sorry for herself, even though she is NOT a million years pregnant."

I heard a beep: another call coming in. Bailey. "Hold on," I said to Trinity, who was sniffling in my ear. "I've got Bailey on the other line."

"Tell her to get over here and take me to the hospital!" she yelled, loud enough to make my dad, halfway across the room, turn and look at me.

"One sec," I said in my best measured voice, to compensate for her near hysteria. Then I clicked over. "Bailey?"

At first, all I heard was whooshing. Then, finally, her voice. "Are you downstairs yet?"

"No, they haven't said anything," I told her. "I've got

413

Trinity on the other line. She's kind of—"

"Freaking out," she finished for me. "I know. But she's not in labor, so there's no point in trying the roads. One way or another, this will be over by tomorrow."

Well, that didn't inspire much confidence. I said, "She's all alone, though."

"Gordon is there."

"She yelled at Gordon."

"Well, my dad's yelling at everyone. It's a storm," she replied. "Look, the wind is really picking up here: we've already got some branches falling. Tell her I said to find Gordon and get to the TV room. They've already reported a tornado touching down in Colby."

"What?" I said, looking back at the TV, where the windbreaker reporter was now literally getting pushed sideways by the wind. "Really?"

"Saylor, wake up. This is a storm. It's going to be bad." She cleared her throat. "Look, just get your dad and grandmother and Tracy and get safe, okay? I'll check back in with you in a bit."

"What about you, though?" I asked as Nana looked at me. "Are you safe?"

"Safe enough," she replied. In the background, I heard a male voice, bellowing. "Shit, I better go. Just stay low and away from windows, okay?"

Before I could answer, the line cut off, bouncing me back to Trinity. Who was still crying.

"I just hate this so much," she said when I told her I was

414

back. "Being alone this whole stupid pregnancy, and now—"

"You're not alone," I told her.

"I am literally standing in this room all by myself!" she yelled so loudly I pulled the phone from my ear. "Nobody cares! If this is like Richard, the house will probably come down around me and my unborn child!"

"Emma?" my dad asked. I looked at him. "What's going on?"

Now Trinity was sobbing, her breath coming in ragged jags. I said, "It's Trinity. She's alone and really pregnant and she wants to go to the hospital."

"Hospital? Now? They're saying to stay off all the roads for emergency vehicles to get through."

Trinity, hearing this, wailed even louder. "I know. But she's so upset, and no one is there to drive her. So she asked if I—"

"You?" Now he gave me his full attention, turning from the TV entirely. "Absolutely not. You're not leaving this hotel."

"I know," I said. More sobbing, louder, and now I felt tears prick my own eyes, I felt so helpless. "But I just—"

He came over, holding out his hand. "Let me talk to her."

I handed it over. He put it to his own ear, blinked at the sobbing, and then cleared his throat. "Trinity? Hello? This is Emma's dad, Matthew. You've got to calm down, okay? This isn't good for you or the baby."

There was a blast of response from the phone, none of which I could make out. He said, "I understand. It's scary.

But the storm will pass and you will be fine. Deep breaths."

I didn't hear breathing, though. Just yelling.

"Is there someone who can keep you company?" my dad was saying now. "Sit with you until the storm passes?"

More wailing. Tracy emerged from the bedroom, where she'd been taking a shower. "Um, I just got a tornado warning on my phone. Should we be worried about that?"

I looked at Nana, who said, "According to the hotel, no."

Outside, there was a crack of lightning, followed by a gust of wind that made the windows creak. "We need to go downstairs," I said. "Now."

"Agreed," my dad said. To Trinity he said, "What? No, we're just discussing if we should take shelter. I'm going to give you back to Emma—"

He pulled the phone away from his ear as she sobbed, loudly, in response to this. He covered the mouthpiece and looked at me. "Does she really not have anyone there?"

I shook my head. "Just Gordon."

"Jesus." He looked out at the lake, which looked mean now, ominous, whitecaps dotting the water, the dark clouds low and thick. "Okay. Look. I'll get you all downstairs and settled, and then I'll ride over there."

"What?" I said. "I want to go."

"No." He looked at Tracy. "Gather up your phone and charger, your purse, anything you might need in the next few hours. Mom and Emma, you too."

"But—"

"*Now*," he said, sounding so firm that I jumped. Tracy

went back into the bedroom, moving quickly, while Nana got to her feet as well. I just stood there, though, as he put the phone back to his ear. "Trinity. Breathe. I'm coming over. Just give me a few minutes, okay?"

I couldn't hear her response, because at that moment another wind gust hit. Then the power went out.

"Go," my dad said to me, and I ran into my room, grabbing my purse, a charger, and my shoes. By the time I got back to the living room, Nana and Tracy were at the door, ready, my dad scrambling for his own things. When we went out into the hallway, it was dark except for the emergency lights, blinking.

"Elevator's out," my dad reported, after trying the button. He turned to Nana. "Mom, can you handle the stairs?"

"Certainly," Nana replied, but I took her arm anyway. "Lead the way."

We went into the stairwell, which was also illuminated by blinking lights, and started down, my dad and Tracy in front, Nana and me following. We'd gone down two flights— slowly—when my phone rang again. Trinity.

"A tree just fell on the porch!" she screamed. "It took out one of the windows and now the rain is pouring in!"

"Okay, okay," I said, reporting this to my dad. "Are you in the middle room? Where's Gordon?"

"I can't find her!" she said. "I've been yelling, but you know how she gets when you scream at her, she just vanishes. My mom's at work freaking out, but she can't leave. God, why is this happening?"

A door on the landing we were passing opened suddenly, a Tides employee with a silver room service tray stepping through. People were ordering food right now?

"Good evening," he said, flashing us a toothy smile. "On your way to dinner?"

"The power's out," my dad told him. "What are you all doing about it?"

"The generator is *just* about to come on," the guy replied cheerfully. "But even if it didn't, we'd be totally safe. The Tides is the most storm-ready structure—"

"Right, right," my dad said, pushing past him. To me he said, "What's happening with Trinity?"

"Tree hit the house," I told him. "And now she can't find Gordon."

He sighed. "Jesus. Okay. Let's get a move on. Mom, you all right?"

"Fine," Nana replied, but she did grip my hand a little harder as we began down the next flight. I squeezed back.

Finally we reached the lobby, where Tides employees were scurrying around, moving plants away from windows and herding guests into a nearby ballroom. "It's a hurricane party!" one girl in a golf shirt told us, waving at the open door. "We have drinks and food and activities for the whole family. Join us, won't you?"

My dad looked in the ballroom, where a total of about eight people, mostly kids, were grouped around one table. The rest were empty. "You need to get everyone down here. This storm is no joke."

"Oh, sir, this is just a precaution," she said as a wall of rain hit the windows, the sound drowning everything out for a moment. "You'd be perfectly safe in your room, as the Tides is—"

My dad hurried past her. "Emma, you and your grandmother get settled. Tracy and I will run over to Mimi's just to check on Trinity and Gordon."

"But—"

"Emma. Do not question me right now."

"Honey." Tracy put her hand on his arm. "It's Emma's family. Her cousin. You can understand why she might want to—"

"This is an emergency," he said.

"Which is why I think it would be better if I stayed with your mother," Tracy replied, more firmly now. "You take Emma and go. Safely. Okay?"

At the desk behind us, all the phones were ringing at once as rain lashed the windows. Someone came in the automatic doors. No one yelled, "Welcome to the Tides!"

"Fine," he said. Then he gave her a kiss. "We'll call once we're on our way. Stay here, yes?"

"Yes," she said, walking to a nearby table and holding out a chair so Nana could sit down. My phone, in my pocket, buzzed again. Trinity.

"We're coming," I said as I answered. "Hang tight."

"I can't find her!" she said. Her voice was high, scared. "I've looked everywhere!"

"Okay, okay," I said, glancing at my dad, who had

overheard this. "Just . . . we'll be there soon."

It was, after all, only three miles. But when we went to the valet stand for the car, no one was there. The rain was coming down sideways.

"Well," my dad said, glancing around for a moment. Then he opened the door to the valet stand, which held all the keys, scanning them until he found his own. "I guess we'll go look for it ourselves."

I followed him down a path to the parking garage. Inside, we looked up at the two stories of cars, some of them double-parked. "Any idea where to start?" I asked.

"At the beginning," he said, starting to jog up to the next level. "Come on."

The good news: we found his Audi at the very start of level two. The bad: it was parked right against a wall and blocked in by a huge SUV directly behind it.

"What the *hell*," he said, eyeing it. "This is insane. We'll never get it out."

My phone was ringing again, but I couldn't stop to answer it. Instead, I walked around to the Audi, which actually had some space ahead of it. "I think I can back it out."

"You can't even get in there!"

"I can try," I said, gesturing for him to throw me the keys. He did, and I unlocked the car, then stuffed myself in the small space on the side away from the wall, inching down between it and the car beside it, a Mercedes. "I think I can crawl in the window, if I can get it open."

"This is crazy and stupid," he said. "We shouldn't even

be trying to get out of here. Doesn't she have family that can come help her?"

"We *are* her family," I said.

He just looked at me as, although my insides felt compressed to the point of flattening, I finally made it to the passenger door. I eased it open about an inch, which was all the give there was, before sticking my hand in and wiggling it around until I found the window button. Because the key was in my hand, it went down. Thank God. I pitched myself in, crawling behind the wheel.

"There's not enough—" my dad was saying, but I ignored him as I started the engine. We'd practiced parking endlessly before my test, in the garage under Nana's building, before I'd hit that car and gotten spooked. No time for fear now. I put the car in reverse, easing back a tiny bit.

"Okay," my dad said, coming around to the front. "That's as far as you've got before the bumper. Now go for—"

I already was, inching up, the wheel turned as far as it would go. Then back. Then up again. Slowly, I began to make a space between the Audi and the SUV, although it took another ten passes or so before it was wide enough to reverse out entirely. But I did it. My phone was ringing the entire time.

"All right," my dad said. He looked as surprised as I'd ever seen him. "Now, let me behind the wheel."

"I'm already here," I said. "Just get in."

He paused, as if he was going to resist this, but then climbed into the passenger seat. I hit the gas as soon as his door swung shut behind him.

Out in front of the hotel, it was crazy windy, the trees bent sideways, rain pelting the glass as I tried to peer through it. We passed a couple of Tides employees, running toward Campus, as I turned onto the road. A layer of water was running across it.

"Flooding," my dad said. "Go very slow and don't brake."

I did as he said until we were past it, then sped up. My phone rang again. "Can you get that?" I asked. "It's probably Trinity."

He picked it up. "Hello? Trinity? Look, we're on our way . . . Celeste? It's Matthew."

I had to slow again to drive over a power line, broken and wiggling like a snake. Yikes. "Ask her if they found Gordon."

". . . yes, we're going there," he said. "Trinity is very upset and Gordon . . . well, she's probably hiding. We'll find her. What? No, we just left the hotel. We should be there . . . what's in the road?"

I waited to hear the answer to this question, but there was none: the line went dead, and he lowered the phone, looking worried. "Sounds like there might be a problem," he said. "We'll see."

A couple of miles later, we did: a tree had fallen across both lanes, bark and leaves scattered all around it. The sky was as dark as I'd ever seen it in my life, and suddenly, probably much later than I should have, I felt my heart begin to race. I was scared.

"Dad," I said as we stopped. "Now what?"

He took a breath. We'd gotten this far—extracting the car, dealing with the weather—and now it was all for nothing. I thought of Trinity, crying in the dark of the TV room. I was about to turn to him and say we should just run the rest of the way when I heard it.

Music.

It was distant, and barely audible above the whipping wind and the rain. But it was there, tinkling piano music, growing louder and louder. It seemed nuts I didn't put together that it was the Yum truck until it appeared on the other side of the tree, its lights blinking.

"Roo," I said, feeling a rush of relief. I pushed my door open.

"What?" my dad asked.

"Just come on." I jumped out and started to run, going around the tree with him following. The rain stung my skin, the howl of the wind filling my ears: it felt like the storm might just carry me away, like Dorothy when *The Wizard of Oz* is in black and white. But then Roo was holding open the door, and I was climbing in. The music was still going.

"It's stuck," he said by way of explanation as my dad piled in behind me. I moved to the cooler, my spot, while he took the front seat, putting on his belt as Roo backed up. "But at least people can hear us coming."

We started driving the final stretch, passing Conroy Market, where the power was also out. Roo stuck his hand out the window and gave a thumbs-up to Celeste, who was standing outside, her phone to her ear. Then she, like everything else, was lost in the wind and rain behind us. But still the music kept playing.

"Apparently, there's a huge tree down on the highway," Roo said as he leaned forward, trying to see through the windshield. The wipers were going full speed, but only pushing the water around. "So Trinity can't get to the hospital."

"She's not in labor, just scared," I said. "And Gordon—"

"Is going to be in *so* much trouble once I find her safe," he finished for me. My dad glanced at him, saying nothing. "Okay, we're almost there. Once we are, you go find Trinity. I'll look for Gordon."

"You take cover," my dad said. "I'll handle looking for Gordon."

Roo jerked the wheel to the right, suddenly, to dodge a branch that was in the road, and I almost slid off the cooler, catching myself at the last minute. The music made it sound like a wacky caper, not an emergency.

Finally, we were at Calvander's, where all the windows facing the water were boarded up, debris from the beach—a shovel, a plastic bag, a beer can—blowing across the yard. Roo jerked to a stop and we all jumped out, running to the main house. The tree that had so scared Trinity was across the porch, water pouring in the one window it had hit, reminding me how serious this actually was.

"Trinity!" I yelled as I came up the steps, throwing the door open. The house was quiet except for the wind, wheezing through any and all cracks. "Where are you?"

"In here!" she said.

I pushed open the door to the TV room to find her on the couch, holding a pillow, tears streaming down her face. "She's not anywhere!" she said. "I've looked all over the god-damn place."

"It's okay," I said, going to her as Roo and my dad took off to the kitchen and the rest of the house. I heard them yelling Gordon's name as I grabbed a blanket from the couch, shaking it out over Trinity, who was trembling. "We'll find her."

"Don't leave me!" she yelled, but I had to, running down the hallway to the kitchen, where the windows were all rain: I couldn't even see the lake. Outside, I could still make out the tinkling music of the Yum truck, or at least I could until another sound grew loud enough to drown it out: a humming, like an engine. Growing closer.

My dad, coming back down the stairs, heard it too. "Tornado," he said. "Into the middle room, both of you. Now!"

I hadn't even realized Roo was there, behind me, until he said, "I can't. We have to find Gordon."

"I will find Gordon," my dad told him. "GO."

I looked at Roo, who nodded and then ran back down the hallway, me following. In the TV room Trinity was rocking back and forth, her eyes squeezed shut.

"Oh, my God," she said as I sat down beside her, taking her hand. Her grip was like a vise, tightening with each boom of thunder from outside. "Where's Gordon? If she's outside, she'll—"

"Shh," Roo said, taking her other hand. "Emma's dad is on it."

He said this so confidently, as if he had all the faith in my father, despite what had happened between them. My dad would handle this. He had to.

Before, the wind had been howling; now, it sounded different. Trinity whimpered, twisting my fingers, and I sucked in a breath, trying to stay calm. Then I heard a crack just outside, followed by a crash.

"Shit," Roo said.

"My dad." I stood up, running to the door. "I should—"

"Saylor!" Roo yelled. "Don't open that!"

I did; I couldn't help it. Nothing can happen to him, I thought, as I ran to the front door and opened it as well, feeling the wind push back against me, hard. "Dad!"

But I couldn't see him. And I knew there was no way he could hear me, over the wind and the howling and the rain smacking the windows. I turned, looking down at the shore: the water was rushing over the dock, foam stuck to everything, and I couldn't make out a single thing. The howling was getting louder.

"Dad!" I yelled again, into the storm. No answer. I stood there, tears in my throat, thinking of the last time I'd seen my mom. That white lace shirt, the way she touched my face. The elevator doors closing as she watched me disappear. Was this another ending I'd remember forever? Where would I imagine him?

"Saylor!" Roo came running up behind me. "Come back inside."

"My dad is out there!" I said, my voice breaking, and then I was crying. "He's—"

There was a whoosh, pushing me back from the door, and I felt Roo grab me, his arms around my waist. The rain was pelting us sideways as I buried my face in his chest, eyes tightly closed, just wanting to hold on to something, someone, as the world seemed to come loose all around me. He put a hand on the back of my head as I turned, looking out in the storm again, and I could hear him speak but couldn't make out the words he was saying. Still, I strained to hear them, holding on tight, and then finally, there was this.

"I see them."

I opened my eyes. He was looking at the shore, so I did too, squinting into the rain and bending trees. At first, I saw nothing, but then, after a beat, then one more, movement in the distance at the dock. I blinked. Twice. And then there was my dad, carrying Gordon as he walked away from the water.

"Oh, my God," I said. She had her arms looped at his neck, legs locked around his waist, as he jogged up the grass, head bent against the storm. In one of her hands, Gordon was holding her Allies book.

Roo let me go, rushing out to open and hold the door as they came up the steps.

"Let's go," my dad said, ducking into the TV room. Gordon was still holding on tightly, her own eyes squeezed shut, as Trinity shrieked, relieved, upon seeing them. "Saylor. You okay?"

I paused. He had never called me that. "Yeah. I'm fine."

He reached out, touching my hair, but couldn't do much more with Gordon attached to him like a spider monkey. Roo shut the living room door. "It's coming," he said as we all got back on the couch, together. We were so close, crammed in together, that I felt like I had a piece of everyone: Trinity's hand in mine, my dad's leg pressed against me, Gordon's skinny elbow at my ear. And then, Roo, sliding in behind me. He took my other hand, squeezing it, as if he'd done it a million times. Maybe, in the deep, lost part of my memory, he had. But it still felt new and familiar all at once as I squeezed back, pressing myself against him. I thought of my mom in that hotel room, on another night years ago, leaving this world with no one even knowing. There were a million ways to go, but the worst would be alone. And I wasn't.

I'd never heard the wind the way it sounded at that moment. Sometimes I still hear it in my dreams. But even then, I have that sense of being part of a greater whole. All of us on the couch, Roo's breath in my ear. Together, we held on.

TWENTY-FOUR

"This is so nice," Bailey said, looking around the room. "You didn't have to."

"Oh, I think I did!" Nana replied, gesturing for us to take our seats at the table before she did the same. "Of course, it's not the Club. But there are oyster forks. See?"

I did. There they were, on the little card table Oxford had brought into room seven, along with three folding chairs. I'd found the tablecloth and napkins in a drawer in Mimi's kitchen, while Nana picked a bunch of gardenias and put them in water for the centerpiece. She was right, it wasn't the Club. It was better.

The Club wasn't an option anyway, as, like the Tides, it had suffered so much damage from the storm it was closed until further notice. Which meant all the guests who'd been so reassured about the hotel's storm readiness suddenly had to find other places to stay, causing everything to be fully booked up. Luckily, we had a connection.

It was Calvander's we'd come to, the night of the storm, after we'd picked up Nana and Tracy, who'd been evacuated as the water rushed into the Tides lobby. We'd taken the Yum truck, me on the cooler seat with Tracy, while Nana rode up front, next to Roo, delighted by the music, which was still playing.

On the day of the storm, Calvander's had two vacancies, so Nana and I bunked in seven while Dad and Tracy took number ten. I'd been a little worried about how my grand-mother would adapt to her new digs. But she took easily to walking over to the main house with me for breakfast each morning with Oxford, who split his paper with her and made all the toast we could ever want. Usually Gordon joined us as well, with her book. She'd become fascinated with every-thing Nana, which I could understand, following her around the way she once had me. Sometimes I'd see them in our room, sitting together and talking quietly, and wonder what they were discussing. But I'd never ask.

The motel itself had withstood the storm with only a little damage, and within a day or two the other guests were back on the beach, slathering themselves with sunscreen as they spread out their towels. From across the lake, we could hear bulldozers and construction equipment going all day long as the Tides and the Club tried to get back up and run-ning. But it would be a while.

And by then, we'd be gone. Back in Lakeview, Nana's remodeled apartment and our new house were both done and waiting for us, as well as the new school year. But I was determined to stay at North Lake, both literally and figuratively, as long as I could.

Which was why we'd scheduled this, our oyster fork meal, on the evening of the second-to-last day, before the chaos of packing and leaving really set in. It wasn't the big group dinner we'd planned, but it didn't matter, as by that point we'd had plenty of those. In the first days after the storm, when the power was still out, we'd sat together at Mimi's big table, eating meals made with everything perishable from the fridge. Oxford grilled hot dogs outside while Mimi and Nana drank boxed wine they'd found in the pantry, sharing stories. Even Trinity was there, still hugely pregnant, counting down the days until the Sergeant arrived home. I was hoping I'd be there when the baby came, but I knew even from the distance of Lakeview I'd still feel part of it, whenever it happened.

A lot of this was because of Roo. That day of the storm, we'd all stayed in the living room, on the couch, until the wind died down and we were sure the danger had passed. Only then did my dad get up, helping Trinity to her feet while Gordon stuck close to his other side.

"Bound to be a lot of branches and power lines down," he told us, crossing the room and opening the door to squint out. "Nobody touch anything, understood?"

Gordon, solemn, nodded, although Trinity was already going to the front door. "Oh, crap," she said a moment later. "That same office window that blew out in Richard is gone again. Mimi is going to be *pissed*."

"Better a window than a person," my dad pointed out. He looked at Gordon, then bent down to her level. "You okay? That was kind of scary."

Hearing his voice as he said this—low, calm, invested— I felt a lump rise in my own throat. We Paynes were a safe people, for sure. And my dad had lots of experience: he could take care of anyone.

Everyone else left to check damage then, leaving just Roo and me on the couch in the dimness of the living room. Distantly, I could hear a siren, as well as someone's phone ringing. But as I turned to face him, his hand still in mine, I blocked that all out. All I could think of were the moments the wind had wailed, the house literally shaking, and we held hands so tightly I could feel both his pulse and mine.

I looked up at him. All those pictures I'd seen of him, from the group shot until the very last one, by the pumps at the Station, and yet this was what I knew I would remember best. This moment, uncaptured, but just as real.

"You okay, storm buddy?" he asked.

I smiled. Then, instead of replying, I leaned in and kissed him. Lightly at first, trying it out, before going deeper, pulling him closer. His lips were so soft as he smoothed a hand over my head, gazing steadily into my eyes while I reached up to touch his face, every bit of us fitting neatly together. It was so perfect—the world falling away, just how I thought a real first kiss should feel—I knew I didn't need a picture, that I would remember it always. Even now, when I thought of it, my heart jumped.

Since then, we'd just sort of slipped easily, wordlessly, into being a couple. A few days later, as we sat on Mimi's steps, he told me he had something for me, picking up the bag he'd brought with him.

"What is it?" I asked.

He handed it over. "Look and see."

It was a photo album, a new one, with a red cover and stiff pages. At first I was confused, until I opened it up to see that same first picture, his dad in his duck pajamas, at the very top.

"Is this—"

"Yep," he said. His leg was warm, pressing against mine. I just felt better with him close by. "Same pictures, same order. I made copies."

"This is incredible," I said, flipping pages.

"I thought you deserved your own album," he told me. "Since the stories are yours, too."

I turned a couple more pages: they were all there. The shot of my mom, somber at day camp. Her dyeing Chris Price's hair. That ill-fated middle school dance. Then Roo and me as kids. Each picture another step toward here, where we were now. I wouldn't be leaving everything behind. Now, I could take the lake with me.

But when I got to the last page, and that final shot of him with his mom and the Christmas tree, I noticed something. "Wait. Are there more pages?"

He grinned. "Look and see."

I turned past the final photo, and sure enough, instead of

the back cover, another page was there, with more behind it. Empty slots, waiting to be filled with the rest of the stories I would tell. I was so touched, moving through them, that at first I almost missed the single picture he'd already included.

It was the two of us, at our makeshift prom, a shot I hadn't even realized was being taken. I was in my dress, barefoot, him holding a hand to spin me out as we danced. I was laughing, my head thrown back, someone blurry and in motion behind me. Like the moment was already passing, even as whoever took the shot captured it.

"This is incredible," I said, barely even able to speak.

"The big photo album in the sky," he replied. "It's like good storm windows. Everyone should have one."

I turned to face him, moving my leg between his. "You are the best."

"I am not," he replied, sliding his arms around my waist. "But I will take the compliment anyway."

I leaned in then, kissing him as the wind blew over us, ruffling the nearby gardenia bushes. I wanted it to last forever, but then I heard Gordon tittering, the way she did when she caught us like this together, and she always caught us like this together.

"Gordon," Roo said, pulling away but keeping his eyes on me. "Don't you have a closet to get into or something?"

"It wasn't a closet!" she shot back as she did every time he said this, which was equally as often. "It was a shed and I was fine."

"Fine." Roo snorted. "You were by the water with a

hurricane coming in and no one could find you."

"Except my dad," I pointed out. I looked at Gordon. "Lucky he knew that place, huh?"

She nodded, solemn. "Lucky."

But it wasn't, not really. I'd assumed he'd found her that day by process of elimination, hunting around the dock until he discovered the small shed built into the side of the motel where, after Trinity had yelled at her, she'd gone to barricade herself with her book. It was only later, when I'd finally had a chance to sit down with my dad, that I found out the real story.

It was a few days after the storm and we were at Mimi's table, having breakfast. Tracy and Nana had gone back over to the Tides to collect our things, so it was my dad and me and my *Bly County News*, where I was reading the obits (Ellis Murdock, 67, died at home with his family around him) while he stared out the window. When Gordon emerged from the motel office, we both watched her walk down to the dock, carrying her book, then take a seat with her legs dangling in the water.

"You saved her life," I said as he nibbled some toast.

"Oh, I don't know about that," he said. "That shed is pretty tough. That's why your mom liked it."

I looked at him. "Mom?"

He nodded, swallowing. "You know how she was into disappearing. She could hide anywhere. But she loved that shed. She told me she always went there when Mimi and Joe were fighting."

I looked back at Gordon, kicking her feet as she read. "And you remembered?"

He looked surprised. "I remember everything about your mom, Emma."

I turned the page of my paper, over to sports. "Me too. But I want to hear all your stories, remember? I mean, sometime."

For a second, he was silent. Then he said, "Right. Yeah, I've been thinking. I'd like that too."

I looked at him. "Really?"

"Really." He smiled, then reached up, rubbing his hand under his glasses. "We can start with this table, right here. Do you know that was my seat?"

He was pointing at the one I was in, to the left of the head. "It was?"

"Yep. Right next to Joe, who did not like PDA of any sort. Your mom sat across from me, but kicked my leg under the table throughout every meal. I had a permanent shin bruise."

I tried to picture him with his own seat in this place I thought *I* knew so well. "Really."

"Oh, yeah." He smiled, a little sadly, looking out at the lake. "It was like a whole new world, being in this crazy house after living with your grandmother. I loved it."

Me too, I thought. Then I kicked him under the table, and he laughed.

The last few days we'd spent packing, getting ready to leave. I slipped my notebook with my family tree in the bottom of my bag, then threw my shoes in on top of it, all jumbled together. Then I took them all out again and put them in neatly. You couldn't change everything all at once. It was good we had time.

The album was one of the last things I packed. Before I did, though, I'd gone up to the office, where I found Mimi standing behind the counter facing the window, her hands on her hips.

"What are you looking at?" I asked her as I came in, the cold air smacking me in the face.

"Oh, just the traffic going by," she said, even though there were no cars at that moment. "Helps me think. What are you up to?"

"I wanted to show you something," I said. "If you have a minute."

"For you, honey?" She gave me a wink. "Always. What is it?"

I walked over, putting the album on the counter between us. As she leaned over it and I opened the cover, I said, "Roo gave me this. But there's something in it I want you to have."

"Oh, my," she breathed softly as I turned the page to that first picture of my mom scowling at church camp. "That brings back some memories."

She was studying the page so intently, her eyes moving across the pictures, that I stayed quiet for a moment. When I saw her eyes get wet, I said quickly, "I didn't mean to upset you."

"Oh, no." She waved her hand in front of her face, turning another page. "I'm not upset. Just remembering."

I looked down too, at all those pictures Roo had told me about, wondering if she recalled the same things. Because the story can change so much, depending on who's telling it. I hoped, over time, I'd hear more of hers.

"This is the one I wanted to give you," I said, flipping to the page I'd marked. There, at the bottom, was the picture of us together on my first visit, sitting in that lawn chair. I'd driven to Delaney to a drugstore to get a good copy of it, which I pulled out now from behind the original. "I thought maybe you could put it under the glass."

She was still for a second. Then, slowly, she moved her hand forward, taking the picture from me. "Well, what do you know," she said, then smiled. "If it isn't George."

We made room for it beside an old shot of Celeste and my mom, right by the register. If I couldn't be there, I liked knowing it was.

Now, back in room seven, I looked around as Nana unpacked the meal she'd ordered from the Club, which was running a shoestring kitchen to try to accommodate all the displaced members. "Oyster salad," she said, handing the container to Bailey, "and cucumber and cream cheese sandwiches. Not too fancy, but it's something."

"It's perfect," Bailey told her as I heard her phone buzz. She glanced down at it, balanced on her bag, then smiled, helping herself to oysters. I looked too: VINCENT, it said on the screen. Apparently, Roo and I weren't the only ones who had found each other during the storm. At the Station, Bailey and Vincent had taken shelter in the snack bar, even as a piece of roof metal blew against the doors, trapping them there. By the time Silas and Jack got them out, something had changed. All I knew was I hadn't heard a word about Colin or Campus since.

"Let's have a toast," Nana said, once we'd each helped ourselves from the carry-out containers and I'd filled our glasses with Pop Soda. She lifted her glass. "To family."

"To family," Bailey said, looking at me.

"To family," I repeated, and I had that feeling again, of being complete, as we clinked our glasses and drank. The next day I'd go home, see Ryan and Bridget, move into a new house and new neighborhood. Even with my wild imagination I couldn't picture it, not yet, but that was okay. The details would come, and then I'd capture and add them, image by image, onto the pages of the book Roo had given me.

What would they be? At that moment, I couldn't say. Only later would I know they would include the In Memoriam I'd write for the *Bly County News*, sending it in so it ran on the Monday after Thanksgiving, the day my mom died. My dad would help me find a picture of her when she was sober and happy. Also to be in those pages, eventually: the day I left, when Trinity and Bailey presented me with my own spray bottle, EMMA SAYLOR—I'd decided to go by both names, not choosing between them anymore— which would be waiting for me the following summer when I returned.

But first, I had to go, and I would. But not as a passenger this time.

Even with all the progress I'd made, my dad wasn't thrilled with the idea of me driving home alone. But Nana had a car coming, and plenty of room for him and Tracy and all their bags, and I had more goodbyes to say than he did. So finally, begrudgingly, he agreed, waving at me as they drove off from Calvander's in a black town car, the blinker flashing as they turned left onto the main road. Which left just Roo and me, my packed bags, and one more thing. A lake thing.

"Hold it out," he said as I gripped the sparkler in my hand. I did, and he put his against it, tip to tip, before striking the lighter. As he waited for them to catch, I took the opportunity to study him. Blond hair, sticking up a bit in the back. The gap in this teeth, trademark. And those numbers, where to find him, across one calf. There were no guarantees of what would happen to us in the coming year, but as my mind started to consider it, there was a spark, another, then a shower between us. I thought of my mom and his dad—both big lives, gone too soon. I was leaving, too. But I knew I'd be back.